PRAISE FOR *ADVERSE EFFECTS*

"*Adverse Effects* is a 'step on the gas pedal and hold on tight' read.
An action-packed medical thriller that doesn't let up
until the very last page."

—**MARY LAWRENCE**, author of *The Alchemist's Daughter*

"When heroine Cristina Silva's nightmares start to become your own,
you know you are reading a good book. *Adverse Effects* is such a book,
an excellent medical thriller."

—**KEN MCCLURE**, author of the Dr. Steven Dunbar series

"A thrilling biotech novel. This is a superb fast-paced book with
excellent depth of characters and scientific background. Lots of easily
understood biotech that provides the foundation for great suspense and
lots surprises that are completely believable."

—**ALESSANDRO BOCCALETTI**, author of *Veritas: The Pharmacological Endgame*

"Riveting from page one, *Adverse Effects* caught my attention from the
very beginning. I couldn't stop reading. You want this book."

—**SHILOH WALKER,** nationally bestselling author

To Cat,

ADVERSE EFFECTS

Thank you

JOEL SHULKIN, MD

ADVERSE EFFECTS

BLACK STONE
PUBLISHING

Copyright © 2020 by Dr. Joel Shulkin
Published in 2021 by Blackstone Publishing
Cover and book design by Alenka Vdovič Linaschke

The characters and events in this book are fictitious.
Any similarity to real persons, living or dead, is coincidental
and not intended by the author.

Printed in the United States of America
Originally published in hardcover by Blackstone Publishing in 2020

First paperback edition: 2021
ISBN 978-1-0940-2287-1
Fiction / Thrillers / Medical

1 3 5 7 9 10 8 6 4 2

CIP data for this book is available
from the Library of Congress

Blackstone Publishing
31 Mistletoe Rd.
Ashland, OR 97520

www.BlackstonePublishing.com

To Geiza, who helps me remember everything.

PROLOGUE

The woman's brown skin rippled like satin beneath Carl Franklin's pale fingertips. Her hair billowed in a black halo against the bedspread. Slender fingers pulled the sheets free from the mattress as she moaned and jerked spasmodically. Her eyes bore into Carl's as his fingers dug into the skin surrounding her neck.

Carl's stomach lurched when his hands tightened around the woman's throat, blocking her screams. Even worse, the growing bulge in his pants confirmed he enjoyed it.

"Stop," he whispered, though it would do no good. The vision continued, relentless. Sitting in the living room of his luxuriant Somerville apartment, Carl gripped his armchair, trying to convince himself the rich leather felt nothing like the skin of her neck. "These aren't my memories."

The woman jabbed her press-on fingernail at his eyeball. Carl tightened his grip. Twisted. Crushed her windpipe. The fight left her body.

"That wasn't me." Carl spoke, though there was no one around to hear him—except for the voice in his head. He doubled over and pressed his fingertips against his skull. "I know who I am. I'm not a killer."

Bullets whizzed past. A soldier rushed at him. Carl slit the man's throat and bolted. Burst through a door. Sprinted outside. Glanced over his shoulder. A mosque exploded behind him. Heat licked Carl's back as he dived for cover.

"I didn't blow up any mosque." Carl dug his knuckles into his temples. The windows shook as a train on Boston's Green Line rattled past. "I've never left the country."

The scene changed. Carl was in an alley, and a submachine gun bucked in his hands. Dark-skinned boys screamed and fell at his feet.

"Get out of my head!" Carl jumped from the chair and stumbled across his apartment to the bathroom. He yanked open the medicine cabinet and found the bottle. With a cry, Carl ripped off the cap and dumped two green capsules into his hand. He popped them into his mouth and swallowed them dry.

"I'm Carl Franklin," he said into the mirror. His rugged, handsome visage was marred by uneven stubble. His eyes were bloodshot, haunted. "I'm a successful accountant. I'm not a killer. Hold onto what you know."

While repeating the mantra, the mental fog lifted. The radiator clattered. A cold breeze blew through the crack under the toilet. His heart rate slowed. The images were gone. For now.

Blinking and shaking his head, Carl stuck the bottle in his pocket and returned to the living room. He needed to call Dr. Silva.

After Carl picked up the phone, he considered what he would say. How could he explain that he no longer knew what was real and what wasn't?

You can't say that.

The cold, hard-edged voice warning him off was his own—but it wasn't. Two weeks ago, the voice had started telling him what to do. Where to go. What to say. Who to fear. Oh, God, why wouldn't it stop?

You know why. You were sick. In pain. You couldn't pay the medical bills.

"No, that's not what happened," Carl pleaded with the voice.

They cured you. And, in exchange, you sold your soul.

"No." Carl flung the phone across the room. The images reappeared one at a time, like stars in a darkening night sky. He recoiled from the sting of his wife slapping him when she discovered the deal he'd made, the horrible things he'd done. His gut twisted at the blood pouring from his wife's forehead after he shot her. "None of this happened. I know who I am."

Do you? Sick laughter echoed in his head. *Are you sure Carl Franklin is real?*

"I have to be. I won't be someone else."

But you are. You always were. The voice amplified, reverberating in his skull. *And you must follow his orders.*

He saw a man with no face, only cruel, menacing eyes. Commanding. Controlling.

"He doesn't exist!" Carl's head swam. The faceless man followed him as Carl stumbled toward the kitchen, losing his balance and cracking his head against the table.

The stench of sour ale from the half-finished beer bottles scattered around the room assaulted Carl's nose, making his stomach heave. Blocking out the smell, he opened the refrigerator and grabbed what remained of a six-pack. He popped open a bottle and chugged the beer.

You can run, but you can't hide. Every word echoed like a concussion grenade. *Sooner or later, you'll have to admit what you did.*

"Never!" Carl grabbed and gulped down another beer. The bottle slipped from his grasp. Crashed. Splattered him with glass shards. He clenched his fists and howled. "I know who I am!"

But you don't. Do what he wants, and you will.

Carl stumbled to the window and gazed out at the frozen

swimming pool below. In a few months, when the ice melted and the flowers bloomed, his neighbors would lounge on deck chairs, listening to reggae music and living the good life. How lucky they were to be free of doubt. They'd never wonder if everything they knew was a lie.

You don't have a choice.

Drops fell from overhanging icicles. Looking at the light snow dusting the courtyard, at squirrels foraging for whatever acorns they'd missed before winter struck, Carl felt calm at last. At peace. He did have a choice.

Hold on. Let's not do anything stupid.

Carl backed up a few steps to get a running start, and then jumped and crashed through the window, plummeting eight stories. His last thought was clear: I know who I am.

CHAPTER ONE

"Now I know who I am," Jerry Peterman said, wiping a tear from his eye. He glanced at the medical licenses and psychiatric board certifications arranged on Cristina's office wall and turned back to her, beaming. "I'm remembering more every day. It's like someone opened the floodgates. I don't know how to thank you, Doctor."

As the affable security guard gushed about his recovered memories, brushing his thinning hair over his bald spot and then rubbing his thick palms together while he talked, Cristina Silva's heart swelled with pride. Nine months earlier, Jerry had been a lost lamb, afraid and unwilling to talk about what little he remembered before the ten-year gap in his memory. Those years had disappeared, as had his confidence. But now he was ready to rejoin the world, and he couldn't stop thanking Cristina and praising her psychiatric skills.

"You're embarrassing me," she said, scribbling on her notepad. She sat on an easy chair opposite Jerry, who was perched on the couch. "Jerry, you've done the hard work, finding mementos to trigger your memories, doing relaxation exercises, staying healthy."

"Sure, all that stuff helped, but none of it would've mattered if you hadn't hooked me up with Recognate. Working bank security these days is going great and I even joined a bowling league—did I tell you that? Still, I keep worrying that one day you'll tell me I can't get the pills anymore, and everything will go back to how it was."

"Don't worry about that. When the study ends, you can keep taking Recognate as long as you need it."

"But will it keep working? What if I wake up one day and—just like before—I have no idea who I am?"

Cristina's skin grew cold. She glanced at the desk photo of a couple in their fifties: attractive, and professional, with Latin features like Cristina's own. Her slender nose and frame perfectly matched the man's, while her dark eyes and curly hair mirrored the woman's. Her parents had died two years ago to the day. Valentine's Day. The day their life ended—and hers began.

Brushing away her thoughts like cobwebs, Cristina turned back to her patient. "Jerry, please don't worry. Even when subjects in earlier studies stopped taking the drug, they experienced no withdrawal or memory loss. I'm just glad it's worked so well for you."

Jerry sighed, visibly relieved. His emotional stability was still erratic. "It definitely worked. You've given me back my life. Do you know what I remembered last night? I ran the Boston Marathon twice. Once in a bunny suit!"

"Yes, you already told me." Cristina couldn't help smiling. "Twice."

His face flushed. "Sorry."

"Don't be. I love your enthusiasm." Cristina's watch beeped. She glanced at it before opening a desk drawer and removing a slim rectangle wrapped in ruby paper. She smiled and handed it to him. "This is for you."

His eyes widened as he accepted the gift. "A Valentine's Day present?"

"More of a token to recognize how far you've come. Open it."

He ripped off the wrapping paper to reveal a book bound in black leather. He ran his fingers over the cover. "It's a journal."

"I think it would be a good idea for you to record both new experiences and regained memories." Leaning forward, Cristina tapped the book cover. "And it's also so you don't need to worry. If for some reason you lose your memory again, you'll have an anchor to quickly pull you back."

Jerry looked at the journal, then at her, eyes brimming with tears. "Thank you. I'm not sure when's the last time someone gave me anything."

"Whatever you remember, write it down." She smiled and turned to her computer. "You're still at the same address?"

"Huh? Oh, yes."

She glanced at him. "Is something wrong?"

"No, it's nothing. It's … Uh …" He studied the floor. "Would you have dinner with me?"

Cristina's face flushed. Unintentionally attracting affections from clients was as much an occupational hazard of working in mental health as getting burnt was when being a firefighter. The clinical term was transference.

Cristina swallowed. Jerry had come so far. And she certainly did not want to damage his still-fragile psyche.

"I appreciate the offer, but because this is a professional relationship with boundaries, I want to be certain that you understand what can and cannot happen between us."

His face fell. He stared again at the floor. "I know. I'm sorry."

"Hey," she said, lightly tapping the journal until he reestablished eye contact. "I'm proud of you. It took a lot for you to ask. Use that newfound courage and keep taking risks. There's someone out there for you. Promise me?"

His mouth twisted before a hint of a smile played at his lips. "Okay, Doc."

"Good. You have my cell number if you ever need a shot of encouragement." She winked. "And since you're a preferred patient, I won't even charge you a co-pay."

He laughed.

Cristina finished typing and printed Jerry's prescriptions before handing them over. "This should hold you for two more months. Be sure to make an appointment with me before you run out. I want to hear more about your college road trip to New Orleans."

After Jerry left, Cristina leaned back in her chair and scanned her notes. So many of her patients foundered no matter what she did. However, her patients like Jerry—those enrolled in the Recognate trials—had experienced dramatic recoveries nothing short of miraculous. And without suffering a single adverse effect.

What a shame the manufacturer had declined so many of her referrals to the trials. ReMind Pharmaceuticals used unusually narrow inclusion criteria for this open trial, but once the results went public, Recognate would be available to everyone. Not only would it help those with total amnesia, it could benefit anyone needing a memory boost.

As she closed Jerry's chart and set it aside, Cristina amused herself with the thought that Recognate was so effective that if ReMind marketed it directly to the consumer, it could cut her patient roster down enough to potentially put her out of business. But there was no sign of a mass patient exodus happening soon. Her patients depended upon her. And Cristina loved helping them find themselves. It got her out of bed each morning and gave her a strong sense of purpose.

Her watch beeped again. She shut it off and glanced at the desktop photo. This time she surrendered to impulse and traced the outline of the man's face, imagining the feel of rough stubble under her fingertips. She did the same with the woman's—almost but not quite smelling the scent of Angel perfume.

"Soon I'll remember everything," she whispered as she stroked the photo. "I won't lose you again."

Cristina pulled her hand away, opening her top desk drawer and removing a bottle of green pills and a water bottle. She popped two capsules in her mouth and chased them with a splash of water. She closed her eyes and tried to remain patient, waiting to discover what she would remember next.

CHAPTER TWO

After finishing her last patient progress note of the day, Cristina leaned back at her desk and massaged her scalp. While psychiatry wasn't as physically grueling as emergency medicine or surgery, the emotional investment of dealing with intractable depression and uncontrolled mania was incredibly taxing. If it weren't for the success with her Recognate patients, she wasn't sure she could get through the day.

A light knock on her office door brought Cristina out of her reverie. She looked up to see her office manager leaning against the jamb. Devi Patel's petite frame was bundled in a ski parka.

"I pulled the referrals for tomorrow and called to confirm your appointments." Devi's voice lilted with a trace of an Indian accent. "If it's okay with you, I'm going to head out."

"Of course, it's okay. It's already six thirty." Devi had been hired six months ago, after Cristina's first office manager quit unexpectedly. Filling the position so quickly had been lucky. To have someone so dedicated and skilled with technology was a double blessing. Cristina certainly didn't want to deal with another employee burning out and urged Devi to leave. "You should've gone home an hour ago."

"I could say the same for you." Devi flipped a strand of straight black hair away from her eyes and pursed her lips. "You're not going to pull another all-nighter, right?"

"No. I just need to review my notes one more time. My report to ReMind is due in a few weeks, and I don't want to leave out anything that could jeopardize their study."

"You? Miss something?" Devi laughed. "Sherlock Holmes didn't have the eye for detail you have. And I'm not just saying that because you're my boss."

"Well, thank you." Cristina blushed. She eyed the pink cashmere scarf wrapped around Devi's neck. "Fancy. Big plans tonight?"

"My boyfriend's taking me to dinner at L'Aromatique for Valentine's Day." Devi furrowed her brow. "You don't have plans?"

"Uh, no, unless you count snuggling with my cat."

The holidays seemed to bring more pain than joy, and Valentine's Day was the worst—a bitter reminder of what she'd lost two years ago.

Push that feeling away, she thought. I need to be complete before I can share myself with anyone else. And I certainly do not need to unload my crap on my assistant.

Forcing a smile, Cristina shrugged. "It's fine. I'll get another chance to celebrate the day in a few months."

"What do you mean?"

"In Brazil, they celebrate Valentine's Day in June. It's called Dia dos Namorados—Lover's Day. I've been thinking of taking a trip to Rio this summer, so …"

An image sparked in her mind so abruptly that Cristina stopped talking: a teenaged Cristiano Ronaldo lookalike held her hand, leading her through a street packed with taxis and tourists. Cristina's other hand clutched a bouquet of red roses. The smell of black beans and seasoned beef wafted from the entrance of a nearby restaurant. The handsome boy caught her eye and pointed up. Towering overhead atop a cliff was at a statue of Christ with outstretched arms.

"Dr. Silva? Are you okay?"

Cristina jumped. She turned, wide-eyed, and found Devi staring at her.

"I'm fine," she said, feeling anything but. She'd gotten used to new memories appearing a few hours after taking Recognate, but this one had been different. It was so vivid and felt more real. Yet her mind told her that wasn't true. It couldn't be.

While growing up, Cristina's parents had often talked about taking her to see Rio de Janeiro, where her mother had been born. They had even taught Cristina Portuguese and made her watch every movie about Brazil they could find. But they never made that trip.

Cristina recognized the statue in the memory from photos of Corcovado. It was Christ the Redeemer, a famous landmark in Rio. But it was something about the boy that struck a chord. It was more than his resemblance to a famous soccer player. He meant something to Cristina. At least, that's how it felt.

Realizing Devi was still eyeing her, Cristina forced a chuckle. "A little headache. It'll go away."

Devi's cell phone chirped.

"That's my guy." She gave Cristina a lingering look. "Are you sure you're okay?"

"Go. Have fun." Cristina shooed her off. "In fact, take your time coming in tomorrow morning. I'll open up."

"But I always check the answering service before anyone gets here."

"I think I can handle a few voicemails on my own."

Devi beamed. "Thanks, boss. Have a good night."

Twenty minutes later, Cristina gave up on her plan to get any work done. Her mind kept drifting back to the vision of

Corcovado. She shut down her computer and donned a black, double-breasted overcoat.

As she stepped from the office building into Boston's wintry night air, she found it easier to chase away the chill than the images of Rio. The experiences Recognate uncovered were comforting, like a warm blanket. But this particular one made her as confused as she was when she had woken in a hospital two years earlier. Could false memory be a side effect of the drug?

Cristina chided herself as she walked to the bus stop in front of her Brookline Avenue office. How many times had she reviewed risks and benefits with her study subjects? ReMind promised genuine memories. And that's what Recognate delivered. Cristina cinched her belt tighter and laughed at her silliness. She was overworked. The memory of Brazil faded away; an odd dream probably stemming from something she'd seen in a commercial.

When she reached the bus stop and stopped to wait, the back of her neck crawled.

Someone was following her. Reaching for her.

She spun and grabbed the man's arm. Twisted it around behind his back.

He cried out in pain.

Cristina wrapped her other arm around his neck. "What do you want?" she demanded. She squeezed his wrist.

He was a head taller than her. Bulky muscles contracted under a flannel jacket.

"I—I wanted …" His voice was strained.

She loosened her grip on his throat.

He coughed. "I wanted to return your book."

He held up his free hand, displaying a dog-eared novel. Jose Lins do Rego's *Menino de Engenho*.

Her face tingled. The book must've fallen out of her purse.

She released him, then stepped back and accepted the book, dropping it into her purse.

The man massaged his neck. A dirty fisherman's cap covered his head, and the collar on his jacket obscured his lower face. Crow's feet lined his obsidian eyes.

"I'm so sorry," said Cristina. "You startled me. I didn't hurt you, did I?"

"I'll be fine." His voice was deep and rough, with a trace of a Latin accent. His clothes were unwashed. Eyes rimmed with redness.

"Do you have a place to stay?"

His gray-flecked eyebrows rose. "You're offering your home to a stranger?"

"Well, no, but I could walk you to the Longwood shelter. It's not far from here."

"You're very kind, but no."

"But—"

He jerked his chin. "Our bus is here."

She turned as the yellow and white 47 bus pulled up, brakes hissing. She nodded. "Again, I'm sorry for my freak-out."

Where had those moves come from? Her friend Andrea had taught her self-defense moves, but nothing as advanced as that—whatever that had been. Cristina shook her head and tapped her monthly T-pass on the reader. First, the weird Rio vision and now this. Maybe it was a good thing she'd be spending some alone time tonight.

She made her way through the empty bus, choosing her usual seat at the midpoint near the heater, the only one with some cushioning. Her heart still pounded.

As he walked by her, the husky man's eyes flicked in her direction. The corner of his mouth twitched. She couldn't read his expression but doubted it was positive.

He plopped into the seat behind her.

Cristina sat up straighter, forearm hairs bristling. An empty bus and he chose to sit there?

The bus started moving. She forced herself to relax. He probably wanted to be near the heater, too. She had no idea why she was so jumpy.

She needed to calm down. She pulled a copy of the *New England Journal of Medicine* from her purse and flipped to an article describing beta-endorphins, naturally occurring opiate-like neurotransmitters. The authors claimed a synthetic version restored memory in mice that had been exposed to toxic drugs. However, the mice became aggressive over time.

Every few years, the journal editors rehashed the beta-endorphin theory, but they were never any closer to finding a viable treatment. Cristina knew their research was close to becoming moot. Once Recognate was approved for mass market, there'd be no need for snake oil and holy water.

The bus stopped and a few more passengers boarded before it continued its route.

The vibrations as the big engine accelerated soothed Cristina. She glanced at the article. There was a reference to a study on gamma-aminobutyric acid agonists for memory restoration. She made a mental note to look that up. It never hurt to follow competing theories.

"You're not who you think you are."

Cristina was startled. The voice came from the seat behind her. She recognized it as the man she'd senselessly attacked. Was he talking to her? No, that was silly. He was probably on his phone. She stuck her nose in the journal and kept reading.

"You may think you know, *Doctor*, but you do not."

The back of her neck prickled. Clearly, he was speaking to her. He knew she was a doctor. Maybe her initial protective instincts had been correct, after all. She'd heard stories about criminals following people home on the bus and then robbing them. Well, she wasn't about to be a victim. She reached out for the stop request wire. Better to catch a cab than take chances.

"If you want to know the truth, stay on this bus," the man said in thick Brazilian Portuguese. "I know who you really are."

His sudden use of her mother's native tongue surprised her. Cristina hardly considered herself fluent, but she knew enough to understand him. And the confidence in his voice—the way he said, *I know who you really are*—made her hesitate.

"The way you attacked me at the bus stop and your confusion afterward prove I'm right. You can feel it, can't you?"

Cristina's heart fluttered. She had felt differently when putting him in that chokehold. It was almost as if someone else had taken over her body. But that was ridiculous. She took a deep breath and gathered her nerves. That false memory must've shaken her more than she thought. Calmly, she turned to face the man. "Look, I don't know what—"

"Don't turn around!"

His tone was so sharp, so commanding, she automatically obeyed, her breath quickening.

After a moment, she chided herself for letting him intimidate her and asked, "Who do you think you—?"

"Keep facing forward and act natural." His voice deepened, becoming more threatening.

"Act natural?" She laughed despite—or maybe because of—her fear. "Why? You'll shoot me if I don't?"

"Yes."

The blood drained from her face. "You have a gun?"

"I won't use it if you remain calm and do as I say."

Her heart pounded. He was serious. How many times had her friend Andrea told her not to take the bus? Cristina had always dismissed these suggestions as being overprotective. She knew how to take care of herself.

Now Cristina regretted ignoring Andrea's warning. Even if she could pull off another move like the one at the bus stop earlier, she couldn't be sure this man wouldn't shoot one of the other passengers first.

But Cristina could get help. Carefully, she slipped her hand into her purse, hunting for her cell phone. While she searched, she needed to keep the man behind her distracted. She'd keep him talking.

"What do you want?"

"I need your help, but we don't have much time."

"Why not?"

"We're being watched."

"By who?" Her fingertips brushed cold plastic. She withdrew her phone. She was vaguely aware of the bus stopping and its doors opening.

"Stop asking questions, Cristina!"

She paused in the middle of dialing 911. "How do you know my name?"

"Because I knew you before your memory was stolen."

Cristina's mouth went dry. The phone slipped from her hand back into her purse. "Who are you?"

"My name is Sebastian dos Santos. Everything you know is a lie," he whispered. "When you find the truth, find me. Trust no one."

A group of teenagers jostled past her seat. One of them, a gangly boy with spiked hair and low-hanging jeans, paused and winked at her. She opened her mouth to plead for help but then stopped herself.

What if the man behind her really knew something? Nearly everything her parents owned had been destroyed in a fire a month before their deaths in a car crash. Since then Cristina had failed to locate any other relatives. And since the head injury she'd sustained from the backseat of that crash had wiped out most of her own memory, all she knew about her parents—and of herself, even her age of 35 years—had been gathered from a few surviving documents, the police detective who investigated the wreck, and her recovered memories. But there were many black holes, even of the crash itself. What if Sebastian dos Santos could provide the missing pieces? Wasn't it worth the risk to be whole again?

After the teenager shrugged and joined his friends at the back of the bus, Cristina gathered her courage. "What do you know?"

No response came.

"I promise I won't call for help. Tell me what you know."

In the back, the teenagers hollered and laughed.

Cristina's cheeks burned. Her knuckles whitened as she gripped the seat. She struggled with her instincts, but they won out. She turned around.

The seat behind her was empty—except for an unmarked manila envelope.

CHAPTER THREE

Paramedics labeled him a DRT: Dead Right There. Male, white, midforties. Eight-story fall from the victim's Somerville apartment window between four and five in the afternoon. Detective Gary Wilson scratched the light stubble growing on his chiseled chin as he surveyed the scene. Lush slate-gray carpet reeking of stale beer. Empty bottles littering the rich hardwood of the kitchen floor. No sign of forced entry. Likely suicide.

The victim's blood stained a few jagged glass shards still clinging to the frame of the shattered window. Cold wind blew inside. Detective Wilson tapped a latex-gloved finger on one of the bigger pieces. Double-pane; it'd take a lot of momentum to break through that. He kept himself in good shape, even by standards for a thirty-seven-year-old cop, but he doubted he could've punched a hole in the glass. He looked over his shoulder to check the angle. Living room was small, and the luxurious leather couch was in the way. Still, a good running start from the kitchen might be enough. He stripped off the gloves.

"Arriving officers found these in the bathroom," Detective Rick Hawkins said as he handed Wilson a baggie containing a pill bottle. The wrinkles around Hawkins' eyes were deeper than ever, his hair winter white. "Dated two weeks ago, but there are only four or five left."

Wilson held the bottle up to the light. A handful of tiny green capsules rolled around inside. He read the label. "Recognate? What the hell's that?"

"Never heard of it."

"It's prescribed by a Dr. Cristina Silva. Let's find out what she knows."

"Gary, it's a suicide. You know, Valentine's Day, death by broken heart. *Wah, wah, wah.* Captain Harris wants us to wrap this up and move on."

"Something about this feels different. Look at this place. Expensive furniture. Fancy clothes. His flat screen TV costs more than my monthly rent. He was living the good life. What would make this guy decide to off himself?"

"Suicide isn't limited to the poor."

"I know." Wilson scratched the bristles covering his cheek. He kept his dark hair cut shorter than police regulations required, but he insisted on keeping the sideburns. "He could've overdosed on the painkillers in his medicine cabinet or hung himself in the closet. Why run through a double-pane window?"

Hawkins shrugged and said, "According to his neighbors, the dude had been shouting nonsense five times a day for the past two weeks. Sounds like he went nuts."

A chill ran down Wilson's neck at the memory: hearing the coroner say, *She just went nuts* … seeing the ghastly look frozen on his mother's face when Wilson identified her and his father at the morgue.

Wilson shook off the painful memories and studied the pill bottle. If the guy had been hearing things, he might've jumped through the window to make it stop. Not a planned suicide, but a suicide all the same. "Are any of the neighbors still around?"

"One's going over his statement with Officer Capshaw outside."

"Let's go talk to him."

A few minutes later, the detectives met in the hallway with Marko Novak. The pasty-skinned man with shaggy blond hair and a goatee lived next door to Carl Franklin. He wore jeans and a *Star Wars* T-shirt.

"How well did you know Mr. Franklin?" Hawkins asked.

"Not well. He didn't talk much to neighbors. Maybe because he always had pretty women over."

"Girlfriends?" Wilson asked.

"At least for the night." Novak sniggered. "The women looked professional, you know?"

Wilson made a mental note. If the victim spent more time with hookers than having actual interpersonal relationships, it could go along with depression. "Tell us again what you overheard."

"Shouting, shouting, and more shouting. Sometimes in the middle of the night."

"Did you ever try to find out what was wrong?" Wilson said.

Novak made a *tsk* sound with his tongue. "One thing I've learned about life, Detective, if you value your nose, you do not stick it into other people's business."

Hawkins gave Wilson a look he took to mean, *Speed it up.*

"All right," Wilson said. "Were you able to make out anything clearly?"

"Most of it was nonsense," Novak said. "But, today, he kept shouting over and over again, *I know who I am* and *I'm not a killer.*"

"He said he wasn't a killer?"

"Yeah."

Wilson turned to Hawkins with a knowing look.

"Also, "I definitely heard two different voices," Novak said. "One of them kept saying the name Quinn."

Wilson committed the name to memory. "Could you tell if that was a first or last name?"

Hawkins shook his head. "It doesn't matter. Door was locked from the inside. Franklin was alone. And crazy."

Wilson ran his fingers through his hair. Was Hawkins right? Even as a kid, Wilson had pissed off his teachers by trying to make the round pegs fit into the square holes. He pissed them off even more when he succeeded. Whenever he had faced an impossible puzzle, an itch started behind his ear. It intensified with every new piece until he solved the whole puzzle.

The back of his ear itched right now.

"Do you know what kind of work Mr. Franklin did?" he asked Novak.

"I think he was an accountant."

Wilson turned to Hawkins again. "He lived an extravagant lifestyle for an accountant. Maybe he embezzled from the wrong client." To Novak, he asked, "Did you ever see anyone suspicious lurking around? Or maybe Franklin invited someone in today?"

"Sorry, Gary. Time's up." Hawkins held up his cell phone to display a text. "There's been a break-in at the Winter Hill stationery store. Perps ran off with a carload of heart-shaped cards and paper flowers. Captain thinks it's tied to the eBay racketeer case we're investigating and wants us to check it out."

After thanking Novak for his statement, the detectives started down the stairs.

Wilson's ear still itched.

"Did you hear Novak say how Franklin was shouting that he wasn't a killer?"

"Carl Franklin was delusional," Hawkins sighed.

"Are there any warrants out for Franklin's arrest? Maybe he's tied to one of our unsolved murders and killed himself because he thought he was about to get caught."

"No criminal records. Not even a parking ticket. C'mon, Gary, let it go."

Wilson sighed and stuffed the baggie into his pocket. He'd leave the pill bottle with the evidence room, but the read he was getting off Hawkins made it clear there was no way anyone else was going to push the investigation any further. Hopefully, Dr. Silva's other patients were more fortunate than Carl Franklin.

"I hate Valentine's Day."

"Why do you ride the bus, anyway?" Andrea Rojas reclined on her red leather couch. Colorful reproductions of paintings by Monet and Gauguin hung on the caramel living room walls of her one-bedroom Porter Square apartment. Flipping her auburn hair over her shoulder, she ran a crimson nail around the edge of her martini glass before taking a sip. "You're a doctor. Shouldn't you—I don't know—have a car service drive you around or something?"

"That costs a lot of money and wealthy patients aren't exactly rolling into my practice." Cristina, who sat next to Andrea, was still trying to keep her still cold hands from shaking. Twenty minutes earlier, she'd come straight to Andrea's apartment after rushing from the bus stop. Now she took a tentative sip of her mojito. It was good, but even her favorite drink couldn't calm her frayed nerves. "I'm still paying off student loans."

"Can't you buy a used car?"

Cristina set the glass onto the coffee table next to a bowl of cinnamon potpourri. "I can't believe you're asking me that. You know why I don't drive."

"*Ay, chica*, I know you're afraid of another accident, but I worry. A totally hot woman like you, dressed to the nines, riding a bus? Draws out all the crazies." Andrea leaned forward and placed her hand on Cristina's knee. "I don't want anything happening to my best friend, okay?"

"I know." Cristina slumped against the seat cushion. "Riding the bus never scared me before, but then I've never been held at gunpoint before either."

"How do you know?"

"That I was scared?"

"No. How do you know he had a gun? Because he told you?"

"Well, yeah."

"Sweetie, working as a paralegal, I get threats all the time. Most are full of crap. He probably just said that to scare you."

"Then it worked." Cristina shivered. "Everything Sebastian dos Santos said was so creepy. He knew my name and where I work. And the way he kept saying that he knows who I really am ..."

"If any of that were true, why all the riddles and threats?"

"He said we were being watched."

Andrea took a swig from her class and wiped her mouth with the back of her hand. "Nobody in real life talks like that. This guy sounds like a total crackpot."

Cristina's cheeks burned. "Didn't you just tell me I need to be more careful?"

"Careful, yes. Take another self-defense class with me or at least carry pepper spray." Andrea narrowed her gaze. "But I know that look from you. What this jerk said is making you doubt yourself—am I right?"

Cristina's irritation faded to embarrassment. Andrea knew her all too well. Shortly after the car crash, they'd met in the laundry room of their apartment building. Cristina couldn't figure out what wash settings to use for her delicates and Andrea rushed to the rescue. That led to dinners together, drinks and late-night talks about everything.

It hadn't been long since the car crash and Andrea had made Cristina feel safe during a time when she was most vulnerable, when she didn't know who to trust. Since then, Cristina felt a

DO NOT USE

need to do everything she could to earn Andrea's trust in return. That meant being honest with her—or at least, mostly honest.

"Sebastian dos Santos said my memory was stolen. Not lost. *Stolen.* What if the hit and run that killed my parents wasn't an accident?"

"Sweetie, you're a shrink so you know some people are sadists. People like this Santos creep enjoy seeing others suffer. You've come so far since we first met, but you still question everything good in your life. Don't you deserve to be happy?"

"Yes, but—"

"But nothing. You've worked hard to recover those memories. They're not fake. You're a good person and deserve the life you've created. Your parents' death wasn't your fault. And neither was Mitchell's."

Cristina flinched. She remembered waking up in a hospital bed two years ago—an IV stuck in her arm, monitors beeping. A man in his midforties wearing a snug charcoal suit and designer shoes sat in a chair beside the bed. He had wavy dark hair and inquisitive blue eyes. Deep facial lines made him look distinguished.

Detective Mitchell Parker from the Framingham PD was investigating the car crash that had killed her parents, Jorge and Claudia Silva. But Cristina recalled nothing about that night, or about her life before. She couldn't even remember her own name. Her memory was blank.

During that awful time, Mitchell had insisted on acting as her personal protector, even blocking intrusions from reporters while the police searched for the other driver that had run them off the road. Some information crept back in, including an understanding of and passion for neuroscience and medicine, but nothing about her personal life.

When she was discharged from the hospital, Mitchell had

escorted her back to her apartment, making sure she had everything she needed. Over the next four months, he checked in on her regularly. Cristina found herself drawn by his self-confidence, his determination to get her life back on track. During visits, he'd even helped her with the paperwork to collect every penny from her parents' life insurance policy, enabling her to reopen the private practice she'd started before the crash. By then, she'd managed to reboot her knowledge of psychiatry using the textbooks she found in her apartment, and Mitchell helped her figure out initial logistics until she hired an office manager to handle the rest. But she still felt nothing when she looked at the picture of her parents, and even her own name felt unfamiliar to her.

"I wish I could help more," he'd told her. "I want to help you reclaim the life you lost."

It was Mitchell who'd heard about a memory drug trial. He insisted it would help her recover personal memories and make her whole.

Too risky, she'd decided at the time. How could Cristina effectively treat her patients if she was taking an experimental drug? At that time, she decided that she could get by without it.

Although Mitchell and Cristina didn't find any more clues about the hit-and-run driver, they found something else: each other. With no memory of her old life, he became the most important part of her new one. When despair over the collision threatened to drown Cristina, Mitchell gave her air to breathe.

Until—with no warning—he withdrew from her. He disappeared for hours, then days. On Labor Day, she found a note slipped under her door. It was long and handwritten. In it, Mitchell apologized for leading her on. He asked for her forgiveness. He regretted not being able to do more to help her. As she read the note, Cristina recognized what it was: a suicide note. Frantic, she phoned him.

No answer.

She tried the police station. He'd failed to report in for the past two weeks.

A few days later, an officer phoned her. Mitchell Parker had been found in a ditch in Callahan State Park, dead of a self-inflicted gunshot wound.

Andrea waved her hand in front of Cristina's face. "Where'd you go?"

Cristina forced away her self-doubt. Mitchell's death had triggered her desperate call to ReMind. With him gone, the need to recover her own memories outweighed any theoretical ethical concerns. And the gamble had paid off. Cristina Silva knew who she was. And Andrea was her rock throughout all of it.

Cristina smiled at her friend. "Are you totally sure you don't want to work for me as a counselor?"

Hooting, Andrea threw herself backward, sloshing wine onto her leopard print pants.

"Shit!" She tried to blot the stain with her hand. After making it worse, she shrugged and set the empty glass onto the table. "Whatever—I got them on clearance. Anyway, no offense, honey, but if I won't let anyone poke around in my head, I'm not going to poke around in someone else's."

"I could sure use the help. My wait list is up to five months now. Which is probably why I'm so stressed. Then add the anniversary of my parents' death to that … " Cristina sighed and took a swig of her mojito. "Let's look at it logically. If Sebastian dos Santos was stalking me, he might know my name and that I'm a doctor and he possibly might have even somehow learned that I suffer from amnesia."

"Exactly!" Andrea scooted closer to Cristina and pulled her in for a hug. "He wants you to run an insurance scam for him or some other dirty scheme, but he's not worth the worry."

"What if he's mentally ill? I'm a psychiatrist. I should've offered to help him."

"*Mami*, you may think you're Mother Teresa and Dr. Phil's love child, but you can't save everyone—especially if it puts you in danger. I don't want you taking that bus tomorrow. Why don't you take the T?"

"It's so far out of the way."

"A little exercise never hurt anyone. And on that note, you're coming to my gym tomorrow after work for a session. It's been weeks since we sparred."

"I know. I've been—"

"So busy, yadda, yadda. No arguments." Andrea gave her a pointed look. "Clear?"

Cristina rolled her eyes and laughed. "Clear. I'll give you a call after work."

After another mojito, Cristina left Andrea's apartment. Walking upstairs to her one-bedroom unit, Cristina glanced over her shoulder to ensure no one was watching before pulling from her bag the folder that Sebastian dos Santos had left behind on the bus seat.

As tempted as she had been to tell Andrea about the folder, her friend's fiery skepticism had made Cristina decide to view its contents alone first.

Once inside her apartment with the door locked, Cristina sat on her suede couch. No fancy paintings or elegant potpourri here. Her place was sparer and less colorful than Andrea's. Maybe Cristina needed to decorate, to try harder, but her office always felt more like home to her than this bare-bones apartment.

Grizabella leaped onto Cristina's lap and curled into a ball. As she stroked the tabby's scruffy neck, the stress seeped from Cristina's bones. She'd rescued the cat from a shelter a few months after she started taking Recognate. Some studies had suggested pet therapy was helpful in restoring memory in Alzheimer's patients. As Cristina had been trying to cope with Mitchell's death, she considered that a feline companion might prove useful. But the moment she saw the little furball at the animal shelter, her motivations were suddenly less utilitarian. It was love at first sight.

Cristina nuzzled Grizabella's back, drinking in her earthy smell before opening the folder and emptying its contents onto her coffee table. A stack of newspaper articles printed from the Internet stared back at her. Her heart beat faster as she recognized the headline on the first: *Local Couple Dies in Hit-and-Run.*

She'd already read that piece and wasn't about to read it again. Setting it aside, Cristina studied the second article. A middle-aged banker in Spokane missing for three days had been found dead in his apartment, his hand gripping the knife he'd used to stab his own eye. Cristina fought the urge to vomit. She tossed the article aside.

Her stomach knotted as she flipped through four more articles. All of them described violent suicides in cities across the country. But for the article on her parents, none of the others had anything to do with her. Had Sebastian dos Santos killed those people? And could he have been the hit and run driver responsible for her parents' deaths?

The last article was dated five years ago and from *O Globo*, a paper out of Rio de Janeiro. In Portuguese, the headline announced a project to study a new treatment for mental health factors causing gang violence in the Rio slums called *favelas*. Alongside the article was a black and white photo of a research team standing next to a Brazilian flag.

Cristina shook her head. What could her parents' death, a handful of suicides and a Brazilian research team possibly have in common?

She sifted through the articles, then checked in vain to see if there was anything else inside the envelope. Chewing her lip,

Cristina nudged Grizabella off her lap and opened her MacBook. After it powered up, she typed the name *Sebastian dos Santos* into the search engine.

Several Facebook profiles popped up with that name. But none of their pictures resembled the man in the fisherman's cap. There was a long-dead French explorer with the same name.

She entered Sebastian dos Santos's name again, but this time added her parents' names. The search engine seemed to work a little harder but produced nothing of substance. She was about to try *Spokane banker*—the first article's suicide—when her phone vibrated. It was a local number, but not one she recognized. Hesitantly, she answered.

"Dr. Silva?"

She relaxed at the soft Southwestern twang, nothing like the rough Latin accent of the man on the bus. "Yes."

"I'm sorry for calling so late. My name is Dr. Lucas Morgan from the Medical Examiner's office. I was wondering if you could come downtown."

"Medical examiner?" She sat up straight. "Why?"

"I'm afraid we need you to identify a body. One of your patients, Carl Franklin, killed himself."

CHAPTER FOUR

Light bluegrass music bounced from overhead speakers, in sharp contrast to the bleak windowless waiting room. A pot of wilted calla lilies rested on a table near the reception desk, their aroma drowned out by the tang of chlorine. Cristina sat alone on a leather bench, staring at the black and white photographs of downtown Boston displayed on the walls. She'd never been in a medical examiner's office before—at least, not that she remembered. Mitchell had spared her from identifying her parents since she wouldn't have recognized them anyway.

And she had never seen Mitchell's body. The heartbreak had been intense. There were even more shocks following his death. He'd led her to believe he was divorced, but the police officer who informed her over the phone about Mitchell's death said he was married. It had been hard enough to accept his suicide, but the fact that he'd lied to Cristina all along left her angry and confused.

Part of her wanted to call his wife for confirmation. Cristina's stomach churned as she recalled how many times she'd nearly picked up the phone, then decided against it. As hurt as Cristina was, she couldn't imagine what Mitchell's wife was suffering. Cristina had only known Mitchell for six months. This woman was married to him. Cristina had stayed away, grieving alone and in silence.

That feeling of loss—more familiar than even the memories of her parents—crept back into her chest. She massaged her chest, trying to relieve the pressure. Carl Franklin couldn't be dead. He would not have killed himself. This had to be a bad dream.

She clenched her fists. *Stay strong.*

The door to the autopsy room opened. A bald, muscular African American man wearing blue scrubs stepped out.

When he spotted her, Lucas Morgan's face lit up with a wide smile radiating warmth. He approached with his hand out. "Thanks again for coming out so late, Dr. Silva. I tried calling your office earlier, but you'd already left."

His handshake was firm. As she noted his square jaw and perfect white teeth set against his dark skin, she found herself at a loss for casual pleasantries "Dr. Morgan, please tell me what happened to Carl."

Morgan led her to the autopsy room, talking as they walked. "The building caretaker was clearing ice off the sidewalk when she heard the window smash overhead. She barely had enough time to get out of the way before Mr. Franklin hit the pavement. He died instantly."

Bitter smells of cleaning fluid and blood assaulted Cristina's nostrils as they entered the autopsy room. The metal tables and overhead floodlights reminded her of a terrifying scene from an alien abduction movie Andrea had made her watch. Cristina's stomach wrenched.

"Here." Morgan offered her a small tube of camphor rub and a surgical mask. "Dab some in each nostril."

She did as instructed and donned the mask. Menthol drifted along her nasal passages. The smell of death was still present but not as strong. "Thanks."

"Follow me." He led her to a table on the far side of the room. A white sheet covered the body. Although Morgan's mask concealed his mouth, his eyes radiated concern for her well-being. "Sure you're ready?"

Cristina bit her lip. Few things troubled a psychiatrist more than a patient threatening suicide. Even worse was when they acted, especially without warning. A thousand questions bounced in her head. Maybe seeing Carl Franklin's body would answer a few of them. She nodded. "Ready."

Morgan pulled back the sheet. A gasp escaped her lips.

Carl's naked body lay on the exam table, his neck twisted to the left. The right side of his head was caved in, right arm bent in an L-shape. What had made Cristina gasp, however, was the smile frozen on his lips.

"That's Carl," she said. "Believe it or not, he looks peaceful."

"I noticed that too. Doesn't match the police report of how he died."

"What do you mean?"

"Neighbors said they heard him ranting and raving. One of the detectives believed Mr. Franklin was having a psychotic break before he ran through the window."

Cristina studied Morgan's face for a sign he was joking. Finding none, she said, "Carl wasn't psychotic."

"The police found a bottle of an antipsychotics he was taking—Recogno or something? It had your name on the script. That's how I knew to call you."

Cristina swallowed hard. Carl had never showed signs of depression or instability. Could Recognate have made him psychotic?

She dismissed the idea. The Phase Three trial reports from ReMind had identified no major adverse effects. Surely, something as significant as psychosis or suicidality would have been reported. There had to be another explanation.

"I prescribed Carl medication, but not for psychosis. This is completely unexpected. Did you find anything in his system?"

"I've only got the preliminary tox back so far. Nothing except a zero point one blood alcohol."

"Carl said he didn't drink."

"That's what they all say." Morgan laughed at his own joke, then grew serious when Cristina didn't laugh with him. "I may be out of line, but it seems Mr. Franklin wasn't exactly forthcoming. Maybe he was trying to manage depression alone and failed."

The idea that Carl had been suffering, and she'd had no idea, was deeply troubling. If Carl were drinking heavily, it would explain his erratic behavior. "I guess you're right. I just feel horrible."

"Don't beat yourself up." Morgan covered the body. "I couldn't find any next of kin—which is why I called you. Did he mention any family I should contact?"

"No, Carl suffered from amnesia. He was an only child and his parents were dead. He never could remember the names of other family members."

"I'm sorry to hear that. Well, he didn't have many personal effects, but you're welcome to look at them."

"Thank you, no. Although, may I take a look at the medicine bottle? Do you know how many pills he took?"

"Cops kept it for evidence."

The shrill chirp of a smartphone woke Quinn from deep sleep. Ambient light from the nearby National Mall spilled through the window into his room at the Willard Intercontinental Hotel. With a growl, Quinn rolled over and snatched the device off the nightstand. After a full day of tense negotiations and unpleasant ass-kissing to potential investors, his forty-six-year-old body longed for one uninterrupted night of rest. That particular chirp was associated with an encrypted chat, warning him that tonight wouldn't be that night.

Operative report received, he read upon entering the chat. Santos active in Boston.

The muscles in Quinn's neck tensed. For two years he'd conducted a manhunt, but the rogue had seemed to vanish off the map. Now he resurfaced in Boston? There could only be one reason. He was after Cristina Silva. Anxiously, he typed: *Has he made contact?*

After a tense moment, the reply came: *Affirmative.*

This could put their entire plan in jeopardy. Santos had to be neutralized. Living in a hotel and operating under an assumed name gave Quinn flexibility to mobilize if needed, but he couldn't abandon his work in Washington right now—not after building up his role in the project over the past year and a half. He'd have to entrust others to handle matters in Boston, and trust didn't come easily to him.

The phone chirped again. Another message: *She tripped an internet packet sniffer. Seeking info on the rogue. She's digging where she shouldn't.*

Quinn caught himself from slamming the phone against the nightstand and instead took a deep breath. He typed: *I'll handle it.*

Grumbling to himself, Quinn tossed the phone onto the nightstand and searched for his pants. No more sleep. He'd deploy his operatives before Dr. Silva learned too much—if she hadn't already. If it was too late and he had to get personally involved, that would be messy for everyone. Quinn hated messy.

CHAPTER FIVE

When her alarm sounded the next morning, Cristina could barely summon enough strength to silence it, let alone crawl out of bed. She'd tossed and turned so much during the night that she wouldn't have been surprised to find bruises covering her body. Every time she'd started drifting off to sleep—she pictured Carl leaping eight floors to his death and jolted awake. When she tried to relax, she'd hear Santos whisper: *You're not who you think you are.*

In the shower, Cristina lathered conditioner in her hair, reciting the mantra she developed to deal with frustrations and setbacks. "You can do this. Yesterday was bad, but today will be better. Every day's another step forward. Every new memory, good or bad, is still progress toward a complete self."

Cristina leaned under the showerhead and closed her eyes, cleansing away stress and fear as warm water trickled down her face. Often a new memory emerged when she did this: a bit of medical school training, an image of a high school track race, maybe even a flash of her mother's face. But today her mind circled back again and again to Carl and her failure to save him. The walls of the tiny shower closed around her. Frustrated, she gave up her search for a new memory and toweled off.

Twenty minutes later, cold wind lashed against Cristina's cheeks as she stepped outside the apartment building. She tucked her hair tighter under a brown stocking cap and wrapped a beige scarf over her mouth. The extra layers protected her from the cold, as well as sheltering her from undue attention at the bus stop.

When the bus pulled up and its door opened, Cristina took a deep breath and reassured herself before boarding. She scanned the aisle of passengers while using her MBTA pass. A group of college students chatted in the back. A Hispanic couple stood near the front with a baby stroller. By the middle door sat an old Indian woman wrapped in a sari and *odhani* veil.

Cristina's usual seat by the heater was empty, but today she instead chose one closer to the front where the driver could clearly see her in the overhead mirror. She loosened her scarf and opened her purse. The can of pepper spray was there, next to the envelope of articles. Cristina had been too exhausted after returning from the medical examiner to review them again. As she pulled out the envelope, she heard a gravelly voice in the back of her mind. *We're being watched.*

She glanced at the Hispanic couple. The woman stuck a pacifier in the baby's mouth and cooed. When the man caught Cristina looking, she glanced away. Better not to take chances. She slipped the envelope back into her purse, found a medical journal and pretended to read it.

A few passengers boarded at each stop, but no husky men with fisherman caps. No one seemed to notice Cristina, let alone try to talk to her. By the time she reached her office, she almost felt disappointed. As frightening as the encounter with Sebastian dos Santos had been, Cristina had questions and wanted answers—perhaps even more now, after losing Carl. Maybe that was why she had ignored Andrea's suggestion to take the T instead of the bus. Despite her friend's reassurances that Santos the stranger was a scammer, Cristina felt sure he knew something about her past.

Or some part of her wanted to believe it.

With a sigh, Cristina hopped off the bus. As she walked to her practice, she reminded herself of her unwritten rule of psychiatry. *Don't listen too closely to your patients' delusions. They might start making sense.*

Devi was starting up her computer when Cristina entered. As expected, her assistant had ignored her offer to take a late morning. She smiled inwardly, grateful for Devi's work ethic. Cristina had not been looking forward to being alone in the office this morning.

Attempting to remain casual, Cristina asked, "How was your date?"

"Amazing. I had no idea leeks could be melted, but they worked so well with the lamb," Devi grinned. Her smile faded as she studied her boss's face. "What happened to you? You look like you didn't sleep at all."

"I didn't. Carl Franklin killed himself yesterday."

"Oh, no." Devi's hand flew to her mouth. "Is that why the medical examiner called? I'm so sorry. What happened?"

"He jumped out a window." The words tasted bitter as they rolled over her tongue. Cristina could feel tears forming and fought them back. "I don't know how I could've missed it."

"Mr. Franklin always looked happy and well put-together. If you missed something, he must have hid it well. If you want, I can pull his file so you can review it."

"Yes, please."

"Or do you need to take the day off? I can reschedule your appointments."

The weight on Cristina's heart lifted. Thank heavens for good friends and loyal employees. "No, it's better if I concentrate on helping the living. When's my first patient?"

"Not for another half hour."

"I'll be reviewing charts in my office until then. Thanks, Devi."

Once inside her office, Cristina sat at her desk and removed the bottle of Recognate from her desk drawer. As she prepared to pop two capsules into her mouth, she paused.

The ReMind researchers had no idea that when Dr. Cristina Silva prescribed Recognate to her patient Catherine Silvers that Catherine Silvers did not actually exist. Cristina had fabricated the fake identity in a moment of desperation. She knew it was wrong, unethical and illegal, but no other medicine had been helping her. When Mitchell died, what was left of Cristina nearly died too. The only thing that had kept her from taking her own life back then was the possibility that maybe, just maybe, she could regain what she'd lost.

Cristina rolled the capsules between her fingers. She'd told herself that she'd try the drug for a few weeks and then stop. But after memories began emerging, she couldn't go back.

Thinking of Carl, she bit her lip and squeezed the hand holding the pills into a fist. The pills weren't dangerous. And like Andrea kept telling her: she needed to stop doubting herself.

Straightening her back, she swallowed the pills.

Cristina was about to pull up her notes on the morning's first patient when she spotted the envelope sticking out of her purse. Curiosity won out. She dumped the contents on her desk. Setting aside the news report about her parents' death, she sifted through the articles about the various suicides. All five had been under psychiatric care but had been reportedly stable. None left next of kin. Just like Carl Franklin.

Her stomach knotted as she finished reading the last article. Had Santos known about Carl's suicide before she did?

Shaken at the thought, she picked up the *O Globo* article. A research team had received private funding to test a new medication to target a key factor they'd identified in class-based gang violence. They called the project *Renascimento*, or "rebirth." The article lacked details but identified the research team leader as a Brazilian, Jose Kobayashi.

The name summoned a flash of memory, but the harder Cristina tried to figure out why the less sure she became of its familiarity. She turned to the photograph, timestamped six years ago. A somber group stood in two rows beside the flag of Brazil—women in front, men in the back. In the center, a man with Japanese features smiled into the camera. Cristina assumed it was Kobayashi.

His face did not register any response from her. None of the other men triggered anything either. But when she focused on the woman on the far left, the one with a confident smile and determination in her eyes, Cristina nearly dropped the printout.

With shoulder-length black hair, high cheekbones and full lips, the woman was a dead ringer for Cristina. Examining the grainy picture even more closely, she became fixated on the thought that this was a photo of herself on a forgotten day.

CHAPTER SIX

Compared to the Boston PD, with its major case division and multiple criminal investigation units, the Somerville precinct felt like a mom and pop shop to Detective Wilson. Crime on the north side of the Charles could be just as violent, but it was nowhere near as high-profile as in the city proper and was more likely to surround local affairs and petty conflicts. At least, that's what Detective Wilson had observed since transferring here three years ago. Though if he was being honest, they'd transferred him. That's what happens when—as Internal Affairs said—you get "personally involved in a case." Wilson knew that his relationship with the witness in the Cambridge murder wasn't as black and white as I.A.'s summary. But he also knew he was lucky to keep his badge.

Wilson sipped his morning coffee—no cream, four sugars—and skimmed through the report on the Valentine theft on his computer. Past making an inventory of what was taken to check against if it popped up for sale online, there wasn't much else for him to do investigation-wise. With a sigh, he saved and closed the file. Getting bounced from Homicide to General Investigations had been a serious blow. Whereas his intuition nearly always led to a homicide arrest, it didn't work properly with other types of crimes. Not to mention that investigating petty thefts and computer crimes didn't produce the same satisfaction as delivering a killer to justice.

Leaning back in his desk chair, he scanned the division floor. The rows of desks were mostly empty; just a handful of uniformed investigators working on their computers. It was almost noon and the other plainclothes detectives were having lunch, or—like his partner, Rick Hawkins—attending an in-service training for the next two hours. Since Wilson wasn't due for his until next month, he had time to follow up on other matters.

Wilson opened his internet browser and typed in a search for "Recognate." After sifting through several pages of results, he frowned. Other than a few entries in an urban dictionary website and the lyrics to a Foo Fighters song, he found no matches. What kind of prescription drug was invisible on the internet?

"Good morning, Detective," a gruff voice said in a thick Boston accent.

Wilson turned to find Sergeant Chip Davis standing over him with his hands on his hips. Davis, a twenty-year veteran of the force, proudly grew up in blue-collar "Slummerville" and probably wore his uniform to bed. He took great pleasure in finding fault with detectives who committed even the most minor of sins. Thanks to his past digresses, Wilson may as well have had a bullseye on his forehead.

"What's up, Sergeant?" Wilson hoped it wasn't another busywork assignment.

"Captain wants everyone in the briefing room. We got company. A Fibbie."

The hairs on Wilson's arms tingled. "FBI? What do they want?"

"Don't know. You been downloading porn again?"

"That's funny. Practicing for open mic night at the Comedy

Stop, I see." Wilson bit his tongue when he saw Davis' blank look. Subtle sarcasm flew over the sergeant's head. "Never mind. Thanks for the heads up."

Entering the briefing room, Wilson understood how cattle felt being led to slaughter. Captain Harris stood at the front, adjusting the lapels on his perfectly pressed uniform as he surveyed the herd. A buff, blond man in a tailored navy suit and a tall, attractive woman with dark hair braided in a bun waited next to him. Wilson recognized Agent Charles Forrester by the bushy eyebrows permanently fixed in a cocky tilt. His thin lips curled into the same smug grin Wilson remembered from when their paths had crossed three years ago on a homicide involving a Boston city councilor. Wilson recognized Agent Charles Forrester by the bushy eyebrows permanently fixed in a cocky tilt. His thin lips were curled into the same smug grin Wilson remembered. A sour taste filled Wilson's mouth. The last case he and Forrester had crossed paths—a homicide case involving a Boston city councilor—had started with constant battles over jurisdiction and ended with Wilson's transfer here. Wilson didn't know for sure that Forrester had gotten Wilson banished. But he knew he preferred a wide berth.

"Take a seat, everyone," Harris said, attacking each syllable. The plainclothes detectives grumbled about having their lunches interrupted but complied. When the last of the nine officers sat down, Harris indicated his guests. "These are Agents Forrester and Vasquez from the Boston office. They've come to request our help tracking down a fugitive operating out of Somerville."

"What kind of fugitive?" asked Detective Miller, a soft-spoken twenty-year veteran from the Anti-Crime Unit.

"Arson," said Agent Forrester. "Along with international terrorism."

Murmurs spread throughout the room. No one liked to hear the T-word used in their backyard.

"Is there an imminent threat?" asked Detective Malone, an

opportunist who always managed to snag the most interesting cases before everyone else.

"To be determined." Vasquez turned on a projector. A photo appeared on the whiteboard of a Latin man with a heavy brow hanging over two eyes like black holes. Deep scars lined his cheeks.

"We're looking for Edward James Olmos?" Wilson asked, struggling to keep a straight face.

"If Olmos has decided to get involved with terrorism, then, yes," Vasquez said without missing a beat. "The suspect has been identified as Francisco Martins, but he may be using another name."

"Detectives Malone and Johnson, "Harris said, nodding at the pair of plainclothes detectives in the back row. "I'm assigning you to work with Agents Forrester and Vasquez on this. The rest of you, keep your eyes and ears open."

As Vasquez handed out BOLO flyers with the wanted man's photo, Captain Harris' gaze locked with Wilson's. "Francisco Martins is extremely dangerous. Do *not* engage him."

Wilson's cheeks burned. Obviously, that last statement had been directed at him. After accepting the flyer from Agent Vasquez, he stuck it in his coat pocket. He had enough to keep him busy. The last thing he needed was to get tangled up in a federal case.

After what she'd seen in the news clippings from Santos, Cristina had been finding it extremely difficult to concentrate on her work for the rest of the morning. At least twice per session, instead of focusing on her patients' stories, her mind drifted back to the *O Globo* article. It seemed impossible that it had been her in the photograph. Could she have a twin? It made her want to track down Santos. What else did he know?

"What do you think, Doctor?" Seventy-year-old Martha Watterson stared intently from the other side of Cristina's desk.

Her white hair clung to her scalp in tight curls. She fidgeted with the cuffs on her cardigan sweater. Despite advancing Alzheimer's, the woman's gaze remained razor sharp.

"I'm sorry, Martha," Cristina said. "Could you repeat that last part?"

"My hairdresser says this plant restores memory. It's called *bacomen* or back pain ... something like that."

"*Bacopa monnieri* It's an Indian herbal remedy."

"That's it. What do you think of it?"

Cristina sighed. "Some studies suggest the herb might be helpful, but it's not proven. I can't recommend something that hasn't been studied or isn't part of a study."

"That's the same thing you said about ginkgo and hawthorn." Tears welled in Martha's eyes. She wiped them away with a shaky finger before taking a deep calming breath the way Cristina had taught her. For a moment, the woman seemed to have regained her composure, but when she spoke, her voice cracked. "I forgot my son's name the other day. I didn't even recognize him. Please, Dr. Silva. There's got to be something I can try."

Cristina's heart broke as she held Martha's pleading gaze. She'd scoured journals for new Alzheimer's treatments and there was nothing ready for market. She'd spent weekends cold-calling researchers, but none could assert Martha would get the study drug instead of placebo. The last thing Cristina wanted to do was give the woman false hope.

She was a perfect candidate for Recognate—good health, no additional comorbid illness to muddy the results, she was still active in her daily routine—yet ReMind excluded subjects with Alzheimer's. As Cristina caught her own reflection in Martha's sad eyes, she remembered how horrible it had been to live without a past. She could only imagine how it would be to feel your past slipping away.

Cristina's thoughts drifted to Carl Franklin. She wouldn't let a tragedy like that happen again. Recovering memory could save one's life. Cristina understood that better than most. She'd risked her career by misleading ReMind for her own treatment, but it had paid off.

"I've got one more thing you can try, Martha." Cristina typed on her keyboard. She paused and smiled warmly. "With any luck, you'll remember more than you realize you've forgotten."

CHAPTER SEVEN

A bare size-eight foot streaked toward Cristina's face. She jerked her head back. Ducked to the right. Deflected with her left arm. Bone thudded against her forearm. She stepped back with her right foot, but before she could recover a fist rammed into her chest. Her breath whooshed out. She fell to the mat.

"That was better." Andrea towered over Cristina, extending a hand to pull her up. "But you're still overcorrecting. Don't think so much. React."

"That's funny, telling a psychiatrist not to think so much." Cristina allowed her friend to help her stand and tried to ignore the bruises to her ribcage and ego. Body odor and sweat thickened the air in Sid's Gym. She was grateful Andrea reserved the space so they could have privacy. "I suck at this."

"Not true. During our first session, you showed me some moves Mitchell taught you that were pretty slick. But you're off your game."

Cristina winced at Mitchell's name. His lie about his marriage made her question if she had ever known him at all. "It's because of that weird photo …"

"Honey, you know that's not you."

"But she looks exactly like me. Let me show you." Cristina fetched the article from her purse and handed it to Andrea.

After a moment's inspection, Andrea laughed. "Mami, she looks like you, like I look like Jennifer Lopez."

"Can you please be serious?"

"I am. Her nose is rounder and her eyebrows thicker. She's got like a unibrow. Everyone has doppelgängers out there if you look hard enough. That weird bus guy must've noticed the resemblance and took advantage of it to scare you."

Cristina studied the photograph. She could see Andrea's point, but the resemblance was still eerie. "I've had a lot to deal with all at once. If anything else happens, they'll have to admit me for inpatient stabilization."

"Don't talk that way." Andrea grabbed Cristina's shoulder and drew up to her full height—six feet—commanding Cristina's attention. "You're a strong, brilliant woman who's rebounded from crises that would destroy most people. You can handle this. Remember that move I showed you last time against a larger opponent?"

"Where I make myself even smaller to draw him in?"

"Exactly. If things seem overwhelming, step back and get low. Change your perspective. By making your opponent even bigger, you have no choice but to find a way to deal with them."

Andrea always knew the right thing to say, and Cristina now felt foolish for letting her fears overcome her. "And I thought I was supposed to be the shrink here."

"Even doctors need a kick in the butt sometimes. Let's go home, clean up, and then you and I are going out to Tangerine."

"I don't think I'm ready for a dance club," said Cristina, picturing Santos lurking in the night's shadows.

As usual, Andrea knew her thoughts. "You're not thinking of that creep again, are you? If we see him, I'll kick his ass." Her friend gave her a hug. "You know I can, right?"

Cristina smiled. "I do. Let's see how the night goes, okay?"

Ten minutes later, they were arriving back at the apartment building when Andrea's phone chirped. After a momentary glance, Andrea frowned.

"Something wrong?" Cristina asked.

"This guy I met last week canceled our date for tomorrow." Andrea dropped the phone back into her purse and started up the stairs. "Jerk doesn't have the manners to call. No, he sends a text."

"And you wonder why I avoid dating?"

"Touché, my dear." They stopped at Andrea's door. "Hey, why don't you come in for a drink first? I could use one and you know I hate drinking alone."

"I need a shower. I stink."

"So do I. It won't bother me."

"I could use a little time alone to unwind." Cristina caught Andrea rolling her eyes. "Don't give me that look. I'll come by after I clean up."

"You better, or you'll have an angry Puerto Rican breaking down your door."

They shared a laugh and then Cristina headed upstairs to her apartment. By the time she reached her door, Cristina decided she needed to stop spending so much time worrying. If she jumped at every shadow, how was she any better off than her patients?

She stuck her key in the lock. At her touch, the door inched open. Her back muscles tensed. She'd locked the door, hadn't she?

She held her breath and listened for movement. Other than outside street noise, she heard only Grizabella softly mewling and pawing at the door.

Pull it together, Cristina. She removed the key from the lock but held it, so the blade stuck out between her fingers.

Cristina nudged open the door. Nothing. She sighed, feeling

relieved and silly. Adjusting her purse strap, she stepped inside and reached for the light switch.

Gloved fingers clamped on her wrist.

Cristina cried out as a dark figure wearing a ski mask tightened his grip. She was dragged inside. The man kicked the apartment door shut.

Grizabella hissed.

Cristina spun, reflexively swinging her free fist. Her key connected with something fleshy.

The dark figure screamed, yanking her arm so she flew across the room. Cristina's shoulder smashed against the wall near the window. Pain jolted across her back. Her purse tumbled away.

She scrambled to her feet. The window light illuminated a square in the center of the room. Darkness engulfed the rest. Her pulse pounded in her ears. He was there. Somewhere.

Something rattled. Cristina spun, ready to strike.

It was the old radiator kicking in. She cursed under her breath.

Slow your breathing, your movements. Don't let him see you're afraid.

The voice spoke in the back of her mind. Female. Whose?

Use the environment to your advantage.

She forced herself to take slow breaths. She knew this apartment better than anyone.

Grizabella yowled. Cristina jumped.

Something scuffled in the dark corners of the room.

Move. Now.

Cristina yanked down the shade and dove to the carpet next to the coffee table. She groped on the table until she found the caduceus paperweight Mitchell had given her. As she clutched it to her chest, she felt a rush of adrenaline.

Unless her attacker had night vision, he was now blind. She had the upper hand.

Cristina listened for any sound that would give him away.

After a few moments, the floorboards creaked.

She pounced. The paperweight crashed into his ribcage.

He roared. Staggered backward against the window. The shade crumpled. A dim beam of light shined into the room.

He wasn't a big man, maybe medium build. She could take him down with a solid punch. His gray eyes glinted as he glared at her. She lunged again with her weapon, but he sidestepped, knocking the paperweight from her hand with a quick chop. The shade fell back into place. The light disappeared.

The man's fist rammed into Cristina's stomach. She screamed and doubled over. He punched her in the cheek, then the side of her head. Cristina fell to the floor. The last thing she saw was her assailant smashing the window and leaping onto the fire escape. The darkness around her faded to gray.

CHAPTER EIGHT

Leaning against the front door jamb, Cristina pressed an icepack against her cheekbone, trying to ignore the throbbing pain and the police officers searching her apartment. In her other arm she held her cat.

When Cristina had regained consciousness, the first thing she'd done was search for Grizabella—who had been found hiding under the bed. Cristina had covered the tabby with kisses, but the joy was short-lived as Cristina took stock of the mess her assailant had made. Books, clothes, and even a pair of pink panties lay on the floor for all to see. She felt violated and called the police.

"We'll be out of your hair soon," said the detective in a South Boston accent. He looked to be in his early thirties, White, with a five-o'clock shadow and jaw-hugging sideburns. "We're doing one more walkthrough to ensure we didn't miss anything."

Andrea stood next to Cristina, seeming at multiple times as if she was about to say something reassuring but failing. Finally, she came out with it: "Do you know who did this, Detective Wilson?" Andrea asked in a husky voice.

Cristina raised her eyebrows.

"Not yet," the detective said. "But we collected some prints from the door lock."

"But he was wearing gloves," Cristina said. "I told the other officers that."

"We'll run the prints, anyway. Sometimes we get lucky." He tapped his chin and studied the living room. "You said nothing is missing?"

"Correct," Cristina said.

"And the only damage was to the window and the lock." He scratched his chin. "Seems like this guy was looking for something specific and didn't find it. Do you take any prescription medications that the burglar could have been looking for?"

Cristina had a brief thought of Recognate, but remembered the bottle was safely stowed inside her purse.

When she shook her head, Wilson said, "You surprised him as he was doing something nefarious—perhaps targeted specifically at you. Can you think of anyone who would want to threaten or harm you?"

"No."

The detective plucked a framed picture off the floor. "Maybe an ex-boyfriend?"

Cristina's mouth went dry. The photo was of Cristina and Mitchell embracing at the New England Aquarium. "He's dead."

The detective handed the photo to her. "I'm sorry. So, no one else then?"

"Actually," Andrea said, "there is someone."

"Andrea, what are you—?"

"Shush, I've got this." Andrea brushed a lock of hair out of her eyes and leaned close enough that her chest grazed the detective's when she inhaled. "A guy accosted Cristina on the bus yesterday. He said he had a gun."

"Wilson turned back to Cristina. "Did you report that incident Ms. Silva?"

"No."

Detective Wilson's eyebrows inched up his forehead. "Why not?"

Cristina's cheeks burned. How do you tell the police that you didn't report a crime because you were curious to know more about the criminal? "He was bigger than the guy who broke in here, and he hasn't bothered me again. I don't know that he really had a gun."

"You should still report any kind of threats. You might not be his only victim." Wilson pulled out his smartphone and began entering notes. "On the bus, you said?"

"Yes, on my way home from work."

"Where do you work?"

"I run a clinic at Longwood."

He looked up. "You're a doctor?"

"Psychiatrist," Andrea said.

He blinked. *Doctor* Cristina Silva?"

Cristina felt uneasy. "Yes …?"

He shook his head. "My partner and I ran the investigation on Carl Franklin's suicide yesterday. One of your patients, right? This is an odd coincidence. I wanted to ask you some questions, and here you are."

Chills ran down Cristina's back. "Was there something suspicious about Carl's death?"

"Cristina," Andrea said, "you got attacked in your own home. I hardly think you should be worrying about anyone else right now. Isn't that right, Detective?" She gave Wilson a pointed look.

"Er, right," Wilson stammered and buried his nose in his smartphone. "What did this guy on the bus who threatened you look like?"

Cristina hesitated. Santos had told her to trust no one. She hadn't told anyone but Andrea. What would happen if she told the police? She struggled with that for a moment, then realized she didn't know that much anyway, so what was the harm? "He had broad shoulders and wore a fisherman's cap. I couldn't see most of his face."

Wilson frowned. "Anything else?"

"He had dark eyes. And he said his name was Sebastian dos Santos."

Wilson wrote down the name and stuck the phone back in his jacket. "I'll put it through the federal databases. The guy who attacked you tonight wore a mask?"

"Yes."

"Okay, we'll run the prints. I'll call you if we find anything." Wilson's hazel eyes glimmered as his gaze met hers. The corner of his mouth twitched.

Something stirred inside her, but Cristina pushed it away. He was handsome, no question. Even as she tried to deny it, she felt the spark of attraction. But now was not the time.

"I still have questions about Mr. Franklin," he said.

"Why don't you give her a call tomorrow, Detective?" Andrea nudged him toward the door. "I'm sure she'll be able to give you better answers when she's not so totally freaked out."

He glanced at Cristina again before nodding. "Good idea. But I suggest you find a safer place to stay tonight, Doctor."

After the detective left with the rest of his crew, Cristina glared at Andrea and offered a sarcastic "Thank you."

"For what?"

"It wasn't your place to tell him about the bus incident."

"Come on, Cristina. A masked man broke into your home and attacked you, and you weren't going to mention to the police that he'd already threatened you?"

"It wasn't the same guy. The man in the ski mask who attacked me had gray eyes."

"Sweetie, it was dark. Everything looks gray in the dark."

"The man on the bus was bigger."

"So, you're saying in the middle of fighting for your life you took measurements?" Andrea threw her hands up. "I don't get what's going on here. Why would you defend this guy unless— You still think Santos knows something about your past!"

"Maybe." As much as Cristina tried to convince herself that her hesitation had only been about safety, she couldn't deny a yearning to discover what Sebastian dos Santos knew. "I don't know what to think."

"Come here." Andrea pulled Cristina into a hug, her Dior Hypnotic Poison perfume assaulting Cristina's nostrils. "I don't know why you're not a bowl of jelly right now. How did you fight him off, anyway? Did you use the moves I taught you?"

Cristina hesitated. It wasn't Andrea she'd heard in her mind. It was a familiar voice, but the more she tried to identify it, the fuzzier it became.

"Yes. They worked great." She lied, feeling horrible the moment the words left her mouth. More lies to her best friend? Cristina really was falling apart.

"Of course, my moves worked, but Detective Wilson had a point." The detective's name rolled off Andrea's tongue like crème brûlée. "It's not safe here. You're staying on my couch tonight."

"Andrea—"

"No arguments. Grizabella too."

Cristina felt relieved. She didn't feel safe in her apartment. At least her friend gave her an excuse. She stroked the cat's head. Grizabella purred.

"Let me pack a bag."

"On the bright side," Andrea said as Cristina searched for a suitcase, "we'll get to have that drink together, after all."

Sebastian dos Santos dragged his overcoat snug across the lower half of his face and leaned around the corner of Cristina's apartment building, taking a look. He ducked back into the alley when he saw the police cruiser pulling away from the curb. Uttering a Portuguese curse, he flattened himself against the wall and waited for the cop to leave, but it was too late. After taking a year to gather the needed information, he'd acted prematurely by contacting her on the bus. Obviously, his enemies had found out.

Sebastian's hand tightened around the locket. He didn't have another year to try again. His only chance of recovering his daughter was to get rid of Cristina Silva.

CHAPTER NINE

Despite drinking two mojitos with Andrea, Cristina lay awake for over an hour. Metal bars under the foldout mattress dug into her back, but even that was less painful than the feeling of being invaded. *Let the cops sort it out.* She curled into a ball on one side of the mattress.

A short time after drifting off to sleep, Cristina dreamed of ramshackle buildings piled atop one another along a narrow litter-strewn street. Rats scampered in and out of garbage bins that reeked. Off in the distance, she heard the ocean's roar and people laughing.

The road wound up a hill, ending at giant colored blocks stacked haphazardly to make a building. Telephone wires snaked around a nearby pole in a tangled mess. Graffiti covered the walls. As Cristina approached, she caught dark eyes peering out of the windows, disappearing the moment she spotted them.

She advanced closer. "Is someone there?"

A teenaged boy appeared in the doorway, wearing only shorts. Dirt and blood covered his cheeks. He clutched a crimson-stained stuffed tiger. He looked suspiciously at Cristina.

She crouched before him. "I won't hurt you."

Bullet holes framed the doorway and glass shards lay beneath a shattered window.

"Where is everyone?" she asked. "Do you need help?"

He tilted his head. "We don't need any more help from you."

Before she could respond, a pistol appeared in the boy's hand.

He aimed the barrel at her forehead. "We trusted you. Now they're all dead."

She stood up, raising her hands and retreating from the gun. Her heart raced in fear. "Who's dead? What happened?"

His hands shook. "You lied to us."

Children's faces appeared in the windows, covered in grime, staring at her with dark eyes. The kids chanted, "Liar, liar."

In the distance there were gunshots.

"I didn't lie." Cristina covered her ears to block out the children's chanting. "Please, tell me what happened."

"Quinn!" shouted a man's voice. "Over there!"

A gun fired and the boy's head whipped back. His body crumpled to the ground.

"No!"

Blood streamed from his forehead. His eyes rolled back.

The chanting grew louder. "Liar! Liar!"

Through tears, Cristina saw the boy's killer holding a smoking rifle. When she focused on his face, she saw it was Carl Franklin.

Her stomach lurched.

"Cristina, wake up," Carl yelled, only it wasn't his voice.

More men mounted the hill, firing the guns wildly. Bullets flew overhead. Children shrieked. A faceless man appeared behind Carl and pointed at Cristina. She threw herself over the boy's dead body, closed her eyes and screamed.

Cristina was still screaming when she felt someone's hands on her shoulders.

"Wake up. What's wrong?"

"Andrea?" Cristina looked around. She was in Andrea's apartment, hugging her pillow on the foldout bed. It took another second for her to register it had been a dream. "Oh, thank God."

"A bad dream?" Andrea sat down next to Cristina on the foldout. Cristina hesitated. "Yes."

"What happened? Tell me about it."

"No. I don't want to think about it. The dream was horrible."

Holding Cristina at arm's length, Andrea held her gaze. "It'll help to talk. Tell me what's going on."

Reluctantly, Cristina recounted the dream. When she finished, Andrea nodded and kissed her forehead. "Honey, with everything that's happened, it's no wonder you're having nightmares. After seeing that article about the Brazilian slums, your mind took all that confusion and fear and created this dreamworld to sort it out. Isn't that what you told me when I dreamed about being a CIA officer after watching *Homeland*?"

"What about Carl? Why was he there?"

"You're the shrink, sweetie. You tell me."

Chewing her lower lip for comfort, Cristina replayed the image of Carl Franklin holding a rifle. "The cop's questions must've drudged up my guilt, and my mind wove him into the dream. In a way, his suicide killed my naïveté. Hence the death of the child. It makes sense, but it's still weird. The whole thing felt so real, familiar—more like a memory than a dream."

"I know what you mean. I have dreams like that myself sometimes. Once the police deal with Santos, everything will go back to normal and your bad dreams will go away." She brushed Cristina's hair off her forehead. "Would some warm milk help you sleep better?"

Cristina allowed herself to smile. "That sounds lovely."

"Good. Settle down and I'll take care of it." As Andrea walked to the kitchen, she called over her shoulder, "By the way, what were you shouting before I woke you up?"

"What do you mean?" Cristina propped the pillow. "I was just screaming."

"No, you were shouting something in Portuguese." Andrea closed the refrigerator and poured a glass of milk. "The only thing I understood was the name *Quinn*."

Quinn watched as a mid-level researcher stood before a whiteboard, babbling about neurotransmitters and inhibitors. The man's hand trembled as he wrote, his scribbled notes resembling an EKG tracing more than a meaningful formula. Every few sentences, he stopped to clear his throat, obviously nervous. As well he should be. ReMind Pharmaceuticals was just weeks away from launching Recognate. Everything had to be perfect before then.

But the latest data on the drug was problematic. The investors gathered in the Executive Boardroom needed to know they had a solution to any potential complication or heads would roll, starting with the research team.

However, that was the least of Quinn's worries as he half listened to the presentation. He still hadn't heard from his operative about the previous night's mission. With Santos on the move, he needed to be sure Cristina Silva wouldn't be a problem, or he'd have to answer to more than dimwitted deep-pocket investors. He checked to ensure no one was watching, then slipped his smartphone out of his pocket for the ninth time and turned it on.

A banner indicated he had a new secure text.

His pulse quickened as he opened the chat. The text was from a different operative than he expected: *Your boy took too long. She surprised him.*

Quinn's shoulders tightened. He'd hoped to avoid confrontation, especially given his operative's violent tendencies. He typed: *Is she dead?*

After a tense pause, he read: She nearly killed him. Barely escaped.

His first reaction was relief and admiration. Even after all this time, she was still resourceful. But aggravation quickly took over. If Cristina Silva remembered too soon, he'd have to take drastic measures. His fingers crushed the keypad as he typed: *Did he find the locket?*

An immediate response: *No.*

Quinn cursed under his breath. Either she didn't have it, or she'd hidden it.

A shriveled man with a dry rasp of a voice interrupted Quinn's thoughts with an indignant question about the violent behavior being reported as an adverse effect of Recognate.

The researcher's face reddened. He stammered, but he did a semireasonable job of providing reassurance that these were isolated events and wouldn't be a problem in the final product. Quinn nodded in agreement, relieved when the elder seemed satisfied with the answer. Everyone there knew too damned well there was a problem, but when there was so much money already invested, it was easy enough to pretend otherwise. As long as no one in the press made a connection, they had time to deal with it.

A disturbing realization buzzed in his mind. If there was anyone capable of foreseeing the chess game he was playing, it was Cristina Silva. And his next move was in her backyard.

Quickly, he sent another text: *Cancel the switch. Abort the next subject.*

For the next two agonizing minutes, the screen remained blank. Finally, the response came: *Too late.*

Quinn's fist tightened around the phone. He needed a new plan before everything came crashing down.

CHAPTER TEN

At Andrea's insistence, Cristina skipped the bus and took a taxi to the office each day, no longer listening to music that might distract her or dull her reflexes, but instead clutching the can of pepper spray inside her purse the entire ride. After arriving at the office unscathed, she tackled her cases, hoping hard work would distract from the tangled mess her life had become.

That was nearly impossible, as Detective Wilson called Cristina daily to check facts and update her on the investigation's progress—which was minimal. Other than Cristina's fingerprints, the only other set of recovered prints remained unidentified. Wilson said he was running it through the FBI system and promised he would have something soon.

She didn't really mind his frequent calls. Wilson was easy to talk to, and he made her feel safe. At times, he almost seemed flirtatious. It was good to feel wanted. Especially when Cristina looked in the mirror each morning and saw the less-than-sexy bruise still lingering on her cheek from the fight. But that feeling of being wanted stirred up others that were less comforting, forcing her to make a reality check. After Mitchell, she couldn't trust her feelings for anyone, especially another cop.

Even though Cristina was sleeping better, it had been a full week since the break-in and she was still jumping every time a patient suddenly crossed their leg. As she wrapped up her last progress notes for the morning, Cristina's cell phone rang. Caller ID said it was her patient, Jerry Peterman.

His voice was tense. "Sorry to bug you, Doctor, but I need a favor."

"How can I help?"

"You told me to keep taking risks, right?"

"Yes, I did," she said, feeling a bit of trepidation.

"Well ..." He cleared his throat and laughed nervously. "Right after our last visit, I remembered I can act, and I took your advice. I auditioned for a small part in a local production of *Long Day's Journey into Night*. I got the part. Isn't that incredible?"

"That's wonderful. I'm so proud of you."

"Please, Dr. Silva, I—I haven't been feeling myself lately. My nerves are getting the best of me. We're performing at six-fifteen tonight. I need that shot of encouragement you promised. I'd feel better knowing someone out in the audience believes in me."

"You want me to be there?" Cristina chewed on her index finger. Jerry was in a delicate state. She had no idea if he could act or not, but if he took this risk and failed, he might need her to pick him back up. After Carl, Cristina would not let down another patient. "Where are you performing?" she asked.

"The opera house off Park Street."

"I'll be there."

"You don't know how much this means to me. Thanks."

Cristina leaned back in her chair and massaged her scalp. She hadn't been out after dark since the attack in her apartment. And the assailant was still out there.

She brushed away the negative thoughts. If Jerry could take a risk, so could she. That was the best way to get her life back on track. Maybe she could convince Andrea to join her.

Devi knocked on her office door. "Hey, boss, I'm going to Fratelli's for lunch. Care to join me?"

"Do they still have that lobster carbonara?"

"Yeah."

Cristina stared at her clinic notes. She should finish them. She should.

"Count me in." Cristina pushed the notes away. "I could use a change of scenery."

Devi grinned. "Great. I'll set the answering service."

After Devi walked away, Cristina opened her desk drawer and withdrew her pill bottle. She poured two capsules in her hand. She had suffered nightmares for three nights after the attack, but then she realized that those were nights she had skipped doses of Recognate. Once she resumed her treatment, the awful dreams disappeared, and happy memories emerged again. That morning, she remembered strutting down the family staircase in a lavender prom gown, her parents beaming with pride at the bottom of the stairs.

Recognate did more than restore memories. It chased away paranoia. It provided perspective. It made Cristina feel whole. Turning the bottle on its side, she poured an extra pill into her palm and swallowed it.

If Cristina needed proof God existed, she found it in Fratelli's lobster carbonara. The North End restaurant always seemed on the verge of folding to its more famous and elegant competitors, but its old country charm, proximity to St. Stephen's Church, and great lunch deals kept the owners from bankruptcy. Throw in a homemade tiramisu that would make the Duke of Florence weep, it was well worth the T ride from Longwood.

Accordion music lilted through the tiny dining room. The only other seated guests were a lovey-dovey tourist couple and an Armani-wearing banker at his own table. Artificial flowering vines hugged the ceiling and pillars and framed a mural of Cinque Terra. Aromas of garlic and oregano hung in the air.

As Cristina speared a chunk of lobster and swirled linguine around it, she knew she'd made the right choice to get away from the office. At the medical examiner's office, Dr. Morgan hadn't uncovered anything to explain Carl's suicide. The police were making regular patrols past her apartment building. And Santos had never resurfaced. Detective Wilson had been unable to find anything on him. Cristina had tried her own online search again, but nothing turned up. He was like a ghost.

The best thing she could do was move on with her life. Her real life, not whatever fantasy that a strange man on a bus had wanted her to believe.

"Thanks for inviting me." Cristina couldn't help but smile while observing Devi wrap her mouth around a giant eggplant Stromboli. "This is the first time we've had lunch together, isn't it?"

Devi finished chewing and wiped her mouth. "You're always so busy, but it seemed like you needed a break."

"You're very perceptive. Someone should hire you."

Devi laughed, and said, "Your cheek's healing nicely."

"Oh, thanks. It doesn't even hurt anymore."

"I hope the bastard who did it can't say the same."

"Yeah." Feelings of being violated resurfaced. "Hey, have you ever dealt with a police detective?"

"Once, when my car was stolen. Why?"

"Well, Detective Wilson, the guy investigating the break-in at my apartment, keeps calling me even though he doesn't have anything new to report."

"Really? Why's he calling you, then?"

"According to him, to gather facts. He asks about my neighbors, the route I take to work, my hobbies ..."

"I suppose that makes sense. You still have no idea who attacked you, right?"

"I guess." Cristina twirled her pasta. "It's …"

"What?"

"Is it normal for them to ask what kind of movies I like?"

Devi lowered her Stromboli in midbite. The corner of her mouth crept upward. "Movies?"

"I told him I like movies about memory, so he mentioned this new action thriller about an international superspy who loses his memory and ends up working for the enemy."

"Oh, yeah, I wanted to see that one."

"So does Detective Wilson. He said it would be quite a coincidence if we ran into each other at the Fenway Theater when it's playing."

Devi snickered. "That's practically an invitation. Is he cute?"

"Wilson?" Cristina toyed with her straw. "I guess."

"You guess? Come on, he's clearly interested in you. Do you like him?"

Cristina blushed. "Yeah, I do."

"So, what did you say to his invitation?"

"I said the premise was farfetched. Memory doesn't work that way."

"What?"

Cristina stopped. Devi was staring at her like she had a chicken on her head.

"You really said that to him?"

Cristina blanched as she imagined how she must have sounded. "More or less."

"And what did he say?"

"Nothing. He said he had to follow up on some leads and hung up. He's been all business since."

Devi's phone chimed. She checked it and looked puzzled.

"What the heck? The delivery guy is waiting outside the office with the new printer I ordered. He's early."

"Should we go?"

"I'll go. You stay and finish your meal." She flagged the waitress and pointed at her Stromboli. "Please box that up."

As the waitress scurried away with the food, Devi stood and pulled out her wallet.

"Don't worry," Cristina said with a hand wave. "It's on me. And I'll get your to-go box."

"Thanks."

Devi turned to go, then stopped and touched Cristina's hand. "You're a great psychiatrist, but you need to stop listening to your head and start listening to your heart."

After Devi left, Cristina stared at the remains of her carbonara. Devi was right. Whenever anyone tried to get close to Cristina, she transformed into an intellectual snob. It kept her from getting hurt, but it was a lousy way to live. Wilson wasn't the first detective to show unusual interest in her. Just because things had gone badly with Mitchell didn't mean they couldn't work out with Wilson. And he was hot.

The background music shifted to a romantic mandolin melody as the server dropped off dessert. Cristina took a spoonful of tiramisu. As mascarpone cheese melted over her taste buds, she thought more about Devi's words. Cristina's head may be able to comprehend the chemical process involved in preparing this dessert, but it was her heart that appreciated the flavor.

Cristina licked cocoa powder off her lips and was about to take another bite when a deep voice whispered in her ear. "Do not run, Cristina. I need your help."

CHAPTER ELEVEN

Alarms blared in Cristina's head, eclipsing the restaurant's lilting mandolin music. She turned to find a broad-shouldered man with Latin features sitting behind her, arms folded on the back of his chair. A coarse beard covered Santos's jaw. Dark hair fell at rough angles over his ears. His overcoat reeked of sweat.

"Get away." She jumped up and grabbed the butter knife, still thick with cream sauce. She scanned the room, surprised to discover they were alone. "What do you want from me?"

"Please don't make a scene," Santos said softly. "I'm not here to hurt you."

"You've a funny way of showing it, sending someone to attack me."

Santos spread his hands out innocently. "I had nothing to do with that. Why would I attack you when I need your help?"

Aiming the knife at him, she searched the room again. "If you are unstable, I can help. I can refer you to some excellent colleagues."

"I appreciate the offer, but I'm not unstable."

"Then why don't you leave me alone? I know who I am. I'm happy with who I am."

"Yet you hesitated when I said your memory was stolen. And

I know you were searching for information about me. At least some part of you wants to know the truth."

"What truth?"

His mouth twisted grimly. "That the Silvas were not your parents."

The words stung. She shook them off. "You're lying."

"I assure you, I'm not."

"Then, convince me I should trust you. How do we know each other?"

After a heavy sigh, he said, "We never met before the other night."

Cristina's blood cooled. "So, you don't know anything about me."

"I know you're the only one who can help me free my daughter."

"Your daughter?"

"In a tragic tale of corruption and betrayal, she's an innocent victim—like you, I'm afraid. I'm sorry you were dragged into this—and that I must involve you again."

"What do you mean *again*?" Her knuckles whitened as she gripped the knife. "Start at the beginning and tell me what the hell is going on."

"That will take time that we don't have. Let me simply ask you this: Have the nightmares started yet? About children being murdered?"

She nearly dropped the knife. "How do you know about that?"

He wiped a smudge off his thumbnail. "The same way I know you're not Cristina Silva."

Detective Wilson skimmed through his emails, then shoved away his keyboard with a grunt. He'd expected a response from the FBI's fingerprint database two days ago on the print found at Cristina Silva's apartment. It was only a partial, but still, what was taking them so long?

Wilson drummed his fingers on his desk. Why was he so fired up over this case? No one was dead. Nothing was stolen. So why couldn't he stop thinking about it? Was it because Dr. Cristina Silva was a brilliant knockout?

Wilson rested his elbows on his desk and rubbed his ears. He'd already been busted once for losing his objectivity. He had no desire to do it again, no matter how silky her hair looked, or how much she smelled like lilacs.

"Hey, partner." Detective Rick Hawkins patted Wilson on the shoulder. "Still puzzling over that suicide?"

"I wasn't. But now that you mention it, you don't think it's weird that the day after a guy kills himself, there's a break-in at his shrink's apartment?"

"I think it's weird that you didn't join me for lunch. You're not on that gluten-free kick like the boys in homicide, are you?"

"I don't even know what the hell gluten is. I had to finish some things here."

"Uh-huh."

"What?"

"Nothing." Hawkins pointed at Wilson's computer screen. "You've got mail."

A new message icon blinked on his inbox. "It's from the Feds." He scrolled through the email. "They found five possible matches for that print."

He closed the email and logged into the fingerprint database A list of names potentially matching the print appeared onscreen. After copying the list onto his notepad, he opened the National Crime Information Center system on the FBI's website and typed them in. The first two had no criminal record. The third was deceased.

After entering the fourth name, Wilson rubbed his chin. "Armed robbery and possession. Could be our guy."

"Doubt it," said Hawkins. "Look. Currently serving ten to twenty in an Ohio prison."

Wilson typed in the last name. "Let's try bachelor number five."

A moment later, they both stared openmouthed at the screen. "I'll be damned," muttered Hawkins.

The prints lifted from Dr. Silva's door matched a familiar FBI mugshot of a Latin man with a thick brow and scarred cheeks. Next to the photo was a list of aliases, including the name Francisco Martins.

CHAPTER TWELVE

The dining room tilted and shifted around Cristina. She gripped the back of her chair. Her other trembling hand still clutching the butter knife. Santos said Jorge and Claudia Silva were not her parents, but that was impossible. Cristina could feel her mother's light, calming caress on the back of her neck during lightning storms. She could hear her father shout "*Goal!*" every time they watched the World Cup game on ESPN. She remembered every major event she shared with her parents since childhood, from her tenth birthday to her completion of residency.

And yet, when she stared at their photo, something was missing. Some element she couldn't pinpoint was absent. And her dream of the teenaged boy had been so real. If Santos knew about that, could he be telling the truth about the rest?

Cristina met his eyes and struggled to keep her voice steady. "So, everything I've remembered over the past two years—none of it's real?"

"Let's just say that those memories were not yours until after your true memories were stolen."

"And why would someone steal my memories?"

"You saw something you shouldn't have. Something that made you a threat."

Cristina felt a chill. "What did I see?"

"I don't know, but it was important enough for them to want you out of the way."

"Why not kill me?"

"You're still valuable to them." His lips pressed together. "And me."

"Because of your daughter," said Cristina, wondering whether it was wise to buy into his delusions. As a psychiatrist, she could detect subtle signs when a patient was lying: avoiding eye contact, fidgeting, tightening vocal pitch. Santos held her gaze like a missile locked on target. His voice and hands remained steadier than her heartbeat. If nothing else, he believed he was telling the truth.

Cautiously, she asked, "Who did this?"

"A mercenary group called Zero Dark. They're responsible for the deaths of Jorge and Claudia Silva."

"That's ridiculous. The crash was an accident."

"It was a hit-and-run, no?"

She nodded.

"And they never found the other driver?"

"No."

"That's because it was not an accident. They were murdered."

Cristina's heart beat faster. As much as she didn't want to believe it, his words rang true. Despite the other memories she'd regained, the crash was one of the few things she still couldn't remember clearly. She'd had flashes—the sound of shattering glass, the pain of a blow to her head, the smell of blood—but nothing substantial. How could she be sure it really had been an accident? "Why would Zero Dark want to murder them?"

Santos opened his mouth as if to answer when Cristina's phone rang. Surprise or fear crossed his face. "Who's calling?"

The caller ID listed Detective Wilson's number.

"A police detective," she said.

He jumped to his feet. "Answer, or he'll think something is wrong. But I cannot stay."

"What? You can't leave. What does Zero Dark want with me? Why did you send me those articles?"

"I'm out of time." He withdrew a cheap burner phone from his pocket and slapped it on the table. "When you're ready for the truth, use this to call me. I'll tell you where we can meet. If I don't hear from you by tonight, or if you involve anyone else, you won't hear from me again."

He swept past her like a gale wind and disappeared into the kitchen. The knife slipped from her grasp. She sank into the chair. The last few minutes felt so surreal she wondered if she'd been daydreaming or had a seizure.

She tried to focus on her parents' faces, but they blurred. She became slowly aware that her phone was still ringing. Shaking off the haze, she accepted the call.

"Dr. Silva, are you okay?"

"Yes, Detective, I'm fine. Why?"

"I called your office, and no one picked up." He spoke rapidly. "When you didn't answer your cell, I thought—"

"Thought what?"

"The print we found on your lock matched a wanted felon. The guy's extremely dangerous. He's wanted for terrorism, attempted murder and arson."

"Oh, my God. What was he doing in my apartment?"

"That's what I wondered, so I dug deeper." He paused. "Francisco Martins was accused of burning down your parents' house."

Cristina felt like she'd been punched in the face. "I'm sorry. He what?"

"You don't know anything about it?"

"No. I mean, I knew their house burned down, but I had no idea it could've been intentional. Why isn't this man in prison?"

"It seems the charges were dropped. But if he's going after you now, that may have been a mistake. I'm going to ramp up the patrols at your apartment and your office. Now that we have a name and a face, we'll find this guy. I promise."

She ended the call and leaned forward, burying her face in her hands. Everything that Santos told her suddenly seemed real. If Francisco Martins worked for Zero Dark, he may even have been the one who had run Cristina and her parents off the road. Why had he returned to her apartment?

"*Signora* ..."

Cristina turned to find the waitress standing next to her with a Styrofoam box: Devi's leftovers.

An impulse nearly drove Cristina to jump up, grab the waitress by her collar, and shake out anything she might know about Santos or Martins or Zero Dark. She managed to fight it back. Instead, she took the box. "Thanks."

"Do you need anything else?"

"No, *grazie*." Cristina pocketed the cell phone Santos had left, withdrew a few bills from her purse and laid them on the table before pushing past the waitress. "I've had enough."

CHAPTER THIRTEEN

When Cristina returned to her office, Devi was scribbling a note while squeezing the phone between her cheek and shoulder. She jumped when she saw Cristina.

"Oh, sir, may I place you on hold?" Devi pressed a button and replaced the phone on the cradle. "That's Mrs. Watterson's son. He sounds worried and was talking so fast that the only part I understood is he needs to speak to you."

"Transfer the call to my office." Cristina handed Devi the to-go box. "When's my next patient?"

"Not until two."

"Thanks."

After closing the office door behind her, Cristina flopped onto her chair, propped her head, and stared at the inactive computer screen. Following her discharge from the hospital after the car crash, her life had seemed like that: blank, empty, meaningless. Until Cristina was able to access those buried memories. Until she knew who she was.

She removed Santos's envelope from the top drawer and dumped the articles on her desk. As she traced her finger over their photo in the article about their death, she heard her parents whispering to her that everything would be okay. She could feel their arms around her.

Yet when she flipped to the *O Globo* article, she felt wind on her face as she rode the tram up Sugarloaf Mountain in Brazil. The tangy smell of feijoada, a stew of black beans and meat, tickled her nostrils. How could Cristina remember so clearly if she'd never been there?

She jumped when her intercom buzzed.

"What is it, Devi?" she snapped into the intercom.

"Mr. Watterson is still waiting on line two." Devi was curt, clearly offended.

Cristina instantly regretted her tone, but Devi hung up before she could apologize.

Cristina took the call. "Mr. Watterson, I'm so sorry to keep you waiting. How can I help you?"

"It's Ma," he said in a thick North Shore accent. "Something's wrong with her."

"Is she sick?"

"Nah, she's healthier than ever. She started riding horses."

"Really?" Cristina couldn't help smiling at the thought of prim and proper Martha on horseback. "I didn't know she rode."

"She doesn't." His voice cracked, on the verge of tears. "She insists she was a champion equestrian back in college but keeps falling out of the saddle. She's lucky she hasn't broken anything. Dr. Silva, before last week, she never rode a horse in her life."

Cristina's smile washed away. "Maybe she never told you before."

"If she was so good, shouldn't it be like riding a bike? She shouldn't forget how, right?"

"Alzheimer's affects both factual and procedural memory. Has she forgotten how to do daily activities like brushing her hair or cooking?"

"No."

"Good. It hasn't progressed that much, then." Despite her reassurance, Cristina's mind nearly overheated as she ran through possible explanations. If Martha was losing procedural memory, perhaps her Alzheimer's was more advanced than Cristina had realized. Maybe even too much for Recognate to have an effect. "Keep close tabs on her and don't let her on any more horses. If her safety becomes at risk, we may need to consider residential treatment."

His breath hissed through the receiver. "I'm not ready for that. Since she saw you last, she's started to forget who I am. What'll happen if she's not living with me?"

"We have to consider all options. Let's focus on preserving as much memory as possible, okay?"

"Of course. It's …" He paused, breathing heavily. "You know, she tried all these herbs and crystals and the therapies with you because she wanted to remember me. She risked everything, and now—it's like she's given up. She yells at me to get out of her house and claims I kidnapped her." He choked back a sob. "I don't understand, Dr. Silva. If something was stealing my memory, I'd fight with everything I had to remember her."

Cristina's heart jumped. "What did you say?"

"I didn't kidnap my mother."

"No, about stealing memory."

"You know, the Alzheimer's—it steals memory."

She shook her head, but it didn't clear anything. "Please, don't give up. Bring your mother in next week, and we'll discuss best options for her treatment."

After hanging up, Cristina rubbed her forehead and tried to figure out when the world had started to fall apart. The only thing left in her life she could trust was her clinical skill, and even that seemed to be waning. She caught sight of her parents' photo and took a calming breath. They wouldn't want her to give up. Even if she doubted everything else, they were and always would be her parents. She needed to remember.

Chewing her lip, she withdrew Santos's cell phone and laid it on her desk. Next to it, she placed her phone and scrolled through the call list to Detective Wilson's number.

Cristina closed her eyes. Memories flitted through her mind: her mother beaming as she received her medical degree, her dad encouraging her to pursue her dreams ...

Cristina picked up the burner cell phone and dialed. When she heard the click on the other end, she said, "We need to talk."

CHAPTER FOURTEEN

Cristina dug her fingernails into her palm as the Green Line T clacked its way to Park Street. Not even Andrea knew where she was going. Santos had been clear about coming alone, and she had Jerry's performance to attend later. But, even if Santos didn't intend her harm, Francisco Martins was still out there.

A sea of black and yellow jerseys filled the train as it zipped down the tracks. Alcohol wafted through the cabin as the passengers pressed against each other and chanted "Let's go, Bruins!" Cristina huddled in her seat and watched them out of the corner of her eye. Any one of them could be Francisco Martins.

Scheduling back-to-back with Santos and Jerry hadn't been the best idea, but she couldn't pass on attending the play, nor could she afford to wait another day to learn the truth from Santos. She checked her cell. Only ten percent battery, so she shut it down. There was no signal in the tunnels anyway.

"Park Street," announced an overhead recording as the train ground to a stop.

Cristina shoved her way through the mass of hockey fans and slipped through the doors a second before they shut. It took another three minutes to climb the nonfunctioning escalator.

The moment Cristina emerged from the station, she was assaulted by the blinding headlights and streetlamps on busy Tremont Street. She glanced at the clock tower. Five thirty-seven. She was already late. The opera house was only a few blocks from the Commons.

After a few minutes on the zigzagging Boston Common paths, she spotted the brightly lit Frog Pond. In the winter, the pond transformed into an ice rink, attracting flocks of visitors. A sea of stocking caps and fur-lined hoods surrounded the pond. Picking Santos out of the crowd seemed difficult. He'd instructed Cristina to wear a green hat and scarf and promised that he'd find her.

She took a position near a statue of a frog with a fishing pole and watched groups of all ages take to the ice. Some floated along, performing pirouettes and double axels. Others clutched the railing like a best friend, trying to move in a straight line without falling. Some of Cristina's tension ebbed as she laughed at the clumsier skaters.

A memory flitted through her mind of ice skating when she was eight. She slipped and would've cracked open her skull if her mother hadn't dived onto the ice and caught her. Before Cristina could cry, her mother made a joke about penguins. As she replayed the memory, Cristina's chest swelled with love, but doubt lingered. What if that memory never happened?

"Continue looking straight ahead," said Santos's gruff voice beside her. "Do *not* react."

"I did as you ordered." Cristina fought the urge to turn. "Now tell me what happened to my parents."

"Are you certain you weren't followed?"

"I wouldn't know if I was. That's why you should appreciate the risk I took coming here, especially with Francisco Martins out there."

"What do you mean?"

The surprise in his voice made her look at him. He wore a

heavy black ski parka and gloves. A knit cap covered his head. Frost clung to his unruly beard and eyebrows.

"That's who broke into my apartment and attacked me. He burned down my parents' house. The police and the FBI are looking for him."

Santos's gaze darted from side to side. He bit down on his lower lip.

"You know him, don't you?" she asked. "Does he work for Zero Dark?"

After a deep breath, Santos said, "He did, but no longer. But he isn't the one who attacked you."

"His fingerprint was on my door lock."

"That print was faked."

"How could you possibly know that? And why are you so sure it wasn't him?"

"Because," he said, looking her square in the eye, "I am Francisco Martins."

"Burning the midnight oil?" Hawkins pulled up a chair next to Wilson, who sat rubbing his chin as he stared at his computer screen. "Time to call it a night, buddy."

"I know, I just …" Wilson threw his hands in the air and grunted. "I've searched every corner of the NCIC website for more information about Martins and keep getting nothing. He disappeared two years ago. There are no reports of recent activity anywhere. So how did Agent Forrester know he was in Somerville?"

"The Feds aren't big on sharing. Maybe that info's classified."

"Yeah, I guess." Wilson scratched behind his ear. That itch had gotten worse over the last couple days. "But how are we going to catch this guy if we don't know where to look?"

"We aren't. You notified Forrester, right?"

Wilson grimaced. "Not yet."

"Gary …"

"I will. But as soon as I contact Forrester, he'll swoop in and take over the entire investigation."

"And that's a bad thing?"

"Not if you are the sort of person who would enjoy boot camp."

"Yeah, not fun. But are you sure that's it? This doesn't have anything to do with a certain sexy shrink?"

Wilson's cheeks flushed. "I have this feeling, okay?"

"Oh, no, not one of your feelings."

"Hear me out. It can't be coincidence that one of Dr. Silva's patients jumped through a window a day before Martins attacks her. Maybe this Martins dude killed Carl Franklin."

"Jesus, Gary, you're not going to rest until you prove this guy was behind the Marathon Bombing and 9/11, are you?"

"Probably not."

"All right, if you want to find something the Feds missed, cross-reference Martins with Silva. Maybe we can find a connection."

"Good idea. Let me try the ICE system." Wilson entered the database and began searching. His screen filled with data. "Around the time he was accused of arson, Martins was working as a mechanic for Manny's Auto in Framingham." Wilson reread the next few lines and scratched his head. "Looks like he kept working there until he disappeared. Why wasn't he in jail?"

"Maybe they didn't have enough evidence."

Another search came up with a smaller return. Wilson frowned as he read. "Martins disappeared the day after the Silvas died in a car wreck. How much you want to bet he ran them off the road?"

"That's a fool's bet. Is there an investigation report?"

Wilson typed a few keys. Two file names appeared. He clicked on the first. "Forensics report says the brake line was severed. Looks like they initially thought it had been cut, but then determined it snapped on its own. Also says there was black paint on the rear bumper. Not much else to go on. Let's see what the police report shows." He clicked the next file. A message appeared in red. "Missing? What the hell?"

"Must be a problem with their server. A hit and run would make the news though. Try public records."

After a few more keystrokes, Wilson's screen lit up.

"There's an obituary for Jorge and Claudia Silva. No mention of Cristina, no details about the crash or any suspects." He pulled up another record. "The police report says the Silvas' car was serviced the day before ..." Wilson scrolled down. "At Manny's Auto. I'll be damned."

"Wait—am I reading that correctly?" Hawkins pointed at the additional lines of text at the bottom of the screen indicating the repairs performed and the technician performing them.

"You are." Wilson gritted his teeth. "Looks like Dr. Silva and I need to have a conversation tomorrow."

CHAPTER FIFTEEN

"What the hell?" Cristina shouted and backed away from Santos. "Are you going to explain why you burned down my parents' house?"

"I will, but you must stop attracting attention."

Cristina fought the urge to punch him. If he was as dangerous as Wilson said, she wouldn't stand a chance against him. She caught people around the ice rink, staring.

"We should move somewhere more discreet," he said.

Cristina held her ground next to the frog statue. "I'm not going anywhere with you," she said quietly enough that only he could hear.

The onlookers lost interest and returned to watching the skaters.

"Answer my questions or, so help me, I'll scream for help."

"Very well," Santos said. "When I was young, I found myself in the wrong place at the wrong time. A powerful man wanted me executed for a crime I didn't commit. I had no chance of proving my innocence. Zero Dark approached me. They promised to clear my name if I vowed to help them. I possessed skills they found desirable." His gaze danced over the heads in the crowd. "I accepted, not believing they could keep their word. They did."

"How?"

"They killed the man who framed me and left evidence proving his guilt. I was free, but not truly free. Zero Dark promised to set me up for killing my accuser if I betrayed them. From that moment on, they owned me."

"So, you committed horrible crimes to stay out of jail?" Acid stung Cristina's throat. "That's why you burned down my parents' house?"

"No. By that time I wanted out of Zero Dark, even if it meant I would be tried for my crimes. But then they found something else to hold against me—something I would do anything to protect."

"Your daughter."

He turned to her, the skin around his eyes wrinkling with a tenderness that reminded her of her father. Or the man she knew as her father. "The director threatened to kill her if I didn't follow his orders. Burn down a house to prove I was still loyal. I didn't even know who owned the house. Only after I obeyed would he trust me to keep silent, or he would silence my daughter instead."

Cristina swallowed. She wanted to hate him but found she couldn't. He wasn't a monster. Just a father left with no options. "What happened once you did as they asked?"

"It wasn't enough. I had to keep serving their needs or they would turn me over to the authorities." His voice cracked. "And they kept my daughter prisoner."

A shiver ran down Cristina's back. "Is she still alive?"

Santos nodded.

"Do you know where she is?"

"I know where she is, but she won't listen to me. That's why I need your help."

"Why would she listen to me? I don't even know her."

"Maybe not, but after you see the truth, after you understand, she'll listen to you."

Cristina threw up her hands to keep from clamping them around his neck. "No more riddles. If you want my help—and

I'm not promising you'll get it—I need details, starting with who ran my parents and I off the road and why?"

Santos stared at her like her nose had fallen off her face. "You were never in that car."

"Of course, I was. I got a head injury that caused my amnesia."

"Your head injury occurred beforehand. You were placed unconscious at the scene of the car crash to replace the third passenger." His stony gaze locked onto hers. "The real Cristina Silva."

Cristina's heart jumped toward her throat. "That's impossible."

"Zero Dark has made you believe you are Cristina Silva to keep you under control. They made me burn down Silvas' house to destroy any evidence that would shatter this illusion. These are dangerous people, Cristina. Only together can we stop them from hurting anyone else."

A thousand thoughts swirled through her mind. Even if she believed nothing else Santos said, certain facts rang true. Someone had killed the people she thought of as her parents; someone had ordered Santos to burn down their house; and something was wrong with her memories, even with Recognate. But a conspiracy involving a shadow organization manipulating her life? The idea would be preposterous if it didn't ignite tiny sparks of familiarity in the recesses of her mind.

"If I'm not Cristina Silva," she said, barely able to work her mouth. "Then who am I?"

A floodlight swung over them. Cristina shielded her eyes. Peeking through her fingers, she saw a reporter interviewing a woman with an expensive-looking fur coat and scarf. Cristina vaguely recognized the woman as a local celebrity, a singer from a popular Boston rock band who'd scored an acting role on a TV courtroom drama. Onlookers crowded around to get a glimpse while the camera recorded their reactions.

"So much for a quiet night at the Pond." She turned back to Santos.

He was gone.

"Damn it," she muttered and searched the crowd. No sign of him.

There was no point sticking around. She started the long walk back to Park Street, angry at herself for not pushing him harder for real answers, and even angrier for allowing herself to believe him. As she trudged down the path, she yanked off a glove. She'd better call Andrea.

When she reached into her pocket for her cell, Cristina's fingertips grazed cold metal. Puzzled, Cristina wrapped her hand around something and withdrew it. She held it in the lamplight. It was a round silver locket, strung on a lightweight chain. An intricate engraving covered the front, depicting a man tied to a tree. Arrows pierced his bare chest. Something about the image sparked recognition, but she couldn't determine why. She flipped the locket over and found the design of a cone-shaped building. Something had been written beneath the building, but the years had worn the writing away. Her finger traced over the design.

Cristina stuck the locket in her pocket and continued walking. As she pulled out her phone and activated it three new voicemail messages popped up. She listened to the first as she continued walking.

"Dr. Silva, it's Jerry. It's almost curtain time. I'm not sure you'll be able to make it, but at least if I talk to you, I can do it. Please call me back as soon as you can."

Cristina's heart jumped. She checked the clock on her phone. Six twenty. She'd spent longer with Santos than anticipated.

She picked up the pace, walking faster as she called Jerry back. No answer.

Her pulsed raced. She proceeded to the next message.

His voice was strained "It was a disaster, Dr. Silva. I couldn't do it." He sounded angry. "He … he said this would happen. I thought I could fight it, but I can't. I'm on my way to Park Street Station. If you're coming, meet me there."

Her grip tightened around the phone. He sounded desperate. She hurried and played the last message.

"Dr. Silva, are you working with them again? Did they get to you?" He broke into spasmodic laughter. "It doesn't matter. This will end tonight."

Cristina stopped. Jerry's voice made her skin crawl—cold, vacant, hopeless.

She verified the voicemail's timestamp. Seven minutes ago.

She hit redial. The phone rang. No answer.

She could not lose Jerry. Not like Carl. Not like Mitchell.

She raced to the Park Street subway station, scolding herself all the way. She'd been so focused on this ridiculous game with Santos she'd forgotten what truly mattered: her patients.

The station exterior was a giant box. She did a full circle around it. No sign of Jerry. He had to be inside. She hoped he wasn't about to do what she feared.

As she pushed her way through the crowded entrance and walked downstairs, she scanned the crowds. Not there. She moved toward the turnstiles, readying her T pass.

A gunshot echoed through the station.

People screamed. Ran in all directions. A heavyset woman crashed into Cristina. Knocked her to the floor. Cristina rolled away onto her knees. Her heart raced. Through the chaos, she couldn't see anything.

Another gunshot. Then two more. More screams. More panic.

Cristina leaped to her feet. Everyone shoved their way to the stairs. A mob swept past like a tidal wave, carrying her with it. She fought to stay on her feet. She swung her arms to keep the others from crushing her.

Someone shouted. He sounded familiar.

"Police!" Four uniformed officers rushed past. "Clear the area!"

"Stay back!"

Even as Cristina fought her way to the stairs, she glanced over her shoulder. She recognized Jerry's voice.

"Stay away or I'll kill him!" he called out.

"Put down the gun!" shouted a uniformed police officer, aiming his weapon. "We want to help you."

"You can't help me. Quinn must die!"

Cristina froze at the base of the stairs. People jostled her as they forced their way past.

"Drop the gun," ordered the policeman. "Now!"

Like a salmon, Cristina maneuvered her way upstream through the crowd. Every instinct told her to get the hell out of there, but her need for answers propelled her forward.

She emerged back in the open area near the turnstiles. Police officers stood shoulder to shoulder, weapons aimed at the far wall. Four inert bodies lay near their feet.

"This man stole my life!" Jerry's voice echoed through the now empty room.

Past the cops, a man in his midthirties knelt on the ground, hands behind his head. One torn shoulder of his jacket hung limply. Tears streaked his cheeks. His eyes were shut tight. Behind him, a balding man wearing a blood-stained parka and jeans held a gun to his head.

"Jerry?"

Jerry's head snapped in Cristina's direction. His expression shifted from anger to confusion. "Dr. Silva?"

"Stay back, ma'am," said one of the officers. "This is a secure area."

"He's my patient, Officer," Cristina said, even as she struggled with the inconceivable reality that sweet mild-mannered Jerry could have killed several people. She'd feared he was about to throw himself in front of a train, but never imagined him capable of this. She forced away her revulsion and focused on the man. "I can help."

Jerry laughed bitterly. "You've done enough already."

Cristina recoiled. "What do you mean?"

"Everything came rushing back. I did horrible things, Dr. Silva. Horrible things."

"It's okay, Jerry. Why don't you put down the gun and we can talk about it?"

"Now you want to talk?" His voice hardened. "I needed your help. You didn't come. Didn't even answer your damn phone. You weren't there for me."

Cristina's cheeks cooled. "I'm here now. Tell me what happened."

"You know what happened. You were there." He pointed the gun barrel at his captive. "And it's his fault." Jerry pointed at the man kneeling in front of him, "He did this to us."

"Please," the man said, sobbing. "I don't know what he's talking about. I've never seen him before in my life."

"Shut up!" Jerry's hand shook as he dug the gun into the back of his victim's head.

The man trembled.

"No more lies," said Jerry.

"Who are you talking about, Jerry?" Cristina stepped closer, telling herself this wasn't the man she knew. Jerry was a good person. He wasn't a murderer. "Who is *he*?"

"Ma'am," the officer said, "you need to stay back."

"I'm a psychiatrist. I know what I'm doing," she said, even though she questioned if that was true with each step she took. "Talk to me, Jerry. Who do you think this man is? What did he do?"

"Don't tell her." Jerry snapped his eyes shut. "She has to know. She's working with Quinn. She did this to us. She needs to pay. Don't make me do this. Please."

Cristina was baffled. Jerry's voice shifted back and forth from that of the mild-mannered security guard she knew to that of a hardened killer. A horrible thought struck her. Could he have dissociative identity disorder, a rare condition once known as split personality? She couldn't have missed something that significant—could she?

"Jerry," she said, using the hypnotic tone she preferred for therapy, despite her heart beating so fast it nearly burst from her chest. "I'm not working with Quinn. I don't know who Quinn is. I need you to tell me what happened. It's not too late to find a way to help you."

He held her gaze, panting heavily. Sweat trickled down the sides of his face. His lips danced as he continued his self-argument in a whisper. Jerry lowered his gun an inch.

"That's it." She took another step, her heart pounding. "Put down the gun and we can talk. You still need to tell me about that New Orleans trip."

A smile played at his lips. Then it vanished, replaced by wild rage. "There was no New Orleans trip. No marathon. None of that was real. I know who I really am: a killer."

The ferocity of his verbal assault forced Cristina to retreat. Her mind raced through possibilities—psychosis, mania, depression. None fully explained his behavior.

"Jerry, you're not a killer. We can sort this out."

The kneeling hostage began to cry.

"That's it," the officer murmured loud enough for Cristina to hear, "we need to put this guy down."

"No," she said. "We need more time."

"We're out of time, Doctor," Jerry said, his voice eerily tranquil. It was a tone Cristina heard before, in patients who'd given up. He jammed the gun behind his captive's ear. "This is the only way we can both be free of his control."

"No!" Cristina shouted.

Jerry pulled the trigger. Blood sprayed his face. His hostage slumped to the ground.

The officers opened fire. Bullets ripped through Jerry's arms and chest. Just before the final bullet tore through his forehead and he crumpled backward, Cristina thought she saw him smile.

CHAPTER SIXTEEN

"Thanks for picking me up." Cristina closed her eyes, focusing on the relaxing scents of the leather seats and cinnamon air freshener. She tried to ignore the jarring movements as Andrea swerved her Mazda Miata back and forth between lanes.

"The T is still shut down, and I couldn't handle taking the bus alone."

"Don't be silly," Andrea said. Gears hummed as she upshifted. "You know I'm always here for you."

"Mm-hmm." Eyes closed, Cristina gripped the console.

"You okay? You look like you're ready to jump out the window."

Cristina forced a smile without opening her eyes. "I'll be fine."

"Relax. We'll be home before you know it."

"Okay." Cristina slowed her breathing, allowing her mind to drift. The moment she started to feel calmer, Jerry Peterman's face jarred her thoughts. He shot his victim again and again. Cristina bolted upright.

Andrea jumped and jerked the steering wheel. The car swerved.

"What? What happened?" They were headed toward the guardrail. Andrea veered back into the lane. "Jesus, you almost gave me a heart attack."

"I'm sorry. I keep seeing Jerry's face. The whole scene was horrible."

"I can only imagine. But don't blame yourself. He was obviously sick."

"That's just it. Jerry Peterman was happy as could be at his last visit. It's my job to tell if someone is a threat to himself or others. He's never seemed unstable. Ever." Again, she saw Jerry's final grin. "And here's the totally bizarre thing: at the end, Jerry had the same smile I saw on Carl Franklin's face after he died, like they were relieved their suffering was finally at an end. How long were they in pain and I had no idea?" She felt like an undead creature had sucked the life from her body. "Maybe I should quit my job before someone else dies."

"Don't talk like that. Damn it!" Andrea slammed on her brakes as the lights turned red. She twisted in her seat to face Cristina. "I know for a fact that you've helped a lot of people who wouldn't have a chance with anyone else."

As much as Cristina wanted to believe that, she kept hearing Jerry's voice, *I needed your help … You weren't there for me.*

"Two patients dead in two weeks, and one of them murdered innocent people," Cristina managed to say without breaking into tears. "Even for a forensic psychiatrist that would be more than bad luck. Clearly, I failed them."

"Enough of that. There's no way you could've known everything, no matter how many questions you asked or how eager they seemed to talk."

The light changed.

Andrea gunned the engine and sped through the intersection. "Everyone has skeletons, you know?"

As the streetlights whipped past, a wave of nausea overtook Cristina, but it wasn't only the movement that affected her. She wondered what Andrea would think if she knew Cristina had been meeting clandestinely with the man who had burned down her parents' house. She snapped her eyes shut. "Could you please slow down?"

"Oh, sorry, honey." Andrea eased off the gas. "Is that better?"

Cristina nodded. Her stomach settled, but she couldn't shake a feeling of dread. Why had Jerry been hunting someone named Quinn—the name she had shouted in her sleep? Her temples throbbed. She sank deeper into the seat. "I want this night to end."

"Did the cops give you a hard time?"

"No, they were very polite. They took a statement and asked to stop by tomorrow to review my medical records on Jerry. When it became clear his rampage was out of the blue, and everything he was babbling was nonsense, they got tired of babysitting me."

"Detective Wilson took care of it, huh?"

"It's not his precinct. They said they'd give him a call in the morning." Cristina brushed a lock of hair out of her eyes and sighed. "Honestly, I'm glad he wasn't there."

"Why?"

"Are you kidding? With everything that's happened, he's going to insist on an escort every time I leave the apartment."

"That's not such a bad idea." Andrea gave Cristina a sideways glance. "What were you doing in the Commons by yourself, anyway?"

Cristina's neck muscles tensed. As much as she wanted to tell Andrea everything—about Zero Dark, the locket, and Santos's claims—the last thing she needed was a lecture on how irrational and careless she was being. If she hadn't met Santos or Martins or whoever he was, she would've answered her phone and maybe could've stopped Jerry. Even though that would haunt her, maybe forever, she was still driven to find the truth. But if she could believe Santos, Zero Dark killed anyone who got in their way. If

Andrea knew the truth, it'd be like painting crosshairs on her forehead. Until Cristina knew what Zero Dark wanted from her, she
couldn't risk involving anyone else.

"This afternoon I remembered skating on the pond with
my parents." As Cristina lied to Andrea, she stared into the side
mirror. Who was this woman staring back with dark circles and
fear in her eyes? She had thought she knew, but now she wasn't so
sure. "I felt this need to connect with them. I'm sorry. I should've
called you, but I needed some alone time."

"Hey, I know that feeling." Andrea exited onto Route 128
toward Somerville. "But with everything going on, you can't take
chances. Next time call me, okay?"

"I will."

"You don't have to suffer alone. You know you can tell me
anything, right?"

"I know."

Nearly a hundred potential investors filled the Marriott Ward-
man Park Hotel ballroom, from advertising executives and movie
producers to entrepreneurial millionaires. Champagne had been
flowing for hours. Quinn recalled attending parties like this nearly
every week up until his third year of college, when his parents cut
him off from his trust fund and inheritance. A weaker man might
have sunken into drunken despair or sought refuge in religion—
but not Quinn. He chose his own path, and now he balanced
on the precipice of being more powerful than his parents could
have ever dreamed. The right pitch could sell every one of these
drunken bastards on the project. He only had to choose the best
offer. The senator he'd been approaching when his phone vibrated
was a prime target, but Quinn knew better than to keep the indi-
vidual on the other end of the secure chat waiting.

After signaling to the senator that he'd return soon, Quinn

slipped into the coat room and checked his smartphone. Three words stared back: *She was there.*

"Shit," Quinn muttered.

The light conversation continued uninterrupted over the string quartet's rendition of a Chopin concerto. News of the Boston shooting had already diffused through the ballroom, although so far no one had traced the crazed shooter's medical prescriptions back to ReMind.

Quinn considered his options. He thought he'd given Santos enough reason to keep his mouth shut—obviously not the case. He should've dealt with him permanently, a mistake he wouldn't make again. But as much as Quinn hated to do it, until he found the rogue, he needed to ensure Cristina Silva would not be a threat.

CHAPTER SEVENTEEN

Outside her apartment building, hailing a taxi, Cristina spotted the front-page headline in the bus stop newspaper dispensers. *Park Street Station Massacre*. Any frail hope that she had imagined the prior night's horrible events vanished. Out of the corner of her eye, Cristina caught an old woman staring at her before looking away.

When Cristina entered her office, Devi was on the phone, scribbling furiously. The office manager widened her eyes when she spotted Cristina and made a flabbergasted expression while indicating an array of sticky notes on her desk.

"Yes," she said into the phone. "I'll give her the message."

"What was all that?" Cristina asked after Devi hung up.

"Robin Roberts' office. They want an interview."

"The newswoman Robin Roberts? Interview about what?"

"Didn't you watch the news? They identified you on TV as Jerry Peterman's psychiatrist."

A knot formed in Cristina's stomach. "The police said they wouldn't give my name to the media until they finished their investigation."

"They didn't. Jerry's sister said your name in an interview on FOX News."

The floor fell away from under Cristina's feet. "Jerry didn't have a sister."

"Apparently he did. Her name's Stacey, and she's pissed. You should've seen her ranting and raving." Devi touched her lip. "Or maybe it's good you didn't see it."

Cristina wiped her hands over her face and fought the urge to scream. "None of this makes sense. Why wouldn't Jerry tell me about his sister?"

"I don't know, but news travels fast. Some of these messages are from Associated Press, the *Globe*, the *New York Times* …" She waved her hand over the sticky notes. "The rest are from patients canceling their appointments."

"Why are they canceling?"

"It might be because on television Stacey Peterman claimed you prescribed a combination of off-label antipsychotics and stimulants that caused her brother to have a psychotic break."

"That's ridiculous."

"Well, apparently he had an empty pill bottle in his pocket, and the police didn't know what it was. If you ask me, his sister is a rattlesnake, looking for an excuse to attack someone."

Cristina fought to control her expression. The pills had to be Recognate.

"Devi, hold my calls."

She shrugged. "I've been doing it all morning. Why stop now?"

Cristina hurried into her office and turned on the computer. She searched her phone directory until she found and called the number for ReMind. They'd changed it twice since she had joined the study, and she hoped they hadn't changed it again.

After a few minutes on hold, a man answered. "ReMind Pharmaceuticals. How can I direct your call?"

"I need to speak to Frank Alvarez in R&D."

"I'm sorry. They're all in a meeting. I can have someone call you back."

"It's urgent. Tell Frank that Dr. Cristina Silva needs to speak to him."

After a sharp intake of breath, the man said, "Please hold, Doctor, while I connect you."

Cristina chewed on her cuticles while she waited. She caught herself and placed her hand on her desk. What kind of psychiatrist chewed her fingers? One whose world was falling apart. She closed her eyes. The operator's reaction was odd, but Cristina didn't care as long as he got Frank Alvarez on the line. Frank had been her contact since day one. Though they'd exchanged numerous emails, she'd never heard his voice. He seemed like a stickler for details and safety protocols. Hopefully, he'd know what to do.

The phone clicked.

"Dr. Silva?" asked a baritone voice.

"Is this Frank? Thank God. I need to give you a heads-up on—"

"Dr. Silva, this is Julius Simmons."

Cristina was startled. Why was she speaking to ReMind's CEO?

"I heard about your connection to the subway shooting." Simmons clucked his tongue. "A tragedy. How are you handling it?"

"Not well, but there's something that didn't make the news. Jerry Peterman, the shooter, was a subject in the Recognate trials."

"I know. Frank Alvarez briefed me an hour ago."

"I'm worried about my other patients. I'll provide whatever information you need for adverse effect reporting, and if you feel we need to suspend the study—"

"That's thoughtful but unnecessary, Doctor. I'm sure you know we found no significant adverse effects during randomized trials." The sound of papers flipping carried over the phone. "But we've only studied Recognate in subjects with stable psychiatric backgrounds. That's why we screen our referrals so carefully."

"Of course, and that's why I've only referred stable patients like Jerry."

Simmons made a *tsk-tsk* sound. "I hardly consider three months in an institution stable."

"What are you talking about?"

"Peterman's sister Stacey announced on the morning news he'd been hospitalized two years ago for attempted suicide."

Cristina reeled as if slapped. "I knew nothing about that."

"So I gathered. A phone call confirmed his stay at Franciscan Hospital." Simmons' tone turned accusatory. "Dr. Silva, how many other subjects have you referred without properly reviewing their histories?"

"None. I know what I'm doing." Cristina braced herself against her desk as her head spun. Two of her patients were dead—she knew what she was doing? "I'm still worried that Recognate may have adverse effects. Another patient of mine—a participant in your study— killed himself two weeks ago. Carl Franklin also had no history of depression. There was no warning."

Simmons hesitated. "How long was he taking Recognate?"

"Almost a year."

"Standard dose?"

"Yes."

"Then Recognate was not at fault. Long-term studies in rats showed no toxic effects at standard dose."

"But those are rats. How many suicidal rats do you see?"

"Doctor, I know you're in a difficult position, but don't blur the issue by pointing fingers. The fact is amnesiac patients sometimes fail to disclose certain facts, making it necessary to dig deeper." Something buzzed in the background. "I'm afraid I have another call."

"Okay, but Mr. Simmons—"

"We'll provide whatever support you require should the

victim's family seek legal action. You've been a valuable resource and we take care of our own, so long as you follow the rules. You have been following the rules?"

Cristina's mouth went dry. "Yes, of course."

"Then you have nothing to worry about. Thank you for your call." With a click, he ended the conversation.

Cristina stared at the phone, more confused than ever. She tried to break it down. Recognate worked on endocannabinoid receptors, the same receptors that bind to marijuana, suppressing norepinephrine—one of the body's fight-or-flight neurotransmitters. Could an overdose overstimulate the brain and cause psychosis?

Chewing her lip, Cristina searched for Dr. Morgan's number on her computer. If the medical examiner found altered neurotransmitter levels in Carl Franklin's autopsy, it might be enough to prove her theory and convince Simmons at ReMind of the crucial need for further study.

As she picked up her phone, the intercom buzzed.

"Devi," she said after pressing the button, "I asked you to hold my calls."

"I know, but you have a visitor."

"I'm not talking to reporters."

"What about Detective Wilson?"

With everyone else seemingly against her, Cristina knew that potentially having a cop on her side was a good thing. "Send him in."

CHAPTER EIGHTEEN

"Detective." Cristina smiled when Wilson entered her office.

His navy twill suit clung nicely to his well-proportioned frame.

She averted her gaze. "Is this about Stacey Peterman's claims? I had no idea—"

"This isn't about Jerry Peterman. I need you to help me with something."

She blinked, taken aback. "Sure. Whatever you need."

"Your parents were killed in a car wreck, right?"

"Yes, I told you that."

"You had a head injury."

"Yes."

"And you lost all memory of events before the wreck."

Her neck muscles tightened. "Where are you going with this?"

"The brake lines were severed. It looked like they'd been cut."

"They weren't cut. They snapped after someone ran us off the road."

"Right. That's what the forensics report said." He nodded and scratched his chin. "Two days before the crash, you took the car to a mechanic. Do you recall his name?"

"Detective, I don't remember anything about that week. I still have partial amnesia."

"Right, right." He glanced at her diplomas. "Francisco Martins."

"What about him?"

"He was the mechanic. The same Francisco Martins that burned down your parents' house." He tapped his temple and flashed a lopsided grin. "Weird coincidence, huh?"

Feeling lightheaded, Cristina sat on the corner of her desk. "I didn't know anything about this."

"Bad things happen to you when this guy pops into your life, and now he's in town and your apartment gets ransacked. It's like you two are connected."

Cristina pressed her fingers against her forehead, fighting to stay in control of her emotions. Santos had admitted to burning down her parents' house as Francisco Martins. Was he responsible for their deaths also? "Are you accusing me of having something to do with the crash that killed my parents?"

"I'm not accusing you of anything. I'm trying to get the facts straight." He stuck his hands in his pockets. "But I learned your parents had a substantial life insurance policy and you were the sole inheritor."

Anger roiled in Cristina's gut. It took all her strength to force it down.

"Detective, I lost everything. I've been living without a past. I had to rebuild my life from the bottom up." Tears lurked at the corners of her eyes, but she fought them back. She wasn't about to let this man see her cry. "I can't explain to you why Francisco Martins keeps appearing in my life, but I assure you there's nothing I want more than to see whoever killed my parents brought to justice."

He held her gaze for a moment, his eyes narrowed, lips twitching. She could tell he was searching her face for clues she was lying. She did the same, scanning him for any sign he believed her, but his expression remained passive.

At last, he looked away. "Amnesiacs are tough to pin down. It's near impossible to tell what's true and what's not. I mean, it's not like you can go inside someone's brain and see what she really remembers, right?"

He had a hideous twist at the end of his nose. How easy it was to overlook that when he was nice and charming, and how quickly it became apparent when the charm wore off. "Unless you're planning to read me my rights, I think this conversation is over."

He shrugged. "I told you, I'm not accusing you. But it would help to have something more to go on."

"Why don't you check my hospital records? They'll confirm my injuries. And everything about the investigation should be in Detective Mitchell Parker's report."

"Parker? Would he have info on Martins?"

Cristina winced. "Detective Parker was the guy in the photo you saw in my apartment. He helped me after the crash, but he didn't know anything about Martins."

Wilson studied her face again. His stony expression softened. "Again, I'm sorry. Well, if you remember anything else that could help us catch Martins, call me."

She considered telling Wilson about Santos, but their trust had already been shattered. Instead, she nodded. After the detective left, she sank into her chair, folded her arms on her desk, and buried her face. There was obviously much more that Santos hadn't told her. And was he involved in making her believe she was Cristina Silva?

How ridiculous did that sound? Of course, she was Cristina Silva. Wilson's news confirmed she couldn't believe everything Santos claimed.

She glanced at her computer screen. Dr. Morgan's number

stared back at her. Whatever happened in the past, she had more pressing threats in the present, including protecting her patients' safety and her own reputation. She pursed her lips and dialed Morgan's number.

"Dr. Silva," he said. "It's good to hear your voice, though I'm guessing you aren't calling to see if I'm free tonight."

Despite her exhaustion, she smiled. "In a way, I am. Did they send Jerry Peterman's body to you for autopsy?"

"He was your patient? You've had an unlucky run, haven't you?"

"Thank you for reminding me."

"Please forgive my dumbass remark. What I meant was, how are you holding up?"

She sighed. "Barely. Please tell me you found something useful when looking at Jerry Peterman."

"Well, he has an odd-looking scar at the base of his neck, but that's years old, so I doubt it's relevant. Blood and urine tox screens were negative except for trace amounts of cannabis and a blood alcohol concentration through the roof."

"He was drunk?" Cristina frowned. Jerry never admitted to a drinking problem, but apparently there was a lot he had withheld. At least he tested negative for stimulants. That would derail his sister's claims.

"What I saw at Park Street Station didn't look like an angry drunk," she said. "Something else happened to him. Are you doing tissue studies?"

"I'm afraid not. His sister is demanding he be transferred to a private pathologist. There's a court order barring me from touching his body until it's settled."

Cristina gasped. "How can she do that? What about the criminal investigation?"

"Boston PD is satisfied with Peterman's psychiatric history and his BAC as the cause of his behavior so they're not fighting her decision. I didn't think a medicolegal autopsy could be refused, so I'm still pushing to overturn the decision, but Ms. Peterman is very persuasive."

"So I've noticed." Cristina chewed her cuticle. Without a full autopsy, she had nothing to exonerate her from Stacey Peterman's claims of malpractice. But maybe there was another way. "Do you still have the blood and urine?"

"Samples are in the cooler."

"This may sound odd, but could you check catecholamine levels?"

"You think he had a pheo?"

Morgan meant a pheochromocytoma—a rare adrenal gland tumor that released high levels of fight-or-flight neurotransmitters like norepinephrine. A tumor like that could manifest as erratic or violent behavior.

"Maybe, or something like it."

"I'm intrigued. Sure, I'll run it. The court only said I couldn't touch his body."

"Great. Could you also do a cannabis quant?"

Morgan hesitated. "I don't usually get specific requests like this from psychiatrists. Is there something you're not telling me?"

Just that I need to know if he was taking the same dose of Recognate I prescribed.

"No, I want to cover all bases," Cristina said. "I need to identify any potential risk to my other patients."

"All right, that's simple enough. It'll take a few days."

"Thank you so much, Dr. Morgan."

"Please, call me Luke."

She smiled. "Thanks, Luke."

As Cristina hung up, she decided it was time to confront Stacey Peterman. If the woman was telling the truth, she was probably in pain. Answering her questions would address her concerns about how Cristina managed Jerry's symptoms and might provide Cristina with some answers as well. She buzzed Devi. "Can you get next of kin information from Jerry Peterman's insurer? I want a number for Stacey."

"I'll see what I can do."

Cristina's cell phone vibrated: Andrea calling.

"This is a bad time," Cristina said. "We'll talk when I get home."

"I don't think this can wait."

"What's wrong? Are you okay?"

"No. I just left a meeting with my supervisor." Andrea paused, as if searching for the right words. "You're being sued."

CHAPTER NINETEEN

"Please tell me you're joking." Cristina massaged her temples. Now she knew what drowning felt like. Every time she came up for air, another wave crashed over her. "Who's suing me? No, let me guess. Stacey Peterman."

"Actually," Andrea said, "it's a combined lawsuit by the families of Jerry's victims. They claim you allowed a psychotic killer to run free."

The blood drained from Cristina's face. "That's ridiculous. Jerry never seemed angry before yesterday, let alone psychotic or homicidal."

"Honey, I believe you, but I can see why a lawyer would jump on the case, with Jerry's history of hospitalization and his sister's accusations. And it was also reported that you were at the crime scene."

"But I didn't know—"

"It looks bad. Still, they need to prove you knew there was a foreseeable threat and didn't warn the victims."

"Then they don't have a case. I feel horrible for those poor people, but how could I warn random victims?"

After a pause, Andrea said, "Are you sure they were random?"

"What do you mean?"

She hesitated again. "Did Jerry refer to his last victim by a name?"

The walls started to close in. "Yes."

"He called him Quinn, right?"

"Yes," she admitted, knowing her failure to mention this to Andrea would piss her off.

"Damn it, Cristina! Why didn't you tell me?"

"I was going to. There was so much going on and … Wait. Was the man Jerry executed named Quinn?"

"No. But a witness told a reporter they heard Jerry shouting '*Quinn must die.*' So even if it was a case of mistaken identity, he was clearly hunting for a specific target."

"Jerry never mentioned anyone named Quinn to me."

"But that's the name you were shouting in your sleep the other night. What aren't you telling me?"

"I don't know anyone named Quinn. I don't know what happened to Jerry." She swallowed back tears. "Andrea, I'm falling apart."

"Calm down." Andrea's tone softened. "Look, with all the trash Stacey Peterman is throwing the media, we need hard proof of your innocence."

"If she was so close to Jerry, where's she been for the past year?"

"That's a good question, but we need to concentrate on you. I'm going to give you the name of a lawyer at another firm, but don't mention my name so there's no conflict of interest. Don't talk to reporters until you talk to him, and for heaven's sake, don't say anything to anyone about Quinn. The last thing we need is a media circus."

Cristina may not have a family, but Andrea was the next best thing. "Thank you. I don't know what I'd do without you."

"Probably end up seeing a shrink, and we both know what a mistake that is." Andrea snickered. "When you get home, I'll fix you a mojito and everything will be fine."

As Cristina considered what lay ahead—an angry sister, a missing daughter, mysteries about her past, the looming threat of Zero Dark, and a lawsuit that could threaten her practice and privacy—for once, the idea of drinking away all memory sounded appealing. "I'll stop by at six."

"Any later though and the rum may be gone by the time you arrive."

Whatever comfort Cristina had found in talking to Andrea ebbed the moment she hung up. Even if she could prove Jerry's rampage was unpredictable and unavoidable, the media attention would take weeks to die down. And Stacey Peterman was stoking the fire.

Cristina keyed the intercom.

"Devi," Cristina said, "did you find anything on Jerry's sister?"

"One of the local news anchors said he'd give me her number if you agreed to an exclusive interview," Devi replied.

"I'm not doing interviews."

"Those were his terms."

"Forget it." Cristina tapped her fingernail on the keyboard. "The insurance company doesn't have it?"

"No next of kin listed."

"Can you search the Internet then? For the names of Jerry's victims too?"

"I can try public records," Devi said. "Why don't you ask Detective Wilson for help?"

"He's busy enough, and I trust you more." Cristina's watch beeped. Time for her pills. She stopped with the drawer halfway open. Andrea's questions about Jerry's rage were valid. Cristina was missing something. "Devi, can you see if we have a chart on someone named Quinn?"

"Is that a first or last name?"

"Check both." Cristina's watch beeped again. She turned off

the intercom and retrieved the pill bottle. Following her routine, she poured three green capsules into her palm, continuing the higher dosage she'd started two days earlier. She stopped short of placing them in her mouth. Two patients were dead. ReMind's CEO insisted Recognate was safe.

Cristina stared at the capsules. A new memory flitted along the back wall of her mind. She snatched at it, willing it to solidify. There it was. She nearly dropped the pills.

She was driving her parents' Lexus. High beams illuminated the wet road ahead. Her mother was in the passenger seat next to her. The smell of *Angel* perfume mingled with the scent of fresh leather. From the backseat, her father was telling a joke.

"So, the psychotherapist goes outside to see his new sign. He's shocked to discover the painter hadn't been able to fit it all on one line, so he broke it up into three lines." Jorge Silva paused for effect. "It read, *Psycho. The. Rapist.*"

Cristina's family all laughed.

Cristina adjusted her rear mirror to dim the glare of the headlights from the SUV behind them. "Do you know why psychotherapy is faster for a man than for a woman?"

Her parents said they didn't.

She turned onto a side road. The car skidded.

Her heart raced, but she forced herself to stay calm. She turned into the skid.

The car obeyed. She exhaled in relief.

"Because when it's time to go back to childhood, the man is already there."

Her parents laughed even louder.

Something rammed them from behind. Cristina's head whipped forward and back.

She checked the rear view. High beams from the SUV nearly blinded her.

"What happened?" her mother asked, clinging to the side console.

"They must've skidded on the ice," Cristina said, looking for a spot to pull over.

The SUV swerved and roared past. Its passenger side clipped the Lexus.

The car juddered. The steering wheel wrenched out of Cristina's grip.

Her mother screamed. Father shouted.

Cristina fought to regain control. The wheel wouldn't respond.

She hit the brakes.

Nothing happened.

They were careening toward the guard rail.

"No!" she shouted.

The Lexus crunched through the guard rail. The windshield shattered.

Her mother was crying. Cristina saw a jagged piece of glass sticking out of her mother's chest. The smell of blood assailed her.

"Mom ..." she said. Then something struck her head, and the world turned upside down.

Cristina stared straight ahead, digesting the memory. How could the smell of blood be so pungent, and the sound of her mother screaming hurt her eardrums, unless she'd been in the car with them?

She opened her fist. The pills seemed to pulsate, beckoning.

Each time Santos's path crossed hers, he had hurt her family. And he'd hidden his involvement with them before the car crash. Maybe Cristina knew more about Sebastian dos Santos than she realized. The answers were deep in her mind. She couldn't give up now.

Closing her eyes, she popped the pills.

In a hostel near Fenway Park, Sebastian dos Santos sat on the common area couch, eyes glued to the television. His heart raced as he watched Stacey Peterman's onscreen rant about negligent doctors. Sweat rolled down his cheek as they flashed Cristina's photo. At best, this would distract her. At worst, it would ruin her.

"What a messed up country," said a traveler lounging on a recliner. "Man goes to doctor because he's crazy, and she gives him drugs that make him crazier. If you ask me, doctors should take these drugs before using us as guinea pigs."

"Then it's good no one asked you." Santos stood and buttoned his overcoat. He had no time to deal with ignorance.

He needed to reveal the truth before it was too late.

CHAPTER TWENTY

As she lingered on the corner of Arlington Street outside the Maharajah Hotel, Cristina's head ached like she'd gone several rounds with a heavyweight champ. She shielded her eyes from the winter sun. Sharing drinks last night with Andrea had seemed like a great idea, but now Cristina was paying for it. The alcohol hadn't chased away the demons, only blurred them together.

Cristina checked the email she'd received early that morning from an anonymous webmail address. It said Stacey Peterman had a change of heart and wanted to meet her to settle their dispute face-to-face. Cristina wondered what the lawyer Andrea had arranged would say about it, but she didn't care. She was certain the woman, as angry as she was, would be more amicable once Cristina explained what Jerry had been through. And, if they could put this matter to rest quickly, without drawn-out legal proceedings, all the better.

For the third time since receiving the email, Cristina studied the screen capture of Stacey Peterman from her FOX News interview. Devi had been right. The woman's hawkish nose and feral blond mane made her look like a harpy. Hopefully, she'd calmed down since.

Sticking her phone in her purse, Cristina climbed the lobby steps to the hotel where she would be meeting with Stacey Peterman. The opulent gold trim and ornate wood inlays caught Cristina's eye as she approached the front desk. Paintings and antiques lined the walls. Lilies and tea lights floated in a huge copper bowl. Even the air smelled expensive, a mixture of orchids and Indian spices. How much would a night cost? Probably more than Cristina could've afforded even before the cost of the potential lawsuit.

The clerk—tall, dark-haired and decked out in an off-white Mandarin-collared suit—finished checking in a guest and nodded to Cristina. "Can I help you?"

"Could you please call up to Stacey Peterman's room?" Cristina smiled.

"Certainly." He began typing. "Your name?"

"Dr. Cristina Silva."

He stopped typing. "The one on the news?"

"No." She struggled to maintain her composure. "The one standing right here. Could you please call Ms. Peterman?"

After an uncomfortable moment, in which the clerk studied Cristina's face in great detail, he picked up the phone and dialed.

"Dr. Cristina Silva is here to see you, ma'am." He paused to listen. "I don't know, but she's here." He listened again. "Yes, ma'am, I'll tell her." He hung up. "She's not accepting visitors."

"She asked me to come here. Could you call again, and I'll talk to her?"

"I'm afraid that's against hotel policy. If you like, I can take your number and give it to Ms. Peterman."

"Fine." Cristina emptied her purse until she found her business cards. She handed him one. "Please make sure she knows it's urgent."

"Yes, I heard you the first time." The clerk stuck the card in an envelope and scribbled a room number on the front.

Cristina tried to see, but he placed his hand over it.

"I'll make sure she gets it. Have a pleasant day."

Cristina had the half-baked notion of distracting him, stealing the envelope, and running upstairs. Instead, she stuffed everything back into her purse and stormed out of the building.

As Cristina made her way to the T station, her anger subsided, and she began to think more clearly. There had to be a reason Stacey had invited her there. If she replied to the email, maybe she'd get some answers. Cristina reached into her purse for her phone.

She froze in the middle of the sidewalk. Her phone was missing. She dug through her purse again. Damn. She must've left it on the check-in counter.

Cristina marched back to the hotel. Had she always been so distracted? Was that how she had missed Jerry's and Carl's warning signs? By the time she reached the top of the staircase, she wondered if even the car crash had been caused by her own carelessness.

Cristina stopped short of entering the lobby. Her heart pounded. She ducked around the corner and spied the man at the check-in desk. Even though his back was turned and he was wearing a navy sport coat, the broad shoulders and the shaggy black hair poking out from under the fisherman's cap were a dead giveaway.

Sebastian dos Santos.

As Cristina watched, the smarmy clerk hung up the phone, said something to Santos, and pointed at the elevator. Santos tipped the brim of his hat and strolled to the lift. After he stepped inside, the doors closed.

Cristina chewed on her fingernail and puzzled over Santos's appearance. Clearly, he wasn't a hotel guest.

The indicator on the wall showed that the elevator stopped on the fourteenth floor.

Whatever Santos's reasons, Cristina had plenty of questions.

Like, why he didn't tell her he'd worked on her parents' car before the accident? And why did Zero Dark want them dead?

Cristina glanced at the check-in desk. The clerk was helping another guest.

There was only one way to find out. Cristina spotted her phone on the counter. Adjusting the belt to her double-breasted coat, she straightened her back and sauntered over to the desk. When the clerk's back was turned, she snatched up her phone and marched to the elevator. With every step, she expected someone to shout out that she should not be there. Cristina kept her chin high and flaunted her budget chic fashion sense.

A security guard eyed her. Did he know her plan? She turned away quickly, then spared a glance over her shoulder.

He was leering at her backside.

Tossing her hair and rolling her eyes, Cristina ignored her pounding heartbeat and continued to the elevator. When the door slid shut, a smile crossed her lips. She was stalking her stalker.

The doors opened on the twelfth floor. She exited and headed for the stairwell.

Two flights later, she cracked open the steel door to the fourteenth floor. The hallway was clear. So far, so good. The elevator was around the corner, so she headed that way.

From the next hallway, she heard a man yell, "You're going to ruin everything!"

Curious, she peered around the corner. What she saw stopped Cristina in her tracks.

Santos was arguing with Stacey Peterman.

CHAPTER TWENTY-ONE

Cristina ducked around the corner. There could be no mistaking Stacey's beak-like nose and short, wild blond hair. Holding her breath, Cristina risked another peek. Santos wagged his finger in Stacey's face. Cristina could make out the harsh tone but not the words.

Santos's six-foot frame towered over the petite woman, but she held her ground. Santos leaned in, his nose inches from hers. She slapped him so hard he staggered against the door.

Covering her mouth with her hand, Cristina retreated again. Clearly, these two knew each other well. Instantly, Cristina remembered the news clippings Santos had given her. All those bizarre suicides—was he involved with them? Perhaps he also had something to do with Jerry's madness.

Cristina chanced another glance. Santos was speaking again. Staring at the floor, Stacey nodded and wiped a tear from her eye. She looked up, smiled sadly and hugged him.

Cristina's shocked gasp shattered the silence.

Stacey's gaze darted her direction. The expletive was clear on her lips. Santos turned too, eyes wide.

"Shit." Cristina dashed toward the stairwell.

Footsteps pounded behind her.

She barreled down the stairs. Ripped off her high heels. Metal steps slammed into her bare feet. A fire door crashed open from above.

"Cristina!" Santos's voice echoed down the stairwell.

She kept moving. Faster. She passed the tenth floor.

"Wait!" Ragged breathing punctuated his shouts. "It's not what you think."

She rounded the next landing. *Ignore his lies.*

By the seventh floor, she started to tire. He was two floors above her but gaining fast.

She ducked through the stairwell door.

There! She dashed across the hall. Pulled the fire alarm. The hallway erupted in flashing lights and ear-splitting sirens.

Panicked guests poured out of their rooms. Cristina raced to the opposite end of the hall. Guests swarmed past. She reached the other stairwell. Looked over her shoulder. Santos's head bobbed over the mass of bodies. Dipping low, she followed the crowd into the stairwell and weaved between the guests as best she could.

The lobby was packed with people, yelling and shoving. Hotel staff struggled to maintain order. Cristina used her thin frame to squeeze her way to the exit, keeping her head down in case Santos was behind her.

It took another minute to reach the front entrance. Cristina's body tingled as the adrenaline wore off.

"Did you smell smoke?" asked a woman in a bathrobe as she trailed behind Cristina. "I didn't smell anything. I don't believe there is a fire."

"Third time this week." Cristina checked over her shoulder as they emerged onto busy Arlington Street.

No sign of Santos.

Cristina forced her knees to stop shaking as she turned to the woman and rolled her eyes. "Last time I stay in this dump."

Sebastian dos Santos pushed his way onto Arlington Street. It only took a moment to realize he'd lost her.

"Merda," he mumbled and glanced at his watch. Fire personnel would arrive soon, followed by authorities when they discovered the hoax. He wouldn't stick around for that.

Someone tugged at Santos's sleeve. He spun around, fist raised. Stacey Peterman stared at him. He lowered his arm.

"Did you find her?"

"No."

She moaned. "What a mess."

"I sent her here for a reason. Why didn't you talk to her when she showed up?" Frustration bubbled in his throat. He fought the urge to yell at her. "We're both at risk."

"I followed orders. They played me. Again."

Avoiding her gaze, Santos willed himself to remain calm. "Now you know."

"I'll take care of it." She touched his arm. "You sure it's not too late for her?"

For the past two weeks, Santos had struggled with that question. Maybe he'd waited too long. Maybe he should've intervened earlier.

"If that's the case, it's too late for all of us."

CHAPTER TWENTY-TWO

As he cruised his Dodge Charger on Route Nine westbound, Detective Wilson tried to shake the feeling of being trapped in a game of Whack-a-Mole. Each time he thought he'd hammered out an answer to the Cristina Silva puzzle, ten more questions popped up.

Wilson turned up the car radio. "Brown-eyed Girl" by Van Morrison filled the car's cabin. Tapping his finger on the wheel, he tried to clear away the fog.

Technically it was his day off, but he'd barely slept the previous night. Conflicting facts and conundrums tossed about in his head. Even when he'd tried being tough, grilling Dr. Silva with sarcasm, she didn't waver, showed no signs of deceit. She clearly believed her story.

But did something like guilt lurk around the corners of her soft, doe-like eyes? Or perhaps it was self-doubt. And the way she got teary-eyed when talking about Detective Parker—Wilson couldn't help feeling sorry for her. It took all his will to resist the urge to offer a comforting hug.

Cursing, he snapped off the radio. It was happening again. He was losing his objectivity. He dug his fingers into the steering wheel and tried to convince himself that his feelings for Dr.

Cristina Silva were not why he was driving to Framingham alone on a Saturday. Nope.

It would've helped if he at least had Mitchell Parker's report. According to Framingham PD, the detective had killed himself without warning. Any information about the Silva crash investigation had died with him. Hard copies had been damaged in a flood and the electronic file was corrupted in a server crash. Hard drive backups were never found.

Wilson passed the sign announcing Framingham. Why hadn't the FBI already done what he was about to do? The answer was obvious, at least to him. The Feds relied too much on their computer tracking systems and spy satellites when sometimes you needed good old-fashioned detective work. While the police report and the officer involved might be gone, there could still be someone who could confirm Martins had tampered with the Silvas' car.

A few minutes later, Wilson pulled into Manny's Auto Center at Irving Square. Icicles hung from the worn-out sign. Inside, he saw, the garage was spotless—not even an oil stain. A well-maintained 1982 Volvo wagon perched on a lift. There were no other vehicles.

When Wilson exited his Charger, he caught suspicious glances from passersby on the sidewalk. He cinched the belt on his overcoat and approached the garage.

"Can I help you?" A stocky man nearly a head shorter than Wilson blocked the way. He wiped his greasy hands on his overalls.

Wilson flashed his badge. "If you're Manny Feldman, you can."

The mechanic's eyes widened. "Please put that away."

Wilson hesitated before returning his badge to his pocket. "I need to ask you some questions."

"Yes, yes, but come inside. Please." Feldman ushered him through the garage into a cramped office. Auto parts littered a simple wooden desk. A pinup calendar of monster trucks hung on the back wall.

After shutting the door, Feldman turned to Wilson, scowling. "Detective, I don't want to tell you how to do your job, but please don't throw that badge around here. It's bad for business."

"I don't understand."

"There's been a rash of Immigration officers coming through here lately. If people see me talking to you and you don't drag me away in handcuffs, they'll think I gave you names. Do you understand?"

Wilson peered out the window. A couple with a baby carriage loitered on the curb, craning their necks to see inside the garage. "Should I take you down to the station to talk?"

The corner of Feldman's mouth twisted. "I'm allergic to precincts. We can talk here—as long as it's brief. What do you want?"

"How long have you owned this garage?"

"Nine years."

"Do you know Francisco Martins?"

He bobbed his head side-to-side. "The name is familiar."

"It should be more than familiar. Didn't he work here?"

"For a short time. Very skilled with his hands. Shame he disappeared."

An itch started behind Wilson's ear. "Do you remember when that was?"

"Maybe three years ago."

Wilson unfolded a flyer and held it out. "Is this him?"

Feldman squinted at it. "Yes."

"Around that time, Mr. Martins was suspected of arson. Did you know this?"

"Yes. The police asked me questions then too."

"Did you keep him on as an employee?"

Feldman's lips puckered. "Detective, those charges were dropped."

"Actually, the Silvas didn't press charges. Unusually kind after he burned down their house, don't you think?"

"Their reasons are none of my business. I saw no reason to keep him from work."

A sour taste filled Wilson's mouth. This wasn't going the way he'd expected. He stuck the flyer in his pocket. "Okay, so you said Martins disappeared. What happened?"

"One day, he didn't show for work. He never came back."

"Did you try and contact him?"

"I called his house." Feldman shrugged. "The number was disconnected."

"Do you have the number? Or his home address?"

Feldman gave him a puzzled look. "Detective, that was years ago. Why would I keep that?"

More plastic moles popped up. Switching tactics, Wilson said, "Did you know the Silva family?"

"They brought their Lexus for service here many times." He half smiled. "Nice car."

"And their daughter?"

"Cristina? Lovely girl. She dated my son Julian in high school."

"Really?" The itch flared. Now he was getting somewhere. "Have you spoken to her lately?"

"No, she moved away after her parents died." Feldman stared at the ground. "Terrible tragedy."

"Do you know how they died?"

"Car crash."

"The day before Francisco Martins disappeared, right?"

Feldman snapped his head up. "What are you implying, Detective?"

"Cristina Silva brought the car here for service the day before it crashed. Francisco Martins worked on the car. The next day, the Silvas died from a hit-and-run and a faulty brake line. But maybe it wasn't faulty. The automotive forensic report I found couldn't clearly determine if the brake line had snapped or if it had been cut." Wilson's pulse raced, the way it did when he was getting close to solving a puzzle. "Since you admired their car so much, you must remember seeing it before the crash."

Feldman pursed his lips. "I remember."

"And did you see Cristina that day?"

"Yes."

"Did she give any money to Mr. Martins?"

Feldman's face twisted like Wilson had told him aliens had landed in downtown Boston. "Cristina dealt only with me. I assigned Francisco to work on the car."

"You assigned him to the family whose house he burned down?"

"He'd been servicing that car for six months. He wanted to win back the family's trust after the charges were dropped, so he offered to take extra care, and the Silvas accepted the arrangement. I inspected the car myself when he was done. It was in perfect condition."

"And yet the brake line broke. Martins was negligent."

"No, he was thorough. He wouldn't miss a faulty brake line."

"So, he cut it."

"As I said, I inspected it after he'd finished. If the line was cut, someone else cut it, not Francisco."

Pop, pop went the moles. Who else could've cut the line? Cristina? "You're positive he didn't tamper with it after you inspected it?"

"Why don't you ask the detective who was here that morning?"

"Detective?"

"The same detective who told me Martins was cleared of all charges. He returned that morning to drop off papers he needed Martins to sign. Spent some time admiring the Silvas' Lexus." Feldman folded his arms across his chest. "He can confirm the car was undamaged."

"What was his name?"

Feldman shrugged. "It was two years ago …"

"Why would you remember?" Despite the cold, Wilson was

sweating. None of this made sense. The moles were whacking him now. "One more question, if you don't mind."

"Please, Detective."

"You said Cristina dated your son. Were you aware of any family conflicts?"

"No, they were very happy." Feldman leveled his gaze. "Is Cristina in trouble?"

"You haven't heard?"

"No."

Wilson turned on his smartphone and activated the news app. When the local headline appeared, he showed it to Ferreira. "See for yourself."

Feldman studied the small screen. He looked up, blinking rapidly. "What does a subway shooting have to do with the Silva family?"

"Dr. Silva was the shooter's psychiatrist." He handed Feldman a business card. "And it seems that she is now being targeted by Mr. Martins. If you hear from him or remember anything else, please give me a call."

Ignoring the card, Feldman scrolled through the article, mumbling incoherently.

"What did you say?"

"Sorry, Detective, but this doesn't make sense. I've known Cristina Silva since she was a child." He held up the phone, pointing at a photo of Cristina in her white coat. "This woman is *not* Cristina Silva."

CHAPTER TWENTY-THREE

The silver locket lurked on Cristina's dining table. She inspected it from every angle. Each time she reached for it, she jerked her hand back as if the locket might electrocute her.

Biting her lip, she tried to summon courage. After the shock of seeing Santos and Stacey Peterman together, Cristina felt lost in a labyrinth. Two seemingly unrelated aspects of her life crashed together, making her question everything she thought she knew. Since returning home, she'd been staring at the locket, her only clue to Santos's daughter. After wiping away some dirt from the worn inscription, Cristina was able to make out the letters *RJ*.

The locket had no latch or clasp. Cristina rubbed it between her hands, tracing over every edge of the engraving. Her finger caught on one of the arrows piercing the man's chest on the front design. She held it close and scraped her fingernail against it. There was a tiny gap, no bigger than a pen tip. Cristina found her sewing kit, chose a needle, and inserted it into the gap. She felt resistance. When she forced the needle inside, it snapped in half.

Cursing, she tapped the locket against the table until the broken tip fell out. She got another needle and tried again. This time, she felt a soft click. The locket popped open.

Nestled into the left half of the locket was a weathered photo of a girl, around five or six years old. Long chestnut hair framed a delicate face. Soft brown eyes peered out. Could this be Santos's daughter?

In the other half was another photo—even more worn and faded—of a beautiful woman with coffee-colored eyes. She looked like the girl's mother. Recognition flashed in the back of Cristina's mind, then vanished. Was that the clue she needed? Had she worked with the girl's mother at some point?

Cristina's phone rang, startling her. The locket clattered onto the table. She seized the phone.

"Turn on the TV," Andrea said.

"What?"

"Turn it on, mami. Channel twelve. Now."

Puzzled, Cristina clicked on her TV. A reporter's face filled the screen. The words *Breaking News* flashed below. "For those tuning in, Stacey Peterman, sister of the Park Street Station shooter, is about to make a public statement."

Cristina's fingertips prickled with apprehension. An announcement only a few hours after she caught Stacey and Santos together couldn't be good.

Stacey Peterman appeared onscreen, wind blowing her blond hair. Cristina wanted to reach through the screen and slap her.

"First," Stacey said into the camera before brushing an errant lock of hair out of her eyes. "I want to apologize to the families who lost their loved ones. As hard as it was to lose my brother, I can't imagine what it must be like for them."

"You bet your perky little ass you don't," Andrea muttered.

"Andrea, please," Cristina said. As much as she appreciated her friend's cheerleading, she wanted to hear whatever venom this snake was about to spit.

"Today, while sorting through Jerry's possessions, I found a journal he'd been keeping since Valentine's Day. Most of it was mundane, until the last entry he wrote two days ago, only a few hours before he ..." She closed her eyes, then managed to gather herself and open them. "Before he went crazy."

Cristina's chest tightened. She had given Jerry that journal.

"Jerry had been struggling with depression for months. He hid it well, even from his psychiatrist. He didn't want her to know that he wasn't making progress and had tried to manage it by drinking." She took a deep breath and exhaled. "When Jerry was fourteen, a school bully hurt him. He carried that pain and anger for so long, it consumed him. But he never told his doctors about it. He was too embarrassed. It's why he attempted suicide two years ago. I thought he'd finally gotten over it, but he hadn't. That's who he was hunting on the night he died. He wrote in the journal the madness would stop once he eliminated the cause."

Stacey's words nearly knocked Cristina out of her chair. Could any of this be true? Was Quinn just a schoolyard bully?

"Jerry would never want someone else to take the blame for his actions, let alone someone he clearly respected." Stacey turned to the camera. "I want to apologize to Dr. Silva for my accusations. She couldn't have known his intentions. None of this was her fault."

"Honey, you're clear." Andrea's voice came through the phone light and airy. "The families have no case for a lawsuit now."

"Yeah, I'm clear." Cristina stared at the TV screen, unable to move. Whatever she expected, this wasn't it. The image changed to the anchorwoman, who summarized the announcement. Cristina switched off the TV.

When Jerry lost his memory, he would've forgotten both the good and the bad. By reliving past trauma, his depression would've returned along with his memories. It was a clear narrative. Cristina could almost believe it herself—if she hadn't seen

Stacey with Santos. What did he say to change Stacey Peterman's attitude?

"We need to celebrate," Andrea said. "Throw on some makeup, and we'll hit the town."

Cristina looked down at the locket, thinking about the photos of the mother and daughter held captive inside. Was this Santos's way of ensuring Cristina kept her promise? "Sure, give me a minute to get ready."

After hanging up, Cristina stuck the locket in a drawer and crossed the room to search her closet for a clean party dress. Her mind was spinning too much to make sense of anything. Better to blow off steam and give her brain a rest.

Once Cristina settled on a silky black sheath dress, she went to the bathroom and pulled out her makeup kit. She frowned when she realized she'd used up her favorite shade of gold eyeshadow. Fortunately, she kept more in her emergency kit.

As Cristina dug through her purse, she discovered her copy of the novel, *Menino de Engenho*. She traced her finger over the cover, remembering the day she had bought it. It was a few weeks after she started taking Recognate, just after recalling her dead mother's love of books in her native Portuguese. Grasping at any thread to connect to her mother, Cristina visited a tiny bookstore in Allston, considered Boston's Little Brazil. The owner recommended this book as a hard-to-find classic.

She chuckled softly. The story was compelling, but the details about social inequalities in rural Brazil were too complex, especially as she fumbled over the Portuguese idioms. And it didn't bring Cristina any closer to her father. With all the craziness of the past weeks, she wasn't likely to finish the rest of the book anytime soon. She carried it to her bookcase and was about to put it on a shelf.

Her gut twisted.

On the next shelf up was another copy of *Menino de Engenho*.

The arteries over her temples throbbed. She removed the book and compared it to the one in her other hand. Similarly worn, almost but not quite torn in the same spots. She flipped to the title page. Same publication date. Both had stamps from an Allston bookshop.

It had all started with Santos, when he returned her book at the bus stop, claiming they'd never met. That he knew nothing about her. Except he knew she had this book and where she had bought it. Maybe he had been there that day at the shop and had been watching her ever since. Maybe he knew everything about her.

She found it hard to breathe. What else was he lying about?

Cristina's phone rang again. She dropped the two books on the floor.

Cursing, she grabbed her phone and answered.

"You ready?" Andrea asked.

Cristina glanced back at the books. No, she wasn't ready for any of this. But she didn't have a choice. If Santos was manipulating her, she needed to fight back. And the best way to do that was to keep him from ruining her happiness.

"Give me five minutes." She hung up.

She scooped up the cocktail dress and headed to change. For one night, she would relax, get her head on straight. Tomorrow, whatever it took, she would find Sebastian dos Santos and get answers.

Quinn sat in a leather recliner in his room at the Willard Inter-Continental hotel in Washington D.C., swirling a glass of cognac. The TV flickered, casting an eerie glow over the hotel room. As Stacey Peterman spoke onscreen, his ears burned. He could see it in her eyes. Santos had gotten to her.

In his glass, amber and crimson waves rolled and twirled in

an elegant, predictable pattern. Quinn's grip tightened, jerking his hand to one side. The cognac sloshed over the edge of the glass. He glared at the puddle next to his foot. One small aberration and everything spills out into a worthless mess.

"There's still time," he muttered.

As much as he hated to lose a valuable asset, Cristina Silva had forced his hand. He set down the glass and picked up his phone. Entering the encrypted chat, he typed, "Eliminate the traitor."

Without waiting for a reply, Quinn tossed the phone on the bed. He reclaimed his glass, leaned back and sipped. His gaze narrowed as the reporter droned on and displayed photos of the two women involved.

The operative's value had ended, and he couldn't protect her.

CHAPTER TWENTY-FOUR

Cristina awoke the next day to her cell phone chirping. Prying open one eye, she rolled over and groaned when she saw the clock. Who calls at seven on a Sunday morning?

Although she'd only had one drink, she had stayed out too late with Andrea, arriving home right as frozen rain began. It took another two hours to wind down. Questions about Santos, Stacey, and her parents swirled like tornadoes through her mind. Only through self-hypnosis had she been able to fall asleep at last.

The phone kept chirping. Cristina felt like she was moving underwater as she groped for it and checked the caller ID. Blocked. Wonderful. For a moment, she considered letting it go to voicemail, but curiosity won out. She rubbed sand from her eyes before answering with a groggy, "hello?"

"Dr. Silva?" The female voice sounded familiar, but in Cristina's sleep-deprived haze, she couldn't place it.

"Yes. Who is this?"

The other woman hesitated, her breathing ragged. "It's Stacey Peterman."

Cristina bolted upright, fully alert. "How did you get my number?"

"The hotel clerk."

"Oh. Right, of course."

"We need to talk." The fiery tone was gone. Stacey sounded afraid. The morning haze dissipated as Cristina recalled the previous day's events.

"Is this about whatever Santos said to you?" she asked.

"I don't know what you're talking about."

"I saw you with him at your hotel."

"I said, I don't know what you're talking about." Her voice had an undertone that said, *Shut up and stop asking questions.* "But it's important that we talk."

Cristina chewed on her cuticle. "Okay, so talk."

"Not here. Somewhere safe. Meet me at Harvard Station at noon."

"Are you crazy? There's an ice storm outside. I'm not going anywhere until you answer a few questions, like what really happened to Jerry. A depressed person wouldn't try something new, like auditioning for a play. And if he was angry at a childhood bully, why not Google him? Why shoot up a T station?"

"I'm sorry, I have to go. I'll answer all your questions at noon."

"Wait—where in Harvard Station?"

The line was dead.

Gritting her teeth, Cristina jumped out of bed, threw on a bathrobe, and brewed a pot of coffee. Whatever Stacey's game, Cristina was determined to get answers.

Wilson scratched his head as he sat at the secondhand kitchen table of his studio apartment, staring at his laptop. He took a swig of black coffee and again scrolled through Francisco Martin's NCIC record. Among his other listed crimes, arson still figured prominently at the top of the list. Why, if the Silvas dropped charges? And which detective told Paolo Ferreira that Martins had been cleared?

Grunting, Wilson clicked out of the record. He fared no better when he dug up Cristina Silva's background. Yes, her medical license was up to date. Yes, Metro West Hospital confirmed her injuries. Yes, she had credit cards, utilities, and a passport in her name. But anything containing photo identification was less than three years old. All records created before the auto crash had been lost or had destroyed.

Wilson went to take another gulp of coffee and scowled when he realized the cup was empty. Just like his search. At the coffeemaker, he found the pot empty too. His cabinets were bare, except for a bag of potato chips and a box of sugary cereal. Damn. Forgot to go grocery shopping. He placed the cup atop the stack of dirty dishes in the sink and returned to stare at his computer. Who was Cristina Silva?

Wilson's phone rang. Grateful for the distraction, he shut down his computer and answered.

"You're not gonna believe this," Hawkins said over the phone. "She's on the move."

"In this weather? Where's she heading?"

"Looks like the T."

Wilson sat up straight, his mind racing. He'd asked his partner to do a drive-by of Cristina's apartment on a hunch. "Follow her, but don't let her spot you. Maybe she's going to her office, but if she's meeting with Martins, she'll lead us right to him."

"Shouldn't we call the Feds?"

"If they show up in their black vans and riot gear, he'll run before they even get close. Silva's only met you once, so she may not recognize you. But if you see Martins, call it in. Don't try to stop him yourself."

"Don't worry. I may be an idiot for letting you talk me into doing this on our day off, but I'm not a total idiot."

After hanging up, Wilson drummed his fingers on the laptop keys. The area behind his right ear was burning red hot.

Ice chunks pelted Cristina's back as she trudged down College Avenue. She pulled her jacket over her face to shield herself from the pellets sweeping under her umbrella. Cold wind bit through her wool overcoat and nibbled on her bones. The street was nearly empty except for a snowplow and a handful of SUVs. Even fewer souls braved the frozen sidewalk. Ahead, a woman in a parka waved her arms and fell on her rump. After climbing back to her feet and brushing herself off, the woman staggered away and ducked into a coffee shop.

Cristina clucked her tongue as she carefully chose her path. Only a fool would be out on a day like this—a fool, or someone desperate for answers.

After stepping through the double doors into the Davis Square T station, Cristina brushed away the ice particles clinging to her coat. She scanned the lobby as she paid her fare and made her way to the trains. On most days, the station was packed with travelers but not today. It would be easy enough to spot Santos if he followed her.

As she waited for the train, Cristina surveyed the platform a third time. A group of Japanese tourists huddled together, appearing uncomfortable in their soggy lightweight jackets and designer jeans. Farther down the platform, a bearded man clad in a camouflage jacket rubbed his hands over a heating vent. Cristina thought she caught movement out of the corner of her eye near the tunnel leading down to the platform, but when she turned, there was no one there. Shivering, she reassured herself.

The train rolled to a stop. The doors opened. Cristina stepped aboard and took the seat closest to the exit. The tourists filled the back of the car.

For the entire ride, Cristina prepared questions for Stacey Peterman. How did she know Santos? Why was he interfering with Cristina's life?

"Harvard Station," the automated voice announced. "Change here for downtown buses."

The doors slid open. Cristina jumped off the train. The tourists chattered behind her. She glanced over her shoulder. They clustered around the giant wall map, jostling for position in a group selfie. Cristina shook her head. The Harvard mystique knew no cultural boundaries.

"Spare change?" A man wearing rags slumped against the wall, holding out a coffee can. His few remaining teeth bore gold caps. He reeked of sweat and grease.

"I'm sorry." Cristina checked her watch. Five minutes past twelve. The train ran slower than usual. "I'm late for an appointment."

As she started for the tunnel, the man asked, "You Silva?"

She froze in midstep. Faced him. "How do you know my name?"

"Some bitch showed me your photo and paid me fifty bucks to give this to you."

He held out his can. Cautiously, she peered inside. At the bottom of the can lay a piece of paper. She looked back. The tourists were still taking photos. The platform was otherwise empty.

"Was this woman blond?" she asked. "Was her name Stacey?"

"Lady, someone gives me fifty bucks, I don't ask questions." He hefted the can. "You gonna take it or not?"

Biting her lip, she reached for the paper, fingers twitching. At last, she withdrew the paper and unfolded it. Her heart raced as she read, *Charles MGH.*

"That's it? Did she say anything else?"

"Yeah, she did say one other thing." He crooked his finger and grinned. When she leaned closer, trying to ignore the stench of old food and beer, he whispered, "You're being followed."

CHAPTER TWENTY-FIVE

Cristina's neck muscles tightened. She turned, looked over her shoulder. The tourists walked toward them, laughing and chattering in Japanese. As they continued past, Cristina spotted the bearded man in the camouflage jacket leaning against the map, trying to figure out his route. He staggered and caught himself. Could be a wandering drunk. Or not.

"Who is he?" she whispered to the homeless man. "What does he want?"

"Who?"

"The guy following me."

"Lady, I got paid to give you a message, which I did." He waved the can under her nose. "You want anything else, contribute to the Save the Homeless fund."

Cristina's heart beat faster. She heard footsteps. Out of the corner of her eye, she saw the bearded man approaching, shuffling and meandering haphazardly. He kept his head down, as if avoiding eye contact.

She dropped a dollar bill into the can. "Who is he?"

The homeless man stuck his nose into the can and then shrugged. "Beats me. Thanks for the buck."

Cristina cursed. She spared another glance. Now the bearded

man was headed toward the tunnel, but he stopped as if he'd forgotten something. He patted his pockets, then reached under his jacket. His hand closed around something that glinted of metal.

Something like the handle of a gun.

Panic washed over Cristina. Her heart pounded.

A voice said deep inside her head, *Act first. Don't be the victim.*

Before she could process the message, her body was already moving. She ran at the bearded man. Jumped. Spun. Kicked him square in the back. He flew forward. His chin smashed into the ground. She touched the floor. Flipped around. Ran back toward the trains. She turned a corner. Crashed into a white-haired man wearing an overcoat. He fell on his back. Cristina rolled away and kept running.

Someone shouted behind her. She blocked everything out. Raced down the stairs. A red line train was waiting. Doors closing.

"Wait!" she yelled, and forced an extra burst of speed.

The doors opened again. Cristina slipped into the empty car. The doors slid shut.

She dived into the seat farthest from the exit. Huddled behind the seat back. Held her breath, waiting for the door to reopen.

It didn't. The train jerked, rolled forward.

Cristina released her breath. Where had that jolt of aggression come from? Not that she wasn't grateful—otherwise she might not be alive. But the ferocity of her own actions terrified her almost as much as the threat of being shot.

As the train clattered down the track, Cristina opened her hand and studied the paper again. *Charles MGH.* She clasped her hands together, finding security in the paper scraping against her palms. Nothing else felt real. Hopefully, whatever Stacey had to tell her would change that.

Wind rattled the casements of Detective Wilson's apartment as he studied the Framingham PD files. Detective Mitchell Parker seemed to be a model cop—decorated for meritorious service, community service, up for promotion. Out of nowhere, he had disappeared for two days and then killed himself. And he left no investigation records on the car wreck that killed Cristina's parents.

Wilson scrolled down to the last page of the employee profile. Parker was survived by his wife of ten years, still living in their house in Framingham. He scratched his chin. He hadn't pegged Cristina as a side gig. But Wilson didn't know that much about her, did he? Maybe she wasn't as innocent as she seemed.

His phone rang, and he picked it up.

"I lost her," Hawkins said.

"What happened?"

"She attacked a vagrant on the Red Line platform while his back was turned and ran off. Practically ran me over on her way to the train. By the time I caught up, it had already pulled out."

"That doesn't make any sense. Did she kill the vagrant?"

"No, knocked him out. Looks like he was reaching for his flask and she flipped out."

Wilson scratched at his ear. He knew something was up with Silva but didn't expect this. Maybe the shock of seeing Jerry Peterman getting gunned down by police had made her snap. "Did she recognize you?"

"I don't think so."

"Any idea where she's headed?"

"A peddler heard her say 'Charles MGH.' I'm waiting for the next southbound train to pursue."

"All right, let me know when you find her, but unless she does anything else disruptive, stay out of sight."

As he hung up, Wilson leaned back in his chair and rubbed his upper lip. If Cristina was a threat to public safety, he'd have to take her in. He hoped he wouldn't have to do that until he found out what was going on. Maybe she was crazy. But he had a hunch there was something bigger. And his hunches were almost never wrong.

When the subway doors slid open at Charles MGH Station, Cristina peered out and checked the platform twice. At every prior station, she'd braced herself when the train stopped. Each time no one else boarded. Each time she chided herself for being paranoid. But now that she was about to leave the safety of the subway car, the paranoia returned full force.

The platform was empty, except for a pair of young women making their way to the staircase. No bearded men.

Sighing with relief, Cristina exited and followed the women upstairs. After passing through the turnstile, she scanned the lobby. It was busier here than at the other stations, mostly filled with doctors in blue scrubs from Mass General Hospital. Not even a blizzard kept surgical interns home. A man groaned and tapped his feet as an elderly couple puzzled over the ticket dispenser. An MBTA worker wandered over to help. A woman wearing a yellow rain slicker and snow boots flitted around the room, passing out flyers. No Stacey.

Cristina started toward the exit. Was this some elaborate joke at her expense? She considered asking the MBTA worker for help, but what would Cristina say? She was meeting with a woman that accused her of killing her brother and who was somehow connected to a man who claimed her memory was stolen? Right. If she mentioned she was a psychiatrist, he could make up a heck of a punch line to tell his friends later at the bar. Cristina shook her head and kept walking. If Stacey wasn't waiting outside, Cristina would have to figure out something else.

"Care to make a donation to fight breast cancer?" The woman

in the yellow slicker blocked Cristina's path, holding a lockbox and hugging a stack of flyers.

"I'm sorry." Cristina dodged to one side. "I don't have time."

"Well, at least take a flyer." The woman stepped in her way again, grinning like the Cheshire cat as she held out a pink paper.

"Fine." Cristina snatched the paper and marched onward. As she neared the door, she heard sleet pounding the pavement outside. She went to open her umbrella and realized she was still holding the flyer. She was about to dump it in the trash when something handwritten on the back caught her eye: *Longfellow.* The penmanship matched the note the homeless man had given her.

She stormed back to the woman in the yellow slicker. Grabbed her shoulder. Waved the flyer in her face. "What the hell is this?"

"I don't know." The Cheshire grin and the blood drained from the woman's face. "This woman made a sizable donation. She showed me your picture and asked me to give you that flyer."

"What was her name?"

"I don't know. She asked to remain anonymous."

"Where is she?" Cristina tightened her grip. "Tell me!"

"Ladies, is there a problem here?" The MBTA worker approached.

Cristina's cheeks flushed. She could imagine what she looked like, holding this woman by the shoulder. Judging by the panicked look on the woman's face, she wouldn't be of any more help anyway.

"No, no problem," Cristina said and released the woman. "I—I'm sorry."

Cristina ran into the freezing rain.

It took fifteen minutes to trod from Cambridge Street to Embankment Road. The clue, Longfellow, was easy enough to decipher. Opposite the Esplanade from MGH, the Longfellow Bridge spanned across the Charles River. How far would she have to cross to find Stacey, or would she have to deal with more cat and mouse games first?

"Over here!" Stacey's voice rose above the pelting rain. She was under the bridge, wearing a hooded raincoat.

Tightening her grip on her umbrella, Cristina picked her way around the puddles and ice patches to join her.

"What's this about?" After shaking the rain from her umbrella, Cristina glared at her. "What's with all this cloak and dagger bullshit?"

Stacey pushed back her hood. Her face was pale. "I'm sorry, but I had to be sure you weren't followed. Were you followed?"

"I don't know. I'm beginning to think everyone is after me."

"That's good. It'll keep you alive."

A shiver ran down Cristina's back. Her resolve wavered. Then she reminded herself this woman had nearly destroyed her career. Heat flushed through her body.

"You sound like someone from a bad spy movie." Cristina wagged a finger in Stacey's face. "Why did you email me, asking me to meet you at your hotel, and then refuse to see me?"

"I didn't send that email. Francisco did."

"What? Why?"

"It's hard to follow his reasoning. Look, I'm sorry I didn't talk to you then, but I will answer your questions now."

"Fine. Let's start with your brother. He was hunting someone named Quinn, and it wasn't some childhood bully."

Stacey nodded.

"Was that Quinn he killed?"

"No."

"So, who's Quinn? Why did Jerry want him dead?"

Stacey's head tilted downward. "Quinn stole Jerry's life."

"That's what Jerry said the night he died. What did he mean?"

"It's complicated."

Cristina scoffed. "I've got time."

Stacey's gaze darted side to side. With a sigh, she said, "Jerry didn't lose his memory in an accident. Quinn stole it."

"Why would Quinn steal his memory?"

"As part of a plan."

"What plan?"

Stacey shook her head. "I don't know all the details. I know Jerry remembering wasn't part of it. That's why he went insane. By the time you saw him, his mind must've been ripping apart at the seams."

Cristina's cheeks grew cold. Was that what Jerry meant when he said it was her fault? By treating his amnesia, had she driven him insane? Recovering memories should bring peace and comfort. Unless those memories were stolen, like Santos claimed hers had been ...

"Why should I believe you?" Cristina asked.

"You shouldn't believe anyone." Stacey handed her a handful of pages torn from a book. "But you might believe these."

"What are they?"

"Entries from Jerry's journal." Stacey gave her a pointed look. "The one you gave him."

Cristina's mouth went dry.

Stacey urged the book into Cristina's hands.

Jaw clenched, Cristina flipped through the pages. Jerry had written in two different styles: one in flowing script, the other chiseled print. But by the last page they looked the same: ragged. Pressured. Cristina's heart thumped as she read his rantings about being a killer, stolen memories, and the name Quinn over and over.

She felt dizzy as she read the last paragraph.

It's like an itch under my skin. The more I scratched at it, the worse it got, until I exposed the raw flesh underneath and realized it wasn't my flesh at all, but someone else's. Jerry Peterman is nothing but a façade. The real me has been itching to escape, and now he has. I know who I am.

The words resonated in her mind, as if he'd shouted them through a megaphone. *The real me ... I know who I am ...*

"Why are you showing me this?" She scrutinized Stacey's face. No signs of deception, but there was something else. Stacey almost never blinked, like she was afraid to let her eyes close even for a millisecond. Like she was afraid for her life. "You're not Jerry's sister."

"No." Stacey stared into the rain for a long moment, hugging herself. When she faced Cristina again, she appeared calmer, more focused. "My name is Anastasia Petrov, and I work for Zero Dark."

CHAPTER TWENTY-SIX

Despite the numbing cold, the back of Cristina's neck burned. Freezing rain pelted the bridge over them. Her body tensed, waiting for some sign the woman standing only a foot away might pull out a weapon. When Stacey remained still, arms folded across her chest, Cristina's anger intensified. "Are you here to kill me?"

Stacey's mouth twisted to one side. "I was only ordered to make you a scapegoat."

"A scapegoat for what?"

"To distract anyone from discovering who Jerry really was."

"Who was he?"

"Jeremy Hammond. In certain international circles, his skill as an assassin was well-known. They called him the Golem."

Cristina wasn't sure she'd heard Stacey right. "The Golem?"

"In the sixteenth century, a Czech rabbi created a man out of clay. It served its master's bidding without question, without fear, no matter how horrible the order." She locked her gaze with Cristina's. "The Golem had no soul."

Cristina shivered as she recalled Jerry's words. *I know who I am. A killer.* "But I analyzed Jerry's psychological profile. He didn't have a violent bone in his body."

"Maybe not the man you knew. But Jeremy Hammond was a coldblooded mercenary. Imagine living a peaceful life as a mild-mannered security guard and then waking one day to realize you are a brutal killer. That would probably send anyone over the edge."

Jerry had been fighting a tug-of-war with two personalities. Literally fighting with himself. No wonder Zero Dark wanted to keep his past buried. "So you defamed me to draw attention away from the truth. What changed? What did Sebastian dos Santos say to you?"

"Sebastian …?" Stacey's gaze narrowed and then a knowing smile played at her lips. "Clever."

"What are you talking about?"

"It's not important." Stacey placed a hand on Cristina's shoulder. Cristina jerked away.

Stacey lowered her hand and drifted toward the other side of the alcove. "I'm sorry. They changed your nose, your face. If Francisco hadn't told me the truth—God, I'm such an idiot."

Cristina's shoulders tightened. "What truth did he tell you?"

"They've been lying to me this whole time."

"Who?" Cristina stomped toward Stacey and slipped on an ice patch. She caught herself on the wall. Forcing herself to stay focused, she turned back to Stacey, clenching the pages from Jerry's journal. "Does Quinn work for Zero Dark? What do they want from—?"

Cristina stopped in midsentence when she saw Stacey's wide eyes and open mouth. A red stain blossomed on the right side of her chest.

"Oh, God!"

Cristina dropped the journal pages and ran to Stacey, who crumpled to the ground, struggling to breathe. As she kneeled over Stacey, Cristina searched every direction for the shooter. All she saw were snowbanks and icy rain. Cursing, Cristina jammed her hand against the wound.

"Get off." Stacey batted away Cristina's hand.

"I need to apply pressure."

With surprising force, Stacey shoved Cristina away and rolled onto her side. She withdrew a slim automatic pistol from her jacket. She checked the clip and fired into the rain.

"What are you doing?" Cristina yelled.

Gunfire echoed against the walls of the bridge.

"You need an ambulance."

"Not with someone shooting at us." Stacey collapsed. Grunting, she switched the gun to her left hand. She propped herself on her elbow and fired again. "Get out of here."

"I can't leave you."

"Go." Stacey grimaced as she held her chest. "You're no good dead."

A bullet ricocheted off one of the bridge girders. Cristina ducked, trying to figure out from which direction the shot originated. What if there was more than one shooter? "Who's trying to kill us, Stacey? What do they want?"

Stacey's breathing became ragged. Between gasps, she said, "Zero—Zero Dark. They—they want to cover up the project."

"What project?"

Stacey doubled over and coughed spasmodically. The gun slipped from her grasp and fell at Cristina's feet. Stacey clamped her lips shut, breathing through her nose. Blood trickled from her mouth and splattered on the wet stone.

Her head jerked up. Her eyes widened.

She caught Cristina's gaze and whispered, "Move."

Gunshots.

Cristina's mind hovered overhead as her body contorted in ways she couldn't imagine. Time slowed. Bullets tore through the air inches from where her head had been. In one fluid movement, Cristina rolled to the ground, snatched up the gun, leaped to a crouching position, took aim and fired.

Cristina snapped back into herself. She knew how to use a gun. She didn't know how she knew. She didn't care. Swinging the pistol in a wide arc, she searched for a target.

A hint of blue behind a snowbank. She sighted down the barrel. Squeezed the trigger. Bullets streaked toward the snowbank. A man in a white ski parka leaped into the air. Dodged the bullets. Twisted as he fell. Landed with his gun trained on her.

Shit.

Cristina dived to the side and slid to the river edge. Slugs hit inches from her shoes. She scrambled to her feet and fired again. The gun burned hot in her hands. She guided it to the target.

The shooter dodged. Milliseconds too slow. A bullet grazed his shoulder. He yelled in pain.

Their eyes met. Cristina's chest tightened. Thin nose, low-set brow, dark hair. Dead ringer for Cristiano Ronaldo. A jagged scar bordered one gray eye, the kind left by a dull knife—or a key.

For another breathless moment, he held her gaze. Then he fired.

Cristina dropped. The bullet screamed overhead. She looked up. He was running away. She bounded after him.

Wait. She glanced over her shoulder. Stacey sprawled, breathing erratically. Dying.

No time, a voice answered, the same one she'd heard during the attack in her apartment. *If he escapes, you'll be next.*

Her feet pounded the slick pavement, slipping and recovering without losing momentum. Sleet pelted her face. The shooter was just ahead, ducking around a corner. A little faster and she would catch him.

Then what? Her legs pumped like pistons. The pistol conformed to her hand like an old lover. She aimed. An image flashed through her mind—bullets ripping through his chest. She tried to force her arm down. It wouldn't respond. Fear gripped her heart. *I'm not a killer.*

You are what the world makes you. The voice grew louder, becoming more defined. It sounded like Cristina, only harder. Colder. Another memory, or was it real? As if in answer to her unspoken question, the voice added, *Memory defines our reality, but what we remember isn't always real.*

Cristina's legs pushed harder, faster. The assailant was in her sights. One squeeze of the trigger, it would be over. Her index finger clenched. She fought it.

No, this isn't me.

You have no idea who you are, shouted the voice. *You don't know anything because you're the one who's not real.*

A half-buried branch poked into Cristina's ankle. She stumbled and fell. Her gun fired repeatedly. Her head struck the ground. The last thing she saw before blacking out was a flash of dark hair disappearing into the white snow.

"Wake up, Doctor," a voice said, interrupting the void. "Wake up and remember."

Cristina opened her eyes. Everything was white.

A shadow moved into her field of vision.

She blinked. The shadow took form. She gasped.

Jerry Peterman stood in the rain, his hands stuffed into the pockets of his jeans. His face was pale, deathly. Blood smears covered his cheek. A scarlet stream trickled from a hole in the center of his forehead.

"I remembered everything, Doctor." Jerry grinned down at her like a shark. "Thanks to you."

"Jerry," said Cristina, unable to tear her gaze away from the trail of blood between his eyes, "how could I have known?"

"Oh, you knew." He spat a wad of blood. "You just forgot. We all forget, but eventually we remember again. That's what Quinn wants."

"What does he want me to remember? What's so important?"

"You're the expert." Jerry threw back his head and laughed, blood spraying between his teeth. His eyes glittered like icicles as his form dissipated. "Move fast. He's coming for you."

A hand grabbed Cristina's shoulder.

She slapped it away. Snatched the gun off the ground. Somersaulted onto her back. Squeezed the trigger again and again.

The gun responded with a series of hollow clicks.

"Dr. Silva! Drop the gun!" A white-haired man in an overcoat shouted at her, pistol trained at her head. She'd seen him in the subway. But his face looked familiar for another reason. Why?

"Do it now," he yelled.

Ice pellets bounced off the gun barrel and splattered against her cheeks. Slowly, as if resurfacing from a deep dive in the ocean, she remembered where she was. "Who are you?"

"Detective Rick Hawkins. I work with Gary Wilson."

"Wilson?"

"I was there after the attack in your apartment, remember? Lower your gun. I'll show you my badge."

Her hands trembled. She kept the gun aimed at him even though it was empty. "How do I know you don't work for Zero Dark?"

"Zero what?"

"The ones trying to kill me." Cristina swallowed hard. It hurt to speak, as if saying it aloud made it real. "The ones who shot Stacey."

"Stacey? Stacey who?"

"Stacey Peterman. But that's not her real name."

"Peterman? You mean the subway shooter's sister?"

"She only pretended to be his sister, so they could use me as a scapegoat."

"Why?"

"I—I don't know." The harder Cristina tried to organize her thoughts, the more jumbled they became. "All I know is she's hurt. I was chasing the man who shot her before I fell and blacked out."

Hawkins studied her, as if trying to decide whether to shoot her or not. "Did you get a good look at him?"

The killer's gray eyes burned like hot coals in her mind. "Yes."

"All right, I'm going to show you my badge. You hand over your gun, okay?"

Cristina breathed slowly and nodded.

Without wavering his aim, Hawkins held up his wallet to display a gold shield.

The gun seemed to weigh a thousand pounds. With a sigh, Cristina twisted it around and held it out, butt first. She didn't resist as he plucked it from her grasp.

"Good." Hawkins stuck Stacey's gun in his holster. "Now, put your hands behind your head."

"What?"

He leveled the gun at her chest. "That wasn't a request. I have to bring you in."

Run.

Cristina's mouth went dry. Her body tensed, eager to follow the voice's commands. But could she outrun Hawkins's bullet?

"Dr. Silva, put your hands behind your head." His brow furrowed. "Please."

"Right. Sorry." She squeezed her eyes shut.

He was following police procedure. He didn't work for Zero Dark. This wasn't a trap. She wasn't seeing dead patients or hearing voices. She clasped her hands behind her head.

Keeping his pistol trained on her, Hawkins lowered one of her arms behind her back and slapped a cuff over her wrist. He repeated with the other. "Let's walk."

"Aren't you supposed to read me my rights?"

"I'm not arresting you. Yet." He lowered his pistol. "Where's Ms. Peterman, or whatever her name is?"

"By the bridge. She's in bad shape."

He activated his walkie-talkie. "Dispatch, this is Hawkins responding to the ten-ten by the Longfellow Bridge. We need an ambulance assist."

The walkie-talkie sputtered. "Copy that, Detective."

Hawkins nudged Cristina's elbow. "Let's go."

They trudged along. Together, they descended the path leading under the bridge, taking care to avoid ice patches. Cristina recognized her footprints in the snow.

As they approached the underside of the bridge, Cristina's heart sank. *It can't be possible.*

Hawkins said into his walkie-talkie, "Dispatch, cancel the ambulance assist." To Cristina, he said, "Do you want to try explaining again?"

She barely registered the question. She could only stare at the damp ground where, minutes ago, she had watched Stacey dying.

Except Stacey wasn't there.

CHAPTER TWENTY-SEVEN

"Honey, what's going on with you?" Andrea asked as she drove Cristina home from the police station.

The sleet had stopped, but the roads were still a mess. Andrea kept to the speed limit, a snail's pace compared to how she normally drove.

"Detective Hawkins said you were talking to yourself and acting crazy. Thank heavens the Esplanade was empty. You could've hurt someone. Where'd you get that gun, anyway?"

Pressing her fingertips against her forehead, Cristina avoided her friend's gaze. The questions hadn't stopped since Andrea picked her up, and Cristina found it increasingly difficult to come up with answers. "I told you. It was Stacey's."

"Right, Stacey's. The dying woman who walked away, leaving behind no bloodstains."

Cristina stared out the window, too rattled by her earlier ordeal to care about being in the front seat of a car. "Hawkins said I was knocked out for at least twenty minutes, from the time someone reported gunshots to the time he found me. That's enough time to hide a body and clean up."

Andrea slammed the brakes sending her Miata into a skid as

the car in front of them took the exit without using its turn signal. Andrea steered out of the skid. She rolled down the window. "Asshole!"

When she'd settled back into the lane, she said, "I'm worried about you, mami. You hit your head pretty hard. Maybe what you think happened didn't happen."

"I didn't imagine it." Cristina pounded her fist against the armrest. "Damn it. I need a friend right now. Don't patronize me."

Spreading her fingers as if she could ward off Cristina's ire, Andrea said, "I'm not patronizing you. I'm saying that with everything that's happened with the lawsuit and Jerry, it's enough to push anyone over the edge. And it all started with that Santos guy getting into your head. He hasn't contacted you again, has he?"

"No." Cristina squeezed her fists. How long could she keep lying to her best friend? What good had it done so far? "Yes, but—"

"Cristina."

"He needs help finding his daughter. And he's the one who got Stacey Peterman to retract her accusations."

Andrea's fury hung between them like a swarm of hornets. Cristina couldn't blame her. Even as Cristina defended Santos, she questioned his intentions. The extra book she'd found confirmed he'd been stalking her long before their first meeting. Could she trust anything he said? There was so much more Cristina had hidden from her friend. And now, after everything that happened, how could she convince anyone she wasn't losing her mind?

"You don't find that at all convenient?" Andrea asked in a controlled voice. "I still think he's the one who broke into your apartment, not Francisco Martins."

"The man in the ski parka broke in."

"So, the man in the ski parka is Francisco Martins?"

"No." Cristina sighed. "Santos is Francisco Martins."

Andrea's face reddened. "Are you kidding me? You've been

skulking around with the guy who burned down your parents' house?"

"He was following the orders of Zero Dark."

"Oh, yes, this mysterious organization who supposedly hired Stacey to discredit you. The ones who stole your memories. Do you even hear yourself?"

Andrea's bitter tone burned a swath through Cristina's heart. She stared out the window. "And you wonder why I don't talk to you about this."

Her friend jammed the shift stick and veered onto the exit for Somerville. "Okay, let me ask you this. If a patient came to you with delusions of being someone else, having violent nightmares, growing careless and disorganized, and insisting someone was trying to destroy their life … What would you think?"

"I'd think they were having a psychotic break, possibly a manifestation of paranoid schizophrenia." Cristina glanced at her friend. She didn't dare mention the voice she'd been hearing or the vision of Jerry, which would only support Andrea's point. "But it's not paranoia if someone is after you. And I was attacked. Twice."

"Honey, that's what you believe, but no one else saw either attack. Yes, they found Martins' prints, but now you're telling me he's Santos. So, maybe you invited Santos there earlier and imagined the attack, like you imagined Stacey and the guy in the ski parka." Before Cristina could argue, Andrea held out her hand. "I'm saying it's possible. You haven't been yourself, and I'm worried about you. When were you planning to tell the police Santos and Martins are the same man?"

Cristina's cheeks burned. "Eventually."

"If it wasn't for Detective Wilson, you'd be in jail right now. Do you know that?"

Cristina recalled Wilson eyeing her like a wolf as she left the holding area. Though he didn't say a word to her, she could tell he knew something. "I'll send him a card."

Andrea opened her mouth, then snapped it shut. With a wave of her hand, she said, "I'm done. If you don't trust me enough to tell me what's going on, then I don't know you as well as I thought."

That makes two of us. Either Santos was right, Zero Dark stole her memory, and the memories she'd regained were fake. Or Andrea was right, and Cristina was going crazy, like Jerry and Carl. Either way, she needed a friend.

"Okay," she said. "I need to tell you something important. Promise you won't get mad."

"Honey, you're scaring me. You know you can tell me anything."

Cristina glanced out the window again. As the snow-covered buildings passed by, she remembered growing up in Framingham, attending college and medical school in Cambridge, suffering through residency in downtown Boston. Those memories that had given her a new life—they felt hollow now. At best, the miracle she believed in so strongly was nothing more than quackery. At worst, Recognate was a curse of insanity.

Taking a deep breath, she said, "I need to tell you about an experimental drug …"

"Tell me again why we let Dr. Silva go?" Detective Hawkins scratched his chin. "We should send her to the Deaconess psych ward. She's not playing with a full deck."

Detective Wilson paced the precinct's cramped breakroom. He needed coffee, but the damned machine was broken, and since the station was running a skeleton crew due to the weather, no one had made a run to the local barista. Smoking to calm his nerves had never crossed his mind, especially after his grandfather died of lung cancer, but the way the case was unraveling he was considering taking it up. "We don't have a body. No one was hurt. What would we charge her with?"

"Unlawful use of a weapon? Creating a disturbance?"

"Then, she does community service. Maybe with a lousy lawyer she serves a few weeks in jail. How does that help us? If we want to draw out Martins or Zero Dark, we have a better chance of doing that with her on the outside."

"Geez, you don't actually believe this stolen memory crap, do you?"

"I told you, I've got a witness insisting that woman is not Cristina Silva, and there are too many corrupted records for it all to be coincidence. Besides, you said she used defensive moves you hadn't seen since you were in Special Forces."

"I've also seen lunatics do unbelievable things. She had a look in her eyes." Hawkins's shoulders trembled. "If that gun hadn't been empty—"

"But it was empty. And that's another thing." Wilson hefted a baggie containing the compact weapon "You said this is some fancy Soviet design?"

"Modified Makarov nine-millimeter."

"Where would Cristina get a gun like that?"

"How about online? They've been importing these for two decades." Hawkins shook his head. "Think about it. She rants to you about an international terrorist called the Golem? Her story is ridiculous. Why are you believing everything she says?"

"I don't believe everything, but I think someone went to a lot of trouble to cover up whatever happened two years ago when her parents crashed—whether it was Martins or Zero Dark or this Mitchell Parker. If her story is true, there's a real threat to the public."

"So, we're going to notify Agent Forrester?"

Wilson flinched. Once they involved the Feds, he'd lose control over the case. But if terrorists were involved, he couldn't keep putting it off. "Like you said, we don't have any evidence yet, except that Martins was in Silva's apartment at some point. Those prints could even be years old. And if she's nuts, the FBI won't be happy we wasted their time. Let's get something tangible before we call in the cavalry, okay?"

Hawkins rubbed the bridge of his nose. "We're devoting way too much time to this case. Don't make the same mistake you made in Boston."

The insinuation cut like a knife in Wilson's back. "This isn't like Boston."

"Prove it," Hawkins said. "If we find hard evidence of terrorist involvement, then we are calling Forrester. And if Dr. Silva loses it again, then you need to start thinking like a cop and stop her from hurting anyone."

As much as Wilson wanted to punch Hawkins in the face at the moment, Wilson still knew his partner was right. If Wilson kept chasing ghosts, they'd come back to haunt him. "Fine, deal," he said. "Until there is hard evidence, we monitor her—but we treat her like a victim, not a suspect."

"Of course." Hawkins patted Wilson on the back. "Now go home and get some rest."

After Hawkins left, Wilson tossed the baggie into the evidence tray and turned on his computer. He logged in and accessed the NCIC database. As Wilson waited for approval of his password, he squeezed his fists until his knuckles turned white. There was one part of Cristina's story that could make or break the rest, the missing puzzle piece he'd been seeking.

The database accepted his password. Wilson cracked his knuckles and searched for any reference to the Golem.

CHAPTER TWENTY-EIGHT

Every morning at dawn, the previous day's tension dissipated as Quinn stretched and focused on breathing in, out, in, out. He'd begun a strict exercise regimen when he rented this hotel room a year ago. Ambient music poured from surround sound speakers and flowed through his body as he folded his legs into a butterfly position and pressed his knees into the floor.

The rising sun peeked around the ivy tower across the way, casting a scarlet sheen over the frost-covered park. An average person might pause and admire the beauty of the capital city stretched out below, but Quinn concentrated on his routine. There would be time for pretty scenery later once the project was complete—after they'd taken care of Santos.

Sharp pain jolted his right knee. He cursed at his distraction and overstretching. He unfolded his legs and massaged his knee.

As much as Quinn wanted to deal with the situation in Boston personally, he had to trust his operatives to handle it. Too much was at stake in Washington and his full attention was needed. He closed his eyes, extended his legs and leaned forward to touch his toes.

The bitter chirp of his smartphone shattered the tranquility.

Quinn's eyes flew open. He roared and shut off the music. He stormed across the bedroom, grabbed the phone off the nightstand, and answered it. "What?"

"You said she wouldn't remember anything," said a male voice with a slight Latin accent.

It took a moment for Quinn to process the statement. The caller wasn't who he expected. "Why are you calling me? You should be going through your handler."

"Fuck that." The caller's voice rose in pitch. "The handler said all I had to do was take out the traitor bitch and escape. No one said the other one would try to kill me."

"Calm down—"

"Don't tell me to calm down. First, she nearly breaks my rib in her apartment when she wasn't even supposed to be there, and now she tries to blow my brains out. This time, she saw my face. When she remembers who I am, she'll come after me."

"No one's coming after you." Quinn fought to maintain his composure. "Just because her training kicked in doesn't mean she remembers. If she did, I would know."

The caller's breathing rate slowed. "You're sure?"

"Quite sure. I have another job for you, unless you no longer think you can handle it."

"Huh?" The caller paused. "No, I'm good. You can trust me."

"I hope so. Expect a call with details and location." Quinn gritted his teeth. "But don't call me directly again."

As he hung up, Quinn wasn't sure how much the caller believed, but soon it wouldn't matter. If the police started listening to Cristina—or worse, if she believed herself—everything would fall apart. He was lucky he'd had someone else trustworthy enough to clean up the mess under the bridge.

Those journal entries alone could've unraveled everything. There was no time left to take chances.

He sent an encrypted text: *Operative compromised. Terminate.*

As Cristina rode the bus to work, she regretted not taking the day off. The more she had told Andrea the previous night, the more terrified Cristina had become. She glanced at the other passengers. Despite yesterday's storm, the bus was full. No Santos, no Cristiano Ronaldo lookalikes, but any one of them could be a Zero Dark assassin.

Cristina shrugged off her paranoia. She had to. She couldn't afford to keep taking taxis. Anyway, if Zero Dark wanted to kill her, they wouldn't do it in a public place. She was safer in crowds than empty subway stations and bridges. And the police were keeping tabs on her, probably to ensure she didn't shoot anyone, but all the same it was good knowing they were there.

A yawn escaped. It had taken most of the night to convince Andrea that Cristina wasn't crazy, and even longer to regain her trust. By the time they'd pulled into the parking lot next to their apartment building, Andrea seemed ready to explode.

"So, all these memories you've regained were because of a drug?" she had asked. "And you never told me?"

Avoiding her friend's gaze as she unbuckled her seatbelt, Cristina said, "Recovering my life has always been my top priority. I had to keep the study secret. Only subjects can know about it until Recognate is approved for public use."

"So, you're also a subject?"

Cristina's cheeks flushed. "Not exactly. The researchers at ReMind don't know I'm taking it. For my prescription, I used the name Catherine Silvers. And if they find out and cut me out of the study, I could lose my memories all over again."

Andrea continued to grip the steering wheel. "You get what you want, and the hell with everyone else."

Cristina stared at the dashboard. "Can we get out of this car? Please?"

"Fine," Andrea said as she opened her door. "Follow me. This conversation isn't over."

They didn't speak again until they entered Andrea's apartment. Andrea broke the silence.

"I need a drink and so do you. Take a seat."

After flopping onto the sofa and hugging a pillow, Cristina said, "I'm sorry I didn't tell you earlier. I'm telling you now because if I am losing my mind, it might be Recognate's fault. I need to talk to someone I trust."

Andrea carried two full glasses from the bar and handed one to Cristina. Andrea then opened her mouth to say something, but stopped. Instead, she sat on an ottoman opposite Cristina, took a swig, and said, "Okay, but now you need to tell me everything."

"I will."

It took an hour and two more mojitos for Cristina to explain how Recognate regulated emotions and memory consolidation, as well as the referral process, how the pills arrived by courier, and Cristina's role in monitoring their response. Then Cristina summarized her conversation with Julius Simmons, everything Santos had told her about Zero Dark, and what Stacey Peterman had told her about Jerry.

"Honey, I know you believe all of this, but bear with me. All of this started when Santos appeared. What if Santos is Quinn? Maybe this drug is poisoning your mind, and all the paranoid crap he's feeding you has taken on its own life."

Tears welled in Cristina's eyes. She turned before Andrea could see them and wiped them away. "You think I'm going crazy."

"That's not it at all, sweetie." Andrea moved closer and put her arm around Cristina's shoulder. "Don't lose sight of what we know is real. You remember the car crash, right?"

Cristina nodded.

"How could you remember so clearly if you weren't there? Has Santos given you any proof?"

Her stomach tensed. All she had was Santos's word and a photograph of someone who looked like her. "What about those memories of Rio?"

"Maybe your parents took you there and you don't remember. If the holes in your memory are big enough, you wouldn't know what you don't know."

"Perhaps." Cristina pressed her fingertips against her lips. Andrea had a point. "What about the way I handled a gun today? Where did I learn that?"

"Maybe you finally paid attention to my self-defense lessons." Andrea had grinned and had given Cristina a hug. "All I know is, we'll figure this out together. But no more secrets, okay?"

"Short Street," announced the bus driver, startling Cristina from her reverie. She looked out the window. Her office building stood less than half a block away. Well, at least no one had tried to kill her. What a way to qualify a successful Monday morning.

When Cristina entered her practice, Devi already had a chart waiting for her. "Mrs. Watterson is here with her son."

"How about I get settled in and then I'll talk to them?" Cristina hung up her coat.

"Um, they're waiting in your office."

Cristina froze in the middle of doffing her hat. "Devi, it's not even eight thirty."

"Under the circumstances, I thought you'd want to see them right away."

"What circumstances?"

Devi shifted papers on her desk. "Mr. Watterson says his mother is getting worse, and he claims it's your fault."

"It's my fault she has Alzheimer's?"

Devi chewed her lower lip. "Maybe you should talk to him yourself."

Stomach fluttering, Cristina ripped off her hat and entered her office. Mrs. Watterson and her son looked up from their magazines. The woman smiled. Her son's pale, doughy face remained stoic.

"Hello, Martha, David." Cristina closed the door behind her and approached them, holding out her hand. "I wasn't expecting you so early."

"Hello, my dear." Martha beamed as she wrapped her hands around Cristina's. "I hope you're ready for your big day."

"Big day?"

"Why, your wedding, of course. To David."

Cristina glanced at Mr. Watterson. "What's she talking about?"

"She thinks we're getting married." David Watterson kept his gaze level through his horn-rimmed glasses. "She also thinks she's the daughter of Charles Lindbergh, Jr."

"Everyone thought he died as a baby." Martha's eyes twinkled. "Not true. Not only did he survive, he fathered me and my twin sister, Isabella. Such a shame he died a few years ago. He would have so loved to have met you, my dear."

Cristina felt her body heat rising. "She wasn't like this before. What happened?"

"I think you know very well, Dr. Silva. You did this to her." He held up a bottle of green capsules. "And it has something to do with these."

CHAPTER TWENTY-NINE

Cristina's heart thumped as she stared at the pill bottle. She sat and folded her hands. "We've discussed your mother's condition at length. This behavior could be a symptom of advanced Alzheimer's."

Anger smoldered in David Watterson's eyes. He twisted the bottle between his fingers. "Ma, when did you say you started taking these?"

"Oh, they're lovely, aren't they?" Martha Watterson winked at Cristina. "The color of emeralds, like my grandmother's necklace. Dr. Silva, you'll wear it for the wedding."

"Ma." He shook the bottle. "When did you start taking them?"

"Oh, yes. Two weeks ago."

"That's how long she's been like this and getting worse. You think it's a coincidence? The damned things aren't even approved by the FDA. I checked online."

Cristina's ears burned. Even if she thought Recognate might be dangerous, disclosing that to the Wattersons before discussing it with the researchers could be disastrous.

"Yes," she said, "Recognate is still being studied, but this has never been reported as an adverse effect. I would've kept your mother carefully monitored for it if it had been."

He slammed the pill bottle onto the desk. Cristina recoiled in surprise. "What gives you the right to experiment on my mother?"

"Now, wait a minute. I counseled her on all the risks and benefits of enrolling. She signed a consent form."

"She's not in her right mind. How can she give consent?"

"Your mother was lucid enough when she came to me, begging me for something, anything, to help her remember." Cristina leaned forward, knuckles white as she gripped the armrests. No more accusations of incompetence. Not today. "She knew what she was doing. And do you know why she was so desperate? She wanted to remember you. Her son. You told me you would do anything for your mother. That's what she did for you."

David Watterson stared at the floor. Had she been too defensive?

"You're right, Dr. Silva." Martha rummaged through her purse. "Those pills have helped me so much. I never would've remembered Isabella without you. As soon as I found this picture, I remembered everything."

She handed Cristina a crumpled photo.

A sinking feeling grew in Cristina's stomach as she unfolded the paper and recognized the raven-haired woman in the picture. "This is Isabella Rossellini."

"Yes, my sister."

"She's a famous actress. Her mother was Ingrid Bergman."

Martha's smile broadened. "Oh, you knew my mother?"

"You see?" The son spread his hands, his face sagging. "Every time she sees a picture in a magazine or on TV, she makes up a story about how it fits into her life. Yesterday, she claimed she babysat Tiger Woods."

"What a nice boy." Martha clucked her tongue. "But he could be a rascal, yes, he could."

Cristina gathered her thoughts as she set down the photo. False memories. But the woman had only been taking Recognate for two weeks, and her other subjects had exhibited no such behavior, even after taking it for months. There had to be another explanation.

"Confabulation. That's the fabrication of false memories. We see it with alcoholics suffering from thiamine deficiency." She turned to Martha. "You said you drink a glass of wine each night with dinner. Have you been drinking more than that?"

"Goodness, no. Too much red wine makes my head spin."

"Okay, so we can rule that out."

"Maybe just two or three tumblers of whiskey now and then ..."

"Ma!" The son gasped.

"All right. Stop." Cristina waved as if she could magically restore order. "Martha, please hold out your hands."

The old woman did so. "I had my nails done. Do you like them?"

Cristina glanced at the haphazard streaks of nail polish.

"Yes, very nice." She focused on Martha's fingers, watching for erratic movements. "No tremor. Speech is fine. It's unlikely she's been drinking enough to affect her thiamine uptake."

"I always take my vitamins." Martha grinned, still stretching out her hands.

"You can put your hands down." As she complied, Cristina sighed. Looking at the son, she said, "When you told me about her obsession with horseback riding, I thought it might be a mild symptom, but it's clearly gotten worse."

"Can Alzheimer's cause this?" The anger in David's eyes was gone, replaced by fear.

"To some extent, yes, but confabulation suggests damage to the frontal lobes and forebrain." The heat drained from Cristina's face as she ran through a frightening differential diagnosis. "I'll need to order neuroimaging right away. Your mother could've suffered an injury to the anterior communicating artery. That could explain her behavior."

David wiped his hand over his face. "Is she going to be okay?"

"It would have to be a slow bleed, but it could already have caused irreparable damage. Did she hit her head recently? Complain of headaches?"

"No, she's been healthy as the horse she tried to ride."

"I forgot about the horse. Did she suffer any head injuries?"

"No. I made her wear a helmet, anyway." He bit his knuckle. "What about the drug? Could it have done something to her brain?"

Though she didn't want to accept the possibility, Cristina knew she had to consider it. "Has she had any hallucinations? Mentioned hearing voices?"

"No."

"How about paranoid delusions? Fear of persecution?"

"Just when she claimed I kidnapped her, but that seems to have stopped." David frowned. "These pills cause all that?"

Heat flushed up the back of Cristina's neck. He seemed more forgiving now, but how would he react if he knew his unstable mother's doctor was also cracking up? "I'm trying to rule things out. Anticholinergic drugs can cause confabulation and sometimes psychotic symptoms, but she doesn't have dry mouth or blurred vision. Anyway, Recognate doesn't have anticholinergic properties. It would be counterproductive to memory restoration."

"But there could be different side effects in different people, right?" David glanced at the pill bottle. "I mean, if it's a new drug maybe it hasn't been studied in people with Alzheimer's."

Cristina opened her mouth to object and closed it again. Many drugs had been pulled a few months or years after entering the market when patients with untested medical illnesses developed life-threatening side effects. Off-label use of medications was always a risk, and if anything happened to this sweet lady ...

"You're right." Cristina switched on her computer and began

typing. "I'm ordering metabolic labs and a brain MRI. Don't let your mother take any more Recognate until we can determine if they're involved." A thought hit her, and Cristina stopped typing. "How did you know Recognate hasn't been studied in Alzheimer's? That information wouldn't be available online."

"No, it's not."

Cristina's chest tightened again. "Then where?"

David licked his lips. "I called the drug company."

CHAPTER THIRTY

"I was scared," said David Watterson. "There was no safety information with the bottle, just a contact number. When I called ReMind, they said Ma had been rejected from the study. I told them I had the bottle in my hand. That's when I noticed you'd misspelled her name. They said you had listed her diagnosis as traumatic amnesia, not Alzheimer's."

The walls crumbled around Cristina, pulling down her degrees and accolades with them. "I was sure she'd respond well to the drug and we'd tried everything else available—"

"I understand. You were only trying to help. Look, I'll call and tell them it wasn't your fault. I want to help Ma."

Images poured into Cristina's mind: the car crash, her psychiatry board exams, a nightmare about monsters in her closet. She squeezed her hands into fists and forced away the memories.

"I appreciate that, Mr. Watterson." She took a deep breath and finished typing her orders. She snatched the printout from the paper tray and handed it to him. "Please call tomorrow with an update."

"Now, dear, don't forget." Martha Watterson gave Cristina a stern look. "Noon tomorrow. Don't be late for your own wedding."

Cristina forced a smile in return. "I wouldn't dream of it."

After the Wattersons left, Cristina sank her forehead into her palms. How was she going to get out of this mess? If her lie had endangered that sweet old lady, she'd never forgive herself. And even if they didn't revoke her license, ReMind would kick her out of the study. No more subjects, no more pills, no more memories …

She picked up her parents' photo and traced the outline of Jorge Silva's face.

"If I'm not your daughter, who am I?"

A buzz from the intercom startled her. "What is it?"

Devi hesitated before answering. "Are you okay? You sound like—"

"I'm fine." Cristina cleared her throat. "Is my ten o'clock here already?"

"No, but Dr. Morgan is waiting for you on line two."

Cristina recalled the tests she had asked the medical examiner to run on Jerry Peterman's blood. She picked up the receiver and switched to line two. "Hello, Dr. Morgan. Sorry to keep you waiting."

"No trouble. And, as I said before, it's Luke."

Cristina allowed herself to smile. He was nothing if not persistent. "Okay, Luke, what do you have for me?"

"Technically, I'm not supposed to tell you any of this without the official paperwork, and this is already complicated because of his sister…"

"Dr. Morgan, please. I just want to be sure this doesn't happen to any of my other patients."

"Okay. Just this once." He snickered. "Anyway, you made quite a good call. Both norepinephrine and epinephrine levels were elevated."

"How high?"

"Five times normal." Luke clucked his tongue. "Wish I could

finish the autopsy. His adrenal gland is probably the size of a golf ball from all those hormones."

"Why can't you? Didn't his sister drop the injunction?"

"Yeah, but she disappeared before making it official. Her lawyer refuses to drop it until she does, so I'm stuck in a holding pattern. I swear, I've never seen a circus like this."

A chill ran down Cristina's back. If Stacey were dead, she wouldn't be approving anything. And Cristina expected lowered norepinephrine by Recognate, or even a mild rebound elevation, not a massive spike. Adrenal tumors were usually rare and slow growing, but Jerry's change in behavior had been so rapid. "Is pheochromocytoma the only explanation?"

"Well, amphetamines and alcohol both can elevate norepinephrine. But his tox was negative for amphetamines, and alcohol doesn't cause that high a spike. Unless Jerry Peterman was smoking two packs a day and guzzling gallons of coffee, I don't know what stressed out his system like that."

Cristina chewed her thumbnail. Stacey said it was the realization he was a murderer that had driven Jerry insane. Could a Recognate overdose have pushed him over the edge? "What about THC?"

"It looks negative."

"I thought you said his tox screen was positive."

"Yes, but inactive THC metabolites remain for up to a month. He's been clean for at least two weeks."

Cristina chewed her fingernail. No active cannabinoids ruled out a Recognate overdose, but if he hadn't been taking it at all, what caused him to suddenly remember his violent past? And she'd written a refill for him a week earlier. Why would he stop taking Recognate?

"Cristina? Still there?"

"Yes. Sorry. I feel like I'm trying to put together a jigsaw puzzle blindfolded."

"I know that feeling." Morgan cleared his throat. "Look, I may be out of line, but this is more than clinical curiosity, isn't it? You sound like you've been through Hell and back."

"You're not out of line. I'm in trouble and I need answers."

"Well, if there's any way I can help, let me know. Unfortunately, my hands are tied with Mr. Peterman."

"Wait. I've got an idea." Cristina forced away her doubts and fears. Time to think like a doctor again, and Jerry wasn't her only patient. "Do you still have samples of Carl Franklin's blood?"

"Sure. I've got the body on ice."

"You do?" Hope for answers to her questions glimmered in Cristina's mind.

"We keep unclaimed bodies for a month, so the police can try to find next of kin. It saves taxpayer money on cremation expenses."

Two Recognate subjects were dead after suffering psychotic breaks. If she couldn't touch one body, perhaps the other could yield some clues as to what went wrong. "Luke, I'd like to request an expanded autopsy."

CHAPTER THIRTY-ONE

The rest of Cristina's morning passed smoother than it had in weeks. No more surprises, odd medication effects or lawsuits. At noon, she set aside her charts with the hope she might get through the afternoon unscathed.

"Devi," she said as she passed the reception desk. "I'm going to lunch. Do you want anything from Mei's Noodle Shop?"

"Hold, please," Devi said into the phone. To Cristina, "Sorry, but it's Julius Simmons from ReMind. He says it's urgent."

Images of the punishment the ReMind CEO was about to inflict on Cristina's career assaulted her. She blocked them out. She wasn't defeated yet. Straightening her blouse, she started back to her office.

"Do you want me to order something from Mei's?"

"No, thanks. I've lost my appetite."

The call waiting light taunted as she approached her desk. She clenched her fists and gathered her strength.

You can do this. Yesterday was bad, but today will be better ... The more Cristina recited her mantra, the less she believed it. She gave up. Willing herself to stay strong, she picked up the phone.

"This is Cristina Silva."

Are you sure? A voice whispered in the back of her mind.

"Dr. Silva. We need to talk."

"Yes, and I understand how upset you must be. It's only because I believe so much in Recognate's potential that I did it."

"Excuse me?"

"I thought it would help that poor lady. I've already told Mrs. Watterson to stop taking it, and it won't happen again—"

"Doctor, what are you talking about?"

"You're calling about Martha Watterson, right?"

"I have no idea who that is." He cleared his throat. "I need you here at our main office in Washington. Right away."

"Washington?" Cristina wondered if she'd misheard. "Why?"

"I'm not at liberty to discuss it over the phone. But we need help with an urgent matter, and ReMind would appreciate your cooperation."

Still trying to grasp the idea she wasn't about to lose her license, Cristina asked, "When do you need me?"

"Tomorrow."

"I have patients. I can't drop everything and fly there without—"

"I've booked a flight for you at eight thirty in the morning."

Cristina's head spun. "I don't think you understand—"

"No, Doctor, you don't understand. I expect to see you here tomorrow with records of every subject you've referred to us." His voice assumed the Darth Vader tone Cristina recognized from their last conversation. "Unless you'd prefer to meet with the medical licensing board …"

The back of Cristina's neck crawled. Clearly, whatever help Simmons needed was more important than Mrs. Watterson, and he wasn't above blackmail to get it. "No, that will be fine. Please give the travel information to my office manager."

"Of course." Though he resumed a congenial tenor, the threatening undertone continued. "Have a pleasant flight."

Cristina placed him on hold. When did her world fall

completely out of orbit? Did she have even a shred of control over anything anymore?

The hold light blinked angrily at her. Let him wait. At least that was something she could control. She opened her desk drawer and pulled out the overstuffed envelope she now carried with her everywhere. The day Santos first appeared—that was the day everything fell apart. Maybe Andrea was right. With her career and her sanity in jeopardy, did she have time for conspiracy stories and a fool's errand?

She glanced at the blinking light again and sighed. If she kept him waiting too long who knew how he'd retaliate? She pressed the intercom button. "Devi, can you get flight information from Mr. Simmons? And you'll need to cancel tomorrow's patients."

"Flight? What's going on?"

"It's a long story, but I'm sure Mr. Simmons will happily fill you in. Can you also gather the records for all of my study subjects?"

"I'll work as quickly as I can. Funny, Mr. Stevens called this morning."

Alarms rang in Cristina's head. Josiah Stevens had been in the Recognate study for eight months. "Did something happen?"

"No, he wanted to confirm his appointment for next week."

Cristina sighed with relief. Crisis averted. But better not take chances. "Do you think you could call the remaining participants to check how they're doing and tell them I'm sending orders for lab work? Just routine. Try not to worry them."

"You're worrying *me*. What's going on?"

"I'm not sure. For now, let's say I'm being cautious."

"Okay. I'm not going to get subpoenaed, am I?"

"Don't worry. Everything's going to be fine."

After turning off the intercom, Cristina toyed with the envelope on her desk. Maybe a day away would be good for her. Despite his subtle threats, Simmons needed her help. If there was a fixable problem with

Recognate, she was all for it. And the trip would get her away from Santos and the madness he and Stacey Peterman had created.

Cristina flipped the envelope open with her finger. The news articles peeked out. She pulled them out and sifted through them. Once more, she skimmed through the multiple suicide reports. It seemed long ago that she was horrified by these gruesome details. Now, after witnessing two murders, the stories barely triggered a reaction. She set them aside and picked up the *O Globo* article. The dark-haired woman in the photo stared back at her. Stacey Peterman said they had changed Cristina's face. Was it possible this woman and Cristina were the same person? The only person identified in the photo was Jose Kobayashi.

The name rang a bell. After searching the Internet, she realized why.

Jose Kobayashi was the first to study beta-endorphins in memory research. Cristina had read his research at least thirty times. Could she even consider it a coincidence that her physical double had worked with a memory expert? She clicked through the list of web pages. After five minutes, she scratched her chin. A statement by the mayor of Rio declared the *Renascimento* project a success three years after its inception. Gang violence was down, and the city had earmarked millions toward improved public services for *favela* residents. That article was dated three years ago. Cristina could find nothing dated after that to identify Kobayashi's whereabouts or activity, nor those of any other team member. It was like they'd vanished.

Cristina slumped against her chair. Another dead end.

She scanned the faces in the photo again. Her mouth went dry. One face was familiar, after all. In the back row, three heads to the left of Cristina's doppelgänger, stood a young man with a thin nose, low-set eyebrows, and a striking resemblance to Cristiano Ronaldo.

Cristina recognized the man who had been in her apartment—the same man who had shot Stacey Peterman.

CHAPTER THIRTY-TWO

"I'm sure it's the same guy." Cristina cupped her hand around the cell phone and peered out the window from the office foyer. From there, she had a clear view of the bus stop—and anyone who might be loitering nearby. "Andrea, this guy knows where I live. He probably knows more about me than I do. What do I do?"

"Don't work yourself into a panic," came Andreas's voice through the phone. "The police are still making runs by your office, right?"

"Yeah, I saw a cruiser pass by two minutes ago."

"You should be fine then. Stay alert like I taught you and don't act like a victim."

"We're talking about a professional assassin, not a mugger."

"I know, it's just …"

Cristina frowned. "You think I imagined him."

"Well, honey, you're all worked up about this trip to Washington. Didn't you tell me this drug jumbles up your emotions and memories?"

"Not exactly, but I get your point." Cristina's heart ached. Her best friend thought she was cracking up, and the worst part was Andrea might be right.

Cristina's bus was approaching. She scanned the street again. All clear.

"Hold on."

She stepped outside and ran to the bus stop, then put the phone back to her ear. "Let's assume for a moment I'm not losing my mind. What if this guy is real and he tries to stop me at the airport? Or does something to the plane?"

Andrea muttered something in Spanish Cristina couldn't make out. After an exasperated sigh, she said, "You'll be fine. I'm going with you."

"Oh, no, that's too much. You have your job. I can't ask you—"

"You're not asking. I have a few vacation days saved up. Let me tell my boss, and I'll head home and pack."

Cristina was so overwhelmed with gratitude that she missed a step as she boarded the bus. The driver caught her arm. She nodded thanks and paid her fare. As she made her way to a seat near the heater, Cristina shook her head. Why hadn't she confided in her friend sooner? "Thank you," she said to Andrea after sitting down." You really are special."

"Whatever. I'll be trolling for cute boys at Georgetown while you deal with the pill pushers. Anyway, if you beat me home, you make the drinks."

Cristina laughed. "Deal," she said and hung up.

After tucking away her phone, Cristina scanned the bus. There was a wheelchair-bound man in a hoodie near the back and an Indian woman with a baby near the front. It would be easy enough to spot the assassin if he appeared.

Cristina confirmed no one was watching her and pulled file folders out of her backpack. Carl Franklin, Jerry Peterman, and Martha Watterson—their names stirred up feelings of failure. At least her other subjects were fine.

She opened Carl's file and searched for clues to something she might have missed.

The Somerville precinct was bustling as officers scurried to respond to fender benders and conflicts due to the icy weather. Detective Miller and his partner shuffled off to file reports from their last case. Sergeant Davis prowled through the station, barking orders at junior officers before returning to his post.

Tucked away at his desk, Detective Wilson studied the CIA file he'd been emailed, feeling like he was reading a Tom Clancy novel. According to the government file, the international assassin Jeremy Hammond, also known as the Golem, was nearly as elusive as his legendary namesake. He had first appeared ten years earlier, poisoning Pakistan's Federal Secretary. While the Golem evaded capture, the Inter-Services Intelligence agency discovered ties to India's Research and Analysis Wing. They launched a bloody attack that lasted four months until the United Nations negotiated a truce.

Assassination after assassination followed. The killings followed no pattern that pointed to a specific geopolitical affiliation. The Golem then dropped from sight after every assassination, only to kill again months later.

Until two years ago. CIA field officers tracked the Golem to Bogota, where informants claimed he was planning to kill the Colombian Defense Minister on behalf of the rebel group FARC. The US operatives arrived minutes after the minister's home exploded, leaving no survivors. Three bodies found in the rubble were never identified, but dental records of one matched Jeremy Hammond's by eighty percent.

After rereading the report, Wilson reflected on Cristina's claims. If Jerry Peterman had been the Golem, the trained killer might not have died in Bogota but perhaps instead lost his memory in the Bogota explosion. But what had made Jeremy Hammond remember the truth?

The ringing of his cell phone interrupted his thoughts. The caller ID read Hawkins.

"What've you got, Rick?"

"Silva's on the move."

Wilson checked his watch. "It's only two thirty. She never leaves the office before five."

"I spotted her on a routine pass and circled back. She boarded the 47 bus."

"Stay on her. She's involved in something big."

"What'd you find?"

"I'll fill you in later, but I think it's time to call Forrester."

"If you're calling the Feds, should I be worried?"

"I hope not. But if things go sour, follow your gut." He ended the call.

Wilson knew he was in over his head. If Martins was in the same league as the Golem, the situation was way out of Somerville PD's jurisdiction. Wilson rubbed his forehead. It was time to call in help.

"Hey, Detective!" Wilson jumped at Sergeant Davis's guttural bark. They heavyset officer waved at him from the doorway. "You've got visitors."

"Who?"

Agents Forrester and Vasquez shoved their way past the sergeant. Forrester's face twisted into a scowl. Vasquez looked cool and controlled.

"Gary Wilson," Forrester said as he approached. "I should've known."

"Agent Forrester, I was about to call you."

"Oh, really? Before or after you fucked up a ten-year investigation?"

Wilson recoiled. "What?"

"Don't play innocent. You've been sitting on leads to Francisco Martins for over a week. And now you're sticking your nose into places it doesn't belong. We're assuming primary authority over all matters relating to Cristina Silva. Effective immediately."

CHAPTER THIRTY-THREE

The brakes of the 47 bus hissed as it pulled to a stop. A group of teenagers boarded and jumped into the front seats. The bus lurched forward and then rattled along the bumpy street.

Cristina closed Martha Watterson's file and stared at the cover. Fifteen minutes of comparing records for all her subjects failed to yield any common threads. Neither Carl nor Jerry had reported anything suggesting false memories. However, Carl had suffered total amnesia, so how would he know if his memories were real or not? Jerry only lost ten years. Wouldn't he be able to tell if his recovered memories didn't match his older ones?

Unless he had lied about everything. Unless he never took the drug.

We're being watched.

The voice whispered in the back of Cristina's mind. She couldn't be sure if it was a warning from her new companion, or an echo of what Santos had said to her that first time on the bus. Either way, the hairs on her neck stood on end. Pretending to check the files again, she scanned the other bus passengers out of the corner of her eye.

The Indian woman remained in her seat. The teenagers

gathered near the front. And the guy in the wheelchair was in the back.

Alarms blared in Cristina's head. That same wheelchair guy had been on the bus that morning.

She grabbed her backpack, walked toward the back of the bus, and dropped into the seat next to the wheelchair.

"You can't make an appointment at my office like normal people?"

Santos pushed back his hoodie, revealing those smoldering obsidian eyes. His clothes reeked of alcohol. "The police have forced me into hiding, but I needed to make certain you were still willing to help me after the unfortunate incident with Ms. Petrov."

"Which incident? The one where you two skulked around behind my back, or where one of Zero Dark's assassins killed her?"

In response, Santos momentarily raised his eyebrows. A moment later, his face was again passive. He remained silent.

"You didn't know she was dead," Cristina said. She pulled the *O Globo* article out of her backpack. "They sent the same guy who broke into my apartment. This one."

"Federico Gomes." Santos nodded. "It makes sense they would send him."

"Why does it make sense?"

"Zero Dark has an unusual sense of humor. You and Gomes share a common history. If they've deployed him, you must take extra care when you travel to Washington."

Cristina noted Santos avoided her question but was more irritated by his apparent belief that he had control over her life. "As if I'm safe here with the guy who killed my parents."

Santos recoiled. "What?"

"I know the brake lines were cut. You worked on the car a day earlier."

"Yes, I worked on the car." He inhaled through his nose. "But

I had nothing to do with the crash killing Jorge and Claudia Silva. I certainly didn't cut the brakes. I swear on my daughter's life."

The conviction in Santos's voice made Cristina pause. He admitted to burning down their house. What reason would he have to lie about that? On the other hand, he'd lied about everything else.

"That night we met, when I attacked you—that wasn't an accident, was it?" She held up a hand before he could answer. "And don't lie. I know about the book. Not only did you use it as an excuse to meet me, but you were there when I bought it."

He sucked in his cheeks, eyes smoldering. "Yes. I'd been watching you for some time, deciding whether or not you possessed what I needed. When you bested me, you proved you had the raw ability, but when you showed me kindness, you proved I could trust you."

"You could trust me?" She choked out a laugh. "How am I supposed to trust you? And how did you know I'm going to Washington?"

"That's not important. What is important is what you need to find when you visit ReMind."

Cristina was startled. "How do you know about ReMind?"

"It was no coincidence they recruited you, Cristina." He sighed heavily. "ReMind is part of Zero Dark."

"Hold on, Forrester." Detective Wilson leaned onto his toes, trying to see eye to eye with the taller agent. "I wanted to be sure we were dealing with Martins before calling you. What gives you the right to barge in here and take over the Silva case?"

"Three things," Forrester said without blinking. "Title Twenty-Eight of the United States Code, Section Five-Three-Three, by order of the Attorney General. Also, Francisco Martins and Jerry Peterman."

"Peterman? What's he got to do with it?"

Forrester opened his mouth to answer but Agent Vasquez stepped between them and placed a folder on Wilson's desk. "We've taken an interest in all mass shootings. We also have reason to believe Jerry Peterman was actually an international terrorist known as the Golem."

Wilson's skin crawled. He tried to act nonchalant. "The Golem, huh?"

"Yeah," said Forrester. "But you already know that, don't you?"

Before Wilson could respond, Vasquez said, "The CIA flagged your request for recently declassified records. They weren't that concerned, but the alert got forwarded to us."

"I was gathering information before I contacted you." Wilson frowned. "What happened to the Freedom of Information Act?"

"That only applies for non-official use," Forrester said. "Not when you're using the information as part of a criminal investigation. Especially one beyond your scope. But you never were much of a team player, were you?"

Wilson's cheeks burned. This was exactly what he wanted to avoid. "I'm sorry you feel that way, but even if Peterman was the Golem, he's dead. What does it have to do with the Silva investigation?"

"That's none of your—" Forrester started to say.

"Charles," Vasquez said, placing a hand on Forrester's shoulder. "Let me handle this."

Forrester glared at Wilson but stayed silent.

Turning back to Wilson, Vasquez said, "Witnesses overheard Peterman shouting the name Quinn before he died."

"Is that supposed to mean something to me?"

"It means something to us. Quinn is the head of a mercenary organization for hire. Zero Dark."

So, Cristina had been telling the truth about the shadow organization. "Are they good guys or bad?"

The corner of Vasquez's mouth twitched. "They started out doing contract work for the military. Security, combat training. For a few years, they did contract work for the CIA. Then there was an incident."

"What happened?"

"On a mission in Lebanon, they got trigger-happy. Fifty-two dead, including twenty-three Americans." Forrester scowled. "Some believe the shootout was a cover for Zero Dark to take out the CIA team since the Zero Dark operatives escaped unscathed, but no one has proof."

"And they're still in operation?"

"They went underground. No official government work anymore. At least, not our government. The bigger problem is Quinn has gone ghost. We think he's using an alias but can't pin him down. Anyone that knows anything about Quinn's whereabouts is either working for him or dead."

"Like Peterman." Wilson took their silence as an answer. "What does this have to do with Cristina Silva?"

"She was Peterman's psychiatrist," Vasquez said. "He may have told her something we can use to track down Quinn."

"I've interviewed her several times. She doesn't know anything."

"That's hard to believe since she's been in contact with Francisco Martins." Forrester's lip curled. "He is also a Zero Dark operative."

Wilson flinched and then cursed himself for reacting. Everything supported Cristina's story, so maybe the rest of her claims were true, too. There was only one way to find out.

"Martins is obsessed with Dr. Silva," he said. "He burned down her parents' house and worked on their car before they died in a crash. Unfortunately, she has amnesia, so I don't know how much help she'll be."

The agents exchanged glances. Forrester seemed ready to make another snide remark, but Vasquez cut him off with a wave. "Detective, I think we got off on the wrong foot. It seems we both have information to bring to the table. Instead of arguing over jurisdiction, how about we work together?"

A voice in the back of Wilson's mind wanted to scream at them to go to hell, but he shooed it away. He had already conceded to himself that he couldn't tackle this alone. And the Feds had access to resources Somerville PD could never match. "You're right. I'll gather everything I've discovered, and we can run through it together."

"Great." Vasquez smiled. "See how nice it is when we play together?"

Wilson cautiously returned her smile but couldn't maintain it when he caught Forrester's dour expression. The agent's eyes shouted a slew of unspoken obscenities at the detective.

"Yeah," Wilson said. "It's going to be a real lovefest."

"Agents," Sergeant Davis shouted from the doorway. He sneered when he spotted Wilson. "And Detective. Malone just called in. He says you both can wrap up your investigations."

"Why's that?" Forrester asked.

"They pulled a stiff out of a dumpster near Porter Square." Davis smirked. "Malone's pretty sure it's Francisco Martins."

CHAPTER THIRTY-FOUR

Cristina gripped the bus seat cushion as if, any moment, she would fly away into the madness now surrounding her. She snapped her eyes shut, praying that when she opened them everything would be normal again. She opened her eyes. Santos was still there on the bus in a wheelchair.

"How is that even possible?" she asked. "How can a pharmaceutical company be part of a terrorist organization?"

"They have little choice." Santos sighed. "ReMind contracted Zero Dark some years ago to cover up a terrible mistake without truly understanding the price involved. When they couldn't make the promised payments, they were condemned to serving Zero Dark's needs."

"Stacey Peterman said they were covering up a project. Does it involve Recognate?"

Santos nodded.

"So, all the work I've been doing with my patients was for Zero Dark? What do they want with Recognate?"

"I don't know." His mouth twisted grimly. "But you do."

"Me? Is that the important information I can't remember?"

"I believe so."

"But you have no idea what that is."

"If I knew, I wouldn't have dragged you into this. Unfortunately, I don't, and you're the only one who can help me."

"To find your daughter." Cristina massaged her forehead. This bus ride couldn't end soon enough. "What's your daughter's name, anyway?"

He scratched his cheek. "That will do you no good. They've changed it. She thinks she's someone else."

"Do you know what name she's using?"

He shook his head.

Cristina's tried to keep it all straight. "You realize when you request someone's help, you need to give them something they can use? How am I supposed to help find her if I don't even know what she looks like?"

"You weren't able to open the locket?"

"It has a photo of a child. Don't you have a more recent photo?"

His lip trembled. "I gave you all that I have. Please keep it safe. Men like Federico Gomes will do whatever is necessary to recover it."

"Is that why he broke into my home?" When Santos nodded, she nearly screamed. "Why do they want her baby picture?"

"There's more to it than that. Did you find nothing else of value?"

"The letters *RJ* inscribed on the locket. Does that mean anything to you?"

"Rio de Janeiro." Santos's eyes drifted, becoming unfocused. "That's where I'm from."

"Is that where your daughter is?"

Santos didn't answer. Instead, he said, "Look past the obvious to find the truth."

Cristina dug her nails into her palms and glanced out the window. She glimpsed the Charles River. They still had a long bus ride ahead. "What does that mean?"

Santos's gaze met hers. "Things aren't as they seem. That also applies to your meeting with ReMind."

"Oh, hell no. I'm not going anywhere near there. If what you say is true, they'll kill me the moment I set foot inside."

"But you must go, Cristina." Pain and regret lingered in the wrinkles around Santos's eyelids. "They won't harm you. They need you. And they don't know you've broken their spell over you. That gives you the advantage. Look, listen, and learn. With any luck, you'll remember the information they seek and can use it against them."

Nothing made sense. "I'm sorry, but this is too much. I'm a psychiatrist, not a spy. Why don't we go to the police and tell them—?"

"Tell them what? That someone stole your memories and gave you a dead woman's identity?" Santos glanced over his shoulder before locking his gaze with hers, eyes blazing. "Even if they don't think you're to blame, why would the police believe a woman who was found waving a gun around, babbling about victims and killers nobody else saw?"

The blood drained from Cristina's face. He was right. Her patients whose appointments Devi hadn't canceled, had not rescheduled. Cristina's professional reputation was eroding. She heard voices and had visions of dead patients. And she could count the number of people she trusted on one hand. Why would anyone believe her?

"My friend Andrea thinks I'm hallucinating, that I imagined Gomes killing Stacey. Is Recognate making me lose my mind?"

His face sagged, the fire fading from his eyes. "You're not crazy. But the drug doesn't work the way you think. And if your question indicates that you have moved past the nightmare stage and onto waking visions and voices, we're running out of time."

The gravity of his voice threatened to crush her chest. "What do you mean?"

"You must find my daughter quickly." He pressed his lips together tightly and swallowed. "Because soon you'll no longer know who you are."

"What's his problem?" Wilson murmured to Agent Vasquez as they waited by his desk. Near the doorway, Agent Forrester spoke to Detective Malone on his cell phone. The male agent's eyebrows seemed to be doing gymnastics as his expression fluctuated between surprised and livid. "Did I spit in his soup in another life, or is he just an asshole?"

A smile played at Vasquez's lips, but then it vanished, and she was all business again. "You know that incident in Lebanon? Forrester's brother was one of the CIA officers killed in the attack."

Wilson glanced again at Forrester, who shook his head and barked orders over the phone.

"No wonder he's so rabid about this case."

"He's been after this guy Quinn for years, even before I started working with him. He's convinced that Martins will lead us to Quinn. Anything and anyone that gets in his way—"

"Is asking for a world of hurt. I get it." Wilson ran a hand over his face. "Look, I want to cooperate. I was just caught off-guard by Forrester's approach."

"Don't worry about it. It's not the first time we've had a conflict of interest with another department. But it's best if we're not adversaries, right?"

Before Wilson could answer, Forrester stormed back over to them.

"I don't buy it." He slammed his phone on the desk. "Malone insists the stiff they found matches Martins' description, but I don't think that dope can tell one Latin guy from another. The man he described sounds too young, and he doesn't have Martins' scars."

"So it's a dead end?" Vasquez said flatly.

"Ha ha. Not necessarily. The corpse has a clean gunshot wound through the forehead. Looks like a professional hit."

"There are a few crime families working locally," Wilson said.

"Yeah, I know. But this was Zero Dark."

"How can you be sure?"

Forrester narrowed his gaze. "Because this guy had Dr. Cristina Silva's address scribbled on a scrap of paper in his pocket."

Wilson was startled. "So, if he's not Martins, who is he?"

"I don't know." He nodded at Agent Vasquez. "They're bringing his body down to the morgue. Why don't you go and find out?"

"I'm on it." Vasquez headed for the door. She stopped and looked over her shoulder. "You two boys play nice."

After she left, Forrester puffed out his chest. "Let's get the doctor here, too. Even if she can't tell us anything about Martins, she can answer questions about Peterman."

"Uh, sure." Wilson pulled out his cell phone. "My partner is in the area."

Hawkins picked up on the third ring. "I'm still tailing the bus," he said. "We're almost to Cambridge, and she hasn't gotten off yet."

"Great," Wilson said. "Can you bring Dr. Silva down to the station right now? Agent Forrester wants to ask her questions."

"Forrester? He's there?"

"I'll explain when you get here." Wilson hung up and turned to Forrester. "It shouldn't take more than twenty minutes. Anything else you need in the meantime?"

Forrester studied Wilson's face two seconds longer than would have been comfortable.

"Collect or write down everything you found on Martins. Don't leave anything out." He jabbed a finger in Wilson's face. "And don't get in my way."

As Forrester stomped toward the restroom, Wilson resisted

the urge to flip him the bird. The whole thing was like a fight on the playground over who got to use the slide. And Forrester seemed exceptionally interested in Cristina. The question was why. Maybe there was something to her fantastic theories, after all.

This woman is not Cristina Silva. Ferreira's words echoed in his mind. When Wilson first confronted her in her office, she seemed certain about her identity. But after the Longfellow Bridge incident, that confidence was gone. What changed?

Wilson sat at his desk and pulled his files for Forrester. The top folder was labeled Cristina Silva. The skin behind his ears burned. If the woman Hawkins was about to bring in wasn't Silva, who was she?

CHAPTER THIRTY-FIVE

The 47 bus's brakes squealed as it stopped at a red light. Cristina stared at Santos, unable to believe what he'd told her. "You're saying I'll forget everything? Who will I become?"

His lips pressed together, and he stared out the window. "If the pattern holds true, you won't become anyone. You'll meet the same fate as the others."

"Others?" The pieces connected in her mind. The blood drained from her cheeks. "Oh, my God. Those articles you gave me, all those violent suicides—they all took Recognate?"

He nodded.

Cristina's stomach lurched. The idea that she played a role in the deaths of Jerry and Carl was bad enough. But the thought that there were others, and she might be next? She fought the urge to vomit. "And this is what Zero Dark wants? To kill people who need help?"

"I don't know their full plan. No employee knows any more than what they need to do their job. Only the one in charge understands how it all fits together."

"Quinn."

Santos arched his eyebrows.

"I know he stole Jerry's memory," Cristina said. "I'm guessing he's in charge of Zero Dark."

The corner of Santos's mouth curled. "It was Quinn who ordered me to burn down the Silvas' home."

She shuddered, more at the way he said their name than at the reminder of what he'd done. "You know who he is."

"Yes."

"How do I find him?"

"Find him?" His eyes widened. "Why would you want to find him?"

"To find another way out instead of the shitty fate you describe."

"That's the last thing you should do. Quinn is a very dangerous man. Even if he doesn't kill you, he'll deceive you, manipulate you, until you willingly serve him without the slightest realization of what he's done."

"So, I'm supposed to sit back and let him keep destroying people's lives?"

"No," Santos said. "You do as I ask and find my daughter."

"Who's manipulating now?" Cristina studied the husky man's face. "How do I know you're not Quinn?"

Santos glanced over Cristina's shoulder. His voice grew cold. "What did you do?"

"What?" She turned to the window. Blue lights flashed. A siren whooped once.

"Ah, Jeez," the bus driver said. "I just paid off my speeding tickets."

The bus slowed and veered toward the right side of the road.

"Filho da puta," Santos muttered. He stared at his feet, nostrils flaring, and whispered, "Please forgive me, Cristina."

"Forgive you?" She turned to him. "For what—?"

Santos's fist connected with Cristina's jaw. White explosions obscured her vision. The back of her head cracked against the window. Pain deafened her. She grabbed onto the seat back. The bus jerked to the side. Her hand slipped. She crashed against the window. Everything went black.

Wilson lingered in the doorway to the special operations room, staring at the top of Forrester's well-coiffed head as the agent bent over a desk, studying a report. It was bad enough that Forrester barked orders like the supreme dictator, but he'd also commandeered the next best private office in the station after the Captain's for his personal use. Wilson considered turning, marching back to his desk, hiding his files and pretending he'd lost them. Slumping his shoulders, he scrubbed the idea. Regardless of his feelings for Forrester, Wilson had to work with the Feds on this one.

"This is what I've got." Wilson entered and held out the files. "I wrote up a summary of my conversation with that mechanic, Manny Feldman, but we might need to interview him again. Maybe he has a record of Martins' home address buried away somewhere."

"Unnecessary." Forrester glanced at the folder before dropping it on the desk. "Martins is too smart to give out a real address. Probably used a burner phone too. If we're going to get this guy, we need to target his current activity. That's why I need to interrogate Dr. Silva."

The way Forrester said *interrogate* made Wilson's neck burn. He bit off a sharp retort. "They'll be here soon. But what do you think Silva can tell you? She says she doesn't remember anything about Francisco Martins."

"And you believe her."

"Well, yes. Her story about having amnesia checks out."

"Did she also forget about her meeting with Martins a week ago?"

"What are you talking about?"

Forrester pulled out his smartphone, swiped across the screen, and offered it to Wilson. "Take a look."

The screen showed a video from a local news affiliate. Curious, Wilson pushed the play button. A reporter held a microphone out to a purple-haired young woman in a fur coat. The woman jabbered about a TV show and then turned around with arms raised. The camera swept over the cheering crowd.

"There," Forrester said. "Pause it."

Wilson studied the tiny screen. In the lower corner, looking startled, stood a woman wearing a green hat and scarf. Cristina.

"Where was this?" he asked.

"The Frog Pond at the Commons." Forrester jutted his chin. "Twenty minutes before Jerry Peterman shot up Park Street Station."

"We already knew she was there. She said she wanted to watch the ice skaters."

"Uh-huh." Forrester jabbed a meaty finger at the screen. "And him?"

Wilson squinted. Someone in a black ski parka was turning away from Cristina, arm raised, making it only possible to make out a thick ice-gilded beard. "What about him?"

"That's Martins," Forrester said.

"How the hell can you tell that?"

Forrester snatched the phone and swiped his finger over the screen. The image reversed and paused again. Now more of the man's face appeared but blurry. "We ran it through face recognition and got a sixty percent match. Not enough for a positive identification, I know, but this footage sure looks like this man and the doctor were caught by surprise and then he ran off. Doesn't that strike you as suspicious?"

After searching for a better explanation, Wilson said, "Yeah, there's something weird going on, but until we confirm that's Martins, we need to treat Dr. Silva like a witness, not a suspect, okay?"

As Forrester opened his mouth to reply, someone shouted from the next room, "Detective, fall back! Don't engage!"

Exchanging a quick glance, Wilson and Forrester ran into dispatch. "What's going on?"

"Detective Hawkins called in after pulling over a bus," said a young, brunette female officer. "When he got close, he spotted a bearded man holding a gun to the driver's head. The driver hit the gas and took off, nearly running him over."

"Give me that." Forrester grabbed the officer's radio. "Detective! Where are you now?"

"I'm trailing behind the 47 bus on Brookline," Hawkins said. "They're swerving all over the road. Who's this?"

"Special Agent Forrester. Why did you pull over that bus? You're supposed to be bringing in Dr. Silva."

"I am. She's on the bus."

Forrester's eyes bulged. "I'm ordering you to stop that bus. Use whatever means necessary."

"Hey," Wilson said. "There are people who could get hurt. Police policy is to minimize risk to bystanders."

"Weren't you paying attention?" Forrester shouted. "That's Martins! If we don't stop him, he'll get away."

The wild look in Forrester's eyes squelched Wilson's retort. Forrester's vendetta against Quinn had made him desperate. Wilson knew how dangerous desperate men could be. He took a step back.

The agent glared at Wilson, recollecting his composure before saying into the handset, "Detective, keep pursuit. We'll send backup to help you capture the gunman."

"You better do it fast," Hawkins said. "Son of a bitch!"

"Hawkins? What's happening? Report."

"He's swerving all over Mass Ave. I got a three-car collision at the Sidney intersection."

"We'll send an ambulance," Forrester said. "You just stay on that bus."

"I'm pulling up alongside them."

A tense silence filled the next three heartbeats. Forrester shot Wilson an anxious glance.

"Gunshots fired!" Hawkins's yell cut through the static. "I'm pulling back. We're in the middle of downtown Cambridge. Too many civilians."

"Damn it." Forrester spun toward the dispatcher. "Where's that backup?"

"Cambridge PD sent three black and whites to intercept."

"Not soon enough," Forrester replied. Then he clicked the handset back on. "Company's coming," he told Hawkins. "Use a PIT when they arrive and then take down the gunman."

"You want him to ram a bus? On an icy street?" Wilson said. "Even if a cruiser had the weight to push a bus, a PIT maneuver could make it skid right into a crowded sidewalk."

"Do you have a better idea, Detective?"

Frowning, Wilson shook his head. They were out of options. If they didn't stop that bus now, it'd ram right into Central Square, one of the busiest intersections in Cambridge. But if Martins were as dangerous as Forrester claimed, then even if they stopped the bus, how would they stop him?

CHAPTER THIRTY-SIX

As Cristina regained consciousness, colors pinwheeled through her field of vision. Cotton clogged her ears. She tried to sit. A gunshot sounded, followed by the crash of broken glass. Someone screamed. The bus swerved beneath her. Cristina thudded against the side of the bus.

Wincing, she dragged herself upright. Santos's wheelchair lay upturned in the aisle. The teenagers cowered in their seat. Santos stood next to the driver, holding a gun to his head as the bus rocketed forward.

Cristina clutched the seat back. "You're going to get us killed!" she shouted at Santos.

"Shut up." Santos said, turning back toward her. His eyes were wild and twitching.

The police siren muddled with her ringing ears and pounding pulse. Cristina glanced at the other passengers, the fear in their eyes chilling her core. She couldn't let anyone else get hurt. Locking her gaze with Santos's, she said, "It's not too late. We can work this out. Put down the gun and let's—"

"Don't analyze me," he said. "I'm not crazy. I came to you for help, and you want to lock me up."

"What are you—?"

"I won't go down without a fight, Doctor." He pressed the gun against the driver's temple. "Lose the cops or you're a dead man."

"Mister, I'm doing the best I can, but this is a bus for crissakes." The driver's hands shook. "It's as maneuverable as—" They hit a pothole. The driver jerked against the steering wheel, then swerved back into the lane. "I'm going as fast as I can, okay?"

"Not good enough." Santos glared over his shoulder. He snarled like a rabid dog. "This is your fault, Dr. Silva. Remember my face. Next time you see me will be your last."

Cristina was too stunned to reply.

Santos held the gun level with the driver's head. "If you value your life, slow the bus to twenty miles per hour, count to ten, and then accelerate again to this speed. After that, don't slow down. Got it?"

"Yes, sir." The driver kept his eyes locked on the road. The bus decelerated. "Anything you say."

Santos marched backward down the aisle. Glancing at Cristina as he passed her, his eyes softened. Before she could react, he sprinted to the back of the bus, shoved open the door and leaped outside.

Forrester hung up his phone. "The Bureau is sending a SWAT team and a hostage negotiator. But it'll take them at least ten minutes to arrive on scene." He grabbed the radio. "Detective, we're out of time. Use the PIT. Now."

"Okay, Agent," Hawkins said. "I'm pulling into position."

"You're sure about this?" Wilson asked with his arms crossed, squeezing his biceps to restrain himself. "There are civilians on that bus."

"You mean, your girlfriend?" Forrester simpered. "Don't you trust your partner?"

"Trust isn't the issue here. You said Martins is highly

dangerous. If he's the gunman, everyone on that bus is at risk—including my partner."

Forrester shot Wilson a withering glance, but then widened his eyes. "You're right. Where's that backup from Cambridge?"

"Intercepting now," said the dispatcher.

"Good. They can secure the scene until SWAT arrives." Forrester's brow furrowed and he looked sincerely worried. "Let's hope your boy can pull this off," he said to Wilson.

Then they waited. Stared at each other. Checked the wall clock. Four minutes since they last heard from Hawkins. The dispatcher coughed nervously. Her partner answered a routine patrol check-in.

Five minutes.

Wilson clenched and unclenched his fingers, feeling helpless. Hating the feeling.

Six minutes.

"Dispatch," Hawkins finally said over the radio. "Hawkins reporting in."

"Go ahead, Detective."

"The bus is secure. Didn't even need the PIT. The driver pulled over."

Forrester snatched the radio. "What about the gunman?"

"Gone. He jumped out the back door while the bus was still moving."

"What? Didn't anyone pursue?"

"Two from Cambridge doubled back, but it sounds like he got away. The driver gave a positive ID of Martins from the BOLO flyer."

"Damn it." Forrester slammed the handset on the dispatcher's desk. "We had him."

Wilson wanted to ask Hawkins if Cristina was okay but knew Forrester would attack him. Instead, he said, "More like Martins had us. He used the bus as a distraction."

"I've got worse news," Hawkins said.

Wilson and Forrester exchanged glances. Forrester shook his head and gestured toward the radio.

Wilson picked up the handset. "Go ahead, Rick."

"Dr. Silva's here. She's got a nasty bruise on her head, but she's okay."

A small sigh escaped Wilson's lips. "What's the worse news?"

"Witnesses say Martins had a heated conversation with the doctor before he freaked out. It looks like their relationship is more complicated than his one-way obsession."

Forrester's lip twitched in what might've been a self-congratulating smile. Wilson clenched the radio, his knuckles whitening. It was Boston all over again. He'd lost his objectivity.

It stopped here and now.

Into the radio, he said, "Bring her in."

CHAPTER THIRTY-SEVEN

"For the last time, I don't know where Martins went." Cristina jammed her fists against her temples. An overhead lamp bathed her and a wooden table in cold white light. The foul tang of nicotine and vomit in the air caused her gut, already agitated by shock and betrayal, to spasm. Each repeated question aggravated her pounding headache. "He didn't say where he was going before he punched me."

Agent Vasquez tapped her index finger against her cheek as she paced by a wall-sized mirror. "But you do admit you've been in recent contact with him. And not only today."

"Yes."

"So, you've been consorting with a wanted terrorist?"

"I already told you. I didn't know who he was."

"Tell me again."

Cristina took a heavy, resigned breath. "He approached me. He used the name Sebastian dos Santos."

Twisting her lips, Vasquez glanced over her shoulder at the mirror and then turned back to Cristina. "And just what did Sebastian dos Santos want with you?"

"He claimed an organization called Zero Dark killed my parents and stole my memories."

"Zero Dark." Vasquez nodded. "What do you know about them?"

"Just that someone named Quinn is their leader."

Vasquez lingered next to Cristina's chair. "Martins worked for Zero Dark."

"I discovered that the other day," said Cristina. The agent's accusatory tone gnawed at her. "Am I being charged with something?"

"No, but you're a primary witness to Martins' crimes." Vasquez tilted her head, studying Cristina's face. "He assaulted you. Don't you want to help us catch him?"

Pain nipped at Cristina's bruised cheek. The memory of Santos's expression before he jumped off the bus made her shudder. Was he insane or in full control? "Of course, I do. But right now, I'm feeling more like a suspect than a victim."

"Well, you haven't been exactly forthcoming."

"I told Detective Wilson everything I know."

"Everything? Are you sure there's nothing else you want to share?"

A cold wind blew onto the back of Cristina's neck from overhead. Santos's voice replayed in her mind. *Why would they believe a woman who was found waving a gun around, babbling about victims and killers nobody saw?* If she was in danger of losing her mind, she needed to be careful about volunteering information. Cristina stared back, saying nothing.

After a moment, when it seemed Vasquez was evaluating the rhythm of Cristina's breathing, the agent reached into her pocket and withdrew an evidence bag containing a crumpled scrap of newsprint. She laid it on the table before Cristina. "Can you identify this?"

Cristina recognized it instantly. "It's an article from a Brazilian newspaper, about a research team studying—"

"I know what it's about, Dr. Silva. Did Martins give you this?"

"Yes."

The agent pointed at a woman in the front row. "Is that you?"

"No."

"She looks like you."

Cristina shrugged.

Vasquez indicated a man in the back row. "What about him?"

"That is Federico Gomes."

"Friend of yours?"

"Hardly. He's the one who attacked me in my own apartment."

"Why?"

"I don't know."

Vasquez leaned on the table with both fists. She squinted at Cristina. "How do you know his name?"

Cristina shifted in her seat. "Santos told me."

"You two sound awfully chummy. What does he want from you in exchange for all this information?"

Cristina caught herself before saying anything about Santos's daughter. Even if they believed the story, it would only make her look guilty. "He seems remorseful. Helping me is like his personal twelve-step program, even though I never asked for it."

"You don't contact him?"

"No. He just appears."

"So he's stalking you."

Cristina shrugged again.

Either frustration or anger crossed Vasquez's face, Cristina wasn't sure. Vasquez tapped the photo. "Could Gomes and Santos have been working together?"

"I don't know," Cristina said. "Santos insists they weren't. He looked surprised when I said that Gomes had shot Stacey Peterman."

"Yes, Ms. Peterman, whom you *claim* tried to defame you on behalf of Zero Dark."

Cristina hesitated at the agent's tone. "That's right."

"How?"

"Stacey said that I had prescribed medications that caused

her brother Jerry to go insane. But he wasn't her brother, and he wasn't taking the medication I prescribed."

"Really?" Vasquez's eyebrows arched. "How do you know?"

"The medical examiner, Dr. Morgan, found no traces of it in his blood."

"Why were you speaking to the medical examiner?"

Cristina stared at her incredulously. "Jerry was my patient. I needed to determine the risk to the other patients I treat."

"I see." Vasquez touched her chin, seeming to digest that. "So, suddenly Stacey Peterman had a change of heart, cleared your name and told you the truth."

"Yes, right before Gomes killed her."

"But her body was never found."

Cristina's breath hitched. Santos was right. They thought she was crazy. Or a threat.

"Gomes must have hidden it—done something with it. I saw her dying."

Vasquez cocked her head. "Maybe you killed her."

Cristina's cheeks grew cold. "I never killed anyone."

"Not that you remember."

They locked gazes. Cristina's pulse raced.

She knows what we did, the voice whispered. *Even if you don't.*

Cristina erected a mental wall to block out the voice. "Do I need a lawyer?"

"Let me just be sure I have this right," Vasquez said. "You're certain Federico Gomes killed Ms. Peterman."

Cristina jutted her chin. "Positive."

"Where is he now?"

"I have no idea. But you should find him. He's more dangerous than Santos."

"Is that right?" Vasquez opened a folder, withdrew a photo, and positioned it on the table in front of Cristina. "Look familiar?"

Despite the grim pallor, the frozen mask of shock and fear, and the gaping wound in his forehead, Cristina recognized Gomes. At the sight of the grim photo, her stomach twisted. "Oh, my God. What happened to him?"

"That's what we want to know. He was shot at close range, head-on, indicating he likely knew the killer." Vasquez circled like a vulture. "Any idea who it might have been?"

Cristina's throat tightened. "You don't think I killed him?"

A thin smile appeared on the agent's face. "If I were a psychologist, I might call your question identifying with the crime. Something you want to confess?"

Images tossed and crashed in Cristina's mind: Gomes, the car crash, the shadow man from her nightmares. She shut her eyes and chased them away. "I'd like to talk to a lawyer."

"Of course, but I have one more question."

Cristina squeezed her fingers together. She could do this. Today was hard. Hell, it couldn't get worse. But she could handle it. "What is it?"

Vasquez leaned over, laid her palms on the table, and looked Cristina in the eye. "If Gomes killed Stacey Peterman, how did she board a plane back to Utah that afternoon?"

"Stacey Peterman's alive?" Detective Wilson tore away from the one-way mirror to face Agent Forrester. Detective Hawkins stood next to him, looking confused. There hadn't been much time to fill him in after he arrived with Cristina in tow. "How long have you known this?"

"Long enough." Forrester trained his gaze on the women in the interrogation room as he sipped his coffee. "We already tasked the Salt Lake City office with tracking her down."

"And when were you planning to include us?"

"When you start acting like team players." Forrester didn't

flinch. "You know, filling in little details like your partner was already tailing Dr. Silva when you called him."

Heat prickled at the back of Wilson's neck. "Okay, I should've told you but—"

"Yes, you should have." Forrester turned, eyes blazing. "Because of you, we lost Martins."

"How is that my fault?"

"If I had known Dr. Silva was on the move, I would've called in SWAT right away. I would've told Hawkins to keep his distance until we had the trap set." He wagged his finger in Wilson's face. "But that's because I'm trying to catch the bad guys, not sleep with them."

The heat burst into wildfire, rushing through Wilson's cheeks. "You son of a—"

"Gary." Hawkins grabbed Wilson's arm. "I need to talk to you outside."

Wilson was startled. He glanced between Hawkins and Forrester before allowing his shoulders to relax. "Yeah, I need some air."

Once in the hallway, Hawkins said, "Spill it."

"What?"

"Whatever's going on between you and Forrester. Why did you lie to him about where I was?"

"I don't know. He stormed in here like Napoleon and took over everything."

"So what? Martins was always their collar. We should've been cooperating right from the start."

Wilson bit back a sharp retort. As usual, his partner knew him too well. "I know, but there's something I didn't tell you about that Boston City Council case."

"What happened?"

"Three days into the investigation, forensics identified the weapon that killed the councilor as a .40-caliber Glock 22." He checked for a reaction before adding, "Used to be FBI standard issue."

"Glocks are pretty common."

"True, but I got one of my hunches. It took a while, but I found an email in the councilor's account from a blocked sender. It seems the councilor had embezzled almost a hundred and twenty million dollars from public funds. The email demanded a quarter of that in exchange for diverting a federal investigation. The councilor countered by threatening to expose the blackmailer—a day before he died."

"What's this got to do with Forrester?"

"Back when I brought the emails to his attention, he got a weird look on his face, told me he'd handle it. Next thing I knew, the case got declared a suicide and the Feds cleared out. A week later, my indiscretion leaked out and I got shipped here."

Hawkins scratched his forehead. "You think Forrester's crooked?"

"I can't prove it, but he's definitely unstable. When he was ordering you to try a PIT on the bus, he looked like his mind had snapped. I know he wants revenge against this dude Quinn, but he seems equally obsessed with Dr. Silva."

"And you're not?"

"It's not like that," Wilson said. "I can't explain it, but I think she is a victim. She's caught up in something big. I have no idea why, but I believe her amnesia story. If that happened to me, you bet your ass I'd do whatever it took to find answers."

Hawkins stared up at the ceiling. "You're going to get us fired or killed before I can retire, aren't you?"

"Sorry," Wilson said. "I can't let this go. I promise I'll be more cooperative, but until I know what's going on, you're the only one I fully trust."

After a tense moment, Hawkins glanced over Wilson's

shoulder. "Looks like Vasquez is taking a break. Dial back your feelings until we know Forrester's angle, okay?"

Wilson nodded. They returned to the observation room, where Vasquez was updating Forrester. Through the one-way mirror, Wilson saw Cristina bury her face in her hands.

"I don't think she's acting," Vasquez said. "She was clearly hiding something about Martins—or Santos, whatever—but her emotions appeared genuine about everything else. She looked shocked to discover that Gomes was dead and Stacey Peterman was alive."

"Work with crazy people long enough," Forrester said as he studied Cristina's face through the mirror, "and you learn how to react to anything. She's our connection to Quinn."

"Whom she knows nothing about," Vasquez said.

"But she knows about Martins and Gomes. That's enough reason to keep at her."

"Detectives." Sergeant Davis stuck his head through the doorway. "There's a call for either one of you."

"You take it, Rick," Wilson said. After Hawkins stepped outside, Wilson said, "Look, either Cristina Silva is a young Meryl Streep and she'll keep playing dumb through another ten hours of interrogation, or she really doesn't remember anything that will help us. Now that we know Martins' alias, we should lock down the city and start a manhunt."

"Worms wait until they think the eagle has gone before resurfacing," Forrester said with a dour expression. "We'll catch Martins. But that's not your real concern, is it? You think we should turn Dr. Silva loose."

"Not loose," Wilson said, "but we're wasting time holding her here. We know Martins wants her help. We can use her to draw him out."

Forrester exchanged glances with Vasquez. She shrugged.

He glared at Wilson. "How do we know she's not dangerous? I'm still not convinced she didn't kill Gomes."

"I don't—" Wilson stopped when he felt Hawkins tap his shoulder with info from the call. As his partner whispered in his ear, Wilson's feet felt lighter. Timing was everything. He said to Forrester, "I can convince you Silva didn't kill Gomes."

"How?"

"Detective Hawkins just spoke to the medical examiner. Gomes' time of death was around ten thirty this morning." Wilson suppressed a smirk. "Three hours after Hawkins saw Dr. Silva arrive at her office."

CHAPTER THIRTY-EIGHT

"Not that I don't appreciate the courtesy," Cristina dug her fingers into the leather seat as her heart raced, "but you didn't have to drive me home."

"Nonsense." Detective Wilson changed lanes. "I doubt very much that you want to take the bus."

Cristina snapped her eyes shut and forced her breathing rate to slow. "I think I'll take the T from now on."

"Am I driving too fast?"

"No, I'm not good around cars. Ever since … the crash."

"Oh, yeah. PTSD, right?"

She opened her eyes and focused on him. It helped a little. "Technically, no, since I don't have flashbacks. But close enough."

"But you remember what happened that day?"

Her head throbbed. Any more questions and it would probably explode. "Can we not talk about it, please?"

Wilson returned his attention to the road. "Sure."

Cristina felt a pang of regret. He was the only one that day who had shown her the slightest compassion. Taking out her frustration on him wouldn't solve anything. "I'm sorry. I'm tired."

"You had a long day."

"The longest." Funny. His nose didn't look so crooked anymore. "I want to thank you."

"I told you, it's not a big deal."

"No, I mean, yes, thank you for the ride, but I mean thank you for taking my side."

"I don't take sides," Wilson said. "I look for the truth. And I think you're telling the truth about your memory being stolen."

"What changed your mind?"

"Too many pieces that don't fit. The Golem. Quinn. Deleted files." He shook his head. "At this point, I wouldn't be shocked if you told me aliens and Bigfoot are involved."

Cristina couldn't help smiling. "Aliens would be less confusing. To be honest, I'm not sure what to believe anymore."

After a pause, Wilson said, "You know, my mom went insane. Killed herself and my dad."

"Oh, my God. I'm so sorry."

"I was a teenager. There were signs that I missed at the time. Everyone did." He swallowed hard. "It's why I became a cop. If someone had listened the first or second or third time she had called for help, things might've been different."

A moment of silence stretched between them. Cristina understood what he meant, but she couldn't stop thinking about Jerry and Carl. What signs had she missed?

"Listen," Wilson said, "I may be able to help, but I need you to come clean about a few things."

An uncomfortable chill spread over her face. "Like what?"

"For starters, what does Martins want from you?"

She hesitated. Could she trust him? Besides Andrea, he was the only one who seemed willing to listen. "He says he needs my help saving his daughter."

"His daughter?"

"He says that she's being held prisoner by Zero Dark. That's how they forced him to do all those horrible things, like burn down our house."

"And cut your brake lines?"

Cristina bristled as she remembered Wilson accusing her of being involved. Softly, she said, "He said that wasn't him."

Wilson steered onto Elm Street and then glanced at her again. "I don't think it was."

"You don't?"

"The car shop's owner said he checked the car after Martins finished and it was fine." Wilson hesitated. "He also said that you are not Cristina Silva."

The air thinned. Cristina rolled down the window and took a deep breath. The cold night air stung her cheeks and forehead. Setting her jaw, she closed the window and turned to him. "So, it's true. Quinn changed my identity, and probably had the Silvas killed."

"So it seems," Wilson said. He pulled up to the curb in front of Cristina's apartment and shut off the engine. "If this guy is as dangerous as Forrester claims, maybe you should enter witness protection."

"I'm not a very good witness when I don't remember anything." She studied her hands. Whose hands were they? Whose faces had they touched? "And, besides, I need to fly to Washington tomorrow."

"Washington? You can't leave town while being investigated."

"But I have to. I'm a principal investigator in a drug trial and there have been some—" She stopped herself. How much should she disclose? If Wilson knew Zero Dark controlled ReMind, he'd be obliged to tell the Feds. They'd confiscate her pills, ban her from traveling, and she'd lose any chance she had of finding a way to hold onto her sanity. She cleared her throat. "Complications. It's only an hour-and-a-half flight. I'll help them get things back on track and be back before anyone misses me."

Wilson's eyes danced, scanning her face. "Sounds like an important drug."

"It is."

He held her gaze for another moment. "All right. I'll cover for you."

Relief washed over her. "Thank you."

"You'll have to sneak out between patrols. Aim for the half hour mark."

"I'll be careful." An idea struck her. Cristina dug through her purse and pulled out a black cell phone, which she offered to him. "Santos gave this to me. The number's no good anymore, but maybe you can use it to find him."

Wilson tucked it into his pocket. "Thanks. I'm sure it's hard for you to trust anyone right now."

"It is. But trust goes both ways." She tried to find a better way to express her gratitude but couldn't. She reached for the door handle.

Wilson's hand grazed her shoulder. Cristina turned back. Found him leaning close, gazing into her eyes. Her heart raced. His head drifted closer. She imagined him grabbing her by the neck and kissing her. Excitement tingled her shoulders. Her lips parted in expectation.

Don't be an idiot. You don't deserve love. You don't even exist.

The voice surged through Cristina's mind, powerful enough to slam her against the seat. Fear and doubt flooded her body. Blinking, she tried to force it away.

"What's wrong?" His brow wrinkled. "Are you okay?"

"I'm sorry, I just—" Cristina closed her eyes and took deep breaths. Her nerves settled. She prayed that when she opened her eyes again, it would be one minute earlier, and Wilson would be by her side, waiting to embrace her. She opened her eyes.

He continued to stare at her like flowers had sprung from her forehead.

Cristina forced a smile. "Like you said, it's been a long day. Thanks again for the ride."

"Yeah." Wilson nodded at the floor several times before looking up and making eye contact. The corner of his mouth pulled upward. "No problem."

After stepping outside, a terrible thought entered Cristina's mind: one that had popped up repeatedly but now seemed terrifyingly more likely.

She stuck her head inside and asked, "What if when I find out who I am ..." She touched her forehead and laughed bitterly. She'd worked so hard to rediscover Cristina Silva. Time wasted on the wrong person. "What if I'm a bad guy?"

Wilson studied her, as if he'd had the same thought. Then he chuckled. "I've dealt with a lot of bad guys. Whoever you are, you're not one of them."

A warm blanket wrapped around her. She smiled. "Good night, Detective."

CHAPTER THIRTY-NINE

"Tell me again why we had to sneak out at five thirty for an eight A.M. flight?" Andrea shook her head as she stuffed her bag under the seat of the Airbus A320. "Or do you have a thing for twenty-four-hour Dunkin' Donuts?"

"I told you." Cristina tightened her seatbelt. "Wilson said I needed to leave early to give him time—"

"Time to stop dreaming about you, I bet."

Cristina's cheeks flushed.

Andrea laughed. "Oh, don't get embarrassed. If that man offered me a ride home, I'd forget everything else, including waking you up to travel with me."

Cristina cringed as she recalled Wilson's hurt look after she pulled away from him. If only she could tell him what she was experiencing. She squeezed Andrea's hand. "No, you wouldn't. You're always there for me. And you didn't have to come. Gomes is dead."

"But Santos is still out there. As long as he's free, I've got your back."

Cristina stuck the patient files she was bringing to ReMind into the seat pocket. "I'm not worried about him."

"You should be, after everything that's happened." Andrea stared at her. "You don't seem worried. Why do you look so calm?"

Cristina hesitated. Despite everything, Wilson's confirmation that she wasn't completely crazy had given her some relief. But how could she share that with her best friend? "I'm eager to get the Recognate study back on track. I left Grizabella enough food for tonight, but I want to return to Boston as soon as possible."

"Not me. I could use a break from the Arctic." Andrea searched overhead. "Where's the call button so I can order us some drinks?"

"It's an early morning commuter flight. They don't serve alcohol."

"No alcohol?" Andrea stood and scanned the compact plane. "What kind of cheap-ass airline is this?"

"It's only a ninety-minute flight. When we land, you can go to the airport bar." Cristina nudged her friend back into her seat. "You do know most people don't start drinking twenty minutes after breakfast?"

"Mami, when this is over, we're checking into a Club Med and partying until we forget our names. Again." She winked.

Cristina smiled, but when her friend turned away, she fingered the silver locket under her blouse. Somewhere out there, a woman had forgotten her father. No matter what kind of man Santos was, his daughter deserved to know the truth.

And so did Cristina. She clutched the locket and closed her eyes. If the key to unraveling her identity was at ReMind Pharmaceuticals, she had to find it.

"Good morning, Detective." Agent Vasquez sidled up to Wilson's desk. She wore her hair down and it draped her shoulders. Her cheeks had a pink flush. She breathed deeply, as if collecting her thoughts. "I want to apologize for my partner's behavior yesterday."

Wilson tilted his head. She was acting like a nervous schoolgirl.

Was she for real? It was a big change from the austere federal agent from yesterday. "That's kind of you, but it's not like you're his keeper."

"No, I'm not. But I can—and should—rein him in when he gets out of line." She sat on the corner of Wilson's desk. "I know this case is personal, but Forrester is letting it consume him."

Wilson could only stare. Was she really coming to him for moral counseling? He caught a whiff of perfume. Or did she have other motives? Like his life wasn't confusing enough already. How stupid had he been, making a move on Cristina? Had he learned nothing from Cambridge? And her reaction had only made it worse. The last thing he needed was to misread another woman's signals.

Hesitantly, he said, "Well, if Zero Dark is operating in our neighborhood, we'll do everything we can to help stop them. Maybe you can convince Forrester we want to help."

A small but warm smile crossed her lips. "I'll try."

Vasquez held Wilson's gaze a second longer than professional comfort allowed.

He coughed onto the back of his hand. "Where is Agent Forrester, anyway?"

Her smile wavered. Vasquez straightened her back and was suddenly all business. "Searching for the murder weapon that killed Gomes."

"CSI already scoured the alley where they discovered him."

"Charles could find a drop of blood in the ocean." She cleared her throat. "He'll be even more obsessed when he learns what I found at the morgue."

"What do you mean?"

"We sent Gomes's prints and dental impressions to Quantico. So far, they've haven't found any domestic records that match them, not even a birth certificate or visa. They're contacting Interpol now."

"He entered the country illegally?"

"It seems so." She glanced over her shoulder before lowering her voice. "But when I arrived, the medical examiner was autopsying another of Dr. Silva's patients. Carl Franklin."

"Franklin?" Wilson cocked his head. "That's the suicide I investigated weeks ago. Why was he autopsying him now?"

"Apparently, Dr. Silva asked him. She seems to think Franklin's and Peterman's deaths are related."

"That doesn't make sense. One jumped out of a window and the other shot up a subway."

"They may have ended up in different places, but she's not wrong." Vasquez pulled a paper from her pocket and handed it to him.

Wilson unfolded it to find a printed mugshot.

"I recognized his face and sent it to records also," Vasquez said. "That man, Carl Franklin—his real name is Carlin Pickens. Number eight on the FBI's Most Wanted list for domestic terrorism. He was involved in the Aryan Nation."

No question it was the same stiff. "How'd Carlin Pickens end up in Cristina's practice? And why'd he kill himself?"

"Maybe you can find out."

"Me?" Wilson said.

"Dr. Silva trusts you. Talk to her. Maybe she'll tell you something she hasn't already shared with others."

Wilson's tongue went numb. Something like Martins' burner phone? Or that she skipped town to visit a drug company in DC? He forced a smile. "Sure. I'll give her a call and let you know what I find out."

"Thanks," Vasquez said. "I'm going to see if our BOLO on Martins turned up any hits." She turned to the door and then stopped, looked back, and grinned. "See how much better things go when we work together?"

After she left, Wilson stared at Carl Franklin's mugshot. At least two of Cristina's patients were terrorists. Was she playing him? At least now he understood why he had gotten a weird vibe from Franklin's suicide. Was it possible that this death was connected to Zero Dark?

Wilson drummed his fingers on his desk, trying to shut out the searing heat behind his ear. He'd found no usable prints on the burner phone Cristina gave him and hitting redial yielded a "number not in service" message. When he called the Salt Lake precinct, he was told Stacey Peterman had disappeared after departing her flight. Martins was still in hiding and Quinn's identity unknown. *Where else am I supposed to look for answers?*

His cell phone rang. Startled, he answered.

"Detective," a thick voice said. "You told me to call if I remembered anything."

Wilson recognized the voice from the mechanic's shop. "Mr. Feldman. That's right."

"The detective who stated Francisco Martins had been cleared of charges. You recall I told you about him?"

"Yes, I do. Did you remember his name?"

"I don't want any problems with the police," Feldman said.

"You won't get in any trouble." Wilson tried to remain calm, hoping he would get straight answers this time. "I'll keep what you tell me strictly confidential."

"You know, I may have forgotten to mention that I had to take a call and left him with the Silvas' car for a few minutes. After speaking to you and thinking about what happened to them—I don't know, maybe he did something to the car. But why would he do that?"

Wilson's pulse quickened. "I don't know. That's a good question, and I promise I'll find out. But I can't do that without knowing the detective's name."

"Yes, yes, of course. I've been trying to remember. It was a long time ago."

"Take your time." Wilson bit his lower lip.

"He was tall, muscular. His face had many wrinkles, as if he'd been to Hell and back."

"Okay."

"It's ... Hold on, I remembered before I called you. Something with a P ..." Another pause. "Parker. His name was Mitchell Parker."

CHAPTER FORTY

Cristina stood outside the boxy office building wedged between a furniture warehouse and a falafel restaurant. She scanned the area. American flags billowed proudly on masts suspended from the historic Mayflower Hotel two blocks away. Cars rushed both ways down the busy street as people hustled to wherever they were headed, blowing on their hands though it was at least twenty degrees warmer in DC than it had been in Boston. Cristina tugged at her scarf and looked back at the building. A sign on the front of the building read *ReMind Pharmaceuticals*.

Cristina stepped through the revolving door and halted, stunned by the surprisingly expansive lobby. Glistening marble floors. Lavish onyx pillars. A sparkling water column tumbling from an ornate glass chandelier into a sandstone basin lined with wrought-iron ivy. Over the basin, a statue carved in Greco-Roman style of a woman holding a book in one hand. A fountain bubbled from her diadem into the basin.

Cristina breathed in the unexpected, luxurious scent of cinnamon. She marveled at the company's ability to afford such opulence.

"Dr. Silva?" A blond woman called from the marble reception desk.

Cristina approached the desk. The name *Kitty* was embla-
zoned in pink script on the left breast of the woman's white lab
coat. On the right, the word *ReMind* overlaid a drawing of a brain
encircled by ivy.

Kitty's teeth glittered between scarlet lips when she smiled.
"Welcome to ReMind."

Cristina swallowed as she prepared for the upcoming confrontation. She could've used Andrea's support. But Simmons had
made it clear to Devi that civilians weren't allowed in the R&D
area, so Andrea had gone to see the modern art exhibit at the
Smithsonian. When Cristina was done, they planned to meet at
Farragut North Metro Station and head from there to the airport.
For now, Cristina was on her own.

"Thanks," Cristina replied to Kitty. "Is Mr. Simmons ready
to see me?"

"He's waiting for you upstairs." Kitty waved and a bear-sized
man with close-cropped hair and a gray uniform lumbered over
to them. He towered nearly a foot over Cristina. An emblem similar to the one on Kitty's coat adorned his left shoulder. His face
was frozen in a scowl. "Mateo, our security chief, will escort you."

"Security?" Cristina spotted a pistol butt poking out beneath
the man's jacket. Her mouth went dry. Santos had reassured Cristina they wouldn't kill her—at least until they had what they
wanted. Forcing herself to remain calm, she faked a smile. "Afraid
I'll walk off with a few samples?"

Not a facial muscle budged on Mateo's face. "Yes. Open
your bag."

Cristina's smile faded. Slowly, she removed her backpack and
unzipped it. Mateo poked around her books, charts and spare
clothes.

He nodded. "Now, spread your arms."

"What?"

He pointed at a sign on the desk. All visitors are subject to search upon entry.

Cristina did as Mateo asked. He ran a wand under her armpits and down her sides. It bleeped over her pocket.

"Remove it," he said.

"It's my phone." She held it out.

"I'll need to keep it until you leave." He snatched it and stuck it in his pocket.

"Hey!"

"No photos, no outside calls. Precautions." He spun on his heel. "Follow me."

Cristina hesitated, recalling Santos's warning. *Listen, observe, and remember.* If ReMind were hiding something, she'd have to rely on her own observations and memory, unreliable as they may be. With a glance at Kitty, who smiled back with saccharine sweetness, Cristina followed Mateo into the elevator. They rode up in silence. After a minute, the doors opened.

"This way." Mateo led the way through a maze of corridors. Down a dim hallway, he stopped at a solid oak door. He knocked twice, then stood at attention.

After an uncomfortable wait, the door swung open, revealing a distinguished African American man with a clean-shaven face. Gray hair curled around his ears. A pair of bushy eyebrows framed gentle amber eyes. When Julius Simmons caught her gaze, an inviting smile bloomed on his face. Cristina tried to mask her surprise. Instead of the monster she had expected, he looked like a shorter Morgan Freeman.

"Dr. Silva, good to meet you face to face at last." Simmons's handshake was warm and firm. He nodded to Mateo. "I'll take it from here. Thanks."

With a grunt, Mateo marched away.

"Please come in." Simmons led Cristina through a modest

foyer, around a corner, and into a more elaborate office framed
by gold-trimmed walls. A leather couch hugged the near wall,
opposite a beautiful cherry desk. On the desk, a Dali-esque melt-
ing clock ticked. The smell of cinnamon permeated the room.
Simmons motioned to a plush office chair as he sat behind his
desk. "Have a seat and let's chat."

Just a friendly chat. Right. She sat.

"Let me get right to the point." Simmons locked his gaze with
hers. "We've run into a few snags, and we're hoping you can help."

"Of course," Cristina said. "That's why I've come."

"You came because I threatened you." Simmons grinned
sheepishly. "I apologize for that. When you deal with politicians
and federal agencies like I do, you're used to playing hardball. I
hope you don't take it personally."

"Not at all." Cristina lifted her chin, relaxing her shoulders.
Maybe Santos had lied. Maybe ReMind had nothing to do with
Zero Dark. "Why does everything smell like cinnamon?"

"A study out of Chicago suggests cinnamon stimulates hippo-
campal plasticity and improves memory." When Cristina stared,
he shrugged. "What? A CEO can't keep up on the hot studies?"

Cristina blushed. No, Julius Simmons was nothing like she
had expected.

He leaned forward. "Did you bring your records?"

"Yes." She pulled the charts from her pack and placed them
on the desk. "What do you hope to find?"

Simmons flipped through the files and looked up. "Are these
all of your patients in the Recognate study?"

"Only six enrolled. You rejected the others."

"How many did you refer?"

"Thirty-two."

"Thirty-two?" Simmons scrunched up his face. "Why where
they rejected?"

"You tell me. I emailed Frank multiple times and he never gave me a good answer. He said they didn't meet inclusion criteria."

"Inclusion rates at our other sites are close to sixty percent." He pushed aside the files. "Yours is eighteen. Of those, a third dropped out."

"They didn't drop out," Cristina said. "They died."

"Another shouldn't have been included."

Cristina's jaw slackened. Did he really brush over their deaths?

"Normally, we conduct a thorough review of subjects who don't fall within inclusion criteria, but Dr. Alvarez decided to approve Mrs. Watterson without a review."

"Why would he do that?"

"He trusted your judgment. Don't worry. I assure you it won't happen again."

Cristina caught the undertone of his comment and cringed. "Again, I apologize for putting you in a difficult position."

"Forget it. We have more important business to discuss." Simmons interlocked his hands against his chin. "What I'm about to tell you is confidential. You're not to share it with anyone, or there will be consequences. Do you understand?"

The way he said *consequences* sent prickles along the hairs on Cristina's arms. "I understand."

Simmons removed a plain brown folder from a desk drawer. He flipped it open and handed her a stack of papers. The front sheet displayed a list of names. Most were unfamiliar, but near the bottom she recognized two: Jerry Peterman and Carl Franklin.

"That's our record of adverse events, Dr. Silva. Over the past six months, fifteen subjects have died or been institutionalized for intractable psychosis." His gaze took on a hard edge. "I need your help finding out why."

CHAPTER FORTY-ONE

As Cristina thumbed through the ream of paper Simmons handed her, her stomach churned. She wasn't as shocked as she might have been. She recalled the news clippings Santos had given her. There had been the man from Spokane—death by self-inflicted stabbing. She swallowed hard and tried to appear surprised. "How has this not been all over the news?"

"Like I said, this is a sensitive matter." Simmons tucked away the folder. "We've kept our involvement out of the media for the good of the project."

"Good of the project? Have you explained to these people's families how you're protecting *the good of the project?*"

"I don't expect you to understand the business. Our marketing director is negotiating with an important client. We need to launch Recognate sooner than expected."

"This isn't about business." Heat crawled up the back of Cristina's neck. "This is about patient safety."

"Everything is about business," Simmons brow furrowed and his nostrils flared. "The first few subjects had unreported histories of mental illness. Then more cases popped up, and we became concerned."

"But not enough to suspend the study to confirm safety?"

"Actually, we very nearly did." Simmons gave Cristina an accusatory look. "When Mr. Peterman drew national attention."

Cristina's cheeks flushed. Simmons knew how to point the finger back at her. "So, why didn't you shut it down then?"

"When you told me about the complications your other patients were having, I realized we had a larger problem."

Here it is, Cristina thought. There's something wrong with the drug. "What is that problem?"

Simmons tilted his head. "Have you been experiencing any headaches?"

"An occasional dull throb. I've been under a lot of stress."

"Mood swings?"

Cristina caught the undertone of his question. "Are you asking if I'm impaired?"

"It's well-known that amnesiacs often suffer from despair and hopelessness. It wouldn't surprise me if you self-medicated."

Cristina squeezed her fingers together, trying to maintain her grip on something tangible. *Give them nothing they don't already know*, Santos had said. If he was right, this was all a game to find out what she remembered. Two could play that game.

"My amnesia is under control," she said. "And I wasn't involved in those thirteen other deaths. Are you asking your other researchers if they're impaired?"

His smile faltered. "This isn't a witch hunt. We're doing a root cause analysis so we can treat the problem."

"Right," Cristina said, "and your goal is to ensure Recognate is safe—not to sweep problems under the carpet before the DSMB audits your outcomes."

A vein bulged on Simmons' forehead. His jaw tightened. Cristina retreated into her chair. Had she pushed too hard?

"Safety is always our number one priority," Simmons said as if reading a script. "I've already notified the Data Safety Monitoring Board that I'm requesting a thorough review, including laboratory analysis, of all subjects. I imagine you've already done the same for your patients."

It took a moment to register his statement. "I'm expecting results soon."

"Please let me know when you get them. Since you asked, I'm also demanding drug screens from all research staff. Can't be too cautious." Simmons rose. "I appreciate your help in this matter. We'll be in touch."

Feeling confused and unsteady, Cristina stood. That was it? No interrogation? No torture? "You don't need anything else from me?"

"If you could leave your files with me, I'll review and return them by courier. I'll contact you if I think anything requires further explanation."

"I see." Cristina puzzled over why she needed to fly all the way down for a brief chat. Simmons' passive expression suggested she wouldn't get anywhere by asking. "Look, I'm sorry about jumping down your throat. It's been—well, I'm not usually—"

"I understand. You've been under a lot of stress." He held out his hand. "I hope you can appreciate our position. Forgive me if I seemed too demanding."

"No, not at all." She shook his hand. "I'm happy to help."

As Cristina turned for the door, Simmons cleared his throat. "Actually, Doctor, there's one more thing."

Cristina's shoulders tensed. "What is it?"

Simmons leered like a starving jackal. "We still need your blood."

Detective Wilson hung up after spending a half hour on the phone with the Massachusetts Internal Affairs office. He scratched that number off his list, leaned back in his desk chair, and massaged his forehead. No complaints against Detective Mitchell Parker before his death. He'd never been accused of or investigated for anything out of line. If they gave out awards for following procedure by the book, Mitchell Parker would've won every one of them.

So, why did he kill himself? And was he involved in the Silvas' deaths?

"Hey, partner." Hawkins pulled up a chair next to Wilson. He wore an uncharacteristic troubled expression. "What're you up to? You missed a briefing on workplace harassment. You been sitting here the whole time?"

"Yeah. Following up a lead. Did they miss me?"

"Nah, I covered for you." He winked. "Said you had explosive diarrhea."

Wilson cringed. "Thanks."

"No problem." Hawkins grew serious again. "Does this lead have something to do with a certain doctor?"

"Yes, but it's more like a wild goose chase. That auto mechanic said Detective Mitchell Parker was in the shop the day before the Silvas' crash, but Cristina told me he knew nothing about Martins." Wilson leaned back in his chair. "The same detective investigating the arson case investigates the car crash, and he doesn't mention the connection to her?"

"Maybe she's lying."

"I don't think so. Parker killed himself and all his records involving Cristina disappeared. This seems bigger. Like Zero Dark bigger."

"You think Detective Parker was involved with them?"

"Maybe." Wilson scratched behind his ear. "Agent Vasquez told me that suicide we investigated—Dr. Silva's patient, Carl Franklin—was a domestic terrorist named Carlin Pickens. A lot of people in this case aren't who they seem to be."

A shadow fell over Hawkins's face. He stared at the desk and nodded.

"What's going on, Rick? You're hiding something."

Hawkins took a deep breath before making eye contact. "Agent Forrester found the gun that killed Gomes in a dumpster a block away from where they discovered his body."

"How does he know it's the murder weapon? He can't have already run ballistics."

"It's a forty caliber. Same as the slug they found in Gomes's skull."

"That's circumstantial," Wilson said.

"I know. Forrester said he's sending it to the FBI lab for expedited analysis." Hawkins's upper lip twitched. "It's a Glock 22—like the one that killed your city councilor."

"No fucking way." Heat burned up the back of Wilson's neck. He jumped out of his seat.

Hawkins grabbed Wilson's shoulder and pushed him back down into his chair. "This is why I hesitated to tell you. We can't assume anything."

"Are you shitting me?" Wilson pointed at the doorway, as if Forrester stood there. "It's the same stunt Forrester pulled in Boston. He's covering something up. Maybe it's his gun."

"Maybe you're right, but we can't do anything until we have more evidence." Hawkins kept pressure on Wilson's shoulder until he stopped fighting. "Have you asked Dr. Silva about Parker or Pickens?"

"Not yet. I tried calling, but she's not answering her phone."

"All right, well, let's start with them. You want to take Parker or Pickens?"

Wilson gripped the arms of his chair. "Parker. I think I know where to go next. But promise me, if we find something that incriminates Forrester, you let me read him his rights."

Hawkins smirked. "You can put the cuffs on him yourself."

After Hawkins walked off, Wilson turned to his computer

and typed a search into the police database. An address and phone number appeared. He dialed.

"Hello?" a female voice asked after the second ring.

"Miranda Parker?"

"Yes. Who's this?"

"Detective Gary Wilson, Somerville PD." He paused, choosing his words carefully. "I was hoping you could answer some questions about your husband, Mitchell."

CHAPTER FORTY-TWO

"Okay, Dr. Silva, we're all done." The ReMind lab technician withdrew the needle and placed a gauze pad over Cristina's arm. "Hold that and I'll get a Band-Aid."

Cristina applied pressure while the tech tossed the needle into a sharps container. "What tests are you running?"

"Chemistry, toxicology, metabolites."

"Why do you need all that for a drug screen?"

"I just draw the blood. If you want to know what they do with it, talk to someone with more letters after their name." The tech removed the gauze and pasted a Band-Aid on Cristina's arm. "Good to go."

"Thanks." Cristina donned her jacket and grabbed her backpack, casting sideways glances at the tube of blood on the countertop. There was a good chance her drug screen would be positive, thanks to Recognate. She'd tried to find a good excuse to avoid being tested but couldn't find any that didn't make her look more suspicious. Her only choice was to comply and try to find answers before they discovered her subterfuge. And she had a good idea where to start. "Since you mentioned it, can I talk to Frank?"

"Dr. Alvarez?" With a shrug, the tech pointed toward the elevator. "He's in R&D, Suite Eighteen. Mateo can show you the way."

The security chief wasn't enthusiastic about escorting Cristina. "My orders were to show you out as soon as you finished the blood draw. Mr. Simmons said nothing about Dr. Alvarez."

"Mr. Simmons flew me here to help with the project that funds your paycheck." Cristina stood on her tiptoes—still shorter than Mateo but enough to make eye contact. "I can't do that without meeting with the head of research."

After a tense moment, Mateo adjusted his holster. "All right, but keep your hands to yourself."

As she followed him through a maze of hallways and stairwells, Cristina's thoughts drifted to Mrs. Watterson's lab results. If Recognate was responsible for the woman's confabulation, Cristina needed to solve the problem before it became irreversible.

"This is it." Mateo stopped before a plain metal door. A sign read *Frank Alvarez, MD/PhD*. The guard rapped twice.

The door cracked open. A male head covered with dark curls and wire-framed glasses peered out.

"Yes?" The man's thick eyebrows met as his eyes darted side to side. "I'm very busy, Mateo. What do you want?"

"Dr. Silva is here to meet you."

"Cristina Silva?" His eyes widened as he spotted her. "Yes, of course. Come in."

He swung the door open, waving her inside.

"Call when you finish." Mateo spun on his heel and marched down the hall.

"Ignore him." Frank closed the door and motioned Cristina to an empty chair. "He did two Marine tours but still couldn't get into the police academy."

Cristina forced a smile and surveyed Frank's office. Stacks of papers and charts cluttered the desk and littered the floor.

"Excuse the mess." Frank sat across from her and shoved aside a mound of charts. "Mr. Simmons ordered us to comb through every Recognate file. I was excited to hear you were coming but never expected to meet you in person. I don't get to interact often with our field researchers."

"Well, I wanted to apologize for the trouble over Mrs. Watterson."

"Oh, that. I should've done a more thorough background check. This is bold new territory. There's bound to be a steep learning curve."

Cristina's smile grew naturally. "I was hoping you'd understand my situation."

"Hey, it's not every day I get a researcher with firsthand amnesia experience." His gaze dropped to her neckline. A curious expression crossed his face. "That's a lovely pendant you're wearing."

Cristina touched her chest in surprise. She hadn't realized the locket had slipped out of her blouse. "Thank you. It's … a family heirloom.

"Might I see it? I'm kind of an aficionado of antique jewelry."

Cristina thought it an odd request but wrote it off as one of the researcher's eccentricities. She tucked the locket back inside her blouse. "If you don't mind, there's something more urgent we need to discuss." She lowered her voice and indicated the door. "Do you think he's listening?"

"Mateo? No, he's finalizing security plans for our grand unveiling."

Cristina imagined a potentially deadly medication being released to the public and shuddered. "That's what I'm worried about. Are you aware one of my patients jumped out of a window, while another became homicidal?"

Frank nodded. "C-252 and W-238."

"What did you call them?"

"Each subject is assigned a random identification number."

Turning to his computer, Frank typed and then swiveled the monitor to face Cristina. "We record dosage, response, adverse effects, and complications."

The alphanumeric characters tumbling down the screen had a dizzying effect. "So, they're just numbers."

"It's the best way to ensure researchers detect trends without interpretation bias." Frank shrugged. "It's standard practice in clinical trials."

"I see." Cristina scanned the list. Somewhere in there was Catherine Silvers, her fake identity. How many others were at risk? "I understand there have been several other … complications."

"You think Recognate is the cause?"

"It crossed my mind."

"Mine, too, but don't tell Mr. Simmons," Frank said. "Recognate is going to help a lot of people, but we need to make sure it's one hundred percent safe."

Santos had to be wrong, Cristina thought. No way could ReMind be part of Zero Dark. "I'm glad to hear you say that."

"That's why I insisted we screen for confounders. I understand you ordered tests on your patients?"

"Yes, but I'm still awaiting the results."

"Can I ask what you ordered?"

Again, Santos's voice echoed in her mind, *Volunteer nothing.* Was this the information they wanted? Did Cristina have the answer and not realize it?

"Electrolytes, metabolic tests," she said carefully. "Anything that could cause delirium."

"Makes sense. Anything else?"

Cristina swallowed before answering. "Norepinephrine levels."

"That's different. Why'd you order that?"

"To see if a Recognate overdose could cause psychosis or homicidal behavior."

"None of our Phase Three subjects showed psychotic or homicidal tendencies."

"Maybe not, but the beta-endorphin studies were discontinued because the rats became aggressive, and endocannabinoids work on a similar pathway so—"

"Hold on." Frank waved his hands. "You're citing Kobayashi's theory? Please. Even Jose abandoned that crap before he joined our team."

Now it was Cristina's turn to be surprised. "Kobayashi worked with ReMind?"

"I thought you knew."

"No."

"He oversaw our Phase Three trials. Persistent total amnesia is uncommon enough that we couldn't reach statistical power in the U.S. alone, so we branched out our study internationally." Frank stood. "Here, let me show you."

Confused, Cristina followed him down the hallway to a display case. A sign on top read Phase Three—Global Success!

"See, we got approval from four different countries. India and Venezuela were easy to persuade. Russia took a little longer and yielded the fewest viable subjects."

Frank pointed one by one at a series of black and white photos. As Cristina surveyed each group, her heart pounded.

"Jose convinced the Brazilian government our research would benefit their people. If it weren't for him, we wouldn't have gotten permission to work in the favelas."

Cristina couldn't hear a word he said over her internal screams as she stared at the photo of the Brazilian research team—the same photo from the *O Globo* article.

CHAPTER FORTY-THREE

Francisco Martins peered from behind a dumpster until the police cruiser disappeared around the corner. He crawled out and brushed frozen food scraps off his pants. A sharp pain bit into his foot. He staggered against the dumpster and hiked up his pant leg. A swollen, red mass surrounded his ankle. Years ago, he could've leaped from a moving bus without injury. He was getting too old for stunts like that.

Grimacing, he scooped a handful of snow and packed it inside his shoe. Using the nearest wall for support, he limped to the end of the alley and looked both ways along the sidewalk. Had his message to Cristina been clear enough? It killed him to inflict pain on her, but he had to make it look like he was no more than a crazed stalker. If the FBI knew she was working with him, they would detain her, and Martins's last hopes of getting through to his daughter would be dashed.

He pulled out his cell phone and typed a message: *How is she?*

After hitting Send, Martins rubbed his forehead with one hand. The alcohol was wearing off and he was feeling the effects. He needed his daily dose.

The cell phone beeped. A new message appeared: *No news.*

With a pained grunt, Martins shuffled down the street in search of food and drink. For now, all he could do was keep to the shadows and wait.

"Cristina, are you okay?" Frank waved his hand before her face. "You're not having a seizure, are you?"

"What?" Slowly, Cristina managed to dispel the shock of recognition enough to process his words. She tore her gaze away from the photo of the research team. "No, I'm good."

"Come sit." Frank ushered her back into his office. "You sure you're okay?"

"I'm fine, just winded from the early flight." Cristina tried to appear calm. "Do you know everyone in those photos?"

"A few. I only communicated directly with the team leaders."

"Who was the Brazilian team leader?"

"Kobayashi, of course."

"Do you two still talk?"

"Not for two years. Not too long ago I tried emailing him, but it bounced back."

Clenching her fingers, Cristina searched Frank's face to see if he knew her double was on the research team. He remained unreadable. "I thought Kobayashi's research centered on gang violence. How does that relate to Recognate?"

"Kobayashi linked slum violence to traumatic memory suppression. He persuaded residents to participate in our trials. They were our biggest and most successful study group."

"Successful how?"

"Highest response rate versus placebo, with a corresponding drop in gang violence. The effects were so dramatic the Institutional Review Board insisted on open trials." Frank grinned. "So, you see, there's no way Recognate could cause aggressive behavior.

Whatever happened to your other patients … there must be another explanation."

"What other explanation could there be?"

"I wish I knew. So far, our workup hasn't revealed anything. What about yours?"

Cristina hesitated to divulge anything. Still, Frank's insight could be helpful. "I don't have all the results, but one patient had elevated norepinephrine levels."

Frank's brow furrowed. "How high?"

"Astronomical."

"Strange. Our animal models never showed elevated norepinephrine."

"Apparently, he wasn't taking his pills. He may have had a pheo."

"An adrenal tumor." Relief washed over Frank's face. "Yes, that would explain everything, wouldn't it?"

"It would," Cristina said, "except we don't have a body to autopsy."

"In other words, you've got nothing."

"I requested an autopsy on Carl Franklin. Maybe they're connected."

"The incidence of a pheo is about two in a million." Frank ran his finger over his lip. "The odds of two of your patients having it would be ridiculous unless—"

A knock on the door startled them both. From outside, Mateo said, "Dr. Alvarez, Mr. Simmons needs to see you."

"I'll be right there." Frank stood and held out his hand. "Thank you, Dr. Silva. You've been quite helpful."

"I have?" For the second time that day, Cristina was befuddled as she shook his hand. It seemed like she'd only uncovered more questions.

"Oh, yes. In fact, I think you've given us the exact information we need." Frank's face grew serious. "Of course, now I'll have to kill you."

Her stomach clenched. Every muscle in her body tensed.

Before she could react, he laughed. "I'm kidding. I meant I'm supposed to find the answers, and now they'll hire you to replace me and—" He looked down. "Sorry. I've been told that as a comedian I make a brilliant researcher."

Cristina touched her chest and searched for breath. "Don't quit your day job."

"I won't." Frank ushered her to the door. "Let me walk you out."

In the hallway, they found Mateo waiting at attention.

"Please let me know if you find anything," she said to Frank.

"Don't worry," he said. "You'll hear from us soon."

As she followed Mateo, Cristina spotted the display case. Gomes had been part of that team. Who else was involved?

"Could we stop a moment?" Cristina flashed her most winning smile. "Dr. Alvarez told me so much about the Phase Three trials. I want to admire your success."

Mateo didn't flinch. "Hurry up."

Cristina studied the display. There in the Brazilian photos was her doppelgänger. Gomes stood behind her. Kobayashi was off to the side. No one else looked familiar.

The Indian photo was too blurry to identify faces. Cristina thought she recognized a dark-haired woman in the Venezuelan photo, but after a moment of study decided she was mistaken. As she moved onto the Russian photo, her heart skipped a beat.

It was a smaller team than in the other photos, making it easy to pick out the woman in the back row. Her hair was darker, not as wild, and she was a few pounds heavier, but there was no mistaking the sharp, thin nose that belonged to Stacey Peterman—AKA Anastasia Petrov.

CHAPTER FORTY-FOUR

The wind stung Cristina's face as she stepped outside, an abrupt change from the morning's balmy climate. She wrapped her jacket tighter around her body and crossed to the sidewalk. A chill ran down her back as she glanced at the ReMind building, but it wasn't from the weather.

Santos was right. If Stacey and Gomes had been involved with ReMind, then ReMind was part of Zero Dark. Cristina turned her collar against the wind and hugged herself. If they had sent Gomes to kill Stacey, why was she still alive in Salt Lake City?

The wind intensified, forcing Cristina to run to the nearest awning. She huddled close to the wall as she searched for her cell phone. She'd had to remind Mateo to return it before he practically shoved her out the door. Maybe Andrea could meet her for lunch in the Adams Morgan district. Cristina had always wanted to try Ethiopian food, and she could get her friend's opinion on her next move.

Mateo had shut down her phone. When Cristina turned it back on, she had two new messages. Curious, she dialed her voicemail and listened. The first was from Andrea.

"Hi, it's me. Listen, since the weather sucks, I'm going

shopping at L'Enfant Plaza. If you get done early, meet me at Market Seafood. Love you!"

So much for Ethiopian. The Plaza was only a few Metro stops away. She started the four-block trek to the station and skipped to the next voicemail.

"Dr. Silva. It's Devi. Please call as soon as you get this message."

The urgency in Devi's voice raised the hairs on the back of Cristina's neck. She dialed her office.

Devi picked up on the first ring. "Dr. Silva's office."

"It's me, Devi. What's wrong?"

"David Watterson just called."

A lump grew in Cristina's throat. "Is his mother worse?"

"Actually, she's calmer now. She's stopped talking about things that aren't real."

Cristina pressed her hand against her chest. The lump dissolved. "Oh, thank God."

"But she's forgetting things again, and it's making her depressed. She's started drinking two to three glasses of wine per night and he can't get her to stop."

"Without the Recognate, her Alzheimer's is returning. Damn! I was afraid of that."

"Her test results came in this morning," Devi said. "The MRI was normal."

"So, no stroke. That's a relief. What about her labs?"

"Nothing flagged as abnormal."

"At least there doesn't seem to be any permanent damage. She'll have the blues for a few days, but she should return to baseline. Then we can find something else to try. Thanks for keeping me updated. Any other fires I need to put out?"

"Dr. Morgan phoned."

Cristina's pulse quickened. "Did he find something?"

"He said you should call him back as soon as possible." Devi lowered her voice. "Are you okay? You sound stressed. Did something happen in the meeting?"

A glance confirmed Cristina was alone. The weather seemed to be discouraging most people from setting foot outdoors. "I can't talk about it over the phone, but something's brewing and I'm at ground zero. Have the police found Santos?"

Devi hesitated before saying, "I haven't heard anything."

"Well, keep the door locked then. If anything happens, call Detective Wilson, okay? He has everything I know on Santos, including a cell phone that he should be able to use to track him down. Call him. Promise me?"

"I promise."

The wind picked up. As Cristina ran across Eighteenth Street, she shouted into the phone, "I have to go. I'll be back tomorrow."

"Be careful, Cristina." Devi disconnected before Cristina could reply.

It had sounded like there was something Devi wasn't telling her. Had the FBI gotten to her? Cristina chided herself. Thinking everyone in her life was part of a giant conspiracy suggested serious paranoia.

As Cristina passed an Indian restaurant, she thought again about the Phase Three trials. Two members of ReMind's international research teams were dead or missing. Make that three, since Kobayashi had also dropped off the map. Something had happened in Brazil that Simmons wanted erased. Maybe that was the information locked in Cristina's brain that could destroy them. But why not kill her? What did she have that they wanted?

Cristina fingered the locket around her neck. In her brief time at ReMind, she hadn't seen or heard about anyone who might have been Santos's daughter. Was the girl on one of those teams as well? Cristina had no idea how she was expected to find her.

Farragut North Station lay on the other side of Connecticut Avenue. As Cristina waited for the light to change, she called Dr. Morgan.

"Luke, what did you find?"

"Cristina! What the heck's going on? The FBI was here this morning. They said you told them to talk to me about Jerry Peterman."

"That's right. I forgot to give you a head's up. What did you tell them?"

"I showed them his labs and they requested a copy. Without a body, I didn't have much else to offer. Was there something else you wanted me to share with them?"

Cristina took a deep breath. If the FBI studied the lab tests and realized she was trying to find out the truth, as they were, maybe they'd be more willing to believe her when she told them what she'd learned about ReMind. "No, that's fine. What happened with Carl Franklin's autopsy?"

"Blood and tissue samples show the same high norepinephrine and epinephrine levels as Peterman's."

Cristina's heart pounded as she crossed to the Metro Station's K Street entrance. "Did you find a pheo?"

"No. I searched the whole abdominal cavity and didn't find any tumors."

"Damn. I was sure you'd find something." She opened the station door and stepped in from the cold.

From the way Frank had reacted back at the ReMind office, Cristina had convinced herself that long-term Recognate use caused adrenal gland overgrowth. But now, with Mrs. Watterson's tests normal and nothing in Carl's body, she was back at square one. "Thanks for checking."

"Actually, I found two other things of interest though," Lucas said.

"Really? What?"

"Carl Franklin has an old wound on his neck like Peterman. I missed it because of the trauma."

"What could that mean?"

"I don't know. It's scarred over."

Cristina frowned. "What's the other thing?"

"Mr. Franklin's liver was a mass of scars and fibrosis. The cells contained Mallory bodies, consistent with alcoholic cirrhosis."

"I don't understand. He never showed any signs of alcoholism."

"I don't know what to tell you, but he was clearly a heavy drinker for some time."

As Cristina swiped her SmarTrip card and walked through the turnstile, Cristina considered this new information. Jerry and Carl were both drunk. Martha Watterson admitted to doing shots. Alcoholic thiamine deficiency caused a condition known as Korsakoff psychosis, leading to amnesia and confabulation. She'd ruled out the diagnosis because Martha didn't show the classic tremors, but what if Recognate masked it? "Luke, could you run two more tests for me?"

"Depends what you need."

"Pyruvate and B1 levels, and check Carl's mamillary bodies for degeneration."

"The blood tests should only take a few minutes. You want me to call you when I'm done, or should I speak directly to those FBI agents?"

Cristina stopped inches from the escalator. "Why would they care about Carl?"

"I'm not sure. They insisted on taking fingerprints and dental X-rays from him and from the guy they brought in yesterday with a gunshot wound to the head." Lucas paused before asking in a low voice, "Are you mixed up in something illegal?"

"I—Luke, I don't—"

"Because if you want me to make something up to throw them off track, I will."

Cristina felt the urge to grin. "Thank you, but you don't have to do that. Look, I have to run, but tomorrow I'll tell you everything, okay?"

"Over dinner?"

"Yes, Luke. Over dinner." As Cristina hung up, apprehension crept along the back of her neck. Why would the FBI be interested in Carl Franklin? If he'd been an alcoholic and she hadn't known, could he have been involved in something else? How much did she know about any of her amnesiac patients?

Cristina entered the line for the escalator. Farragut North was the third busiest station on the Metro line, and today was no exception. She tucked her cell phone into her pocket. Hopefully, she'd make it to L'Enfant Plaza in time to grab a bite before they had to rush to the airport.

As the mass of people pressed against her, something poked into Cristina's back.

"Watch it," she said over her shoulder.

The crowd shuffled forward and stopped. As Cristina waited, she got poked again.

"Excuse me." She started to turn.

A gloved hand clamped onto her arm.

"Don't turn around," a robotic voice said in her ear. "Or I'll shoot you right here."

CHAPTER FORTY-FIVE

After ringing the doorbell, Detective Wilson assessed the scene as he awaited a response. Modest white colonial home complete with black shutters and an antique rocking chair on a white porch. Quiet Framingham neighborhood, lots of manicured hedges and trees. Exactly as Wilson had pictured Mitchell Parker's house on the drive from Somerville—except for the "No Trespassing" signs and the electric fence bordering the security gate. At least Miranda Parker buzzed him through the gate without hassle.

The red oak front door cracked open, half-revealing a feminine face below the safety chain. An intense pair of green eyes analyzed him. "Show me your badge."

"I held it up to the monitor when I drove up."

"I want to see it up close."

Wilson displayed his badge. After a moment, Miranda closed the door. He heard a sliding sound. The door swung open. A small woman stood inside, wearing a sweatshirt and jeans. Midlength blond hair fell over a forehead riddled with worry lines. She clutched a Beretta pocket gun, her fingers trembling. A shotgun rested against the wall behind her.

Tension crawled up Wilson's back. He kept his hand on his

hip, near his holster. "I'm not here to hurt you, Mrs. Parker. I just wanted to ask you a few questions."

She aimed the pistol at his groin. "I'm a cop's wife and a good shot. Move your hand."

Wilson lowered his hand to his side.

Without dropping the gun, Miranda waved Wilson inside and shut the door. She studied him up and down. "Tell me why a Somerville cop is interested in my husband's death."

"I'm actually more interested in a case he was investigating."

"Why would I know about that?"

"Well …" He swallowed. "It seems your husband was involved with a victim in the case."

She fiddled with her collar with her free hand. "Involved how?"

"They were having an affair before he died."

Her fingers stopped moving. "No."

"I'm sorry to have to break it to you like this but—"

"I mean no, he wasn't having an affair."

He poked his tongue against his cheek. "Well, she said—"

"I know my husband. We had problems, sure, and we spent some time apart for a few months four years ago, but Mitchell was never unfaithful. When we got back together, we were stronger than ever." Her lips twisted. "At least until he went missing again for two months, right before he …" Miranda Parker shook her head and stopped.

The back of Wilson's ear started to itch. "You're sure he didn't have an affair while you were apart? He never mentioned a woman named Cristina?"

"Never."

"How about Jorge and Claudia Silva? He investigated an arson case involving their home and later their deaths in a car crash."

Miranda's already pale complexion lightened another two shades. She lowered the gun. "Those are the names that agent mentioned."

Wilson drew back in surprise. "Agent? What agent?"

"He showed up four weeks ago. Said he was FBI."

Possibilities swirled through Wilson's mind. Had Forrester already been there? "What did this agent ask you?"

"He said Mitchell had been working with the FBI on a case involving the Silvas. He insisted Mitchell had something they needed. When I said I didn't know what he was talking about, he threatened me. Said if I was hiding anything or talked to anyone, he'd kill me." She shuddered. "I know that's not how the FBI operates. He's lying, or he's dirty. Either way, I could tell he had the resources to follow through on his threat. That's when I installed that electric fence. I haven't left the house since."

Those plastic whack-a-moles popped up again. Wilson tried brushing them away. "I hate to tell you, but I can think of at least twenty ways around your defense system. Has this agent visited you again?"

"No."

"Do you remember his name?"

"Something like Gomez."

Wilson was startled. "Could his name have been Federico Gomes?"

"Yeah, that's it."

The moles started whacking him. "At least you won't have to worry about him. He's dead."

Miranda stared. If she felt relieved, she didn't show it.

"Mrs. Parker, Gomes was involved in a criminal organization. Is it possible that your husband was involved in something illegal?"

Her eyes widened. "No!"

"Maybe he made a bad deal, betrayed the shield." The moles toppled like dominoes. "And then he tried to deal with it, failed, couldn't live with the guilt, and took his own life."

She stared at the floor. "That's not what happened."

"You can't know what he was going through if he didn't talk to you."

"That's not what I mean." When she looked up, tears clung to her eyelids. "Mitchell didn't kill himself. He was murdered."

"Keep moving, Doctor." The assailant's words were filtered through a voice changer. "Nothing sudden."

"What do you want?" Cristina shuffled with the crowd toward the Farragut North Station subway escalator. "Who are you?"

The gun jammed into her back again. "Don't talk."

Cristina's mind raced as she searched for a way to escape. There were too many people around. If she ran, one of them might get caught in crossfire. "I know you think I have something you want, but I don't know anything."

Her abductor didn't answer. The pressure in her back eased. Cristina turned her head, hoping to glimpse him.

"Face front and shut up." The gun barrel prodded her. "I won't warn you again."

Cristina clutched her backpack. Her knees shook as she stopped in front of the escalator.

The attacker nudged Cristina forward. She stepped onto the escalator. He boarded the same step, bumping up against her, looming over her. His bulky ski parka prevented her from getting any sense of his body shape. A whiff of cinnamon passed her nostrils.

They reached the platform. The gunman grabbed her elbow and pushed her toward the nearest track. The other passengers jostled back without making eye contact.

The train pulled up. The door slid open. An automated voice announced, "Red Line to Silver Spring."

The assailant shoved her onto the train. The other passengers were busy reading newspapers, playing with their mobile devices, or otherwise disconnecting from the world around them.

The last passenger squeezed into the car. The doors closed automatically. With a jerk, the train rolled forward. Cristina held tight to the pole. She felt her assailant take a step back with the train's movement. He squeezed her arm as he regained his posture.

Over her shoulder, she asked, "Where we going?"

"My employers want to speak to you."

"Do you work for ReMind or Zero Dark?"

He didn't answer. The gun jammed harder into her back. Cristina gritted her teeth.

"I'll tell you what I know, okay? Please don't hurt me." Cristina's shoulders trembled. "I want this whole situation to end."

The grip on her elbow relaxed. "It'll end when you give us the key to fixing the drug."

"Fix Recognate? How do you mean?"

"I know you have it on you." The train veered around a corner. He shifted his weight. "I want it."

"All right." Cristina kept her tone level, hoping he couldn't tell she was bluffing. "Whatever you want."

"Not here. When we get off the train."

Cristina nodded and squeezed the pole, her pulse racing. The train slowed as it approached the station. An overhead display read *Metro Center*.

The conductor applied the brakes, and the train jerked backward. The assailant shifted his weight. The pressure on Cristina's back lightened.

Now.

The voice commanded Cristina's body into action. She threw herself forward. Swung around the pole like a tetherball.

Her attacker fell forward. He let go of her elbow. Groped for the pole.

She revolved behind him. Shoved as hard as she could against his back. He collapsed onto the laps of nearby passengers.

Use your advantage.

"He grabbed my ass!" Cristina pointed at him. "Pervert!"

The assailant struggled to disentangle himself from the surprised passengers. Two men and a woman stepped between him and Cristina, blocking her view.

Run!

The doors slid open. She dived between the remaining passengers. Slipped outside. Hit the platform running. Behind her, shouting and cursing.

Dodging and weaving, Cristina sprinted up the escalator to the turnstiles. Slapped her SmarTrip card against the reader. The bars retracted. She squeezed through.

"Hey," someone yelled behind her. "Stop her!"

Both escalators were packed. She ran up the stairs.

Feet pounded the steps just behind her.

Halfway there. Move faster.

The abductor grabbed her pack from behind. Jerked her shoulder backward.

That's it. Let me handle this.

The voice shoved Cristina's mind aside. Her body wheeled around on its own. She chopped the assailant's arm with her free hand. He let go. His brown eyes widened beneath a cold weather mask, igniting a faint spark of familiarity. He swung at her. She dodged and shoved the pack at him. He tumbled backward. Ignoring stares from the escalator riders, she sprinted up the stairs.

By the time she reached the top, Cristina had regained control. She found the strength for one last surge. She threw open the station door and dashed onto the sidewalk.

Flashing lights off to the right. Police. They could help. Cristina ignored her aching legs and ran to the corner of Twelfth and

G streets. Cars sped through the intersection. If she waited for the light, the man would catch her. She had no choice. She'd have to risk crossing the street.

A black sedan squealed around the corner. Screeched to a stop in front of her. The passenger door opened.

"Get in!" the driver shouted.

Cristina's heart pounded in her ears. She recognized his wavy dark hair, the distinguished facial lines, and those eyes—blue as a clear sky. His name caught in her throat. When it finally passed her lips, she still didn't really believe he was there.

"Mitchell?"

CHAPTER FORTY-SIX

As Miranda Parker buried her face in her hands and wept, Detective Wilson fidgeted. Square him off against a combative drunk or a narcissistic felon, he'd win every time. But dealing effectively with a crying widow? Clueless.

"I'm sorry," she murmured and wiped her eyes. "I need to sit for a moment."

He awkwardly escorted her to the next room. Subdued blues and lavenders matched a somber gloom hanging in the air. A cluttered wooden desk sulked in the corner. No knickknacks, no pictures on the wall. It was clean and utilitarian.

Miranda stumbled. Wilson shifted his attention to helping her onto the suede couch.

"Can I get you anything?" he asked.

"No, thank you. I'll be fine." She rubbed her forehead and motioned for him to sit next to her. "I haven't been able to sleep. I keep thinking about Mitchell."

"Why do you think he was murdered?"

"I'm a paralegal. I've reviewed tons of police reports. The medical examiner found no gunpowder residue on Mitchell's fingers."

The itching behind Wilson's ear intensified. "Which they should have if he shot himself. Did you request an autopsy?"

"I was in shock and Mitchell's captain convinced me it wasn't necessary." She shook her head. "But in my heart, I always felt something was wrong. Mitchell seemed happy. The suicide note sounded nothing like him. And then, after Gomes threatened me, I went through Mitchell's things."

"You found something?"

"An empty pill bottle tucked away in an old overnight bag. I think it was something called Recognate."

Wilson's heart jumped. "Recognate? You're sure?"

"I can check. The bottle is upstairs."

The moles started to line up, goading him to knock them down. "Can I see it?"

A puzzled look crossed her face. "Sure. Hold on."

As Miranda climbed the stairs, Wilson mused over this new information. He stood and crossed over to the desk. Folders with labels *Tax stuff* and *Utilities* lay atop a pile of books and loose papers. A simple cream-white photo album half-poked out of the pile. He wiggled it loose and opened it. The first few pages showed pictures of Miranda Parker in a flowing white wedding dress. The next pages displayed bridesmaids, followed by groomsmen.

"Found it." Miranda reentered the room, holding out a small bottle. "What do you think it is?"

"I'm not sure." He took it and inspected it. The word *Recognate* was handwritten in small print on a plain white label. No other markings except for a date and a phone number. "This was filled three years ago. You didn't find any others?"

"No."

"That would've been long before the Silvas died." Wilson squeezed the bottle. "Did your husband ever mention Francisco Martins?"

"No."

"He never told you about working with the FBI?"

"No." Tears reappeared in the widow's eyes. "I didn't know about any of this. It's like he had two different lives."

Wilson nodded empathetically and looked around for a box of tissues. His gaze fell on the photo album. His pulse quickened.

"Mrs. Parker, did you remarry?"

"No, why?"

He pointed at the photo. Miranda stood in her wedding gown, smiling, holding hands with a dashing young man in a black tuxedo—close-cropped blond hair, chiseled features, baby-smooth cheeks. "Who is this man?"

Her brow furrowed. "That's not funny."

"I'm not trying to be funny. I'm trying to understand what's going on." He pointed at the man again, a man completely unfamiliar. "Please, tell me his name."

She visibly struggled to maintain her composure as she studied his face. At last, she said, "That's my husband. Mitchell."

"Get in!" Mitchell pulled Cristina into the car.

She tumbled into the seat and pushed him away. "How are you alive? What are you doing here?"

"Rescuing you." He floored the gas pedal, and the sedan rocketed forward. Cristina's door swung shut. He readjusted the GPS on his dashboard and glared at her. "Fasten your seat belt."

"Answer my question." Cristina studied Mitchell's face. A few gray hairs at the temples and extra wrinkles around the eyes but otherwise he looked the same. "You're dead."

"I know. I'll explain later. Right now, we need to move." He checked his rearview mirror. "Crap."

"What?" In the side mirror, Cristina spotted the masked gunman giving chase on a Kawasaki Ninja. He was wearing her backpack.

"Hold on." Mitchell gunned it. He swerved around a tractor-trailer.

Inertia flattened Cristina against the seat. "You're going to get us killed!"

"That's what I'm trying to prevent." He drew a gun.

"Oh, my God." Her chest tightened.

"Sit tight." Mitchell rolled down his window. As he steered with his right hand, he fired behind them with his left.

Cristina covered her ears. Mitchell stopped firing. She looked out her window. The assailant was coming up fast on their right. He aimed a pistol.

"Get down!" Mitchell pressed her head down. Fired his gun.

The window shattered. Cristina screamed.

"All right." Mitchell released her head. "He's gone."

Cristina sat up. The gunman was gone. She shook glass from her hair. Fear and anger wrestled inside her chest. Tears welled in her eyes. "What the hell's going on? Why did you fake suicide? Why did you lie to me about being divorced? How did you know where to find me?"

Her phone rang.

"Don't answer that," Mitchell said.

"Don't you dare give me orders." She sniffled and checked the caller ID. *Wilson.* Trembling, she held the phone to her ear and answered.

"Cristina? Are you okay? You sound scared to death."

"I'm okay, I just—"

"Who are you talking to?" Mitchell asked, his face reddening. "Give me the phone."

Ignoring him, she said to Wilson, "Someone attacked me."

"What? Where are you?"

"Still in Washington."

"You need to get back here."

Mitchell grabbed at her. "Cristina, give me the phone."

She switched the phone to the other ear and deflected him with her elbow. Mitchell scowled and changed lanes.

"Who is that?" Wilson's voice rose in pitch. "What's going on?"

"I don't know how to explain, but I had help from Mitchell Parker. He's right here."

"Parker? Cristina, I think Federico Gomes murdered Mitchell Parker—the real Mitchell Parker, that is."

"What?" Cristina's gaze drifted to Mitchell. He glared at her out of the corner of his eye. Her throat swelled. "I don't understand."

"Whoever's with you, it's not Parker. Get out of there. Somewhere safe. Get—"

Mitchell seized her arm. Yanked her over. Snatched the phone.

"Give that back." She batted at him.

He tossed it out the window.

"Why'd you do that?" she asked.

"ReMind planted a tracer on your phone. See?" He pointed at the GPS. A blue car icon blinked in the screen's center. A blinking red dot crept toward the bottom of the screen. "I tapped into their signal. It's how I knew where to find you."

Cristina stared at the screen and then at him. Blood drained from her face. "Who are you?"

"Cristina—"

"No, no more bullshit. I know you're not Mitchell Parker. Who are you?"

"I can explain."

"Who are you and what do you want from me?"

"This is a mistake."

"Tell me or I'm jumping out of this car." Cristina reached for the door handle.

"Stop." He slammed his fist against the steering wheel. "Damn it, Cristina. I'm with the CIA."

CHAPTER FORTY-SEVEN

"Cristina?" Wilson hit redial. Her voicemail answered immediately. He disconnected. Hundreds of scenarios playing in his mind. All bad.

"What's going on?" Miranda Parker asked, her face pale. "Is someone impersonating my husband?"

"I'm not sure, but right now I think we need to get you someplace safe."

"You said Gomes was dead."

"He is, but he wasn't working alone. I'm going to take you back to the station, and we'll try to sort all this out."

As Wilson took Miranda's elbow, his phone rang. He put it to his ear. "Cristina? Are you okay?"

"I'm not Cristina," answered a familiar male voice.

"Rick." Wilson rapped his fist against his forehead. "Sorry."

"What's going on?" Hawkins asked. "Where are you?"

"I'll explain it all when we get back there. I'm bringing in Parker's wife. I want her to talk to Forrester and Vasquez."

"Yeah, that's why I was calling. They're getting ready to start an interrogation."

"Interrogation? Of who?"

"Devi Patel, Dr. Silva's office manager."

"What do they want to know from her?"

"They went to Silva's office to sift through her files. Patel put up a fight and they dragged her in." He paused. "She told them that Dr. Silva hadn't been in all day."

Wilson's cheeks cooled. He should've coordinated with the office manager after promising to cover for Cristina. What a rookie move.

"Where is she? And don't lie to me."

Wilson grunted. "DC. Meeting with a pharmaceutical company about her research. She was supposed to fly back later today, but something's happened."

"What the fuck, Gary?" His partner sounded pissed. "When were you going to tell me?"

"I didn't want word to get out. Sorry. I should've trusted you."

"You're damned right. Now what?"

"Do a GPS trace on Cristina's phone, and find out what drug companies are in the area." He ushered Miranda toward the door. "What about Stacey Peterman? Did you find out anything more?"

"You're not going to like it."

"Tell me."

"Peterman checked into Flight 337 to Salt Lake, but then flight logs showed her seat stayed empty."

"What?"

"Someone bought her ticket in cash thirty minutes before the flight."

"So, it's a cover-up." Wilson stopped short in the walkway. To Miranda, he said, "You said Gomes showed you an FBI badge?"

"Yes."

Wilson's throat constricted. Into the phone, he said, "Rick, stall Forrester until I get there. Don't let them interview Devi."

"I'll do my best."

After disconnecting, Wilson helped Miranda into his Charger's front seat and jumped in. He activated the dashboard light and sped toward the highway.

"CIA?" Cristina shook her head, as if she could shake away the madness. "You're full of shit."

"It's true," Mitchell said without taking his eyes off the road. "I didn't want you to find out like this."

"Stop lying. If you're CIA, show me your badge."

"We don't carry badges. You'll have to trust me, okay?"

"Trust you? Very funny. After you faked your death?"

"I was deep undercover. If you knew the truth, they would've gone after you."

"Who? Zero Dark?"

He glanced at her, eyebrows raised. "Yes. How do you know about them?"

"A lot has happened, Mitchell." Cristina pressed her palm against her forehead. "What the hell's your real name, anyway?"

"James, but you can stick with Mitchell. I've grown accustomed to it." He tugged at his collar. "I know this is all confusing—"

"Confusing doesn't even come close. How do I know you're not Zero Dark?"

His lips pressed into a thin line. He veered onto the beltway. "Because I worked with Jorge Silva."

Her mouth went dry. "Dad?"

"Jorge was our lead agent on Zero Dark. He had the most intel on their operations, their technology." His cheek twitched. "Two years ago, he called me. Told me he'd learned the identity of Zero Dark's leader."

"Quinn."

He nodded, apparently unsurprised Cristina knew the name. "Jorge arranged a meeting the next day with me and our field director to reveal all the names and identities of those involved in Quinn's network. But Quinn killed Jorge and his wife two hours after we spoke."

Cristina's heart sunk. Santos was right. Everything she knew was a lie. She analyzed Mitchell's face, hands, tone of voice. He seemed to be telling the truth. She wasn't sure if that made anything better or worse. "So, you still don't know who Quinn is?"

"I've got a pretty good idea. Jorge discovered a connection between Zero Dark and a DC-based pharmaceutical company."

"ReMind."

"Exactly. Quinn uses an encrypted chat protocol to communicate with his team. I can't crack the encryption, but I was able to triangulate their origin. He's here in DC under an alias."

"You think he's hiding as a ReMind employee?"

"I think he's in control of ReMind."

Cristina's heart beat faster. "Julius Simmons."

"Zero Dark has a vested interest in ReMind's research. Their new drug plays a major role in Quinn's plans. He'd want to oversee it personally."

Cristina's pulse pounded in her ears. Recognate—that was the drug. It wasn't working properly, and people were dying. Zero Dark believed she knew how to fix it. But she didn't, even if she might have once upon a time. What would they do to her if she never remembered? "Why did you visit me in the hospital? Don't lie to me."

"You know you're not Cristina Silva."

"Yes." She swallowed hard. "Did you know? When you met me?"

"Not at first. I knew Jorge had a daughter Cristina, but I never met her."

"Do you know where she is?"

"I assume dead."

Her throat constricted. What kind of people was she dealing with? "Do you know my real name?"

"No. I have no idea who you are, but it's obvious you're important to Quinn. I heard about the attacks. I've been keeping tabs on you."

"Because you care so much about me, right?" Tears wet her cheeks. "So much you made me believe you were dead?"

"Cristina, I fell in love with you." His fingers clenched the wheel so tightly his knuckles turned white. "I know that's hard to believe, but it's true. A Zero Dark agent found out about me. To protect you, I had to disappear."

Trust your heart, the voice said in her mind. *Do you believe him?*

Even as Cristina tried to block out the words, she realized that—despite everything—she wanted to believe him. After all, didn't he just save her life? "What happened to the real Mitchell Parker?"

"Another Zero Dark agent pretended to be FBI and recruited him. When Parker found out the truth, he called us." He grunted as he changed lanes. "So, we took him in for protection."

"And then you pretended to be him?"

"It's easier to assume an established identity than to create one from scratch. Plus, it made it look like he was still active. For a couple of months, it threw off Zero Dark."

"But then they found out."

"Mitchell Parker disappeared during the transfer to an FBI safehouse." He jammed the stick shift to high gear. "Quinn was Green Beret Special Ops. Most of his operatives are turncoats he recruited through Special Operations allies, including our own agencies. He's got at least two FBI field agents under his thumb."

Cristina's cheeks cooled.

He glanced at her and then did a double take. "What's wrong?"

"Two FBI agents interrogated me in Boston. They asked me what I knew about Quinn."

His jaw clenched. "What were their names?"

"I don't—I don't remember."

"Think."

Cristina drew back. His face had turned crimson, eyes bulging.

He inhaled through his nose, relaxed his grip on the steering wheel. "This is important. What do you remember?"

"There was a woman named … Vasquez, and a man named Forest. No, Forrester."

After a silent moment, he asked, "Do they know you're here?"

"I don't think so. Do you know them?"

He stamped on the gas pedal. The car shot down the expressway.

"Where are we going? The airport's the other way."

"Who booked your flight?"

Her skin prickled. "ReMind."

"Right. I'll warn TSA to check your plane, but you won't be on it. I need to get you somewhere safe." He met her gaze, his eyes haunted. "You can't go back to Boston."

CHAPTER FORTY-EIGHT

"Where is Dr. Silva?" Agent Vasquez shouted into Devi Patel's face. She leaned over the wooden interrogation table, inching her nose closer to Devi's. "Answer me."

Devi stared back; eyes cold, expressionless. "I want to speak to a lawyer."

"Oh, we can get you a lawyer. Or we can make a deal that benefits both of us."

"What deal?"

"Did you recruit Carl Franklin and Jerry Peterman to Dr. Silva's practice?"

"I'm her office manager. I schedule her appointments."

"But did you know those men before they began seeing her?"

"No."

"Did you know they were terrorists?"

"No."

Vasquez held up a slim black phone. "Who gave you this?"

"I told you, it's mine."

"It's unregistered. We call it a burner phone."

Devi shrugged. "My phone is in the shop. I needed something temporary."

"Right." Vasquez turned on the phone and faced the screen toward Devi. "Read that message aloud."

Devi glared silently.

"Read it or I'm charging you with obstruction of justice."

Eyes smoldering, Devi held the agent's gaze another moment before reading the text. "Take everything and get out."

"Who sent that?"

"I don't know. Probably a wrong number."

"You may have deleted your other messages, but our tech guys can still find them. We can reduce your charges if you come clean now."

Jaw clenched, Devi hesitated, seeming to study every pore on the agent's face. She looked down at the table. "I want my lawyer."

Vasquez clenched her fists. Slowly, she lowered them. "If you don't start cooperating, we might charge you with accessory to murder. Think about it." She turned and left the interrogation room.

As Vasquez burst into the observation room, Detective Wilson glanced at Devi through the one-way mirror. The diminutive office manager sat erect, hands folded, staring straight ahead. Hawkins had been unable to keep the Feds from starting their interrogation, but Ms. Patel seemed capable of defying them on her own. Wilson didn't know whether to be impressed or worried.

"She's tough." Vasquez leaned against a wall. "We need to request a warrant to search her phone and email."

"We don't have that kind of time." Forrester studied Devi through the window. He turned to Vasquez. "Dr. Silva's missing, and she's implicated in Gomes's death."

"Wait a minute," Wilson said. "Implicated how?"

"A vagrant claims to have seen a woman follow Gomes into the alley where they found him. She left ten minutes later, alone."

Wilson's stomach fluttered. "And you think it was Cristina?"

"The woman had tan skin, possibly Latina."

"Did he give any other description?"

"She was wearing a brown hat and overcoat," Vasquez said. "Taller side. He didn't get a good enough look at her face to create a composite."

"That describes a quarter of the Boston population," Wilson said. "And, anyway, Cristina's average height."

"She could've been wearing heels. The witness couldn't recall."

Wilson pushed the hair off his forehead. "Did this witness hear the gunshot?"

"No." Vasquez dipped her chin. "There's construction in the area. Too much noise."

"Ballistics on the gun we found match the slug in Gomes' chest," Forrester said. "She killed him with his own weapon."

"But there were no signs of a struggle, which means Gomes allowed the killer to get close. Why would he do that to someone like Silva, who he had attacked twice?"

Forrester shrugged. "Maybe they were working together."

"That makes no sense. Besides, she has an alibi."

"Well, Gomes was killed two blocks from Dr. Silva's home, and she's our only lead. I want a BOLO and no-fly on her *yesterday*."

Wilson bit his inner cheek. If Cristina was in trouble, a BOLO was in her best interest. He'd have to trust she wouldn't divulge his role in her escape. "Fine. Let's do it. But we've got a bigger problem. I've got a witness here who says Gomes threatened her, claiming to be FBI."

Vasquez and Forrester exchanged glances.

"You knew?" Wilson said.

"Gomes's dental records matched a special agent who's been missing for nearly two years," Vasquez said. "But his prints belong to an ex-ABI."

"ABI?"

"*Agência Brasileira de Inteligência*," Forrester said. "Brazil's CIA."

"So, which is he?" Wilson asked.

"We're trying to figure that out," said Vasquez. "But we need to discover who sent Devi Patel that message."

"It has to be Silva," Forrester said.

"I don't think so." Vasquez ticked off the points on her fingers. "The number doesn't match Silva's. And phone logs show Patel called Silva twice from the office—the last was only a few minutes before we arrived."

"Did you try calling Silva's phone?" Forrester asked.

"It goes straight to voicemail," Vasquez said.

Forrester grunted. "Keep grilling the secretary. If it wasn't Silva, someone else arranged for Pickens and Peterman to be her clients. I want to know why."

He stormed off, leaving Vasquez and Wilson uncomfortably alone.

After another moment of awkward silence, Vasquez said, "Well, I better get back to work."

"Hold on." Wilson grabbed her arm.

Vasquez's hair flipped over her forehead as she turned to him. Her lips parted expectantly.

Wilson flushed and released her arm. "I wanted to talk to you about Forrester."

"Oh." Vasquez pouted briefly. "I know. He's on the hunt again."

"No, that's not it." He checked to make sure they were alone. "I think he planted that gun at the Gomes crime scene."

"Why would he do that?"

"I don't know, but he's done it before. And if Gomes was working for both the FBI and Zero Dark—"

"You don't trust him."

Wilson shook his head.

She sighed. "Thank you for coming to me. I'll keep my eye out for anything suspicious. Who's that witness you mentioned?"

"The wife of Mitchell Parker. Did you know him?"

Vasquez stared blankly. "Nope. Who was he?"

"A detective investigating Francisco Martins a few years ago. His wife Miranda says he was working with the Bureau."

"Strange. I didn't see his name mentioned in the files. Maybe Charles knew him."

"Yeah, maybe." Wilson rubbed his chin. Forrester knew him, all right. And probably what really happened to him. "She's pretty shaken. I'm going to recommend she be put in witness protection."

"Good idea. I'll set up that BOLO on Silva." Vasquez turned to leave and then stopped. She lightly squeezed his arm. "I know you think the pretty doctor is innocent, but we need to protect the public. There's a good chance she's crazy or playing a deadly game. Maybe both."

"But if she is innocent," Wilson said, "we have a duty to protect her, too."

Vasquez's smile faltered. She released his arm and left without another word.

Wilson pressed his fist against the wall, leaned his forehead against it. Vasquez was right. After all, Cristina was treating two terrorists and having clandestine meetings with a third. But he still believed her. And now she'd disappeared. Which meant she could be in trouble and he was powerless to help.

No, not powerless. Wilson straightened his shirt, then glanced at Devi Patel who still staring straight ahead. Forrester was right about one thing. Devi knew more than she was telling. He just needed to ask the right questions.

Cristina twisted the pay phone's cord between her fingers. "Andrea, it's me."

"Where are you? I've been calling you for hours. And what number is this?"

The cacophony of travelers rushing through the Dulles Airport international terminal made Andrea's voice hard to hear.

Cristina touched her forehead. "It's a long story."

"I hope it's a good one," said Andrea. "I'm already at Reagan Airport."

"I'm not going back to Boston. You have to leave without me."

"What? Are you okay?"

"I'm fine." Cristina swallowed hard and glanced over her shoulder at her rescuer, who stood watch a few feet away. "I'm with Mitchell."

The silence on the other end of the phone deafened her. Cristina braced herself for the imminent onslaught of questions.

"Mitchell Parker? Are you seeing dead people now?"

"He's not dead. It's hard to explain."

"Oh, I bet it's hard. What I'm hearing is either he lied to you or you lied to me about his death. And neither possibility makes me happy."

Cristina cringed. "I know, and I promise I'll tell you everything, but I can't do it now."

"Are you in trouble?"

Cristina glanced at Mitchell, who was typing something on his phone. "I'm handling it. But I have to disappear for a little while."

"You once told me that if you feed delusions, like superhero fantasies, you disconnect from reality entirely. You see everyone, even your friends, as enemies. Promise me that won't happen."

Andrea's words struck like a knife to Cristina's chest. "I'm not delusional."

Andrea sighed. "Fine. I believe you. Is there anything I can do to help?"

"Can you please take care of Grizabella? The landlord has a standing order to let you into my apartment in emergencies."

"Of course, I will."

"Thank you." Cristina fought the urge to sob. "Stay alert. And don't talk to anyone, especially the FBI."

"FBI? Jesus, Cristina, what've you gotten yourself into?"

"I don't know."

After she hung up, Mitchell said to Cristina, "Do you have a passport?"

"Yes. I used it to board the flight here since I never renewed my driver's license. You want me to leave the country?"

"Quinn's operatives can find you anywhere within U.S. borders. Your best bet is off-grid."

"But what about my patients? I can't disappear—"

"Your life is in danger and you're worried about your patients?" He chuckled. "You're something special, Cristina."

They held each other's gaze for a breathless moment.

She turned away and brushed a lock of hair behind her ear. "Let's go."

"Right." Mitchell tucked his hand under his elbow and nudged Cristina forward. "We've got a private jet waiting at the special departure gate. They'll take you wherever you want to go."

"You're not coming with?"

"If I disappear, Quinn will figure out I'm a mole." Mitchell withdrew a squat black device from his pocket. "Keep this safe. Use it when you find something against him."

"Is it a weapon?" She studied it. "What does it do?"

He flipped it open to reveal a keypad. "When you push these numbers, it sends your voice through the air to my phone."

Cristina fought the urge to slap him. "You're still an arrogant jerk."

"Part of my charm." He handed her the phone. "It's a satellite phone with a GPS ghost. Use it anywhere in the word and anyone not using a special decoder will think you're five thousand miles away."

Cristina pocketed the phone. "Clever."

"Don't contact anyone but me, including that detective."

"Gary Wilson? But he's been helping me."

"If he's working with those FBI agents, you can't trust him. You know nothing about him."

Cristina clucked her tongue. "I could say the same about you."

"I'm sorry I misled you, but others will do much worse." Mitchell clasped his hands around hers. "Promise to be careful."

An uncomfortable thrill ran up Cristina's arms, recalling the same feeling when they'd first touched. She studied the fine wrinkles around Mitchell's eyes. He seemed sincere. And he had saved her life.

Softly, she said, "I promise."

"Good." He released her hands. "We better get you to the gate."

"Wait. My pills were in my backpack."

"Forget them."

"I can't. There's an extra bottle in my desk. If we call Devi—"

"There's no time." He held her elbow again and ushered her forward.

"But I could lose everything. I'll forget who I am."

Mitchell stopped short. Grabbed her shoulders. Looked in her eyes. "No pills can define who you are. Okay?" His lip trembled, almost imperceptibly. "You're the woman I fell in love with."

"Oh, Mitchell—"

He waved her off. "I know, it's bad timing. But when we get through this, I want to make it up to you. Maybe we can start again?"

For just a moment, Cristina wanted to forgive him, to start again, or maybe hold onto something from her past that wasn't a complete lie. Then she remembered how he had used her, the hell he had put her through when she thought he was dead. And despite his warning, she trusted Detective Wilson, maybe more than she did Mitchell.

After a glance at the security line, Cristina adjusted her coat. "Let's get through this madness and see what happens."

"All right," Mitchell said, disappointment tugging at the corners of his eyes even as he tried to remain unflappable. "We have safehouses everywhere. Have you figured out where you want to go?"

With her life unraveling, her only hope was to find a clue about what Quinn wanted from her, something she could use against him. Or maybe someone. Her fingers brushed over the locket under her blouse.

"Brazil, of course."

CHAPTER FORTY-NINE

"*Bem vindo ao* Rio de Janeiro," the pilot said over the intercom after the sleek Lear jet touched down at Galeão-Antonio Carlos Jobim International Airport. "Welcome to Rio, Dr. Silva. Please remain in your seat until Jimmy gives you the okay."

Cristina fought to remain calm as she placed her declaration card inside her passport and clutched it against her chest. Jimmy, the copilot, had already briefed her on the customs process. While it wouldn't be as simple as they made it seem in spy movies, it would be faster than going through the main terminal.

"It's *Carnival*. They're so used to celebrities and diplomats coming by private jet." He laughed. "They'll assume you're a supermodel."

Despite his reassurance, Cristina's neck muscles tightened when she saw the uniformed officer waiting at the hangar entrance. She scanned her passport for the tenth time. Her visa was good for another year. Good thing her parents had been planning that trip ...

Cristina gripped the passport more tightly. Were they really her parents?

The cockpit door opened. Jimmy appeared with a mannequin-quality smile. "You're good to go. Remember, your ticket says you return in three weeks, but we can come get you whenever you need."

"Right."

"You've got the address for the safehouse?"

She recited the Alto Leblon address he'd given her.

"That's it." He ushered her to the hatch. "Don't worry. They'll have everything you need. We do this all the time."

As Cristina stepped onto the air stairs, the summer heat assaulted her, making her winter clothes feel ten times heavier. She glanced over her shoulder.

Jimmy waved. "You'll be fine. Don't forget to stop by Zuma's. They have the best stroganoff around."

She half-smiled and continued down the stairs. Her heart pounded as she approached the customs officer. A local meal was the last thing on her mind.

When Cristina reached the bottom of the stairs, she forced a smile and handed her passport to the officer with a warm, "*Bom dia.*"

"*Bom dia.*" He plucked the passport from her fingers.

As he flipped through the pages, she held her breath. What if he doubted her identity? What if he ran fingerprints? At any moment, Cristina expected him to rip off a mask, revealing Agent Forrester, and shout, "Gotcha!"

The officer looked up. "How long is your stay in Rio?"

"Three weeks."

"Business or pleasure?"

She wanted to say neither. "Pleasure."

He studied Cristina's face, then the passport, then her face again. Seconds ticked by. Cristina tried to keep her expression neutral, to pretend the sweat running down her forehead was from the heat.

The officer pounded a stamp onto her passport and again on her arrival card. "Welcome to Rio."

Fifteen minutes later, Cristina stepped again into the sticky outdoors. She'd thought the CIA would've provided her a private vehicle, maybe a limo, but Jimmy told her she needed to rely on local transportation. Zero Dark had discovered all the agency's Rio contacts. For their own protection, they had to disavow themselves of any connection. Inside the safehouse, the agents could protect her, but in public Cristina was on her own. Still, Jimmy warned her to ignore the gypsy cab drivers who bombarded her as she left the terminal and only use an official yellow taxi.

After a minute of searching, Cristina found one. As the young driver opened the door for her, he looked puzzled.

"*Não tem* baggage?"

She shook her head. In Portuguese, she said, "I travel light."

He helped her inside, closed the door, climbed into the driver's seat, and turned back to face her. "*Ipanema?*"

When the driver smiled, Cristina saw a half dozen missing teeth.

Cristina started to recite the address Jimmy gave her but stopped. Once she entered the safehouse, they'd probably keep her there. And she had one question she needed to answer before that happened. She removed the locket from around her neck and held it out to the driver. "Actually, do you know where this is?"

"Of course! Very famous place in Rio. But very boring." His eyebrows bounced up and down. "You prefer to go to *Copacabana*, no? Much better party."

"Thank you, but no. If you know where this is, please take me there."

The driver shrugged and started the taxi. "*Tudo bem.* But do not complain to me when you miss out on good samba."

A ringing woke Gary Wilson from deep sleep. He slammed the snooze button on his alarm clock and buried his face in his pillow. He tried to return to sleep and failed. His mind had remained full throttle for hours after he dropped into bed, and now he was paying for the lack of sleep. Every time Wilson had closed his eyes, he'd thought of another possible connection between Agent Forrester and Zero Dark. And when he'd finally manage to stop thinking about that, he'd worry about Cristina and what might've happened to her. Reports said that she'd boarded a private jet bound for Paris before the no-fly went into effect, and then disappeared. What the hell could she be doing in France?

Groaning, Wilson rolled over and pressed his thumbs against his forehead. He'd hoped interrogating Devi Patel would yield low-lying fruit, but the woman had remained harder to shake than a granite pillar. It was only near the very end, after he'd asked for the fourth time where Cristina was, that Devi's demeanor softened.

"You care about her, don't you?" she asked, searching his face.

"I care about her safety, as I would any victim's," he answered quickly, hoping anyone watching wouldn't pick up on the subtext of her question. "And I know you do, too. That's why I need you to tell me anything that might help us find her."

Devi swirled her tongue inside her mouth and then motioned him closer. Cautiously, keeping his fists ready in case she tried to attack him, he leaned in.

She whispered, "You know where she was, right? She told you?"

Keeping his expression passive, he nodded.

"She said to trust you. Did she give you something before she left?"

Remembering the burner phone—hidden in his apartment until he figured out what to with it—Wilson nodded again.

"Don't lose it."

Devi leaned back and crossed her arms, staring straight ahead. Wilson tried pressing her, but she remained silent after that. When he left the room, he found Agent Vasquez watching through the one-way mirror.

"What was that about?" she asked, brow furrowed.

He shrugged. "A few choice words about your agency. Not worth repeating."

The ringing restarted, shocking him back to the present. He snatched up the alarm clock and realized it was turned off. He traced the ringing back to the cell phone on his nightstand.

"Cristina," he said after activating the phone. "Where are you?"

"It's not Cristina." The voice was deep and masculine, with a heavy accent.

"Who the hell is this?" Wilson checked the caller ID and realized he wasn't holding his phone. He was holding the phone that Santos had given Cristina.

"Detective Wilson, my associate told me to trust you, and so I'm reaching out to you because I fear Cristina is in danger." The caller breathed heavily into the mouthpiece. "I need your help."

CHAPTER FIFTY

Blaring horns and thrumming engines surrounded the taxi as they crept along the bustling Avenida Republico do Chile through the center of town. Devils, superheroes, birds and natives mingled with throngs of whooping partygoers dancing and taking selfies. Cristina's taxi turned off the packed street, passing through a metal gate and up a narrow lane. Cristina marveled at the conical pyramid directly ahead. Off to the right stood another tower comprised of layered rings, topped with a simple cross. They rolled to a stop in front of the pyramid.

"*Chegamos.*" The driver engaged the emergency brake, then turned and gesticulated at the pyramid. "Metropolitan Cathedral. *Oitenta Reais.*"

"Eighty?" Cristina frowned. "You said sixty."

"Yes." He gave an apologetic smile. "But traffic was very bad, you know? That is the risk when you visit Rio during Carnival."

Sighing, Cristina flipped through a roll of colorful bills. She'd been surprised when copilot Jimmy had handed her a giant wad of Brazilian currency.

"Ten thousand Reais," he'd said. "Plenty to get to the safehouse. Once there, our agents can get you whatever you need."

"You had this lying around?"

"We keep over fifty different currencies available so agents don't have to deal with local exchanges or bank cards that can be tracked or hacked. Once you leave the Rio airport, use cash only. No hired cars, no plastic, nothing traceable. It will be easy to disappear in a crowd of two million tourists." Jimmy had given her a pointed look. "Cristina Silva needs to become a ghost."

Now, she shuddered at the irony of his statement. Cristina Silva was already a ghost. So, what did that make her now?

"Here." She counted out five bills and handed them to the driver. "Keep the change."

"If you get bored praying, a samba parade runs through here in twenty minutes." He gave a thumbs-up. "Free party!"

Cristina managed a faint smile. "Thanks. I'll keep that in mind."

As she stepped out of the cab, the air stuck to her skin like hot oil.

"*Boa sorte!*" He drove off.

Cristina fingered the locket around her neck as she studied the cathedral. What could this place have to do with Santos's daughter? Maybe the origin of the locket wasn't important, which meant Cristina had wasted a trip. But as long as she was there, she would check it out.

Two men stood at the entrance, dressed all in black, with heavy bulletproof vests and combat boots. Each held a semiautomatic rifle. Badges on their shoulders identified them as Civil Police. Cristina tried to look like a casual tourist—not a fugitive who still wore long sleeves and dress slacks in summer heat because she had no other clothes. As she passed, their mirrored sunglasses reflected everything. Their mouths, set in grim lines, revealed nothing. Cristina caught their heads shift briefly, following her as she entered. She held her breath and kept walking. Her body tensed involuntarily.

No footsteps behind her. She dared a glance back. The guards remained in position.

Her tension ebbing, Cristina looked forward again and gasped. Gorgeous stained-glass windows stretched in columns along the four walls of the cathedral from the floor all the way to the ceiling, casting a vibrant glow over the rows of pews in the center of the chamber. The ceiling formed a cross, white light spilling through. A handful of other tourists meandered about, their footfalls echoing and reverberating.

Cautiously, Cristina took the long way around the room to the other side, staring up at the glass arcs. A fresco depicted two cardinals smiling at what she assumed was Christ, while what appeared to be a brown rope twisted between them. She figured it had some religious meaning that escaped her. She scanned the other frescoes.

By the time Cristina reached the opposite wall, her chest felt heavy with disappointment. None of this sparked any personal recognition or memory, and she had no idea how it connected to Santos or his daughter. She sat on a pew and stared at the fresco. Now what? Go to the safehouse and hide?

Her watch beeped. She cursed and shut it off. She'd already missed another three doses of Recognate. How long before she started losing memories?

As Cristina trudged back to the entrance, she passed a tour group taking photos in front of a statue. She glanced at the statue and did a double take. The statue was of a man tied to a tree. Arrows pierced his chest and thigh. She pulled the locket out from under her shirt. The statue matched the engraving.

"Excuse me," she asked the woman she decided was the tour group leader. Cristina pointed at the statue. "Who is this?"

"*Sao Sebastião*," the woman said with a hint of annoyance at being interrupted. "Rio's patron saint."

The guide continued her spiel, but Cristina wasn't listening.

She stared at the statue, her mind hearing the clicking of pieces falling into place.

"Sebastian dos Santos," she whispered. "Sebastian of the saints."

Cristina's pulse pounded as she waited for the guide to finish. She was in the right place, after all. As soon as the tour group moved on, she sprang to the statue and inspected it. No obvious imperfections. She crouched and ran her finger along the base, hoping to find a note tucked away, or maybe a secret switch.

As she touched the marble surface, the scene changed. Organ music channeled through hidden pipes. Worshippers filed in to fill every pew, rubbing against each other. The pungent odor of sweat hung heavy in the air. An archbishop raised his arms, leading the congregation in prayer. A woman sat beside her, seeming vaguely familiar though Cristina couldn't see her face.

What is this? The organ music swelled into a majestic coda. *A memory?*

Yes, said the voice in her mind. *But not yours.*

Outside the church, someone shouted. Then gunfire at the entrance.

Everyone screamed. Scattered in all directions. Some stumbled, fell, only to be trampled by others fleeing. Cristina knelt, throwing her hands over her head. More gunshots echoed. She shrieked.

She heard her name. Gazed upward. A giant stood over her, dressed in black. She tried to focus on his face but could not make it out. From his back sprouted two wings. He spoke, his voice thick with an accent she couldn't place, but gentle. "It'll be all right. You can trust me …"

Look out!

The image vanished. Cristina heard footsteps behind her.

Her body reacted. She spun. Her fist shot out. Connected

with bone. The police officer staggered backward, hands covering his nose. His sunglasses clattered on the ground.

Behind him, his partner retreated. The officer swung his rifle toward Cristina.

She lunged. Somersaulted. Wrapped her thighs around his head. Squeezed as they toppled.

The Brazilian policeman howled. Dropped his rifle. Cristina jammed her knees against the base of his neck. The policeman dug at her legs, choking. She squeezed tighter. He collapsed. She tumbled off. Snatched up his rifle. Clutched it by the muzzle. Twirled, swinging it like a baseball bat. The butt crashed into the first officer's temple. He collapsed.

Cristina sprinted, clutching the rifle. Her heart raced, senses heightened. The congregation parted, allowing her to pass. Their frightened murmurs reverberated in her ears. She pressed on until reaching the exit.

Sunlight blinded her. Drumbeats echoed up the hill from the street below. She shielded her eyes. A mass of partygoers paraded, singing and dancing around floats filled with samba bands and costumed revelers.

"Stop," someone shouted from behind.

Cristina glanced back. A woman appeared at the cathedral entrance. Dark hair spilled over the shoulders of her bright pink sundress.

Keep running. You're not safe.

The woman transformed, morphing into Carl Franklin, dressed in fatigues and a combat helmet. An assault rifle appeared in his hand. Blood streamed down the side of Carl's face. His brow furrowed. Lips twisted into a snarl.

"You did this," he said, his voice sounding distant, filtered. "You'll pay."

Cristina fired her rifle at the Carl apparition, and he scrambled for cover. Cristina threw away the gun. Bolted down the hill toward the street. She reached the parade, dived into the crowd. Fell in step with a group of revelers.

A girl in a bikini and blue afro locked arms with Cristina and handed her a plastic cup overflowing with greenish liquid and mashed-up limes.

Drink it, the voice commanded.

Cristina's eyes darted side to side. No sign of Carl Franklin lookalikes or the police. But the people dancing around her had noticed her odd clothing choice. They eyed her suspiciously, whispering among themselves. Up ahead, Cristina spotted three police officers dragging away unruly carousers, beating them with billy clubs.

Blend in! If you don't look like you belong, they'll turn you in.

A powerful craving overtook Cristina. She threw back the drink. The afro girl cheered her on. A cold tingle rushed over her. She drained the glass. Her feet felt lighter. The voice ceased.

Cristina.

This time it wasn't from inside her head. Her heart pounded as she looked around. Someone was calling her name. She scanned the crowd.

Cristina.

Her senses heightened. Alcohol, sweat and urine assaulted her nostrils. She pushed her way through a sea of dancing bodies.

Cristina.

Her name resounded from every direction. She covered her ears, snapped her eyes shut.

Liar. You lied to us.

Cristina's eyes flew open. Everyone around her was dressed in rags. Blood streamed from their foreheads. They pointed at her with bony fingers.

You did this to us.

"No!" Her temples throbbed, bass drums pounding. "I don't know what you want."

Cristina.

"Stop. Please stop." She covered her ears again. Their shouts permeated her fingers, over and over. *Liar! Liar!*

"Sabrina."

A hand wrapped around her wrist.

Cristina jammed her nails into the assailant's fingers. Heard a pained cry. Spun around. Slammed her fist against the attacker's elbow. Another howl. Cristina rolled to the ground. Jumped up to face her attacker.

"*Ai! Puta que pariu!*" It was the woman in the pink sundress. She clutched her hand and pressed it against full lips. Her dark hair fell away, revealing warm coffee-colored eyes and a regal nose. "*Ta doida?*"

The voices stopped. The bloody specters vanished. The pounding in Cristina's head subsided. Merrymakers jostled her as they shoved past.

"I'm sorry," Cristina said. "I thought you were trying to hurt me."

"I only wanted to speak to you." The woman surveyed Cristina from head to toe and shook her head. "*Não acredito.* I didn't believe it was you, but it is. I thought I'd never see you again, Sabrina."

Apprehension crawled up the back of Cristina's neck. "What did you call me?"

The woman tilted her head. "Sabrina. That's your name."

Cristina's cheeks cooled. It hadn't been her name she'd heard being called. It was Sabrina. Somehow her mind had changed it, made it familiar.

Cristina's fingers clenched. "How do you know me?"

"It's me, Maria." The woman touched her chest. "Your sister."

CHAPTER FIFTY-ONE

Detective Gary Wilson studied the other T passengers as he descended the stairwell at Government Center Station. College students and union workers mingled with straitlaced executives, all bundled in scarves and parkas. An E line train arrived and quickly filled, leaving a dozen passengers waiting for the next. Wilson wanted to plug his ears. The constant clacking, flickering fluorescents, and stench of body odor made it tough to keep down his meager breakfast of corn flakes and coffee. He meandered to a bench and waited.

Santos had chosen this meeting place wisely. Wilson watched passengers force their way aboard a B line train. Cell phones were useless underground. It was easy to blend into the crowd. And there were ample escape routes.

Wilson knew the signs of surveillance from years of stakeouts: the businessman who never turned the newspaper page, the woman drinking the same cup of coffee long after it's been emptied, or the panhandler who didn't seem to care about how much money was coming in. Wilson didn't spot anyone out of place.

"Excuse me."

A blind man wobbled before Wilson, tapping his white cane against the bench. He was tall, broad shouldered. Sunglasses shielded his eyes. A wool hat covered his ears.

As Wilson shifted to make room, he noticed the man's swollen ankle. "Hey, you should get that foot looked at."

"I'll be fine, Detective."

Wilson was startled. "Santos?"

"Avoid eye contact or names. I've ensured no one's followed us, but let's not take any chances."

Facing forward, Wilson side-eyed Santos. Now he recognized the broad chin, the heavy eyebrows and the bulbous nose from the BOLO. It took all Wilson's will not to punch him in the face. "What makes you think I won't haul your ass to the station?"

Santos remained placid. "If you thought it ended with me, you wouldn't have come alone."

Wilson tried to think of a good response but came up empty. "All right, where's Cristina?"

"I thought you knew."

"Last I heard, she was headed for Paris."

"Paris?" Santos's lip quivered. "I doubt it. I expect she's on track to find the truth."

"Do you always speak in riddles?"

"Detective, only when I'm sure I can trust you will I give you a direct answer." Santos winced as he shifted his foot. "I'm in no condition to run if we're caught, so we must make this brief. Did Cristina tell you why she went to Washington?"

"It had to do with an experimental drug—Recognate, right?"

"Yes. The memory drug she prescribed for Carl Franklin, Jerry Peterman, and herself."

"Wait—she's taking it?"

"Yes. Which means she faces imminent danger." Santos leaned down to scratch his leg. As he did, he said, "All these deaths are because of the drug. If you want to help, learn whatever you can about it."

"How? The prescription bottle didn't have a company name or an address, and I can't find anything online. I tried calling the number on the bottle, but no one answered."

"If you cannot find where something is, start by looking where it is not." Santos straightened his cane and prepared to stand. "When you find it, contact me again."

"Wait." Wilson pretended to help the old man to his feet and yanked his arm, pulling Santos closer. "What about Devi? The Feds still have her."

"Talented young woman, yes? She's an aspiring actress I hired to monitor Cristina, but she knows nothing that can help us." Santos withdrew his arm. "Do not tell the FBI about this meeting. Trust no one."

"So why should I trust you?"

"You shouldn't. However, desperation makes for strange bedfellows. Cristina had faith in you, so I must do the same." Santos slipped a burner phone into Wilson's hand. "You may call me just once. Betray my trust and you'll never find me again."

Wilson casually slipped the phone into his pocket. "Betray my trust, and I'll see you in Hell."

"Don't fear, Detective. We have one thing in common."

"What's that?"

Santos made eye contact. "We both want to find Cristina alive."

Cristina pressed a trembling hand against her forehead. The world seemed to spin as the samba parade surged around her. "I have a sister?"

"You look terribly ill." Maria grabbed Cristina's hand. "I'll take you to a hospital."

"No." Cristina ripped her hand away. "No hospitals."

"You need a doctor."

"I am a doctor. I'm not letting someone I don't know drug me."

"Don't you trust me?"

As Cristina scanned Maria's face, she felt a twinge of recognition, but it faded. "I don't know you."

Frowning, Maria glanced side to side before holding out her hand. "Then we must change that. Come with me."

Cristina hesitated. Could she trust this woman? Ever since she left Washington, she had been forgetting the people she knew best. She could no longer remember the color of Claudia Silva's eyes. Who was left to help her, before she forgot her own name?

"All right." Cristina took Maria's hand. "But no hospitals."

"You have my word." Maria led Cristina through the crowd to the sidewalk and then to a side street. As they walked, Cristina's gaze darted, searching for attackers. Nothing happened. Her paranoia ebbed, but she remained alert.

After another block, Maria led Cristina into a parking lot and over to a green Ford Ka. They buckled in. Maria revved the engine and honked as she squeezed into the traffic.

They drove in silence, and Cristina tried to sort reality from fiction. How much of what she had seen in the cathedral was memory and how much was hallucination? Was she remembering her past life or was she losing her mind?

A few minutes later, they arrived at a gated community. A lofty apartment building towered beyond a gate bordered by manicured trees and hedges. Maria rolled down her window.

The guard peeked in and nodded. "Bem vindo de volta, Senhora Carvalho."

He waved them through.

They parked in front of the building. Cristina's fingers tingled with apprehension, and she suddenly feared she could be walking into a trap.

"Our last name is Carvalho?" she asked.

"Yes, but it's complicated." Maria led Cristina up two flights and down a short hallway. They stopped at Apartment Twelve. Maria glanced over her shoulder before unlocking and opening the door. "Inside. Quickly."

Entering the apartment, Cristina felt like she'd stepped through a funhouse mirror. A flat-screen TV overlooked sleek leather couches and a glass-top coffee table with a heavy bronze statuette of Christ the Redeemer. Mint-colored paint covered the walls. Luxuriant silk drapes framed the windows. The place was familiar and yet it wasn't.

She turned to Maria. "How did you happen to be at the cathedral right when—?"

Maria slapped her across the face. Cristina recoiled in shock, her hand to her cheek.

Maria said, "That's for letting me think you were dead."

"Dead?"

"You told me you were in trouble and then refused to let me help you. You said if I didn't hear from you in three days to assume you were dead." She clenched her fists. Her lip trembled. "That was three years ago. Once before, you ran off to study English in America for a year, but this time, you didn't return. Every Carnival since then, I've gone to the cathedral and lit a candle for you. And now here you are."

Cristina forced down the rage swelling from being slapped. Her cheek stung, but what hurt more was the unexplainable sense of guilt to this woman she didn't know. "For the past two years I've thought I was Cristina Silva. I didn't even know you existed."

"Who's Cristina Silva?"

"She, I mean me, I mean—it doesn't matter. Until a few weeks ago, I knew who I was and then that changed. Now I don't know what's real and what's not." Cristina studied Maria's unassuming elliptical eyes, her prominent cheekbones, the creamy mocha color of her skin—yes, she could be her sister but with plastic surgery, so could anyone. "I don't know who I am, and I'm losing my mind."

Maria stared back. After several beats, she approached. Cristina retreated, muscles tensed.

Maria stopped, tilted her head, and then spread her arms. "*Vem ca.*"

Cristina didn't move. What trick was this?

Muttering to herself, Maria advanced, pulling Cristina into her arms. "You're not losing your mind. You're regaining it."

A warm feeling of security and belonging rushed over Cristina in a way her memories of Jorge and Claudia Silva never had. Her body relaxed. She hugged back.

After a moment, Maria released her. "Who did this to you?"

"Some dangerous people. Did I ever mention anyone named Quinn to you?"

"No."

"Zero Dark?"

"No."

The locket brushed against Cristina's skin. She wrapped her hand around it. The image of a winged man resurfaced, stretching out his hand as chaos rocked the cathedral. Again, she tried to focus on his face but failed. "What about Sebastian dos Santos?"

Maria's gaze narrowed. "So it was no coincidence you were at the cathedral."

"No. I was trying to find someone: a girl. But instead, I remembered a man with wings."

"Sebastian dos Santos." Maria made the sign of a cross. "You were very young when gang members attacked the cathedral. A man rescued you, carried you outside, and then fled. We never learned his name. You called him Sebastian dos Santos."

"After Saint Sebastian." The vision intensified, but now

Cristina could see that the wings belonged to the fresco behind the man. "I thought he was my guardian angel. So, what I saw in my vision at the cathedral really happened."

"Yes, but years ago." Maria's brow furrowed. She placed a hand on Cristina's forehead. "What's wrong? Your skin is pale and wet."

The room started spinning. Thoughts and memories clashed in Cristina's mind. She tried to control her breathing and nudged away Maria's hand. "I'm fine."

"I should call a doctor," Maria said.

"No doctors." Cristina leaned against the wall, clenching her fist, willing the man's face to clarify. What if Santos had been her savior? Had he been in her life all along? A powerful craving struck, stronger than the one in the samba parade. She relaxed her fist and tried to smile. "It's a lot to absorb. I could use something to drink."

"Of course." Maria escorted her to the sofa. "*Caiparinha?*"

"Excuse me?"

"A drink made from *cachaça* sugar. I make them strong."

"Great. Thank you." As Maria entered the kitchen, Cristina shut her eyes. Memories of the Silvas swirled away as she clutched at them. Shadows swelled without form. "You live here alone?"

"Yes," Maria said over chopping sounds. "Ever since you disappeared … and Mother died."

Cristina bolted upright. Her heart ached in a way it never had when she learned about the Silvas' deaths. "She died?"

Maria appeared holding two glasses filled with cloudy liquid and crushed limes. She handed one to Cristina and sat beside her. Cristina took a sip. A pleasant rush of sweet and sour rolled over her tongue. She took a bigger gulp. The cravings subsided.

"She died of dengue last year." Maria sipped her drink. "Father's death stole her will to live."

"Father—?"

"My father. Your stepfather. He died shortly after you left." Maria sighed. "It has been very difficult."

More dead ends. Frustrated, Cristina drained the glass. "I'm sorry. But what about my father? Do you know where he is?"

Maria shook her head. "No. I don't even know his name. Father adopted you when he married Mother. My entire life, you've been Sabrina Carvalho."

Cristina slowly twisted the glass in her hand. How could she know if anything Maria said was true? "Tell me about our mother. I can't even picture her."

"She was beautiful inside and out. She loved you very much." Maria pointed across the room. "There's a picture of her."

The glass slipped from Cristina's fingers and crashed to the floor. Her mind shattered, spraying memory fragments in all directions. She shook her head. It wasn't possible.

In a silver frame was a portrait similar to a smaller one she'd found nestled in a locket—a smiling woman with chestnut hair, delicate features, and coffee-colored eyes.

Dazed, she turned back to Maria, who had rushed to clean up the broken glass. How could Cristina not see it before? They had the same eyes.

"Maria."

Maria looked up. "Are you okay? Your hands are shaking."

Unable to speak, Cristina removed the chain from her neck. Fingers trembling, she opened the locket and showed it to Maria. "Are you the girl in this photo?"

"No." look of puzzlement spread over Maria's face. "This girl is you."

CHAPTER FIFTY-TWO

Detective Wilson sat at his desk, staring at the mess he'd doodled on a yellow notepad. Quinn. Gomes. Parker. Cristina and her patients. He'd written their names and drawn lines of varying thickness between them, trying to understand the connections. Parker was the key. Was he FBI? Zero Dark? Or something else?

"Gary." Hawkins waved his hand in Wilson's face. "Anyone home?"

"Sorry. I was trying to figure this out."

"What is it? A spiderweb?"

"It's sort of a string theory chart. I think if we find the fake Parker, we'll find out who Quinn is. And maybe even how Agent Forrester fits in."

Hawkins pursed his lips.

"What?"

"Captain Harris thinks we're dedicating too much time to this. He wants us to work with Vice on finding the source of a new designer drug popping up at the high schools."

Wilson's cheeks cooled. "Why would he think that?"

"Dunno. But I saw Forrester buddying up to him this morn-ing while you were—Where were you, anyway?"

"Overslept." Wilson thumped his fist on the desk. He had to

keep his meeting with Santos secret. No point giving Forrester more ammunition to use against him. "Bastard must know we're onto him."

"Maybe he just doesn't like you."

"Do you believe that?"

"Nah, what decent person could resist your sparkling personality?" Hawkins's serious expression betrayed his joke. "Even if Forrester is dirty, he's a Fed. He probably covered his tracks."

"I know, but even the best criminal masterminds slip up." Wilson frowned at his scribbles. "And I still don't get how this drug fits into the picture."

"The *R* stands for the drug?"

"Recognate. Yeah."

"Why didn't you write one over Peterman? I thought he was taking it."

"Don't you remember? Cristina told Vasquez the coroner didn't find it in his …" Wilson trailed off. Moles lined up and then fell one by one. He heard Santos's voice: *If you cannot find where something is, start by looking where it is not.* "Son of a bitch."

"What?"

"What's the medical examiner's name?"

"Morgan, I think. He's at the downtown office."

Wilson jumped up and grabbed his coat. "Cover for me?"

"What do you want from the M.E.?"

"If Harris asks, better you don't know."

As he ran out the door, Wilson made sure he had both burner phones in his coat pocket. If Morgan could answer his questions, he might be one step closer to finding Cristina and a solution to the case.

"This isn't possible." Cristina paced the room, pounding her fists against her skull in a vain attempt to force the idea of Santos as her father out of her head. "Fuck."

"Stop." Maria grabbed Cristina's wrists.

Maria's hands felt like ants crawling across Cristina's skin. She pushed her sister away. "Don't touch me."

"What's happening to you? Why are you doing this?"

"Don't you see? This has all been for nothing." Cristina ripped the locket from her neck and held it high. "The woman I was trying to find for Santos is me. Get it? I came all the way here to find his daughter, but I'm his daughter."

"Your father died in a car accident before I was born."

"A car accident." Cristina snorted. "Where have I heard that one before?"

"How can you be certain this man is who he claims?"

"I just know. I ..." Cristina glanced again at her mother's picture. "Do you have pictures of my father here?"

"I've never seen one."

"Naturally." Each strand Cristina grabbed at shredded into a million unusable threads. She ground her fist into her palm. "It has to be him."

"So, if he is your father, why not tell you?"

"I don't know. He said I'd find the information I needed to convince his daughter who she really was, and ..." Cold beads of sweat trailed down Cristina's forehead as she made the connection. "I'm Zero Dark's prisoner."

"Who?

"A mercenary group. ReMind. That's what he meant. They've been using me all along. Maybe they even planned for me to come here."

"You're not making sense. What's ReMind?"

"A drug company. They're tied to Zero Dark." Images of Simmons, Stacey and Jerry Peterman, and Santos clicked into place like a game of Connect Four. "They used me to keep Jerry Peterman under control. They threw me under the bus when it all to hell. That's what Santos wanted me to see. There must be something here in Brazil that will expose them."

Maria sat on the couch and took a swig of caipirinha. She wiped her mouth and placed the glass on the table before looking up. "Does this involve your research?"

Cristina did a double take. "You know about my research?"

"Of course," Maria said. "Your work was supposed to solve Rio's problems with violence. I assumed that failure was why you disappeared."

"Violence?" Cristina recalled the *O Globo* article. "I *was* working with Kobayashi. But what failure? The favelas are supposed to be safe now."

"Safe? Ha!" Maria spat at the floor. "The government wants tourists to believe they're safe, so they'll come enjoy sporting events and spend much money. All lies. Just because the pacification police units have expelled the gangs doesn't mean the favelas are safe. They're more dangerous now than they were before."

Liar. You lied to us.

Once again, ghostly faces surrounded Cristina, mouths gaping. Children chanted as they shot at each other. The smell of charred flesh assaulted her. She screamed.

Maria blinked rapidly. "What's happening?"

The images vanished. Cristina staggered over to the couch. Afterimages of the violence smoldered on her retina and then faded. Sweat streamed down both cheeks. "Why is it more dangerous now?"

"I don't think now is—"

"Tell me." Cristina stumbled and fell against Maria. She squeezed her sister's arm. "What happened to them?"

Maria pressed her lips together. "For all their terrible deeds, the gangs kept their home in order. The government only cared about proving they're in charge. Your research didn't decrease violence in the favelas. It gave the government an excuse to control the gangs."

Don't listen to anything she says.

"Shut up." Cristina covered her ears and backed away. "You're not real."

"Who are you talking to?"

"No one." Cristina held her breath. The voice stayed silent. "No one, it's … I'm fine now, but I need to speak to someone from the research team. One of them must know what happened. Can you help me?"

Maria's upper lip twitched. "I'm sorry, but I don't know anyone."

She's lying.

"Enough." Cristina jammed her fingers into her ears. She caught movement near the window. An apparition materialized, mutating into the figure of an armed man. Another appeared, and then another. They aimed heavy rifles at her. "No! They found me!"

"There's no one else here." Maria placed her hands over Cristina's wrists. "No one is going to hurt you."

Lowering her hands, Cristina tried to focus on the light scent of mango in Maria's hair, the soft touch of her skin. This was real. She had to remember that.

Nothing is real, Cristina.

A cold chill ran down Cristina's back. This voice was different—male, familiar. Like moving through molasses, she turned and saw Jerry Peterman, blood trickling from his forehead. Next to him was Carl Franklin, his head twisted at an impossible angle, one side of his face caved in.

"No. No, no, no."

It won't be long. You can't fight it, just like you can't fight Quinn.

"No!" Cristina shut her eyes and rocked—anything to block out their voices, the smell of their decaying flesh. "Focus on what you know. Focus on what you know."

Maria shook Cristina's shoulders. "What should I do?"

What do you know? You don't know anything.

"I know who I am." Cristina shoved her sister aside and leaped from the couch at her former patients. She passed through them and tumbled to the ground. She bounced to her feet, punching and kicking. They mocked her. She fought back even harder. "I know who I am. I know who—"

Pain exploded in the back of Cristina's skull. She staggered and fell. The last thing she saw before losing consciousness was Maria standing over her, wielding the statuette of Christ the Redeemer.

CHAPTER FIFTY-THREE

Every time Detective Wilson had to set foot in the morgue, he flashed back to being a sullen sixteen-year-old staring at the cold bodies of his parents. After that experience—even though he reminded himself they were long gone—he could never shake the feeling they were still there, watching him with those empty eyes. As Wilson sat on the leather couch at the Boston Medical Examiner's office, mesmerized by the fresh calla lilies, he steeled himself for what he would see inside the autopsy room.

"Detective Wilson." Dr. Morgan entered the room, wearing blue scrubs and a white lab coat. He stretched out his hand. "I'm Luke Morgan, Chief Medical Examiner."

Wilson glanced at Morgan's hand. "You weren't just, you know …?"

"I wear gloves, Detective," Morgan said. "Besides, you carry more active germs than a cadaver."

Grimacing at the image, Wilson shook Morgan's hand. "Thanks for agreeing to talk to me. I'm sure you're busy."

"Unfortunately, that's true, but I'm always available to assist law enforcement. How can I help?"

"I have questions about Jerry Peterman."

Morgan flinched. "I already told the FBI everything I knew about him."

"Well, let's see if they missed anything. Cristina said you didn't find anything unusual in his blood."

"Cristina?" Morgan seemed to survey Wilson up and down before jutting out his lip. "Huh. Makes sense now."

"What does?"

"Nothing," Morgan said. "Anyway, that's not entirely true. Jerry Peterman had abnormally high catecholamines."

"What are those?"

"Fight-or-flight neurotransmitters. High levels can cause restlessness, poor decision-making and aggressive behavior."

"You mean like a shooting rampage?"

"That's putting it bluntly."

"What could cause that?"

"Trauma, stimulants, fear, prolonged stress—although before that I had never seen levels that high. Some antidepressants raise norepinephrine but not like that."

"What about a drug you haven't seen before?"

Morgan's eyebrows knitted together. "What do you mean?"

"Cristina—Dr. Silva—was testing an experimental memory drug called Recognate. She prescribed it for Peterman and another patient who committed suicide, Carl Franklin."

The color faded from Morgan's cheeks. "I didn't know."

Wilson leaned close. "I can see you're trying to protect Cristina, but if you want to help her, I need you to be completely honest."

Morgan opened and closed his mouth before shaking his head. "I don't know anything. Why don't you ask Dr. Silva?"

"I would, but I don't know where she is."

Morgan's eyes widened. "Did something happen to her?"

"She flew to DC for a visit to the drug company that makes

Recognate. In Washington, someone attacked her, and it now seems she has fled the country."

Morgan stared at the floor. "What's the name of this company?"

"I don't know. I was hoping if we knew more about the drug, we could track it down. Did Cristina tell you anything about it?"

"No, but she kept perseverating on the trace THC."

"Tetrahydrocannabinol, the psychoactive ingredient in marijuana." Wilson scratched his chin. "She didn't know Peterman smoked pot?"

"Quite the opposite. She seemed perplexed because the quantitative analysis was negative—almost like she expected it to be high."

"Did you find THC in Carl Franklin's blood also?"

Morgan shrugged. "Trace amounts, yes."

"Did you do a quantitative analysis on him too?"

"No, she didn't request it. Anyway, alcoholics often use pot, so I assumed ..."

"Carl Franklin was an alcoholic?"

"His liver was pickled. I told Cristina yesterday."

"You talked to her yesterday?"

"Yes, but I had no idea she was out of town."

Wilson tried to get a grip on Morgan's information roller coaster. "Look, I'm not trying to bust you. Tell me what you and she discussed."

"She wanted me to examine Carl Franklin for signs of alcoholic brain degeneration. It can cause memory loss and psychosis."

"Did he have it?"

"Franklin's labs were normal, but I haven't finished autopsying his brain. If his mammillary bodies are damaged, that would make it likely."

The skin behind Wilson's ear itched. How did it all tie together? "Could someone create a drug that causes everything you found?"

"I'm sure they could, but why would they? That doesn't sound like a good memory drug."

"You're right." Wilson thumped his fists together in thought. "If I can get some Recognate pills, can you figure out what's in them?"

"I'm not a pharmacist, but I can test for the basic compounds."

"Finish your autopsy. I'll call you when I have the pills." As Morgan left the room, Wilson pulled out his cell phone and dialed. When he heard a voice on the other end, he said, "Rick, it's me."

His partner's voice was stressed. "Gary, where are you? Hell's breaking out here."

"What do you mean?"

"The tech team cracked Devi Patel's phone. They found months of deleted text messages from Patel to her contact. Most were garbled, but the most recent one was intact." Hawkins paused. "The message Patel received said to call you and you would handle everything."

Wilson's throat constricted. "Rick, I only met Devi once before. I didn't …"

"It doesn't matter. Forrester has convinced Sergeant Harris that you're the one who's dirty. Don't come back to the station."

"But—"

"Gary, they've got a BOLO on you."

The blood drained from Wilson's cheeks. "Son of a bitch. Forrester probably planted that message. He knows I'm onto him."

"I'm doing what I can, but you should stay low. They're casing your house right now."

Wilson clenched his fist. Forrester was sending him a message: Back off or else. But Wilson couldn't back off. Not when Cristina was in danger. Not when there was so much at stake.

"I'll stay in hiding, but I need a favor."

CHAPTER FIFTY-FOUR

Everything you know is a lie. Find the truth. Trust no one.

Trust no one.

Cristina jolted awake, Santos's words resonating. Pain throbbed in the back of her skull. She went to rub it and found she couldn't move her arm. Her arms and legs were tied to a chair. Maria sat on the edge of the leather couch, holding a bowl.

"Relax." The woman's lips twisted with worry. "How do you feel?"

"Like I've been drugged and tied up by someone claiming to be my sister."

"I am your sister." Maria leaned forward and held a spoonful of thick liquid near Cristina's lips. "Eat this."

"So you can drug me again?"

"It's *escaldado*. Mother's favorite soup. It will nourish you." Maria made a show of draining the spoon, swishing it around her mouth, and swallowing. "See?"

After a moment, Cristina tasted the soup. Flavors of chicken, egg, and vegetables rolled over her tongue pleasantly. She took another bite.

"I didn't drug you," Maria said as Cristina ate. "You were raving about ghosts trying to kill you. I had to knock you out and bind you for your own safety."

Dream fragments twinkled in the dark areas of Cristina's mind. She remembered crashing through a window to attack a faceless killer. She turned her head and spotted the broken glass table. Swallowing hard, she noticed Maria had changed into a T-shirt and shorts. "How long was I out?"

"Nearly twelve hours." Maria set the bowl on the couch. "Several times you woke and screamed about someone named Quinn or demanded alcohol. I didn't think you needed any more to drink."

"Good decision." The craving was gone, along with the voices. "What did I say about Quinn?"

"Nothing that made sense. Who is he?"

"Someone dangerous who wants something that I know—only I don't know what it is. My only hope is to figure out what happened with the favela project and whether or not it had anything to do with Recognate. If I can find out why *Renascimento* failed, maybe I can figure out why the drug is failing now."

"If I untie you, do you promise not to attack me?"

Cristina nodded.

Maria undid the ropes.

Cristina rubbed her arms in relief. "Thank you."

"Don't thank me yet. I wasn't entirely truthful. I know how to find a *Renascimento* researcher."

Cristina leaped from the chair. She staggered and caught herself. "Show me."

"We must wait until you've recovered. It's important you're at your best."

"Why's that?"

"Because he is hiding in one of Rio's most dangerous favelas."

A cold wind hit Gary Wilson's face as he sat on a bench. He pulled a wool stocking cap lower over his ears and bundled the tattered overcoat tighter. The Mattapan Trolley Station platform was packed with downtown commuters, allowing him to blend into the crowd. At least here, the city hadn't yet installed surveillance cameras everywhere, making it high-risk for crime but low risk for being spotted on the run.

Detective Rick Hawkins approached, similarly bundled against the chill, and sat next to Wilson. He stared straight ahead, as Wilson had instructed, following a play from Santos's book.

"This is risky," Rick said under his breath. "I saw you blacked out your plates, but your Charger still sticks out like a sore thumb."

"I'll take my chances. What about you? Any tails?"

Hawkins shook his head. "Drove through Dorchester and took every side road I could find."

"Good. Did you bring it?"

Hawkins reached into his pocket, withdrew a plastic baggie, and pressed it against Wilson's. Feeling the slick crinkle of the plastic, Wilson grabbed it and stuck it into his own pocket.

Hawkins said, "You look like shit."

"I slept in my car last night. Got the new threads at Goodwill." Wilson chanced brief eye contact. "Thanks for helping out."

"You're still my partner. And with the shit at the station—"

"What shit? About me?"

"Worse." Hawkins sighed. "Miranda Parker's gone missing."

Forgetting his own rule, Wilson stared at Hawkins. "I thought she was in witness protection."

"Someone intercepted the transport team. One agent was killed and three more are in intensive care."

"Jesus!" Wilson rubbed his forehead. "Any idea who did it?"

"No witnesses able to talk. But the Feds arranged the transport. They're the only ones who knew where the team would be and when."

"Forrester." Wilson clenched his fists. "Son of a bitch. Be careful, Rick."

"I'll watch my back, but are you sure you don't want to pull in Vasquez? She's been defending you, insisting that the message on Devi's phone doesn't incriminate you."

"Really?" Wilson considered for two seconds. "No, Forrester wouldn't hesitate to destroy her, too. I can't risk anyone else. But I want you to take this." He pulled a slim plastic device out of his pocket and handed it to Hawkins.

"What's this?"

"One of Santos's burner phones. I've got another one. I programmed the number into yours. Don't call my phone again until this blows over."

"Santos? Why do you have two of his phones?"

"I can't tell you, Rick. Trust me, okay?"

After a moment of silence, Hawkins said, "All right. What do you want me to do?"

"Did you find anything about whoever made that drug?"

"The number on Franklin's pill bottle was different from the one Miranda Parker gave you. I tried it. No answer, no voicemail. It's registered to a bakery in Washington, DC."

"Keep looking. If we find them, maybe we can uncover a connection to Forrester and clear my name."

"Okay." Hawkins stood and checked his watch. "Damn trolley never runs on time. I'm calling a cab."

Wilson waited for his partner to leave. After an old woman took the open seat, Wilson shuffled out to the parking lot. He climbed into his Charger and slipped the bag out of his pocket. Inside were three tiny green pills. With a grim smile, he replaced the bag, started the car, and drove off.

Less than a minute later, a black shape shot into the air and flew overhead, following the Charger like a hawk chasing a field mouse.

CHAPTER FIFTY-FIVE

Quinn was in his hotel room, cleaning his Beretta, when his phone vibrated. He calmly finished lubricating the recoil spring, then lined up the slide and clicked it into place. He wiped his hands with a rag before snatching the phone, logging into the secure chat and reading the message.

Detective isn't giving up.

Quinn swelled with rage. He'd thought his contacts capable of distracting the remaining liabilities. Jabbing the buttons, he wrote: *You're certain?*

The tracker on the other cop led me right to him. The drone is following him now.

Quinn slammed his fist against the table, knocking the oilcan to the floor. A dark stain spread across the carpet. He'd thought the detective would be easier to scare, but clearly, he required more convincing. Jabbing the keypad, Quinn typed: *Deal with him. No mistakes.*

Without awaiting a reply, Quinn tossed aside the phone, grabbed the cloth and mopped the oil stain. When he finished, he lifted the pistol and snapped the magazine into place. If his operative failed, Quinn would have to stop worrying about getting his hands dirty.

"Here." Maria entered the living room, carrying a bundle of clothes. "These will be more comfortable, and you will not stand out so much."

"Thanks." Cristina accepted the garments and laid them on the couch. She started to remove her pants and stopped.

Maria was watching.

"I'm sorry. I know you're my sister but—"

"You see me as a stranger." Maria turned her back. "I understand."

"Thanks. Again." As Cristina disrobed, she recalled how, for so long, she wanted to know her family. Now she had a sister—one she couldn't remember anything about. Cristina sighed as she pulled on a pair of jean shorts. Nothing in her life would ever be simple. "How far is it to where we're going?"

"Less than an hour drive, but the roads are too dangerous for cars."

"So how will we get there?"

"*Par motocicleta.*"

Cristina paused in the middle of zipping up ankle boots. "A motorcycle?"

"I kept your Sherco in perfect condition."

"*My* Sherco? You can't be serious. I can't even stand riding in cars."

Maria shrugged. "I'll drive. I'm sorry, but there's no other way."

Cristina removed her long-sleeved blouse and tossed it onto the couch. The locket bounced on her chest. She held it, the engraving caressing her palm like an old friend. Memories flitted through her mind—some familiar, some not.

Maria glanced over her shoulder. "Are you okay?"

"Trying to make sense of something." Cristina threw on a blue T-shirt. "You can turn around."

When Maria faced her, Cristina showed her the locket again. "Even if Santos gave me this to make me remember who I am, why would Zero Dark send Gomes to steal it? Why would it matter to them?"

"Because they don't want you to remember."

"It's more than that. Santos said it was important." She opened the locket, displaying the photos inside. "But it's just family pictures."

"You wore that same necklace ever since you were twelve. Mother gave it to you, so she'd always be with you and—"

"What's wrong?" asked Cristina.

"This picture of Mother. It's not the same."

"Are you sure?"

"Look." Maria pointed at the framed photo. "This part is different."

Cristina reexamined the photo. Sure enough, the lower corner was a lighter shade. A thin line indicated where it had been torn and reglued. Cristina tugged at the photo until it lifted out of the locket. She flipped it over. On the back, someone had written $C20H23NO4+C13H16N2$.

"What does that mean?" Maria asked.

"I have no idea, but the handwriting looks familiar."

"It should," said Maria. "It's yours."

Cristina puzzled over the message. Perhaps this was the secret Zero Dark wanted.

"Maybe the *Renascimento* researcher will be able to help." She looked Cristina up and down. "Good. You only need one more thing."

Maria opened an armoire door, revealing a safe. After spinning the combination dial, she reached into the safe and removed a pair of semiautomatic pistols.

"Why do you have those?"

"We'll need them in the favela."

"But why do *you* have them?"

"My father worked for Tropa de Elite, Rio's special forces. He trained us both in self-defense." Maria stared at the guns and tightened her grip. "He was a good man."

"What happened?"

"His commander ordered him to flush a nest of Barracudas—a dangerous gang. When his troops arrived, they found the Barracudas engaged in battle with Comando Novo."

"Who?"

"The New Command, an even more powerful gang. After you disappeared, the gangs went to war. They didn't care who was caught in the crossfire." Maria turned to Cristina, her eyes hollow. "Father tried to rescue a six-year-old boy. Both were killed."

Cristina felt sick. "Oh, no."

"Father wouldn't take chances. I always believed it wasn't an accident but never found proof." Maria offered the pistol again to Cristina. "That's why I'll help you. To find out why my father died, so his spirit can rest."

Cristina held her gaze another moment, then accepted the gun. The cold metal jolted through her arm and up to her brain. Images of intensive combat training flashed through her mind. She saw herself standing side-by-side with Maria in target practice. A man with close-cropped hair and strong features instructed them. He was firm but kind.

Then a shadowy figure appeared. He shouted in her ear. Ordered her to set aside fear and compassion. To focus on self-preservation. Nothing else mattered. Follow orders. The only way to survive. She aimed not at targets but the faces of men and women. She pulled the trigger.

A hand touched Cristina's shoulder. She jumped. Twisted around. Raised the pistol. Shadow Man stood before her. White teeth glittered. She aimed.

"Sabrina!" Maria's voice shattered the illusion. "What are you doing?"

The shadow man dissipated. Sweat streamed down Cristina's cheeks. Her hands shook. She lowered the pistol. "I'm sorry. I—I don't think your father was the only one who trained me."

Releasing her breath, Maria removed the gun from Cristina's hand and placed it next to hers on the couch. "Maybe you're not ready yet. I'll return it when I'm certain you won't shoot me by mistake."

"Again, smart." Cristina concentrated on slowing her breathing. Three days without Recognate and she was losing self-control. She needed answers fast. "What else do we need?"

"Only one thing." Maria held Cristina's hands. "We must help you become whole before you lose anything else."

CHAPTER FIFTY-SIX

The best thing about the Albany Street homeless shelter was its anonymity. The missionaries had a strict motto of "Love unconditionally." That meant no questions asked or ID required. When Francisco Martins limped in, they ensured he had a bed, food and antibiotics. It wasn't the Maharajah Hotel, but it was a good place to hide.

After another spoonful of beef stew, he wiped his mouth with a paper napkin and carried his tray to the kitchen.

The kitchen volunteer accepted it. "Feeling better?"

"Yes, thank you," Martins said. "A good shower always helps."

"Don't leave anything valuable lying around. Cecil lost an iPhone last week—still not sure how he got one in the first place."

"Thanks for the warning, but I have nothing of value." Martins donned a stocking cap. "I'm leaving now to look for work."

"Try the burger joint on the corner. They always need someone." The volunteer wiped his hands.

As he stepped outside, Martins wrapped a scarf around his face and turned up his collar. He stumbled from awning to awning. When possible, he waited for a large vehicle to pass and rushed alongside it before ducking into an alley.

Ten minutes later, he stopped at a nondescript brick building two blocks from Andrew Station. Upon entering, he walked directly through the first door on the left, where a sign announced *U-Save Self-Storage.*

"Can I help you?" a teenage girl asked without looking up from her phone.

Martins held up a tiny key. "Withdrawing my items from locker 32."

She checked her computer. "You're paid until the end of the month."

"I no longer need it."

"Whatever. Drop off the key when you leave." She returned to her texting.

Martins smiled inwardly as he passed the desk and veered into the first row of lockers. He'd investigated five storage facilities. This one had only one security camera behind the counter and it accepted cash with no ID checks. He'd carefully selected the locker, far from the desk and out of line of sight.

He crouched before locker 32. He turned his key and the door popped open. He slid out the box, removed and unzipped a duffel bag, then activated a small black device contained inside. A map appeared, displaying a blinking red light. He deactivated the device and stuffed it into his pocket.

Digging through the bag, Martins located his Ruger and three clips. He inspected the gun and started to load it. His hand shook. He paused and took slow breaths. When the shaking ceased, he tried again. This time, the magazine clicked into place. Setting aside the weapon, he removed a tightly rolled pair of socks. He unrolled them and withdrew a pill bottle.

Martins poured a handful of green capsules into his palm. As he studied one, he considered how such a tiny package could be so valuable—and so dangerous. Yes, if it weren't for the pills, he might never have found his daughter, but at what cost? Even now, he could feel control slipping away. He had to stay focused, and there was only one way to do that.

He popped a pill into his mouth.

Wind whipped against Cristina's face. Sand and gravel splattered off her legs. Even closing her eyes and imagining sunbathing on a tropical beach wasn't enough to block out every bump, every whine of the Sherco's engine. The roads had been bad, but the dirt mountain road to the favela was intolerable. She buried her face in Maria's back and wished they'd taken the car.

After another five minutes of struggling uphill, Maria skidded to a stop. The engine shut off. She said, "You can let go. We're here."

Cristina opened her eyes. Her heart sank. Broken cars and trucks sulked on both sides of the ruined street. Dilapidated hovels crumbled around them, built one atop another all the way up the mountainside. The bitter tang of garbage hung in the air. Men, women and children meandered in shorts and T-shirts, some wearing shoes, some not. They wore a haunted look, as if waiting for their world to end.

"Why do they look so afraid?" she asked.

"*Fala portugues!*" Maria got closer and then said in Portuguese, "Don't speak English. You must appear as if you belong. They target tourists first."

Across the street, three young men lingered, menace radiating from their eyes. A pistol butt protruded from the shorts of the smallest man.

Cristina swallowed hard. Since she'd been in the country, Portuguese was becoming more comfortable for her. But would it be convincing enough? In Portuguese, she said to her sister, "Can I have the gun now?"

"Soon. First, we must get past them."

Just uphill, two men in black uniforms leaned against a police car. They caressed their assault rifles while they chatted.

"Many officers truly want to help the people who live here," Maria said. "But they cannot watch everywhere. The gang leaders may be gone, but there isn't peace."

"How do we know who we can trust?"

"We do what those here have learned to do. Trust no one."

The color drained from Cristina's cheeks. Santos's warning became all too clear. Against so much corruption, what chance did she have?

Maria motioned for Cristina to follow as she approached the officers. "Let me do the talking."

Cristina kept her head down, only glancing at the officers. Neither was older than twenty, but the tightly coiled way they seemed to study everything made them seem older, hardened.

The two women halted a few feet from the police car. The men stopped chatting.

"This road is restricted," said the darker one with a black beret. He tightened his grip on the rifle barrel. "Residents only."

"We're volunteers at the Casa do Coração orphanage." Maria smiled and indicated a backpack strapped to the motorcycle. "We bring supplies."

The lighter-skinned officer scratched his goatee. "What supplies?"

"Toothbrushes, crayons, clean clothes. Things that children need."

"We must inspect everything."

"Of course."

Maria stepped back and motioned to Cristina to do the same. The goateed officer opened the backpack. The darker one trained his sights on the women. After sifting through the bag, the officer nodded at his partner, who relaxed.

"If you're carrying drugs or weapons," Goatee said, "declare them now."

"What would children do with drugs and weapons?"

A hint of a smile appeared. He stepped away. "Okay, you're clear."

"Thank you." Maria led Cristina by the hand back to the bike.

"Hold up!" Beret approached. He examined Cristina's face. "Why are you bruised?"

"She's visiting from Belo Horizonte," Maria began. "She was—"

The officer held up his hand. "Let her speak."

Cristina's cheeks cooled. At least, her Portuguese had improved to fluency, most likely an effect of her restored memories. "I … went rock climbing at Sugar Loaf. I slipped and crashed against the mountain. The doctor said it'll be fine in a few days."

Beret studied her. To his partner he made a gesture with his thumb and pinky. Goatee nodded and spoke into his radio. Beads of sweat formed on Cristina's forehead.

They know who you are. They're going to kill you. Run!

The voice roared in her head. Cristina ignored it.

After what felt like several minutes, Goatee murmured to his partner. Beret nodded and waved. "Don't keep the children waiting."

"Thank you, Officers." Maria grabbed the motorcycle's handlebars. "You're doing fine work keeping us safe."

As the women passed, Beret caught Cristina's eye. "You should be more careful. Rio is a dangerous place."

Once they were out of earshot, Cristina said, "Where are the guns?"

"Better you don't know." Maria kept her eyes on the road as they walked the bike up the mountainside and onto a dirt path. "Don't look back and make eye contact with no one."

"You sound like you know your way around."

"For the past two years, I've been studying the effects of Rio's policies on the favelas. The system is designed to keep the poor from moving beyond their caste, starting with the children." She pointed ahead. "That's why we're going there."

The ground fell away beneath Cristina's feet. Ahead stood a building composed of colored blocks covered with tangled telephone wires and graffiti.

It was the same building from her horrible nightmare.

CHAPTER FIFTY-SEVEN

Trash littered the ground. Bullet holes riddled the building's front wall. Odors of sweat and urine drifted toward Cristina's nostrils. When she squinted, she saw children's dirty faces staring out at her. When she listened, she heard voices chanting, *Liar, liar* ...

Maria nudged Cristina's shoulder. "What's wrong?"

"I've been here before." The voices faded; the faces disappeared. Now Cristina saw two young boys and a girl—all around seven or eight years old—sitting on the front stoop, making crafts out of paper and bent pieces of metal. Neither of the boys wore a shirt. The girl's tank top and shorts were covered in dirt. Something fluttered in her belly. "What is this place?"

"Casa do Coração." Maria half-smiled. "Why do you think I brought crayons and toothbrushes?"

"Your contact is hiding here?"

"This orphanage was once under Comando Novo protection. Even in their absence, the police know better than to tear apart a home for children. Wait here."

Maria pulled the motorcycle up to the orphanage. The children looked up and said something Cristina couldn't hear. Maria replied and the kids laughed. Maria looped a chain through the front tire and secured it with a padlock before removing the backpack. She handed it to one of the boys, who unzipped it and pulled out a box of crayons. He held it over his head like a trophy and ran into the building. The others squealed and chased after him.

"That should keep them busy." Maria ran her fingers under the motorcycle seat. Something clicked. She lifted the seat, revealing a secret compartment. She removed one of the handguns, loaded it, and handed it to Cristina.

The moment Cristina touched the gun, a chill ran through her body. Voices whispered in her ear, *Liar, liar.* She smelled blood and gun smoke. Children's faces appeared again, scarlet stains over empty eyes, accusing her. *Liar, liar.*

"Sabrina?" Maria's voice dispelled the visions.

Shaking, Cristina turned to her. "Children died here, didn't they?"

Pursing her lips, Maria nodded.

Cristina's eyes filled with tears. Her stomach churned. "Was it my fault?"

Maria used her thumb to wipe the tears away from Cristina's eyes. "You made poor decisions. But you wouldn't harm children."

Something stirred inside Cristina, something warm and pleasant. Comforting. A sister's love. But whether it was a memory or a new feeling, she couldn't tell. Steeling herself against what she might find inside, she stuck the pistol into her waistband. Maria prepped her own weapon and did the same.

Together, they entered the building. The green and pink interior walls lifted Cristina's heart but only slightly. Someone had started to paint a red and white fish on the concrete floor but had never finished. Half of a princess doll lay in a dusty corner. Cristina detected a hint of bleach. At least the inside was clean.

"*Ei, você!*"

Two young men, neither older than seventeen, strolled toward them. The younger boy wore shorts and a tank top. The taller wore only a pair of torn jeans. Deep scars lined his bare chest. They stopped in the middle of the doorway.

"Who is she?" the shorter one asked in Portuguese, eyeing Cristina.

"We don't mean any harm, Tiago," Maria said. "This is my sister."

"You come with guns and expect us to believe you?"

"You know the streets aren't safe. We must protect ourselves."

"The rich always protect themselves from the poor," said the taller boy. "But how can we protect ourselves from the rich?"

"This isn't about rich or poor, Eduardo. This is about ending the cycle of violence. Isn't that what we discussed?"

Eduardo's mouth twisted. He turned to Tiago and jerked his head toward the hallway. The shorter boy ran off while Eduardo stood with his arms folded. "We'll see what Dona Luisa has to say."

Moments later, Tiago returned. Following him was a woman wearing jeans, a plain white blouse, and a red headscarf. She studied the women over wirerimmed glasses. "Why did you bring her here?"

"Please, Luisa," Maria said. "My sister must speak to him."

"He speaks to no one." Luisa appeared to be in her midthirties, but her scowl made her look ten years older. "Isn't it enough that we allow him to live?"

"He will answer her questions—and ours. I'm certain of it."

Luisa remained steadfast.

Cristina set her jaw. She understood why Luisa didn't trust her. These children were fighting for survival, thanks to the *Renascimento* project of which she'd been a part.

Cristina pushed her shoulders back. "If he can explain what went wrong here, I may be able to find a way to fix it. I promise, I'm not here to endanger you or the children."

Luisa arched her eyebrows. She glanced at the boys, who shrugged. Without another word, she led the sisters to a massive bookcase filled with children's books. Tiago and Eduardo shoved the bookcase to one side, revealing a wooden door.

"Talk to him," Luisa said. "But do not scare the children."

Cristina glanced over her shoulder in time to see several young children spying on them from around the corner. Their eyes widened, and they ran off.

"As you say," Maria said.

Dona Luisa glared at Cristina for another uncomfortable moment and then left with the boys in tow. Maria approached the door and rapped three times, waited, and then rapped twice more.

"*Quem é aí?*" a voice called from inside.

"Maria."

Wood scraped against concrete. Someone stumbled toward them. Heavy breathing came through the keyhole. "*Tem mais cachaça?*"

"Yes. Please let us in."

The door swung open, releasing a pungent gust of alcohol and sweat. A worn, soot-covered face appeared in the doorway. Cristina gasped as she peered through the dirt and recognized the man. "Dr. Kobayashi?"

He blinked three times. His gaze drifted until at last he focused on Cristina. His features hardened. In a low voice tainted with bitterness, he said, "You."

For the third time since he entered the morgue waiting area, Wilson checked his pocket to ensure the pills were still there. He let out a breath of air and resumed his incessant pacing. His career was already in ruins. But if Mitchell Parker and his wife Miranda were examples of how Forrester and Zero Dark dealt with problems, his life was also in jeopardy. His only hope was to find out more about these pills before it was too late.

"Detective." Dr. Morgan emerged through the doors. "Did you get it?"

Wilson handed the medical examiner the bag of pills. "How long will it take?"

"It depends on their composition, but if I start the analysis now, I should be able to give you preliminary results before you leave."

"Great." Wilson followed Morgan through the doorway to a machine that resembled a cross between a photocopier and a food processor.

At the touch of a button, a drawer slid out. Morgan inserted a pill and pushed another button. The drawer slid back.

Wilson coughed, never at ease in the morgue. "Should I wait out there?"

"Actually, I have something to show you." Morgan pushed another button. The machine lit up and emitted a low humming sound. He walked away and held open the autopsy room door.

Wilson's gut lurched. "In there?"

"I assure you, everyone in there is very much dead."

"That's what bothers me." Wilson summoned his courage and entered the autopsy room. The stench of formaldehyde and decaying flesh assaulted him.

Morgan offered him the menthol gel. Wilson shoved it into his nostrils.

In the center of the room, a body lay on a metal table, covered by a white sheet.

"Detective Wilson," Morgan said, "meet Carl Franklin."

Morgan drew back the sheet, revealing a partially dissected white male in his midforties. The right side of his face was smashed in, his left leg twisted. Wilson covered his mouth.

"I've finished autopsying his brain." Morgan donned a pair of gloves and removed the top of Franklin's skull. "Come here, please."

"Seriously?"

Morgan gave Wilson a once-over and rolled his eyes.

Cheeks flushed, Wilson forced himself to look. Spasms rocked his esophagus. The cadaver's skull seemed to be stuffed with pasta and marinara sauce.

"What am I looking at?"

Morgan used a probe to push aside one of the cerebral lobes and pointed at the underlying structures. "This is the hippocampus. That's the amygdala. Both are important in learning and encoding new memories. Look here." He made a circling motion with his finger. "They're twice their normal size."

"What does that mean?"

"Let me show you something first." Morgan turned the mass of brain tissue over, then stuck his probe inside and pried it open. "This is the left temporal lobe. When I was checking the mammillary bodies as Cristina requested—which are fine, by the way—I found this."

Daring to lean over Morgan's shoulder, Wilson spotted a blackened patch of tissue. "It looks like charcoal."

"It's necrotic. A third of his temporal lobe had eroded."

"What would cause that?"

"Not sure." Morgan flipped the lobe back. "I found similar scars on the hippocampus, but if you look here …" He indicated a glistening lump of grayish tissue overlying the dead patch. "It seems he managed to rebuild the tissue."

Wilson whistled softly. "So that drug does restore memories."

"Not entirely." Morgan prodded the fresh tissue with the probe. "Microscopically, the cell column structures are completely different. The newer tissue is unregulated and uneven, invading the old tissue like a cancer."

"What does that mean?"

"Whatever Recognate is designed to do, it doesn't recover damaged memories." Morgan poked the gray mass again to emphasize his point. "It replaces them."

CHAPTER FIFTY-EIGHT

Kobayashi's eyes smoldered. Upper lip quivered. Fingers trembled. At last, he said in Portuguese, "So, they've sent you to kill me. Fitting justice, I suppose."

"I'm not here to kill you," Cristina said in English, in case anyone was listening. "You're the only one who can tell me what went wrong with the *Renascimento* project."

"Why are you speaking in English? And why do you look different?"

"I'm not who you think I am." Cristina took a step closer.

Kobayashi flinched like he expected her to beat him. Cristina's chest tightened. What kind of person did he think she was? What kind of person had she been?

"Please," she said. "I need your help."

After another moment, Kobayashi leaned close as if sniffing her. He studied her eyes and withdrew, chuckling softly. His laughter intensified. He rested against the doorjamb and guffawed into his elbow.

"What's so funny?" Maria asked.

"'God has given you one face. And you make yourself another.'

How right Shakespeare was." Kobayashi looked at Cristina and burst again into laughter.

Cristina seized his tattered collar. "I'm tired of being the butt of jokes I don't understand. Someone did this to me. I want to know why. Will you help or not?"

Kobayashi stopped laughing. His eyes widened, rimmed with fear. "You were taking Recognate. But you're not anymore. Are you?"

"Not for three days."

He touched his chin in thought and nudged her away. "Then we have time—though just barely. Come inside."

The women started toward the door. Kobayashi blocked Maria's way. "Only her."

"I haven't seen my sister for three years," Maria said. "I won't lose her again."

"You won't. But what I must say is only for her ears." He leaned out and scanned the hallway. "If you found me, others will come. Someone must warn us if they do."

Maria glanced at Cristina, who nodded.

Frowning, Maria jabbed her finger at Kobayashi's chest. "If she's harmed, you will answer to me."

Kobayashi raised his withered arms. "Do I look like I could harm her?"

Muttering under her breath, Maria drew her pistol and stood guard.

Cristina and Kobayashi entered his room. Barely larger than a pantry, it had a single window allowing sparse light inside. He closed the door and invited her to sit on a bench next to a rickety table. He parked himself across from her. A ratty mattress covered by torn blankets was on the floor beside them. The room reeked of human waste. She fought the urge to gag.

Kobayashi rested his elbows on his thighs and folded his hands together. He studied her, his eyes sharp and probing. She squirmed, feeling like she was back in the interrogation room at the police station.

"So, you've returned. Why?"

"To discover who I am."

"Who do you think you are?"

"Until recently, I thought I was a psychiatrist from Boston named Cristina Silva."

"Silva?" He smiled. "Clever."

"I said I'd had enough jokes. Don't make me hurt you."

"I apologize. It isn't that funny." With a long sigh, he smoothed his fingers over his cheeks. "How did you find out?"

"A man named Sebastian dos Santos showed me a photo of your—*our*—research team and told me I wasn't who I think I am."

"Santos?"

"You know him?"

"No, but names are meaningless. What did he tell you about our research?"

"Nothing, but I know you weren't studying gang violence. You were working for ReMind."

"Five years researching endorphins and all I created were aggressive rats. My career was slipping away from me." Kobayashi rested his forehead on his thumbs. "Then ReMind found me. They played to my ego. Even then, I was skeptical, until they showed me the animal studies."

"What did they show?"

"No aggression, not even on withdrawal. Just a little jitteriness and tachycardia. A much better response rate than I ever achieved."

"So, you pushed to hold human trials in Rio."

"Who told you that?" He snorted. "ReMind wanted to operate without Institutional Review Board oversight. Twice I refused. On the third request, they promised to fund everything. Give me top credit. Donate a sizeable amount to rebuilding the favelas."

He leaned back and spread his hands apart. "Win-win for everyone. How could I refuse?"

Children's voices echoed in her mind. *Liar, liar.* "ReMind claims its Recognate trials in Rio were their most successful."

"Oh, very successful, depending on how you look at it."

"What do you mean?"

"More than half of the gang members enrolled recovered memories and ceased violent activity." He rubbed his hands together as if trying to remove a stain. "Then members of Comando Novo started turning up dead. Murdered. Then, Barracuda members also died." Kobayashi stopped rubbing and studied his fingertips. "After the Pacification Police Units moved in, the gangs declared war on each other. They no longer fought for territory. They fought for revenge."

"The police incited a gang war?"

"No. The police didn't kill those gang members." His eyes blazed. "We did."

CHAPTER FIFTY-NINE

Beneath the layers of dirt and grime, the lines around Kobayashi's eyes and mouth remained serious. "Do you know what happens to research subjects in a test group when a clinical trial ends, the ones who still need treatment?"

"Well, I …" Cristina searched for an answer. "I guess they could keep taking the drug."

"Yes, that would be an excellent idea. What if they can't afford it?"

"ReMind didn't offer to continue treatment?"

"As I said, they used a convenience sample. Once they had their data, it was no longer convenient to keep providing free samples." He clenched his fists. "I had been so excited about the prospect of success, I had never considered its aftermath."

"What aftermath?"

"The subjects became violent. More violent than ever before."

"But you said the lab animals didn't become aggressive."

"True," Kobayashi said. "But the animals hadn't spent their lives wallowing in poverty, watching loved ones tortured and murdered. The animals hadn't blocked traumatic memories only for them to be forced back into their minds later."

Cristina's head spun. "I don't understand. Why did the people here recover traumatic memories after stopping the drug?"

Kobayashi exhaled against his clenched fist and stared at the floor. At last, he staggered to the mattress. Reaching underneath, he withdrew a crumpled sheaf of papers. He handed them to Cristina. "These are my interviews during the study. Each subject describes wonderful, long-forgotten childhood events. The looks of joy on their faces as they remembered them for the first time were incredible."

As Cristina sifted through the narratives, a lump grew in her throat. The descriptions mirrored what Jerry, Carl and Martha had reported, and how she had felt while taking Recognate. Cristina's hands shook. "Their happy memories—they weren't real."

"Recognate turns the brain into putty, susceptible to the power of suggestion. At the mention of something remotely plausible, the drug molds that putty into new memory. But it only lasts as long as the subject keeps taking the drug."

I remember everything, Jerry had said. Cristina recalled his face changing, as if he were two minds trapped in one body. "And when they stop taking it," she said, "they remember the truth, and it drives them mad."

"It's more about the emotions attached to what they remember. The lab animals didn't become aggressive because their new memories were indistinct from their old ones. To suddenly remember that your mother was killed by your best friend, however, or that you once held your sister's still-beating heart in your hand …" He closed his eyes. "It was devastating."

The images seeping into Cristina's brain, the voices she was hearing—were they true memories, shreds of a past life knitting themselves back together? "When did you discover this?"

"Too late to stop what was to come. Like everyone else, I assumed the Pacification Police Units executed those people. It wasn't until a CIA officer knocked on my door that I learned the truth." Kobayashi searched under the mattress again. "Someone gave him a tip that mercenaries were operating out of Rio. He believed they were responsible for murdering the gang members … Ah, here it is." He hobbled back to Cristina and handed her a business card. "This is the man who visited me."

Her heart sank. The card read Jorge Silva.

She ran her finger over the name and withdrew it as if shocked. Trembling, she set the card on the table. "For two years I've believed he was my father."

"Now you understand the joke. I told you it wasn't funny." He plopped on the bench and folded his hands together. "The name of the man he was after was—"

"Quinn." When Kobayashi's eyebrows rose in surprise, she shrugged. "Lucky guess. So, Dad—I mean, Silva—believed Quinn killed the gang members? Why?"

"ReMind hired him to clean up their mess. If word got out Recognate didn't work in Brazil the way they claimed, they'd look like fools."

"The company killed those people to avoid reporting bad results?" In her mind, she heard Simmons's voice: *We've been working overtime to keep it out of the headlines for the good of the project.* She shuddered. "But no matter how much they cover it up, Recognate doesn't work."

"Do you think that matters to them? All they care is that people pay for something they believe works. The world is full of desperate people."

People like you.

Cristina bit her lip. "Santos said I had information locked away in my brain—something Zero Dark needs and fears."

"You were one of our team's most promising neuroscientists. We were lucky Federico introduced you to us."

"Federico?" Cristina's jaw slackened. "Federico Gomes?"

"Yes. Apparently, you two knew each other since you were teenagers."

Cristina flashed back to the waking dream of Corcovado, running hand-in-hand with a young Cristiano Ronaldo—the first true memory, after all. She felt queasy. How could a childhood friend have tried to kill her?

"Right before you disappeared," Kobayashi said, "you told me you'd found a way to make Recognate stable. No adverse effects. No withdrawal."

Her heart raced. "And did I tell you what that was?"

"I'm afraid that secret disappeared with you. If you had a stable form of the drug, you could safely discontinue it without losing your mind. Unfortunately, that requires you to regain your true memories. Which means losing your mind."

"But you said I was just a neuroscientist. I wasn't a mercenary or a gang member. I should be fine, right?"

For a long time, Kobayashi held her gaze. Finally, he stood and withdrew from his pocket a pill bottle. "I saved these to bargain for survival. Take them and return to your new life. Forget all this."

She stared at the green capsules inside the bottle. A craving worked its way from her inner core outward. It would be so easy to return to being Cristina Silva.

Or she could create a new life here in Brazil. She could be anyone she wanted.

But you won't be you. The voice whispered from every corner of her brain. *And you're not me. Quinn took that from us. He won't let you walk away.*

Ripping her gaze from the bottle, she glared at Kobayashi. It took every ounce of effort to speak. "I can't walk away when others are in danger. What aren't you telling me?"

Kobayashi sucked his lower lip, seeming to be fighting an

inner battle. At last, he said, "We've all done things we'd like to forget, yet they're part of who we are. If you truly wish to find yourself, you may uncover things you won't like, things you may even detest. Are you prepared for that?"

Was she? Could anyone be? "I am."

Kobayashi drew in a deep breath and released it in a forceful sigh. He seemed about to speak and then stopped. He was staring at her chest. "What is that?"

"What?" She looked down. The locket rested against her T-shirt. Instantly, she remembered what she'd found inside. "It contains formulas."

His eyes bulged. He backed away, waving his hands. "You gave that locket to someone to keep it out of Quinn's hands. Quinn must know you have it now. We're not safe. Quinn is—"

The tiny window exploded. Kobayashi's head jerked backward and bounced off the wall behind him. Before Cristina could scream, his lifeless body toppled toward her.

CHAPTER SIXTY

Staring at Carl Franklin's brain was bad enough, but Dr. Morgan's revelation stirred up every urge in Detective Wilson's gut to vomit. "You're telling me Recognate can erase people's minds and reprogram them as someone else?"

"Not exactly." Dr. Morgan stripped off his gloves and tossed them in a bin. "You've heard of stem cells?"

"They use them to treat spinal cord injuries, right?"

"Among other uses. Stem cells are precursors. With the right manipulation, they can become anything we want."

Wilson indicated Franklin's new brain tissue. "Those are stem cells?"

"In a manner of speaking. Recognate turned Mr. Franklin's mind into a blank slate. If I'm right, someone then fed him new memories."

"Jesus, what kind of drug could do that?"

Something chimed in the other room. Morgan jerked his head. "Looks like we're about to find out."

They left the autopsy room. Morgan walked to the analyzer and pressed a button. A display screen lit up. Morgan studied it. His gaze narrowed. He mumbled to himself.

"Something wrong?"

Morgan pressed another button. The drawer slid back out. He plucked the capsule, opened it, and touched it to his tongue.

"Are you crazy?" Wilson grabbed Morgan's wrist. "What the hell are you doing?"

Morgan snickered and offered the capsule. "It's sugar."

"What?"

"It's a placebo. A fake pill. Researchers use them in studies to prove the effects of the test drug aren't due to random chance."

"Cristina was prescribing Carl Franklin a fake drug?"

"She may not have known. Often the researchers blind both the prescriber and the subject as to who gets the actual drug."

"But he must've gotten the real thing at some point, right? Sugar couldn't do that to his brain."

"You're correct. Someone switched the pills." Morgan scratched his chin. "Cristina's patients had barely detectable THC levels. They were probably taking placebo for at least a week. He was effectively going through withdrawal, causing his emotional instability. But it might also explain …"

"Doctor?" Morgan's look unsettled Wilson.

Morgan suddenly dashed across the room and flipped through a box of glass slides. He chose one and placed it on a microscope, then fiddled with knobs.

"Detective, come here."

When Wilson approached, Morgan stepped back.

"Take a look."

Wilson peered through the viewfinder. A pink blob floated. "Help me out, Doc."

"Those are cells from Franklin's hippocampus. The organized columns are the damaged tissue. The irregular tissue is new."

"Yeah, you said that."

"But what I missed was that the old tissue was undergoing active mitosis at the time of death."

"Meaning?"

"The old tissue was growing back. Don't you see?" Morgan's eyes danced. "This explains the catecholamine surge, the psychosis, everything. They were regaining their real memories after they stopped taking the drug."

Before Wilson could reply, the wall behind them exploded.

Kobayashi crumpled into Cristina's arms. Bullets blazed across the floor. Riddled the researcher's back. Cristina crouched, using his body as a shield. Drew her gun. Fired back.

The bullets stopped. She shoved him aside. Rolled under the table. More gunfire. Bullets tore through the tabletop. Wood chips spattered. The shooting stopped again. Cristina panted. Checked her magazine.

The door burst open.

"Sabrina!" Maria shouted on entering.

Another barrage of bullets slammed into the wall. Maria sidestepped. Fired at the window. Someone outside yelled. The gunfire ceased.

More shouting. Maria fired at the window.

"Wait," Cristina said, holding up a finger. They listened.

Sounds of fistfighting came from outside.

"Come." Maria pulled Cristina out from under the table.

As they turned toward the door, Cristina spotted the pill bottle. Voices shouted in her head. Some said to grab it. Others warned her to forget it. The loudest won. She pocketed the bottle and followed Maria outside.

In the hallway, the sounds of fighting grew louder. Luisa rushed toward them.

"What have you done?" She pushed past them and peered

inside Kobayashi's room. She covered her mouth and crossed her chest. "*Meu Deus.*"

"Luisa." Cristina touched the woman's shoulder.

Luisa spun, eyes blazing.

"We didn't kill him."

"You may not have fired the bullet, but you led the wolves to our door. Now the Tropa do Elite will take away our babies."

Maria frowned. "You think this was the police?"

"The officer attacking Eduardo and Tiago is not here to bring milk and cookies."

Cristina's chest tightened. She couldn't allow any more innocents to be harmed. "Get the children somewhere safe. Don't come out until you're sure it's clear."

The corner of Luisa's lip twisted. She withdrew a slim pistol from her jeans' back pocket. "We take care of ourselves."

Respect bloomed in Cristina's chest for this woman, who protected the children and even the man who endangered them in the first place.

"Let's go." Maria pulled Cristina away. To Luisa, "Is there another exit?"

"No."

"Then we must move quickly." Maria cocked her handgun. "Don't hesitate to fire. They won't."

The women ducked into archways along the hall. Outside, the thudding and pounding intensified. A loud *crack* sounded, followed by a groan, an angry shout and an engine whine.

When Cristina and Maria reached the entrance, they flattened themselves against the wall. Someone outside was crying.

"Eduardo! *Ta bem?*" Maria shouted.

"Yes," he said between sobs. "But Tiago—that bastard killed him."

Cristina's heart pounded as she followed Maria outside,

gripping her pistol. Eduardo knelt, cradling Tiago's lifeless body. A bloody knife rested on the stoop.

"It's my fault." Tears streamed down Eduardo's face. "We heard gunfire. I wanted to protect the others."

"What were you thinking?" Maria asked. "Why would you fight a police officer?"

"No officer fights like him." Eduardo wiped snot from his nose. Blood streaked his cheek. "He was a wild animal. Tiago stabbed him in the shoulder. He pulled out the knife, killed Tiago, and escaped on a motorcycle."

"Tropa de Elite doesn't send officers alone. He must have been bought."

"By a man named Quinn, I'm betting," Cristina said. "Which way did this killer go?"

Eduardo pointed up the hill.

"Then there's still time to catch him. He can tell us who Quinn is. Maria, how fast can the bike go?"

"Fast enough." Maria placed her hand on the boy's shoulder. "I'm sorry, Eduardo."

Eduardo turned away and hugged Tiago.

Maria snapped open the chain lock and hopped onto the motorcycle. Cristina jumped on behind her. Maria kick-started the Sherco and veered down the short driveway. Blood stained the ground ahead. Another blotch lay a few feet farther.

"Follow the blood trail," Cristina said.

They rolled down the small dirt road. Maria gunned the engine. The Sherco rocketed forward. Cristina clung to her sister and shut her eyes. A moment later, she forced them open. Cristina could no longer afford fear. She and Maria needed to work together to find the killer and get answers.

They zigzagged up the hill, dodging motorcycle taxis and potholes. The engine whined.

"We're near the mountaintop," Maria shouted over the wind. "Hold on."

A crosswind whipped against them. Cristina tightened her grip around Maria's waist. They shot forward and skidded around a torn-up stretch of road, then came to a hard stop.

Several feet ahead, a stone barrier blocked their way. A red Yamaha cycle lay beside it, front wheel rotating. Footprints trailed through the dirt behind a crumbling brick house into the trees.

Maria shut off the engine. Both women dismounted and readied their handguns.

"This used to be a Barracudas hideout," Maria whispered as they tracked the footprints around the side of the house. "A checkpoint to invade Comando Novo territory." She held up her hand. Cristina stayed still. Maria crouched and touched a patch of grass. She lifted her index finger, revealing a red stain. "It's fresh."

The hairs on Cristina's neck pricked. Kobayashi's killer couldn't be far.

They continued behind the house. Maria searched side to side. Again, she halted.

"I saw movement … up there." She aimed at the highest window.

Cristina's heart pounded.

After two seconds, Maria relaxed and stood. "It must have been a reflection. We'll need to move quickly to catch up—"

Gunshots echoed in the woods.

"Move!" Maria dived at Cristina and dragged her down.

Bullets tore up the ground. Dirt scattered over them.

The gunfire stopped. Someone cursed.

Cristina spotted someone in a black military uniform and face mask struggling with a submachine pistol. One arm hung by his waist. His gaze met Cristina's.

Recognition jolted Cristina. She'd seen those eyes before— her kidnapper in Washington! And something else was familiar.

The assassin turned and ran into the woods.

"He's getting away." Cristina leaped to her feet. "We need to go."

"Not we," Maria said through gritted teeth.

Cristina's gut knotted. Blood streamed from a hole in Maria's jeans below the knee.

Maria forced a smile. "It's not that bad."

"It's bad." Cristina knelt beside her and covered the wound. "You need a hospital."

"No time." Maria shrugged off her shirt. Ripped it in half. "Tie it off. Quickly."

Cristina lashed the fabric around Maria's femur and tied it.

Maria blotted the other half of her shirt against the wound. She hugged her pistol. "I'll be fine. Don't let him escape. You need your answers. Go!"

Heart pounding, Cristina raced through the woods. Adrenaline surged. Her body shifted into cruise control. She dodged tree stumps and rocks. Euphoria washed over her. It felt good to let her body do all the work.

That's right. Let go of the wheel. Take a break.

If I do, what happens to me?

The same thing that happened to me. You'll be here, buried away at peace. Doesn't that sound nice?

It did. So many people had died because of her. It would be a relief to not be responsible anymore.

A tree branch slammed into Cristina's chest.

She fell to the ground. Her elbow crashed against a rock. Pain shot up her arm. The gun slipped from her fingers, bounced away.

The assassin loomed over her. He tossed aside the branch and reached for a knife on his belt.

Don't think. Act.

Cristina flung a handful of dirt at his eyes. He raised his arm. She somersaulted toward him. Twisted. Kicked him in the chest. He staggered backward.

She swung at his jaw. He grabbed her arm. Rammed his knee into her side. Shoved her back. Charged. Slapped her face.

She blocked high. He chopped at her stomach. She covered her abdomen. He punched her jaw.

Pain blinded her. He was too big. Too fast.

What do you do against a bigger opponent?

Cristina was startled. It was a different voice. Her best friend's.

She knew the answer: *Make yourself smaller to draw him in.*

The assailant coiled to strike. Cristina curled into a ball.

He hesitated, then lunged. At the last second, she rolled backward. Kicked him in the face. He staggered. She grabbed a pointy rock. Sprang forward. Jammed the rock into his wounded right arm.

The assailant shrieked. Cristina froze. Her attacker was a woman.

An elbow rammed into Cristina's nose. She stumbled. The assassin tackled her. Clawed at her eyes. Cristina swatted the hand away, then jabbed her finger into the assailant's knife wound. The assassin screamed again. Cristina flung her to the ground. Straddled her chest. Wrapped her hands around the opponent's neck and squeezed.

"You ... were paying attention," the assassin said. "Good for you, mami."

Whatever remained of Cristina's world collapsed. *Please, no.*

Cristina loosened her grip on the assassin's neck. She pinched one corner of the black face mask and lifted. Auburn curls spilled out and fanned the ground like a halo. The blood drained from Cristina's face. She stared into the eyes of the one person she trusted most.

"Andrea," she whispered. A mix of anger and confusion made it almost impossible to speak. "Why did you do this?"

CHAPTER SIXTY-ONE

"You should've let it go, Cristina," Andrea said between ragged coughs. She wriggled against Cristina's weight. "At least, let me go."

"Shut up. Don't talk unless I tell you to talk." Even as Cristina pinned her to the ground, she tried to convince herself this wasn't Andrea. Not her best friend. Not the woman who shared all her secrets. Andrea had never lied to her. This had to be another hallucination.

"Didn't think you'd fight dirty." Andrea sniggered. "You'd never beat me in a fair fight."

Cristina slapped Andrea's face. She stopped herself from doing it again. Every strike made it more real. She lowered her hand. "You used me."

Andrea turned her head and spat blood. "Don't take it personally."

"You pretend to be my best friend, try and kill me in DC, follow me to Brazil—*again* to kill me—and I'm not supposed to take it personally?"

"I wasn't sent to kill you. Okay, I *was* sent to kill you in DC—but that was before Quinn convinced me that was a bad idea."

"What are you talking about? Don't you work for Quinn?"

"No, I work *with* Quinn," Andrea said. "I planned to take that locket of yours and kill you, but Quinn wanted you alive. I thought he was making a mistake, acting out of some kind of chauvinistic chivalry, but then he told me why he wanted you kept alive at all costs."

"And why is that? To get the secret formula?"

Andrea managed a slight shrug.

"Well, he's not getting it. If he comes after me again, I'll ..." She searched for a threat that would hold any weight. "I'll kill myself. The secret will die with me."

Andrea laughed. "Forget who you're talking to? You're a survivor like me, girlfriend."

"Don't call me girlfriend."

"Fair enough. But you haven't taken Recognate consistently in—what, a week or two, now? Soon you'll remember your old self, and then you'll run back to your old boss and beg him to take you back under his wing."

Ice formed in Cristina's blood. "Old boss?"

Andrea laughed. "You've always been working for Quinn. You're only in Rio because he wanted you here."

"That's a lie. I'm no puppet."

"Oh, you think you can cut your strings and become a real girl? Who do you think trained you, made you who you are? No one disobeys Zero Dark and lives."

Ghosts of Carl Franklin and Jerry Peterman drifted between the trees. "Jerry and Carl were compromised," Cristina said. "Quinn made them Recognate subjects to hide them from the CIA so, even if they were caught, they couldn't reveal his identity."

A sarcastic smile twisted Andrea's lip. "You always were the smart one."

Cristina wanted to wring Andrea's neck. Instead, she studied the face of the woman who had pretended to be her friend. What-ever Cristina had once loved about her was gone.

A glint of metal caught Cristina's eye. Her gun was only a few feet away, nestled in a bed of leaves. It would be so easy to blow that backstabbing smirk off Andrea's face.

As if reading Cristina's mind, the hard edges around Andrea's eyes softened. "For what it's worth, I'm sorry. I did see you as my friend. I never wanted to hurt you."

For a moment, Cristina glimpsed the friend she'd known for three years. Whatever Andrea had done, she wasn't the one pull-ing the strings. Slowly, Cristina released Andrea's shoulders and sat back. "What am I supposed to do with you?"

"First, you release me, and then we return to Quinn together. You give him what he wants, he lets you go back to whatever life you choose. Then he and I get rich and buy an island somewhere, and everyone lives happily ever after."

Cristina's gut twisted another turn. "You and Quinn?"

"I'm still pissed at him for shooting at me in DC, but we've come to an understanding." Andrea shrugged. "Hey, you know I like 'em wild."

"I don't know anything about you, and I'm not going back to Quinn." Cristina stood and held out her hand. Andrea eyed it with-out moving. Cristina offered it again. "I'm letting you limp back to your master. Tell him to stay away from me and anyone I care about. If I see your face again, I'm putting a bullet through it. Clear?"

"As clear as the sparkling water in a mojito." She grabbed Cris-tina's hand and pulled herself up. After brushing off her pants, she limped away three steps and then stopped. "You're a good person, Cristina."

Cristina could feel her heart breaking. She turned away. "Go before I change my mind."

Anger and hurt boiled in Cristina's chest as Andrea shuffled through dirt and dried leaves. Cristina looked down at her hands. Only a minute ago they were throttling the neck of a woman she once loved and now never wanted to see again. If Andrea was right, and she had worked for Quinn, what horrible things might those hands have done?

"Oh, Cristina, one more thing—"

"Andrea, get the hell out—"

The knife zinged through the air and buried itself in Cristina's shoulder. She stared at it, dumbfounded as blood trickled down her shirt. Ten feet away, Andrea leaned against a tree. A smile played at her lips as she pulled a second knife out of her belt and waved it by the tip.

"Quinn convinced me not to kill you," Andrea said with a wicked gleam in her eye. "He didn't say you needed all your limbs."

CHAPTER SIXTY-TWO

"Don't do this, Andrea," Cristina said, trying to keep her voice steady, ignoring the throbbing pain where the knife protruded from her shoulder.

"You're giving orders now?" Andrea flipped the knife around in her hand. "I'm done with orders. Do you know how painful it was to listen to your endless whining about how much you remembered? The whole time I wanted to rip off your goddamned lips."

Keep her talking. Try to get the weapon.

Cristina fought the urge to look at the gun. She figured she could grab it with one strong leap. "What did I do to you?"

"Quinn's obsessed. We could've ended this weeks ago if he hadn't interfered, all to keep you alive."

"Because I know how to fix the drug so his mercenaries don't go crazy when they stop taking it?"

"Is that what you think?" Andrea laughed. "You're dumber than I thought. Quinn ordered them dead."

"Why?" She coiled, ready to spring.

"He said it was an experiment gone wrong—case closed. Move toward that gun and you're dead."

Cristina froze. Something scurried up the nearby tree.

Andrea grazed the knife blade across her lips. "I think he just wants to tie up loose ends. Like he's doing now with the medical examiner."

The muscles in Cristina's neck tightened. "Luke Morgan?"

"Poor Cristina. You're losing all your friends." Andrea raised the knife over her head. "Better to cut ties now, starting with that pretty little nose they gave you."

Gunfire sounded. Birds squawked as they flew away.

Andrea's body shook. A slug tore through her neck. Blood spattered her black vest. The knife slipped from her hands. She toppled to the ground.

Cristina jumped, as if the bullets had struck her. She stared at Andrea's body, unable to move. She wanted and didn't want to rush over to help her former best friend. She couldn't seem to summon any reaction at all.

Three young men wearing bandanas over their faces stepped forward, bearing AK-47s. One approached Andrea's twitching body. He studied it, then spat and turned to Cristina.

"Please, don't kill me," she said, hands raised.

He scanned her up and down and then jerked his head.

Another teenaged boy ran to her. He inspected her knife wound and said in Portuguese, "It's not deep, but it will hurt."

He yanked the knife. It slid out of her shoulder. Cristina screamed.

The boy slapped a rolled-up shirt over the wound and indicated for her to apply pressure before bringing the knife to his leader.

"When Eduardo called, we thought Tiago's murderer was long gone," the leader said. He inspected the knife and tucked it into his belt. "But Filipe saw everything from the Barracudas den. He told us where to find you."

Try as she might, Cristina couldn't summon the slightest grief as she stared at Andrea's lifeless body. Instead she spoke to the gang leader in Portuguese. "You're Comando Novo?"

"Next generation. The government wants to control the favelas, but we *are* the favelas. Until they eliminate corruption and poverty, they'll never eliminate us." He held out his hand. "Will you help us?"

"I want to get home and ... Dr. Morgan!" She fumbled in her pockets until she found Mitchell's satellite phone. "I need to warn him."

Cristina dialed the number from memory. The phone rang once and then she heard, "We're sorry, but the number you dialed is not in service. Please check—"

Cristina disconnected. Her cheeks went numb with fear for Morgan. She realized the boys were watching her. "Go help my sister Maria. She needs medical attention."

The gang members exchanged glances. Two trotted back downhill. The leader remained behind, checking his rifle. Cristina ignored him, wincing from the pain in her shoulder as she pressed the balled-up cloth against it and thought of her next plan. She could call Wilson. But could he get to Morgan in time?

Something underneath Andrea vibrated. Cristina started forward, but the gang leader stopped her. He used his rifle to turn over her body. They spotted a phone on her belt.

Cristina pushed him aside and snatched the phone. No identification showed on the display. Clenching her jaw, she hit Answer.

For thirty seconds, she heard silence. At last, she said, "Who is this?"

"Ah, Cristina. Nice ... your voice. We are overdue ... chat."

Cristina's blood froze. The phone had a weak signal, the voice fuzzy and broken by static, but familiarity glimmered in the shadowy recesses of her mind. It could be only one person. "Quinn."

CHAPTER SIXTY-THREE

"Is Luke Morgan alright?" Cristina's upper back wound tight with the knowledge there wasn't anything she could do from Brazil to help. The movement sent another pained twinge through her shoulder. "If you hurt him—"

"I'm afraid … dead …" Static hissed. " … your detective friend."

Cristina reeled, as if a cannonball had slammed into her chest. The gang leader caught her, but she shrugged him off. It took another second for her to speak. "You're lying. You must be lying."

"Don't believe me? Call … I'll wait."

A warm breeze blew, but Cristina's bones chilled.

The gang leader cocked his head. She held up her index finger and mouthed, *Wait.*

Her hands seemed to be encased in ice as she fumbled for the satellite phone and dialed Wilson's number. Shrill chirps sounded in her ear, each unanswered ring jabbing like a knife. Her hand trembled.

Click. "Who is this?"

"Cristina Silva. Who is this?"

"Detective Hawkins. Where the hell are you?"

"Never mind that. Where's Wilson?"

He paused. "I don't know. There was an incident at the morgue. Someone blew it up. Killed Dr. Morgan. I found Wilson's phone, but we haven't found him. He could be anywhere under this rubble."

Cristina covered her mouth. Her throat constricted so she couldn't speak.

"Tell me where you are, and I'll help you," said Officer Hawkins.

It took several tries before she could say, "You can't help me."

Cristina hung up. Stared at Andrea's phone. The display indicated Quinn was still online.

Heat flushed through her veins. She put the other phone to her ear. "You son of a bitch."

"Now, my turn. Where's Andrea?"

Swallowing hard, Cristina said, "Dead."

Two heartbeats of silence followed. "That's unexpected but … fortunate. Every vestige … life as Cristina Silva is gone … have no choice … return to me."

"The only way I'll return to you is to see you dead."

"Ah, there's the firebrand … .Without me … Recognate, you're doomed to madness."

"I'll take my chances."

"Oh, Cristina, don't … foolish. Why waste two lives?"

He's right. You're losing it. At least one of us can survive.

Cristina withdrew Kobayashi's bottle from her pocket. She squinted at the green capsules. If she took them all, could she start fresh? Maybe this time would be better. Maybe she wouldn't be so driven to remember. Maybe …

"You're considering, aren't you?" Quinn's voice dripped with self-congratulation. "Go back … ReMind. Give … the answer. Then, I … help you reclaim … life you lost."

Reclaim the life you lost …

Cristina's throat constricted. She couldn't breathe.

Another man had used that exact phrase before. In the same tone of voice. In fact, the same voice.

The shadow man materialized before her, clutching a rifle, barking orders. Only now the shadows dissipated, revealing a strong brow, penetrating blue eyes, and deeply fissured cheeks.

Mitchell.

Staggering, numb, she stared at the satellite phone. How else could Andrea find her so easily? How could Mitchell have known where she'd be in Washington? Who had convinced her from the start she was Cristina Silva, all the while knowing she wasn't?

A scream formed in the pit of Cristina's stomach. She tamped it down. She had to stay in control. Couldn't let him know she knew.

"Cristina? What … you say?"

Images flitted through her mind. Wilson. Morgan. Jorge Silva. Maria. Her real mother.

Tightening her fist around the bottle, she said into the phone, "I'll go to ReMind. But then I want to meet you. Face to face."

"Of course. It's … long time. I can't wait."

She disconnected the call. "I can't wait to see you in Hell."

Cristina's hands shook. Her legs buckled, and she fell to her knees.

The gang leader rushed to her. She shoved him away.

Tears trickled, then streamed down her cheeks. A bubble grew in her chest, crushing her heart, until it burst at last. She cried for Wilson and Morgan. She cried for Carl and Jerry. She cried for Andrea. Most of all, she cried for Cristina Silva, the poor woman whose life she'd inadvertently stolen.

When she had no tears left, she sat back on her heels and took slow deep breaths. Her body felt stronger, her head clearer. She saw now that every choice she'd made since Sebastian dos Santos entered her life had led her to this decision.

She looked at the gang leader. "I'll help you—by destroying the man who did this to you. To us."

The mingled odors of blood, gun smoke, and formaldehyde stung Francisco Martins's nostrils as he knelt behind a dumpster near the hole in the outer wall. Yellow crime scene tape surrounded the area. A conspicuous trio held his attention: two men and a woman. They were picking their way through the debris.

When the morgue exploded, he'd been a block away, on his way back to the shelter. So far no one had spotted him. He adjusted his earpiece. He was lucky enough to be in range of the bug he'd hidden inside the burner phone he gave Detective Wilson, so he could overhear everything, including the white-haired cop's phone conversation with Cristina.

"Agents?" A uniformed officer held out a baggie containing a green capsule. "We found this under the analysis machine. It looks like someone ground another into dust."

The taller man studied the baggie. He scowled. "Detective Hawkins, how the hell did the medical examiner get a hold of this?"

"What?" asked the white-haired cop. "You know what that is?"

"Yeah, but it's top secret." To the woman, "We need to get going."

"Going where?" asked the white-haired cop.

"Washington." The taller man held up the baggie. "To deal with this."

"If you know where they make that, I'm coming with you."

"This is Bureau business and doesn't involve you, Detective." The blond man's face reddened. "If you want to help, tell the reporters outside a gas line exploded."

He and the woman marched away.

On a hunch, Martins withdrew the black device and activated

it. As he expected, a blinking red light indicated a position directly inside the lab. He flipped a switch. A green light appeared, moving south. He turned on his phone and dialed.

The detective on scene jumped. He checked his pockets and pulled out a black burner phone. He answered and said, "Who is this?"

"Detective, this is Francisco Martins."

"Martins? Where the hell's my partner?"

"I know how to find Detective Wilson. He's alive." Martins watched the blinking light drifting offscreen. "But we must move quickly before that's no longer the case."

CHAPTER SIXTY-FOUR

When Detective Gary Wilson opened his eyes, he saw nothing but darkness. He couldn't tell up from down. Sharp pain bit at the base of his neck. He tried to sit up. His head banged something hard. He went to rub his head. His hands were bound behind his back. He wriggled his feet. Tied, also.

He managed to run his fingers over what felt like zipties binding his ankles. Metal scraped his wrists—handcuffs. He knew a few escape tricks, but the confined space meant it would take a while.

Something moved beneath him. He held still. Vibration. Subtle shifts in inertia. He was locked in the trunk of a motor vehicle.

He had no idea why he was still alive. But he wasn't going to wait to find out.

Gritting his teeth, Wilson pulled his knees to his chest and groped for his shoelaces.

As they raced down I-95 in a beat-up Crown Vic, headlights illuminating a small chunk of the dark highway, Francisco Martins hunched over in the passenger seat, studying the tracking device. He tried to ignore the wary glances Detective Hawkins kept giving him. At least it hadn't been as difficult as Martins feared to convince the detective not to turn him into the authorities. The seeds of mistrust were deeply planted—all Martins needed to do was nourish them. Nevertheless, the way Hawkins drove with pistol in hand unnerved Martins.

"I told you, I don't intend to escape."

"Yeah," Hawkins said. "Well, forgive me for not fully trusting a terrorist. Maybe I should've called for backup, after all."

"By the time you convinced someone to help, your colleague Detective Wilson would be dead."

Hawkins quieted, jaw clenched. Martins tensed, fearing the detective might change his mind.

Hawkins indicated the tracking device. "You're sure that'll lead us to Wilson?"

"The GPS in the other burner phone is active—which either means your FBI friends didn't find it, or they're using it to lure us in."

"I don't like that second option."

"You needn't fear." Martins closed his eyes and mentally prepared for the imminent confrontation. "Before today ends, Quinn will pay for his crimes."

CHAPTER SIXTY-FIVE

The bright lights of the Reagan National Airport assaulted Cristina as she passed by the baggage claim area. She wore a platinum wig and eyeglasses as a disguise, but no one paid attention to her. Half-asleep passengers yawned and leaned against each other as they waited for their suitcases to arrive. Limo drivers circulated, holding up white signs with names written on them.

Since she had no bags, Cristina went directly to the pay phones. She'd had time during the ten-hour overnight flight to reconsider her plan to take Quinn down. Maria had tried in vain to convince her to stay in Brazil.

"We can move to Recife," her sister had said, pleading with her from her hospital bed. "Or Minas Gerais. Even the Amazon."

"You're in no condition to travel," Cristina said, indicating the cast on her sister's leg. Maria had been lucky that the bullet missed the actual kneecap, but it fractured the top of her fibula. The doctors said Maria needed two weeks of bedrest to heal. "And, anyway, Quinn knows I'm in Brazil," Cristina said. "He won't stop until he finds me. We'll never be safe."

"I just got my sister back," Maria said, tears filling her eyes. "I don't want to lose you again."

Cristina had held her hand and said solemnly, "You won't. I promise."

Now that promise felt empty. Cristina had used the satellite phone to call Mitchell for a ride home, careful not to reveal that she knew his real identity. Her plan was to pretend to go along with exposing Simmons as Quinn—then get the real Quinn alone and kill him. But she now saw it was foolish to think she could attack Quinn and whoever else was working with him alone. But who could she trust? Not the FBI. Not the CIA. Not Santos. With Wilson dead, there was only one person left who might be able to help.

She dialed Wilson's number and waited for an answer. After four rings, she heard Detective Hawkins say, "Hello?"

"It's Cristina Silva. I need your help."

"Dr. Silva? Where are you?"

"Washington. I know who Quinn is, and I know where to find him."

"We're a half hour out from Washington."

Cristina stiffened. "We?"

"You need to—Hey!"

There was what sounded like a brief scuffle, then a familiar rough voice said, "Hello, Cristina."

"Santos. What are you doing with Detective Hawkins?"

"Tracking Detective Wilson."

Cristina felt breathless. "Quinn said he was dead."

"I believe he's still alive."

A wave of euphoria washed over her. Wilson, alive! That changed everything.

"According to my tracker," Santos continued, "I think they are taking him to ReMind."

"He's a prisoner?" Her brief joy vanished, replaced by fear. "What do they want with him?"

"I imagine they plan to use him to force your hand. Don't worry. We'll help you deal with them."

"There's not enough time. Quinn's expecting me." Cristina's mind flooded with images of Wilson, bloodied and beaten. "If I don't go with him, he'll figure out I learned the truth and kill Wilson."

"Go with him? Cristina, what did you do?"

"I made a mistake, but I'm going to fix it." She massaged her wounded shoulder. The ibuprofen she'd taken on the flight helped dull the pain, but it wouldn't last—and neither would her memories if she didn't act quickly. "Just get here as soon as you can."

"Wait, Cristina, you can't—"

She hung up.

Are you sure about this?

Cristina straightened her back and gathered her courage.

"To save Wilson," she murmured, touching the locket around her neck. "I'll do whatever it takes."

CHAPTER SIXTY-SIX

A sleek black limousine purred alongside the curb as Cristina emerged from the airport exit. After she gave the driver a nod, he opened the door.

Mitchell poked out his grinning face. "Good morning, Doctor. I hope you had a pleasant trip."

It took every iota of strength for Cristina to refrain from choking him. At least he didn't seem to suspect she knew the truth about him.

"Unforgettable."

She climbed inside and sat across from Mitchell. The driver shut the door.

Mitchell raised the privacy screen and deactivated the intercom.

Cristina ripped off the wig and glasses. "I've wanted to do that for ten hours."

"Too bad. I think it's sexy."

Cristina cringed at his repartee. On the flight back, she'd analyzed everything he'd ever said to her—from their first meeting in the hospital to their reunion in DC. No question remained in her mind that he had orchestrated everything. And here he was, still pretending to be her savior. At least he didn't seem to know she'd learned the truth. As much as it repulsed her, she had to play along for now. Pretend to be working with him. At least until she found out where they were keeping Wilson.

"The immigration officer thought so, too. He was too busy checking out my legs and asking if I danced samba to inspect my passport."

"Let me see it."

The thought of his finger grazing hers made Cristina want to vomit. She handed it to him.

He scanned it. "Sabrina Carvalho. Where'd you get it?"

"My sister Maria had it. She found it in my apartment after I disappeared."

"I see. Well, lucky for that." He returned the passport.

"Yes. I'm so lucky." She tucked the passport in her purse. "Quinn said he'd meet me after I went to ReMind. Are you sure he's actually Julius Simmons?"

"Positive. Halfway through clinical trials, Russian locals killed four researchers. The Chief Security Officer hired private contractors for protection. Two months later, each city experienced surges in gang violence, sparked by police assassinations. And get this: they'd hired the CSO only two weeks earlier, and he surged up the corporate ladder. Then the CEO disappeared, and the CSO took the helm. Guess who?"

"Julius Simmons."

"Naturally. Who else would be obsessed with fixing Recognate?"

Who else, indeed? Cristina studied his airbrushed smile, marveling at how someone could lie so easily. She slipped one hand inside her coat, probing for the inner pocket where she'd smuggled the letter opener bought at an airport shop. It wasn't sharp, but if she caught him by surprise, she could drive it through his windpipe. Her pulse raced. "Quinn has stolen everything from me. I want to destroy him."

His smile faltered, briefly, and then he grinned. "I always loved your passion. I wouldn't trust anyone else."

It took all Cristina's will to keep her expression stoic. Bracing herself against the cabin, her shoulder twinging, she leaned over and crawled into the seat next to him. His eyebrows raised but he otherwise didn't react. She leaned closer, her hand tightening around the letter opener.

You really think you can kill him in cold blood? Sabrina's laughter filled Cristina's mind. *You couldn't even kill Andrea.*

Cristina's resolve wavered.

Before she could react, Mitchell yanked her closer, pressing his lips against hers. Cristina recoiled, repulsed. But Sabrina shoved her mind away and returned his kiss. Fireworks exploded in her head. Her arms wrapped around his neck, devouring him. The touch of his fingertips against her cheeks thrilled her.

Cristina looked down, watching her body embrace his.

What's happening?

I'm taking back control. Before you ruin everything.

Mitchell's tongue probed her mouth. His hands explored her waist and hips. She tried to pull away, but her body wouldn't respond.

We have to stop him. He did this to us.

You don't know anything. You have no idea who you are.

Carl Franklin and Jerry Peterman materialized nearby. They offered a rifle and started firing. Bullets whizzed past her head. A dark-skinned boy appeared, running toward her, crying for his mother. He fell, dead, a knife protruding from his back.

No. Stop.

You need to give him the formula. He can fix Recognate. Make these memories go away. He can fix me.

Cristina's stomach hardened. *You mean us.*

I mean me. You're just a shadow. And it's time to turn on the lights.

"No!" She shoved Mitchell away and scrambled to a corner of the limo seat, gasping for breath.

He stared at her, tense, as if afraid to touch her. "What's wrong?"

"It's starting. The memories are returning." She clutched her chest, trying to reassure herself she was still whole. "And I don't think I'll survive."

CHAPTER SIXTY-SEVEN

As the limo stopped in front of the ReMind building, Mitchell touched Cristina's shoulder. She withdrew reflexively, regretting it when his face darkened. Did he suspect she knew who he was?

"I injured it in Rio." She massaged her shoulder. "And it's hurting pretty bad. I think I should stay here."

What are you doing? You need to go in there and give him what he wants.

Why? So you can get rid of me?

If you cooperate, I'll let you stay in the background. But if you defy me, I'll tell him your plan and he'll kill Wilson.

"Is there something else going on?" Mitchell asked, his face screwed up with concern. "Something you're not telling me?"

Cristina hesitated.

Tick, tock.

"No, nothing." She forced a smile. "I guess I can handle the pain, after all."

"Okay." His face remained stoic for another moment and then he smiled back and helped her out of the car. As they approached the entry, he said, "Remember, our plan is to trick Simmons into confessing he ordered the murders to cover up his Recognate problems. The CIA isn't allowed to operate on U.S. soil, and we can't trust the FBI, so this is the only way we can get the truth."

"And he's just going to confess to us?" If Mitchell was Quinn, perhaps Simmons could be an ally.

"He will if you tell him how to fix Recognate," said Mitchell.

"But I don't know how to fix it."

"Lie. At least until you remember. With any luck, he'll slip first. Once we take down Simmons, the CIA has researchers who can study Recognate and produce it properly." Mitchell gave Cristina a grin she presumed was meant to be reassuring but came off smug. "Don't worry. We'll get you the right treatment."

Cristina's heart pounded as she followed Mitchell inside. She still didn't know what role Simmons played or what awaited her. A letter opener wouldn't be enough against the two of them. Her only hope was to bluff until she could bargain for Wilson's life, or Santos arrived.

"Welcome back, Doctor," Kitty said as they approached the reception desk. She lifted the phone. "I'll call Mateo to escort her."

"I'll take her there myself," Mitchell said. "I need to update him on a client."

"Of course, sir." Her teeth glittered. "Have a nice day."

They rode up the elevator. Cristina noticed a bulge under Mitchell's jacket. Had to be a gun. Her nerves shot into overload. The walls were crushing her. She needed to escape.

Uh, uh. No escape now. You run, you're done.

Her stomach fluttered.

Mitchell eyed her. "What's wrong?"

"Nothing," she said. "Just nervous."

"Keep it together. This will all be over soon."

The doors opened. They traversed the long hallway and stopped at the oak door. Mitchell opened it, and Cristina entered.

"Dr. Silva." Simmons rounded the corner into his office foyer, arms spread wide. "I hear you have excellent news to share ..." His grin faltered as Mitchell appeared. "Oh, I didn't expect you."

"I ran into Dr. Silva downstairs," Mitchell said. "I wanted to hear what she has to say. Our client is demanding a working product."

"Yes. Of course." Simmons's mouth twitched, then he was all business. "Let's talk."

They sat across from each other. Simmons folded his hands in his lap. Mitchell crossed his leg over his knee. Cristina clenched her fists, desperately trying to think of a way out of this mess without losing control to Sabrina.

At last, Simmons asked, "Well? What's the answer?"

She glanced at Mitchell. He gave her a blank stare in response.

Slowly, she said, "Neither Jerry nor Carl had active metabolites in their bloodstream. They suffered acute withdrawal."

"Impossible. Frank insisted they received their monthly supply uninterrupted."

Kobayashi's story replayed in her mind. There was only one possibility. "What if they received placeboes?"

"Placeboes? We don't use placeboes in an open label trial."

She swallowed. It was a dangerous card to play, but she had more up her sleeve. "I know about Rio."

"*Cristina*," Mitchell murmured.

Simmons scowled. "What about Rio?"

"The subjects went insane when their supply was cut off. That's why ReMind hired a mercenary group to take care of it."

The CEO's eyes burned. Prickles ran up and down her arms.

Unexpectedly, Simmons burst into laughter. "You've got a great imagination, young lady." To Mitchell, "Did you put her up to this?"

"You're denying it?" she asked.

He pulled a file out of his desk. "We reviewed your blood tests. THC levels are markedly elevated, and chromatography confirms synthetic cannabinoids. Since you don't seem like a spice user, I assume you've been taking Recognate. At high doses."

Her cheeks cooled. "Yes."

"You stole from us. But that's not the immediate problem." He shut the folder. "You're diaphoretic and your pupils are dilated. How long since your last dose?"

"Four days."

He sighed. "Then you need my help as much as I need yours."

The intercom buzzed. Simmons pushed a button. "What is it, Kitty?"

"Two federal agents are here to see you."

Cristina glanced at Mitchell. He looked as surprised as she was.

"Fine. Send them up." Simmons leaned across the desk. "Now, no more games. If the problem is withdrawal, as you claim, how do we fix it?"

"There might be a way," she began, trying to stall. "But it may cause more deaths."

He pressed his fist against his lips and stared at his desk. "Then we'll have to shut down the study."

"Why would you do that?" Mitchell asked. "The investor is ready to sign."

"I know, but Dr. Silva is right. Too many lives have been lost already. We need damage control, or we're screwed."

The office door clicked open.

Mateo appeared. "They're here."

"Send them in." Simmons looked at Mitchell. "We may as well deal with this all at once."

Mateo disappeared. Footsteps plodded on the hardwood floor. Cristina turned.

Agent Forrester stormed into the office, followed by Vasquez. Cristina's mouth went dry.

"This is unacceptable, Julius," said Forrester. "You should've told us this drug was flawed before we agreed to use it for witness protection ..." Forrester stopped in his tracks. He glared at Cristina. "What are you doing here?"

"Please sit, Agent," Simmons said. "She's here to help."

"This whole mess is because of her." He pointed at Cristina. "You're under arrest."

"I don't think so," Mitchell said.

Forrester wheeled around. Focused on Mitchell. Cheeks reddened. "I recognize you."

Mitchell sighed. "Well, that's a shame."

Something clicked behind Forrester. He turned. Agent Vasquez held a gun to his head. A silencer hugged the barrel.

"Grace?" he whispered.

"Sorry, Charles." She fired.

Agent Forrester crumpled to the floor.

"What the hell?" Simmons yelled. "You can't—"

"Quiet!" Agent Vasquez trained the gun on him, then glanced at Mitchell. "What now, Mr. Quinn?"

CHAPTER SIXTY-EIGHT

The stink of gun smoke and blood lingered. Each tick of the desk clock reverberated in the room's deadly quiet. Quinn held Cristina's gaze for what seemed to be forever. Her heart pounded.

"Well, shit," he said, grimacing. "That was an unfortunate twist. I hadn't expected you to find out quite like that."

She continued to stare at him, fearing what he might do next.

"Hold on. You don't seem surprised." He squinted. "You already knew who I was, didn't you? What gave me away?"

Cristina stayed silent. Let him fret over how he slipped up.

"What's going on?" Simmons cowered behind his desk. "Why did you kill Agent Forrester?"

"Business, Julius." Quinn shrugged. "Isn't that what you always say? Charles Forrester would've shut us down once he found out who I was. Instead, I shut him down. Just like in Rio."

Simmons balled his fists. "This isn't what we agreed."

"We agreed you'd get a fancy desk and a figurehead position. You didn't care how you got it." Quinn jabbed his thumb against his chest. "I've held this company together. Not you. Now I need Cristina's help."

Cristina was startled. "What makes you think I'd help you after what you've done?"

"What I've done is keep you alive. You'd be dead if it weren't for my orders. Hell, I saved your life in DC when Andrea tried to kill you."

"Only because you want to know how to fix Recognate."

"Information that will benefit all of us. With a working drug, we can save you and change the world."

"You're insane," Simmons said. "Change the world? You just killed our FBI liaison."

"We don't need him," Quinn said. "Vasquez will handle the Bureau. Anyway, I've got a dozen other potential buyers lined up."

"Who?"

"That doesn't matter until we have a stable drug." Quinn turned to Cristina. "That's why I need you. I tried to keep you out of it. The best minds worked nonstop and failed every field test."

"Field test." Something in Cristina's mind clicked. "You switched Carl's and Jerry's Recognate for placeboes."

"I did what had to be done. If they tried calling the number on those bottles, they would've reached an inoperative number. I had to keep Simmons out of the loop."

"Those others, the psychotic breaks Simmons told me about. That was all you." Cristina's stomach heaved. "You killed your own men."

"When you remember, you'll understand."

"I'll never understand a monster like you."

"Sabrina Carvalho did. She wanted adventure. Excitement. A new life." Quinn leered. "That's why she suggested we test Recognate on ourselves."

Cristina's body warped inside out. "What?"

"Jorge Silva got too close. The only way to hide you from him and the rest of the CIA was to turn you into someone else. Carl, Jerry, Federico and you."

Cristina swallowed hard. She asked her other self: *Is this true?* There was no answer.

"This is outrageous," Simmons said. "You never told me any of this."

"You didn't need to know, Julius, but Cristina does. She needs to understand so she can remember who she was." Quinn regarded Cristina coldly. "Who she still is."

Her hands shook. New memories seeped into her mind, swirling and blending with false ones. She was laughing over drinks with Andrea and Kobayashi. She watched old movies with Jorge and Claudia Silva on Maria's sixteenth birthday. Her mind was suddenly balancing on a precipice over an abyss. Molten lava spurted all around her, licking at her feet. Her friends and family yanked her arms in a tug of war. Cristina knew that no matter which way she fell, she was doomed.

She clenched her fists. *I won't give up.*

The locket seemed to scald her chest under her blouse. Pressing her fist against it, she built a mental wall to hold back the lava. Pushed away her conflicting thoughts. Straightened her shoulders. "Even if I remember, I won't tell you anything."

"Oh, I think you will." He lifted his smartphone to his ear. "Bring him in."

After fumbling in the darkness for who knew how long, Gary Wilson removed one shoelace. He dropped it on the floor. Wriggled into a prone position. Bit the lacing and chewed at the aglet. Half broke off in his mouth. He spat it out and rolled over again. Twisted the plastic piece between his fingers. Maneuvered it into the cuff lock. Wiggled and turned it until he felt a click. The cuff popped open.

Wilson shimmed the other cuff and rubbed his wrists. Next, he grabbed the zip tie around his ankles with both hands and snapped it. He checked his pockets and holster. Empty. He searched the confined space for a tire iron, wrench—anything he could use to break free. Nothing. He felt around for what he thought was the trunk lock. Kicked. Again.

The hatch opened. Sunlight blinded him. He covered his eyes.

A shadow moved into view. Big.

"*Que es esto?*" the shadow asked in a baritone, leaning forward. He reached out his left arm, displaying an emblem portraying a brain surrounded by ivy. A nametag on his chest read, *Mateo*. "Let me help you."

The man's eyes bulged. He gagged. Blood streamed from his mouth. He fell.

Wilson scrambled to the hatch. He froze.

Mateo lay on the ground, bleeding, a knife protruding from his back.

"I hope you weren't planning to leave," said a thin man with wire-framed glasses, aiming a pistol at Wilson's forehead. "The fun's about to start."

CHAPTER SIXTY-NINE

"This is it." Francisco Martins rushed to the ReMind building with Detective Hawkins. "Cristina and your partner should be inside."

"All right." Hawkins held Martins's elbow and nudged him forward. "Nothing funny."

"I'm quite humorless."

As they entered an opulent lobby, the detective let out a low whistle. Martins led him to the front desk.

The receptionist smiled. "How can I—?"

"Save it." Hawkins flashed his badge. "Somerville PD."

Her smile didn't falter. "You're out of your jurisdiction."

"I'm with a special task force. On Recognate."

Her grin wavered. "Are you with those feds?"

"What feds?"

"The ones I sent to Mr. Simmons's office. Let me see." She ran her finger down a list. "Forrester and Vasquez."

Hawkins was startled. "They're here?"

"You're not with them?"

"They told us to handle it." Martins smiled. "They must have become impatient and gone ahead without us."

The receptionist studied their faces. "Hold on."

They waited while she dialed. The detective looked nervous. Understandable, but they had no time for error. Martins surveyed the lobby.

"I tried calling Security, but Mateo won't answer," the receptionist said. "Let me check the monitor. Okay, there's someone in admin—Oh, my God! He has a gun!"

"Call 911," Hawkins said. "How do I get there?"

Martins didn't wait to hear the receptionist's answer. Ignoring the ache in his twisted ankle, he darted into the elevator. Once inside, he readied the pistol he'd hidden in his underpants and prepared for the worst.

"Here's a choice," Quinn said with a theatrical flourish. "Help me fix Recognate and you can continue as Cristina Silva or whoever you want. Or wait until Sabrina takes over and helps me—I'm sure she'll be more cooperative."

Tears welled in Cristina's eyes. The idea that her prior identity had helped create this mess—it was too much. She couldn't let that person regain control. But she couldn't help this madman either. Teenaged boys screamed in her mind. Her brain swelled and threatened to rupture her skull. Sweat rolled down her cheeks.

You're not real, kid. Time to disappear.

She dug her nails into her palms. The pain was real. She was real.

"Cristina." Quinn tapped his watch. "Clock's ticking."

"Go to Hell."

Quinn's face darkened. He raised his fist but stopped himself. "We'll see about that."

A man stumbled around the corner as if pushed, holding his hands by his head. His gaze met Cristina's.

Cristina's heart leaped into her throat. "Wilson?"

"Keep moving." The man behind the detective used a gun to

urge Wilson forward. The captor's face came into view: Dr. Frank Alvarez.

Cristina's mouth went dry.

An odd look crossed Wilson's face. He mouthed, *Run.*

Wilson ducked under Frank's gun. Spun. Knocked his pistol away. The policeman connected his fist with Frank's groin. Frank howled and doubled over.

Cristina tried to run, but her feet had rooted to the floor.

We're not going anywhere. Not until Quinn cures us.

Quinn and Vasquez aimed their weapons at Wilson, but he raised his hands over his head.

"Valiant effort," Quinn said. "But ill-advised."

A sliding sound came from Simmons's desk.

Quinn whipped around. Fired.

The bullet struck below Simmons's clavicle. He screamed. Clutched his chest. Fell into his chair. A pistol dropped onto the floor.

"Julius, Julius …" Quinn kept his gun trained on Simmons. "I understand the detective's misguided action, but you know me. What were you thinking?"

"Kill me," Simmons said. Blood stained his shirt. "I deserve it for inviting a sociopath into my house."

"Why waste the bullet? You'll be dead soon enough." Quinn turned to Cristina. "You could've run. I guess you realized you need my help."

"No," Cristina said, keeping her voice level. "I realized you won't kill me because you need my help."

"True, but I don't need him." Quinn grabbed Wilson's neck and dragged him to face Cristina. He pressed the muzzle against Wilson's temple. "You thought you lost your boyfriend once. Give me what I want, or this time you'll get to watch him die."

CHAPTER SEVENTY

"Get your pistol," Quinn said to Frank, who clambered to his feet. "And make sure no one heard those gunshots."

"But—"

"Do it!"

As Frank stumbled away, Quinn asked, "What do you say, Cristina?"

A powerful craving struck Cristina, worse than the ones in Rio. The thought of Maria's *caipirinha* made her salivate. The more she fought it, the worse it became. "Will you let him go?"

"Don't trust him, Cristina," Wilson shouted. "He's a murderer."

"Shut up." Quinn pressed the muzzle harder against Wilson's skull. He met Cristina's gaze. "Yes, I'll let him go."

Give him what he wants, and this'll all be over. We'll drink ourselves into a stupor and forget everything.

Every corner of her brain lit up. Dr. Morgan said about Carl that he was clearly a heavy drinker for some time. Stacey said Jerry was drunk, but that wasn't why he went crazy. Devi said Mrs. Watterson had started drinking two to three glasses of red wine per night.

The formula from the locket whirled in her mind, expanding, rotating, pulsing.

Her heart raced. She understood.

"You remember, don't you?" Quinn eyed her. "You know how to fix it."

"No. I don't."

"Don't lie to me." He ground the barrel against Wilson's cheek. "Tell me."

"Don't tell him anything, Cristina," a familiar husky baritone said from behind Vasquez.

Sebastian dos Santos pressed a gun against the agent's back.

A mixture of relief and anger washed over Cristina. Relief that he was there. Anger that he had hidden the truth from her—that he was her father.

"What are you doing here?" Quinn asked, still holding Wilson. "Can't you see we're negotiating?"

"Then negotiate your surrender." Santos jabbed the gun against Vasquez. "Or I'll kill her."

"Go ahead," Quinn said. "She's a liability, anyway, seeing as she's linked to the murders of special agents Gomes and Forrester."

Vasquez blanched. "But ... You can't—"

"Sorry, dear. You were a tremendous help, but I don't need you anymore." Quinn turned back toward Santos. "Once I've got a stable drug, I can brainwash anyone to work for me. Besides ..." He patted Wilson's shoulder. "My ante trumps yours."

"I've been in this game far longer than you, boy," Santos said. "I only care that Cristina is free. Once that happens, you and I will cleanse our souls in Hell."

"Jesus, you're still a walking fortune cookie. You know what?" Quinn drew a second pistol from his jacket. Fired three times. Bullets ripped through Vasquez's chest.

The FBI agent screamed and slumped to the floor. Quinn fired again. He struck Santos in the abdomen. The man crumpled.

"No!" Cristina started for Santos.

Quinn swung a gun toward her. She froze.

Santos writhed in agony. Cristina's heart nearly burst. No matter what he'd done, she couldn't let him die. "If you want the answer, let me help my father."

"Your father?" Quinn's eyes widened. He stared, then snickered. "I don't believe it."

"You didn't think I'd find out?"

"Oh, I'd be surprised if he didn't tell you himself. What I don't believe is how someone so brilliant could believe something so ridiculous." He pointed at Santos. "That man's not your father."

CHAPTER SEVENTY-ONE

Cristina fought to stay in control. "How would you know if he's my father or not?"

"Because I made him believe he was," Quinn said. "We went underground because the CIA was onto us."

"Jorge Silva was tracking you. I know."

"Who do you think tipped him off?"

She stiffened. "Santos?"

"He'd been helping Silva for months in exchange for asylum. No wonder he botched my order to burn them in their own home. He didn't want to kill his golden goose." Quinn glared at Santos's writhing form. "But I couldn't lose an asset. I made sure he wouldn't betray me again."

"You made Santos believe I was his daughter."

"All I had to do was steal a little of his memory. Just enough to make him question his past. Then I got him hooked on Recognate, gave him the locket, and fed him the story about your savior. Once Jorge Silva trusted him again, even enough to service his car, I set him in position to take out the Silvas." Quinn scowled. "But Martins ran, so I had to get my hands dirty. I hate getting my hands dirty."

"You cut the brake lines," Wilson said. "You killed the Silvas. You're full of lies."

"Shut up." Quinn cracked the pistol butt against Wilson's skull and looked at Cristina. "You see? You don't owe him anything."

"I'm sorry, Cristina," Santos whispered.

"Does he even have a daughter?" Cristina asked, breathless.

Quinn simpered. "Nope."

Waves of nausea swept over her, each stronger than the previous. Nothing was real. Not in this life. Not in the other life. All she had left were lies. If she didn't do something, she would lose even those.

"Let Santos and Wilson go, and I'll tell you."

Quinn grinned. "You got it."

She took a deep breath. "Alcohol."

His grin faltered. "Excuse me?"

"Alcohol blocks the cannabinoid receptors. The more alcohol, the weaker the drug's effect over time. Old memories start returning. If you then stop the drug suddenly, the receptors scream for stimulation, causing the subject to crave anything with the same effect."

"So, they get drunk."

"Intoxication causes psychosis. When combined with a surge of violent memories—"

"They go nuts." Quinn gaped. "How do we fix it?"

Wilson's eyes pleaded with her. Santos barely clung to life. She couldn't let them die. She couldn't let Sabrina take over. Cristina's only hope was to help the man who ruined her. "The formula's hidden in the locket. A combination of benzodiazepine agonist to block the alcohol effects and a third-generation sedative to relieve the anxiety. Build it into the drug and it'll work."

Quinn nodded. "Thank you, Cristina."

His finger moved toward the trigger.

Gunshots. Quinn yelped. The gun dropped from his hand. Blood spurted from his arm.

"That's a warning shot." Officer Hawkins appeared around the corner. "Now put your hands up."

Quinn glanced from his wounded arm to Cristina. Fire danced in his eyes. Wordlessly, he swung around. Fired the other gun.

Hawkins ducked around the corner. Bullets slammed into the wall.

Wilson threw himself backward. He crashed into Quinn and they both fell.

Quinn wrapped his good arm around Wilson's neck. Wilson rammed his elbow against Quinn's abdomen. Quinn grunted, held tight.

Cristina watched, frozen in place. Memories tossed and crashed.

Simmons's gun lay inches away.

Do it. Stop that madman.

You said we needed him. He's our chance for sanity.

We don't need him. I remember now. We can't trust him.

Why should I listen to you? You helped him. You loved him.

Yes, I loved him. And I paid for it.

The office vanished. Now, Cristina was inside a sparsely furnished shack. Artillery covered a wooden table. A younger James Quinn pressed his fingertips against his forehead. Blood stained his shirt.

"You're terrorists," Cristina heard herself saying. "You ordered Jeremy to kill a boy."

"We have a job—"

"You kill children! Everything Francisco told me is true."

"Why were you talking to him?" He threw a glass against the wall. It shattered. "Do you know what you've done?"

"I know what I'm going to do." She started for the door. "I'm leaving."

"You can't leave." He grabbed her arm. "I can't lose you."

"You already have."

Quinn's face twisted with rage. He grabbed a rifle. Rammed the handle into her nose. She cried out. Blood streamed from her nostrils. The gun crashed into her skull. Again and again.

Cristina flashed back to Simmons's office at ReMind. She gasped for air, as if she'd been ten feet underwater for years and only now had broken free to the surface. Everything became clear.

Eight feet away Quinn stood with his back to her, squeezing Wilson's neck. The hand hanging from his wounded arm jammed the pistol into Wilson's back. Anger flared in her gut and then as quickly cooled.

"Kick the gun here and come out," Quinn said. "No heroics. I only need one arm to kill you both."

A pistol slid across the floor. Hawkins emerged with his hands by his head.

"Good. Thank you for making it easier to—"

Cristina plunged the letter opener into Quinn's wounded arm. He screamed. Wilson broke free.

Quinn staggered. Turned to face Cristina. His face contorted into a mask of confusion and shock. "You—you need me. You can't both exist in the same mind."

Cristina smiled thinly. "We made peace."

Quinn's eyes blazed. He lunged. Tackled her. Rammed his forehead against hers.

Pain exploded in Cristina's skull. She kicked. Connected with Quinn's groin. He howled.

She rolled away. Sprang to her feet. Kicked again.

He caught her foot. Lifted. Threw her against the desk.

"I made you, bitch." He stormed toward her. "You're nothing."

Gunfire rang out.

Quinn's mouth gaped. He clutched his chest. Blood stained his shirt. He collapsed.

Crouched a few feet away, Wilson lowered the smoking pistol.

Whatever strength Cristina had left drained from her body. She slumped against the desk.

Wilson scrambled to her side. "Stay with me."

Cristina opened her mouth to say she was fine, but she wasn't fine. She couldn't speak. She might never be fine again. She wanted to cry. No tears would come.

Hawkins knelt next to Santos. "This guy needs help."

Cristina's mind shifted into clinical mode. She pushed away Wilson and crawled over to Santos. His skin was ashen. His chest barely moved.

While she fumbled for a pulse, Wilson asked Hawkins, "How'd you find us?"

"Dead lab tech outside. Shot through his glasses. Figured it was Santos's work."

Santos's carotid thrummed weakly. Cristina ripped open his shirt. Her heart sank. Blood streamed from a wound below his ribcage.

"It hit his liver. I can't stop the bleeding."

"It's … as it should be," Santos said. "My work is done. You … are free."

A whiff of alcohol on his breath reminded her of their last meeting on the bus, when he'd attacked her. Instantly, she understood. "You stopped taking Recognate. You knew you weren't my father."

"I tracked down subjects and stole their pills, but … it became too difficult. I stopped for eight months."

"How did you not go crazy?"

"They did not steal my entire memory. I always knew who I was. The only thing they gave me … was you." Santos coughed violently. "My feelings for you … were still there. I was driven …

to release you … to help you restore your … true self. To become Sabrina Carvalho once again … But after we spoke in the Boston Commons … when you showed compassion for me … even after learning the truth … I couldn't lose you, either. I … started taking them again."

"Why?" Tears blurred her vision. She wiped them away. "You were free. Why would you risk everything for me when I'm not your daughter?"

With great effort, he placed his hand on hers. "You're the daughter I always dreamed …" Santos's voice faded to a wheeze. His eyes closed.

Cristina laid her head on his chest. Her sobs drowned out his final breath.

CHAPTER SEVENTY-TWO

"Do you see her?" Wilson asked as they stood by the baggage claim exit at Boston Logan Airport.

"Not yet." Passengers shuffled past. Cristina stood on tiptoes to look over their heads. "There she is."

Maria Carvalho waved from the bottom of the escalator and approached. The automatic door swung open. "*Oi! Cheguei!*"

"*Bemvindo!*" Cristina embraced her sister. "I can't believe you're here."

"Nor can I. *Ta frio!*" Maria pantomimed a shiver.

"I brought you a coat." Cristina indicated Wilson. "I'd like you to meet Gary."

"*Mootoo prazer.*" Wilson blushed at his bad Portuguese. "That was off, wasn't it?"

"Close enough." Maria laughed.

"I'll get your bags." He headed for the carousel.

"*Bonito,*" Maria said as they watched him go.

"Yeah, he's a good catch. So, how was your first international flight?"

"Long but good. Enough about me. How are you, really?"

"Every day's another step forward. That's what I tell my patients."

"Are you working again?"

"Not yet, but I plan to reopen soon. I'm even bringing Devi back once she finishes her community service."

In a low voice, Maria said, "Did they arrest you?"

"No. Anyone else who knew about my past is dead. As far as the government is concerned, I'm an innocent victim."

"*Gracias a Deus.*" Maria squeezed her hand. "Mother would be proud of you."

"My memory's still spotty, but I remember her as well as I remember the Silvas.

I wish they were still alive." Cristina squeezed back and smiled. "At least I have you."

"Always, but how did you remain sane?"

Once again, Cristina saw Quinn hovering over her, wielding the rifle. She grimaced and forced the memory away. "Sabrina made mistakes, but she wasn't a bad person. Instead of fighting for dominance, we accepted each other. We're part of each other. I know who I am now—who I really am. But …"

"But what?"

"There are still some things that don't add up. There are still some things that don't add up. You said I disappeared three years ago—but I only showed up in Boston as Cristina Silva two years ago. Where was I in that missing year? And what did Quinn use to steal memory? Santos said—"

Wilson approached, dragging a bulging suitcase. "You sure you brought enough clothes?"

"I'm Brazilian." Maria laughed again. "Most of it is shoes."

He glanced at Cristina's face and frowned. "You're not unloading your life's questions on her, are you?"

"No." Cristina held his hand, savoring the warmth. "I've got all the answers I need."

They chatted as they walked to the parking garage. Halfway up the fourth parking row, Wilson handed Cristina a set of car keys. She pressed a button. The taillights on a red Mini Cooper flashed.

"Nice car," Maria said.

"Thanks. It's a birthday present to myself."

"It's yours?" Maria gaped. "I thought you hated driving."

Cristina grinned. "After runaway cars, buses and motorcycles, I think I can handle a Mini." They loaded the car and climbed in. Cristina's hands trembled as she gripped the steering wheel, but this time it wasn't due to withdrawal. *I'm in control.*

"Whose birthday are we celebrating?" Maria buckled up. "Sabrina Carvalho's or Cristina Silva's?"

"Neither. We're celebrating my rebirth." Cristina wrinkled her nose as she turned the key. "Better hold on tight."

With a whoop, Cristina hit the accelerator and they raced off to face the world.

EXCERPT FROM
TOXIC EFFECTS
THE MEMORY THIEVES SERIES: BOOK 2

CHAPTER ONE

Chilled September rain bounced off DB's black balaclava and drizzled down her cheeks as she skulked in a grove of oak trees. From her vantage point in the darkness, she could see Meridian Hill Parks' illuminated statue of Saint Joan astride her horse, sword raised overhead. DB's shoulders stiffened, chin lifted. She and Joan were kindred spirits. Both trained as warriors. Neither could rest until they finished what had to be done.

And both were plagued by visions that drove them mad.

She forced away those thoughts and donned leather gloves, focusing on the matter at hand. She had a job to do.

Before long, a big man stumbled past the statue wearing a gray hoodie, torn jeans, and white high-top sneakers. A ratty backpack slung over his shoulder. He twice glanced behind him with the jerky movement of a fearful man, granting her a brief look at his face. She recognized him from the photo her handler had sent as Mateo Gonzalez. Several days' growth of stubble clung to his cheeks and chin. His eyes darted everywhere, as if Death itself were hot on his tail.

It wasn't far from the truth. He'd been reported dead six months ago.

She gave him a thirty-second lead before following. The smell of musk lingered in the air behind him. Raindrops bounced off her skin, pale as the moon rising over the treetops.

Mateo blundered down the stone steps, kicking up mud and gravel as he went, before turning north onto the path running parallel to the street. He stopped and leaned forward, hands on his knees, panting and looking back in her direction.

DB slipped into the shadows.

His gaze narrowed.

She didn't move.

Mateo let out a few more ragged breaths, then he straightened and started jogging down the path, his white sneakers flashing in the moonlight.

Creeping down the stairs, she followed.

His footfalls echoed on the wet pavement. *Thud. Thud. Thud.*

DB stayed on the grass, careful not to snap a stray twig or trip on a branch.

His head jerked to the right. He listed that way, headed for the park's east entrance.

He was going to chicken out of the meeting, as she'd feared. If he disappeared again, it could take months to relocate him, and her employers would hold her responsible. As much as she wanted to find out who he was meeting, she couldn't let Mateo Gonzalez escape or she herself would be in trouble with her bosses at Zero Dark. She slipped her hand under the back of her black t-shirt, feeling for the cold metal strapped there, picking up her pace.

As if suddenly realizing where he was, Mateo veered to the left.

She removed her hand. He was back on track. Good. She held back and waited under an oak tree. The rain lightened to a sprinkle.

Mateo followed the path to the next intersection, then turned right, heading north again. His head rotated side-to-side as he ran, like a child's toy robot.

A child's toy robot...

An image formed in her mind. A playroom in a New England colonial house. There was a chalkboard on an easel and a bookcase lined with picture books and stuffed animals. She sat crisscross-applesauce on a Minnie Mouse carpet, playing with the robot and laughing. A man sat on a white couch with his back to her, watching a soccer match. He turned, but she couldn't see his face. He called her by a different name, but she couldn't make it out.

DB jolted back to the present. The glitches, as she'd nicknamed them, had recently become more frequent. Memories, hallucinations—she didn't know what they were, but she couldn't deal with them now, not with her prey slipping away. If this mission fell to shit, there'd be Hell to pay.

She cut across the grass, chiding herself for getting sidetracked. Her employer promised to eliminate the glitches for good, but only if DB obeyed. She clenched her fist. One day, she'd be done following orders. One day—but not today.

The abstract white lump that was the Serenity sculpture loomed atop the hill ahead. As DB approached, her breathing hitched. She couldn't see her target. Had he already made the drop? Had he fled, after all? Or did he know she was tailing him and was now hiding in the bushes, waiting for her to get close enough to ambush?

Her hand returned to her back, muscles tensing as she crested the hill.

She relaxed. There he was, next to the statue like a good little soldier.

Keeping to the trees, she crept closer. She stopped behind the bushes, where she could make out the worn marble of the statue, the missing hand, the cracks at its base. The seated figure's face had all but worn away, leaving only two vacant holes for eyes that seemed to be observing from afar. It looked anything but serene. A fitting place for this rendezvous.

Mateo paced next to the sculpture, fumbling with the strap on his backpack, eyes wild. He mumbled under his breath.

DB inched closer.

His head snapped in her direction.

She froze. Still as the sculpture.

He squinted, staring straight at her.

She held her breath.

A twig cracked off to the side.

Mateo whirled around.

"Easy," said another man, this one in a business suit—Armani, DB guessed. He held a briefcase in one hand, the other extended palm-forward to show it was empty. "It's me."

"Were you followed?"

"Were you?"

Mateo wheezed, eyes bouncing around like rubber balls. He spoke with a Mexican accent, his voice rough, almost a growl. "I feel like I'm being followed all the time. You told me they wouldn't find me."

"How about a thank-you? Do you know how much red tape I had to go through to pronounce you dead on arrival and transfer you to a secure location to patch you up?"

Mateo glowered at Armani. "Thank you."

Straightening his back, Armani said, "You're welcome. If you hadn't bolted afterward, you could've been under safety watch for the past six months instead of hiding in dumpsters and tunnels. At least you were smart enough to call me. I promise your identity will be safe."

"Did you make that same promise to Kitty and the others?" Mateo bit off each word as if it were dripping with wormwood. "Is that why they're all dead?"

As she listened, DB reached under the back of her shirt once more, removing a slim Kahr CM9 pocket pistol from a holster taped to her spine. She checked the magazine. Satisfied, she threaded a suppressor onto the barrel.

"That's why I asked you to meet me alone," Armani said. "We had a breach, but it's been handled. You need to—"

A silver gun appeared in Mateo's hand, glittering in the moonlight. "I need to stop listening to people like you."

DB paused. This man was braver than she'd thought.

Armani raised his hands again. "Take it easy, Mateo. We'll figure this out. We'll move you into full witness protection and—"

"Protection?" Mateo barked out a sharp laugh. "You can't protect me from them. They are the *Nagual*. Shapeshifters. They steal your mind and make you one of them. Friends, lovers, employers—none of them can be trusted." He aimed at Armani's forehead. "You could be one of them and you would never know until it's too late."

The guy sounded like a raving lunatic, yet his words resonated in DB's ears. *They steal your mind...*

"I promise: I'm not one of them," Armani said. "We'll get you out of the country, under twenty-four-hour security. I'll guard you myself."

Mateo's grip on the gun slackened. "I'm finding it very difficult to trust you or anyone else."

"I have the papers right here, in my briefcase." Armani set the satchel on the ground. "Everything you need to create a new identity. You can take it and run. Or you can come with me, and I'll make sure you're safe."

For another tense moment, Mateo kept the gun trained on Armani's face, his hand wavering a bit. At last, he lowered it. "All right."

"Thank goodness you've come to your senses." Armani

buttoned his jacket. "But first, don't you have something to tell me? You said on the phone someone else was involved in the Re-Mind affair—someone not dead. So who would that be?"

DB raised the CM9 and adjusted the night sight, aiming at Mateo's forehead until a ring appeared on the scope. As soon as handed over the information, she could eliminate them both, collect what she needed to satisfy her employers, and head home.

Mateo stared at the ground, his chest rising and falling. He looked up at Armani and said, in a voice so low she almost couldn't hear, "You promise my wife and daughter will be safe?"

She froze.

Daughter? They didn't say anything about a daughter.

Armani tilted his head. "You have my word. They'll be under the best of care. They already think you're dead. They'll never know they were in danger."

Blood coursed through the arteries in her temples. *He has a daughter.*

Daughter.

Another vision erupted in DB's mind. This time, she was driving. Rain pelted the windshield. A stately dark-haired woman with refined features rode next to her. A man's gruff voice came from the rear seat. Her heart swelled with something she couldn't describe, not at first, but as she homed in on it, she understood what it was: love.

Hot, white light flooded her field of vision. The sound of metal crunching against metal filled her ears. The woman screamed.

DB jerked back to the moment at hand. Her heart raced. She forced her breathing rate to slow.

Stay in control, she ordered herself. *You have a mission.*

Clenching her jaw, she raised the gun again, telling herself not to think about Mateo's family. His wife. His daughter.

Damn it.

She could do this. It was what Zero Dark had trained her to do. If she failed, she would be next.

But DB would not fail. She never failed.

Mateo was holding something out to Armani. It looked like a printout from the Internet.

"Everything crashed down when she showed up," he was saying. "If you want to know what happened that day, find her. She's the reason for all of it."

Armani grinned as if possessed by a demon. "I knew you'd come through."

His hand slipped inside his jacket.

DB shifted her sights and fired.

A hole appeared in the center of Armani's forehead, filling with blood. His mouth contorted and puckered. He crumpled to the ground.

Mateo whirled, raising his pistol. He moved into a fighter's stance.

She leaped from the bushes.

As she expected, he took a step backwards, off-guard.

Before he could recover, she dropped to the ground, rolled, and kicked out his legs.

He tumbled and dropped his gun.

She lunged like an anaconda. Her arm constricted around his throat. She pressed the gun barrel against his temple.

"Please," he said, voice cracking with tears. "I don't know anything. I was only a security guard."

"I won't tell Zero Dark about your family," she whispered. "They'll be safe."

His body stiffened. Then he nodded.

He understood. That made it easier.

She pulled the trigger.

His body sagged.

Her stomach heaved. DB closed her eyes and counted to twenty. The nausea passed. She laid him on the ground and searched him, removing his wallet, and stuffing it into her pocket. She took his gun and replaced it with hers—unregistered, serial number wiped clean. Covering his fingers with hers, she fired into the ground, allowing residue to coat Mateo's hand.

She crossed over to Armani, slid a hand into his jacket, and removed the Sig-Sauer P226 with attached suppressor he'd been seeking. She stuck it in her waistband next to Mateo's and searched the rest of his pockets. Empty. No ID.

She unfurled Armani's fingers and withdrew the paper Mateo had given him. Her mind started racing as she read, the moonlight on her pale skin giving her a ghostly appearance befitting her name: Dama Branca. The White Lady.

Her phone vibrated.

When she picked up, the caller asked in a distorted voice, "Is it done?"

"Affirmative. But why send me? Your mole seemed to have it covered."

There was a pause. "Mole?"

"The one the target was meeting. He was one of ours, wasn't he?"

Another pause. "You eliminated both?"

Her chest tightened. "You told me to leave no witnesses. Why'd you order me to kill one of our own?"

"That's not your concern."

"But I think—"

"You're not paid to think. Now, any loose ends?"

DB glanced at Mateo's body, imagining his wife driving their kids to school, blissfully unaware of what had happened to her husband, moments before a truck rammed into their car and killed them all. She wrinkled her nose. This operation stunk. There was more her handler wasn't telling her.

"I said, any loose ends?"

She set her jaw. It would do DB no good to lie. Her bosses would find Mateo's family anyway. The only thing that would happen would be she'd be next on Zero Dark's hit list.

Unless she gave them something else to worry about.

"Who is Cristina Silva?" she asked, trying to sound indifferent.

No response.

"Why does that name sound familiar?" asked DB.

"Never mind." She could hear the hitch in the caller's voice over the distortion. Anger? Aggravation? "She's not your mission. Proceed to the next target."

"Copy. I'll call when I've arrived in Salt Lake."

The caller disconnected without a response.

"Dick."

She stuck the phone back in her pocket and studied the news article again. The *Boston Herald* headline read, "*Psychiatrist Cristina Silva to join Longwood Memory Center.*"

DB outlined the photo with her fingertip, memorizing the contours of the woman's face, the shape of her eyes, the line of her nose.

"But first," she whispered, her voice like a stranger's to her ears, "I need to make a side trip to Boston."

ACKNOWLEDGMENTS

It all started with a random person sitting behind me on an empty bus.

Over the next fifteen years, that seemingly innocuous chance encounter has evolved into the story of a desperate woman seeking the pieces of her past, no matter the cost. Although I'm not a memory specialist, I drew heavily on my training and experience as a developmental-behavioral pediatrician and interaction with psychiatrist and other mental health professionals to craft this book and, in particular, to breathe life into Dr. Cristina Silva.

Although this book is a work of fiction, and there is no drug of which I'm aware that works like Recognate, scientists are constantly publishing new studies on memory and potential memory enhancers. As I was writing this book, I was taking courses on medical law, global ethics and human rights at the Harvard School of Public Health, where I learned about the real-life threat of absent Institutional Review Board oversight of pharmaceutical studies in third world countries.

In addition to my numerous instructors in creative writing and medicine, and of course my parents who always supported my love of writing, there are several other specific individuals without whose help this book would have remained incomplete. First, a big thank you to Lynnette Novak, who served as sounding board, editor, and advocate. Also, thanks to Nicole Resciniti and the rest of the Seymour Agency for all of your support.

Thank you to Dana Isaacson, whose feedback as a developmental editor elevated this book to a new level, and to Josh Gross, whose line edits prevented minor discrepancies from derailing the story. Thank you as well to Rick Bleiweiss, Josie Woodbridge, and Josh Stanton at Blackstone for believing in this book.

Huge shouts to my beta readers, Christina Clemetson, Rebecca Fujikawa, and Cheryl Wyatt, and to everyone at FanStory.com and QueryTracker.com who provided feedback when I was first developing the story and preparing my query letters. I'd also like to thank Ann Collette, Barbara Poelle, and Carly Watters who were all extremely helpful and positive.

Thanks to the #writingcommunity for supporting me as an author and connecting me with some amazing writers and readers.

A very special thank you to the late Michael Palmer, who not only inspired me with his writing, but served as a mentor and friend as I first embarked on this journey. His son, Daniel, has carried on in his stead and has also been a great source of support, as have my fellow physician authors Tess Geritsen, Gary Birken, and Leonard Goldberg.

And last, but never least, thank you to my amazing wife, Geiza, for being my muse, first editor, and cheerleader; and to you and our incredible daughters, Valentina and Isabella, for being patient throughout this long process, even when I had to lock myself away to finish this book. I can't wait for you all to read it.